the
BOOKWRM
box

Helping the community, one book at a time

THE NOT-OUTCAST

TIJAN

For anyone who struggles with something that is invisible to the eye, difficult to explain, and is outside the box for normal comprehension. For those who love those individuals.
For the readers!

PROLOGUE

THE PAST

I 'd loved Cut Ryder all my life.

Okay. That's a lie.

I'd only known him for this last year, and if I were being fully, fully honest here, I've only talked to him a handful of times.

...

Yeah.

I'm lying again.

I mean, I've seen him *loads* of times. He's Pine Valley High School's star hockey player, and we're a school where hockey isn't that big of a deal. Football and baseball are. But when Cut started playing for the team, everything changed.

I mean, that's what I'm told.

I actually didn't go to school there until this last year, but it felt like I'd been there all my life. Just like I felt like I'd known Cut all my life. The real, real truth is that he's my brother's best friend, and see, that's why I thought I'd known him all my life. Except I hadn't. Just like I haven't really known my brother either.

I mean, not until this year. This was the first time I came to stay with my father.

Chad. That's my stepbrother's name. He's the same age as me.

But I didn't see him a whole lot. Like, hardly ever.

I mean, he didn't really talk to me.

He didn't talk to me in school either.

But I did get rides to school from my stepmother (Chad's real mom), and sometimes Chad would be at the school when we arrived because Natalie (his mom) needed to talk to him or ask him to do something. And Cut was there with him most of the time.

Or some of the time.

Okay. Cut only came to the car once the whole year, but it didn't matter.

I was sure he knew who I was.

I mean, I was his best friend's sister. Or stepsister. Did it matter? We were siblings.

Cut never really looked at me. He frowned at me once, in a hallway, when I yelled out, "Hey!" He passed me right by, but there was a flicker in his eyes. He so knew me.

See? We were friends. We were tight.

Or we were just in my head.

I guess, when I think about it, a lot of things this past year only happened in my head.

Like that I had loads of friends at Pine Valley. The truth is, I didn't, but it was because everyone knew Chad was my brother. He'd told them not to befriend me. He was trying to protect me. At least in my head that's what he was doing.

And he was super good at it, because he only talked to me once that year in school. It was at my locker. I was there, shutting it, and I knew Natalie was supposed to pick me up because I had to stay after for a meeting about my mom. Chad shoved a stocking cap at me. "Here."

He didn't wait for me to grab it, so it fell to the ground, but I scrambled—a big smile on my face—and I looked up. "Hey! Than—"

He was already walking away, not giving me a second glance.

He was carrying a bag, and Cut was at the lockers. A couple girls were standing with Cut, but he looked at me then.

He saw me and acknowledged me.

See? He did know me! I totally forgot about that time. There was no frown on his face then. Just his eyebrows pinching together, and he looked from me to Chad. Actually, now that I thought about it, he looked kinda confused.

I mean... What was that about?

Chad had told him about me.

Hadn't he?

No way. Of course, he had.

How do you not tell your best friend about your sister?

Your half-sister.

Your stepsister.

To be fair, my dad didn't know about me until I was eleven. And that was five years ago. There had been minimal phone calls or birthday cards since then. It wasn't my dad's fault. I heard him calling. Or more specifically, I heard my mom fighting with him.

Like, all the time.

Then again, that's all my mom really did.

She fought with people, then she smoked up. She liked to lock herself in her bedroom.

Or she liked to lock me out of the house.

One time it lasted a whole week. Other times, not as long. Other times, longer.

There was one time where she locked herself in her room for a full week.

I knocked and asked if she was okay. Sometimes she'd yell at me to go away. Sometimes she didn't say anything, but she always got mad when I went to check on her. And I didn't think she'd eaten that week or had any water, so I left sandwiches outside her door, and I stole a couple bottles of water from the neighbors.

I stole other things, too.

I always hated doing that, but if I were being honest, I didn't think I was really stealing them. Mrs. Johanson saw me take a water one time, and she didn't say a word. There were two bottles there the next day.

Sometimes I swiped them, but I didn't like to. And I'd only do that if I was in dire straits.

I didn't like seeing my mom like that or doing those things, so I spent as much time at school as possible. The water fountain there was free, you know?

But anyway, back to Cut and how much I loved him.

Because I did. A lot.

I mean, he's gorgeous. He has this dirty blond hair, and he keeps it shaved on the sides of his head. He lets it get a little longer on top, and he's always running his hands through it. It looks messily rumpled, and it's just so adorable. Although, I bet being a hockey player he'd not want to be known as adorable, but in my mind, he was.

I know I wasn't the only girl in school who thought so either.

Cut and Chad were both popular. They're hockey players, so of course they were popular. But Chad was grumpy a lot of the time. Or at least, he was grumpy to me. You know, when he actually talked to me. But not Cut. He was always grinning or joking around his popular friends, and everyone loved Cut.

How could you not?

He was going into the NHL. Everyone knew it. I heard Chad talking about it to our dad one night at the house. It was one of the few times he was there. At first, I thought that Chad not living here with us was weird, but then I heard Natalie mention to one of her friends that they thought it was best if he stayed at Cut's house while *Donna's kid* was staying with them.

That's how she said it; those were her words exactly.

I mean, I knew she was talking about me, but it made sense. Everything made sense after that.

I was Donna's kid.

I was also Deek's kid. So that meant I was Chad's stepsister.

So even though Natalie didn't like calling me her stepdaughter, that's what I was.

But yeah, everyone's been great to me this whole time I was at their house.

The food was great every night.

I could drink water any time of the day, and get this—it was endless, coming out of their fridge. I just had to grab a glass and push it against the button, and voila: instant water. It was good water, too, so I didn't need to stay at school that long after classes ended.

I never got locked out.

I never had to find a warm place on the streets.

I did look up the local shelter, just in case. One never knew.

But back to the family, because I found out that I had another little brother. Can you believe that?

I had no clue where he'd been this whole time. Maybe like Chad, he'd been sent somewhere else while they needed to take care of me? Oh man. I hoped I hadn't put them out, or him out, or used his room? That'd be awful if they brought me in and sent him away because I took his room, but that didn't make sense.

Their house was epically big.

I mean, Chad could've stayed there, and I probably wouldn't have even seen him.

Though, thinking on it now, Natalie was also gone a lot. There were a ton of nights when it was me at the house and Deek was working in his office. I mean, yeah, I spent time with my dad. That was super, über cool, you know? We had meals together, or some meals.

We had meals in the beginning together.

After a while, not so much.

He kinda stopped talking to me toward the end.

Except snapping.

He liked to snap a lot.

But in the beginning he talked to me about my mom, and

when he did, he'd get all tense in the face. His words would come out clipped, but I got it. I really and truly did.

Donna was...well, let's just say Donna was a lot.

I'm her daughter, and she only talked civilly to me after she'd been away at one of those clinics. She stayed there a long time. This time was the longest, and my dad thought it'd be best if I spent it with them, but usually I stayed at my uncle's house, but this time was cool. It was like seeing how the other half lives.

The high school was nicer, too. There weren't gangs at Pine Valley.

Can you imagine? How Chad would be at my normal school? With the gangs there?

I started laughing, just thinking about it, and then I thought about Cut. It wasn't funny anymore.

Cut would've still been popular and pretty, but he probably wouldn't have laughed as much.

That was sad to think about because I liked his laugh. I listened for it in the hallways.

"Cheyenne."

Crap. They're talking to me.

"Cheyenne." My counselor leaned over, putting her hand on my arm. "This is important. You need to focus on being present with us."

They're always preaching that. Being present.

What did that even mean?

So what if my mind wandered? So what if I'm hyper and sometimes so hyper I missed what's going on around me? They would be, too, if they grew up where I did, the way I did.

Being present sucked, especially now. I mean, more so now than ever.

Could we go back to talking about Cut?

"Cheyenne."

That was my dad talking.

"What?" I looked at him. He was frowning at me, sitting in the corner with his arms crossed over his chest. He dressed up for this meeting—a business suit. Natalie's here, too, heaving a sigh, like she usually did when she's around me. I've noticed she didn't do that when Chad was around. I couldn't say how she was around my other brother because I obviously didn't know him.

I didn't think they even knew that *I* knew about him.

Let's talk about that.

Why *haven't* they told me?

It's not like I'm this horrible person.

I didn't do anything. I mean, the worst I did was think, think and talk to myself, be not present—which I could see my dad knew I was doing again.

He got the same look on his face every time he's exasperated with me.

His mouth flattens. His nose wrinkles a little, and it looks like he's constipated or something.

Now he's uncrossing his arms, rubbing a hand over his forehead.

He does that a lot when I *really* frustrate him.

"Cheyenne."

Aw crap. It was the counselor again. She was being more insistent, and I needed to focus. If I didn't, she'd get mad. Then I'd be asked to leave so they could talk, and nothing good was discussed when I wasn't in the room.

"Yeah?"

She was trying. I could see the effort, but even her face was tight and rigid. She nodded toward Deek and Natalie. "Your father is wondering if you feel comfortable enough to return to your mother's care?"

That.

I felt a knot coming up my throat.

I knew I didn't want to come to this meeting.

Deek cleared his throat, leaned forward, and rested his elbows on his knees. "You've been at our house for six months, and we've made accommodations and changes so you'd feel comfortable there. If you choose to remain there, we do need to discuss bringing Chad and Hunter back into the house."

Hunter! That was his name.

I didn't think my dad realized that was the first time he'd referenced him in front of me.

Natalie wasn't looking at him. She had that same blank and somewhat peeved look directed at me. Thinking on it now, she looked similar to my dad whenever they had to deal with me.

Maybe they had mentioned the other brother before, but I didn't think so. I would've remembered. Who forgets their own brother's name? Not me. Especially not me. I'd never had a brother before.

Hunter.

Now I knew his name, I was never forgetting it.

"Cheyenne."

I messed up again. My counselor sighed.

It wasn't my fault that I was like this.

But it was on me to control it, so okay...

I had to concentrate here.

A deep breath in.

Hold—that never worked for me.

"My mom's good again?" I asked.

Crap. That was a question, not a statement from me. I messed up there, too.

The counselor looked relieved. I was participating. She always got less snippy when I responded to her.

"She's graduated to the halfway house, and she'll be able to leave as early as this week. She's reached out and requested to see you."

I frowned. *Why?* I shrugged. "Nah. I'm good."

All three adults shared a look at that.

See! I'm so focused here. Noticing everything. Every. Thing.

"What do you mean, you're good? You don't want to see your mother, or you don't want to live with her?"

See her. Duh. It's always the same. She'd come out of those places happy and hippie and seeing rainbows and talking about angels. She'd be nice, promising to keep with her yoga and meditation and the rules. Always the rules.

Life would be decent, for a while.

But she'd start smoking again.

Or she'd meet a guy and *then* start smoking again. I'm not talking the cigarette kind of smoking.

Same old, same old.

Then I'd get locked out.

I'd be on the streets.

I'd spend time with Herb. He lived on the corner two blocks from the house.

"I guess I'm good with living with her, but can I come back to Deek's the next time?"

A look flickered in my counselor's eyes. She knew what I was talking about.

Natalie's voice hitched high. "Next time? What does she mean, 'next time'?"

Oh boy.

That answered my question. Natalie looked all panicky at the thought that I could be coming back. It was cool. I could stay at my uncle's, I guess. My cousins liked me. They thought I was funny. Plus, I wasn't scared to walk from my room to go get water there, though they didn't have the fancy fridge water that Deek did.

Still. It was all cool.

I'd miss looking at Cut.

Gah.

I loved Cut. I think I loved him all my life.

❄

So I WENT BACK to live with my mom.

She was nice, like I knew she would be.

Until she got bored, like I knew she would get.

Then she found a new guy, like I knew would happen.

So, the same old, same old happened.

This time I went to the shelter, but I wasn't there long.

Something happened, so I stayed with Herb for a bit. Herb was cool.

He's got a nice dog, too.

But somehow the cops found out where I was. I got picked up.

I knew not to ask Natalie or Deek, so that time I went to my uncle's.

Things were good, until they weren't.

Same old, same old.

But turns out, not this time.

I COULDN'T BELIEVE they came for me.

I was more grounded this time. It was a whole year later. I was going into my senior year of high school, and this time I was with the normal kids. They got me meds. My uncle got me in to see a therapist who worked with me. There was a new county program where they paid for those services. There was group therapy, and yeah, okay, they sent me somewhere for a bit. But I came out, and it was like the world was shining brighter.

I've never felt like this.

People would say things, and I understood them. I responded, and they replied.

I felt like one of them, you know?

If you know, you know. If you don't, that's cool. That meant you're blessed.

The place said I was misdiagnosed, and my symptoms were because my mom was a junkie when I was inside of her. And I got all that. It made sense, but it was awesome. I mean, it wasn't. The reason I was there and all of us were there wasn't cool at all.

Though, could I tell you a secret?

I was relieved. And I felt bad saying that. I'd never admit that to anyone else, but I was.

There were no more ups and downs, threats, screams, violence, the streets, shelters, cops, or fostering. From the time I lived with my dad, and the times I've been with my uncle, I got that I needed structure. It said a lot that a kid like me got that. Like, it said a *lot*.

"Cheyenne."

Oh, boy. My dad. He looked wary to talk to me.

"Hi, Deek."

He smiled, and he blinked a few times before he came the rest of the way to where I was waiting.

He reached for me, and like a normal person (who can read that this is what he wanted), I moved in, and he hugged me.

I hugged him back.

It was all so cool.

Then Natalie was here, and she smiled at me with all this gentleness. Who knew she could be like that? Not that she was *mean* mean, but she was at least slightly bitchy mean. If that made sense?

And holy crapola I'm-gonna-crap-my-pants crap!

There's a little dude next to her, and he looked just like Chad. His hair even had a slight twinge of red in it.

I thought Natalie was reaching for a hug, but no way. I dropped to my knees, smiling wide at this little guy, and I reached for him (because I can now, because I'm a normal person now— there are so many benefits to hanging in the normal, cool crowd), and he *came to me!*

"Hey, buddy." *Keep it quiet, Cheyenne. Calm. Don't scare the little dude away.* "I'm your big sister."

"I know!"

I always wanted a sibling.

A little dude to love and look over.

I was almost bowled over by his excitement.

"Hunter," Natalie reprimanded him.

I didn't know why, but he stared at her and then he must've remembered.

"Oh." He lifted his arms, wound them around my neck, and squeezed me tight. He said in a rush, "I'msorryaboutyourmomI-heardshewasn'tnicebutI'mstillsorry."

Okay.

I replayed it back silently, put in the spaces, and I got it.

I eased back and held up my pinkie finger.

He was watching me. Wide eyes. Then, grinning, he lifted his pinkie, and we locked.

"Put it there, dude."

Could I tell you another secret?

I didn't like talking about my mom or the reason everyone was here.

There was sadness, and I felt it, but right now I was riding the wave of meeting my little brother. Now I've not only met Hunter, hugged Hunter, but we pinkie-duded each other.

Little Dude leaned forward and whispered in my ear, "Do you like koalas?"

I leaned back, giving him the biggest and brightest smile ever. "You serious? I love koalas!"

His whole face lit up. "Me too."

I looked up, but no Chad. Or Cut. (I was really hoping Cut would come.)

As if reading my mind, Natalie coughed. "Chad's at a hockey camp where he's going to college next year."

I stood, but I had to squeeze little dude's shoulder.

He looked up, bumping into my leg, and I'm calling it. We're going to be the best koala-loving friends.

Then he moved over to his mom, and I got that, too. She seemed pretty chill this time.

"Silvard, right?" I asked.

Natalie's eyes got big.

Me. Normal. I was loving it. "You told me last year that's where he's going. Early acceptance?"

"Yeah." She blinked some more, then shook her head. "Uh. Yeah." She regained her footing, and her smile was more genuine. "Cut got a ride there until he goes to the NHL. Chad doesn't think he'll make the team. He's not as good as Cut, but he's hoping for one last year with him."

I got it. I'd want one last year with Cut, too.

Honestly, I'd take one last moment with him at this point. I still loved the guy, though I've realized he had no clue who I was that year and we never actually talked. Like, ever.

I was a bit delusional that year.

"That's cool." I was bobbing my head, acting just like what I said.

It's my new favorite word.

Deek cleared his throat, suddenly all serious. "I've talked to your uncle, and he mentioned the agreement we worked out. That works with you?"

I knew what he was talking about, and I nodded. "I'll stay with my uncle. I'm guessing you want me to go to Silvard next year?"

He relaxed. Dude did not want me in the house. I got it. I understood.

His shoulders lowered, and the lines of tension in his forehead eased at my words.

"We're figuring since Chad will be there, you might want to get to know your brother a bit."

Now that I'm better...

Now that my mother wasn't...

"That'd be great." I winked at Little Dude. "But only if Koala Dude and I can hang sometimes."

He giggled at his name.

Deek's head jerked to the side. "We can talk later about that."

With a clearer head, it turned out that I was smart, and I might even be a little super-duper smart. I would need to work hard and work a lot, but I could probably graduate like one of those normal people.

The agreement was that I stayed away and Deek would pay for my college.

He was choosing Silvard.

My uncle thought I'd be pissed about that, but I was down.

I wasn't like one of those girls. I didn't have plans, dreams, or Pinterest boards about anything. I was just happy to be able to go to college, and Silvard is no slouch school. They're D1 and pretty fancy-pants. I knew it'd be hard, but as long as I kept current with therapy and meds, I was down for the pound.

I could get a degree, and whadda ya know? I could get a decent job at the end of all this.

I saw my uncle approaching, and I knew what that meant. It was time to get this shindig going.

My dad hugged me. He was still so tense. I didn't know why.

Natalie hugged me. "I'm so sorry for your loss, Cheyenne." She smoothed my hair, her hands fell to my shoulders, and then Little Dude hugged my knees.

I didn't tell anyone, but my shoulders tingled after that touch from her.

My mom used to be nice like that, but that was a long time ago.

Like, ages ago.

Like, I couldn't remember now, but she must've been at some point.

She had to be.

All moms hugged their kids, right...?

But I didn't want to deal with that. I got my Little Dude here.

I crouched down and held up my pinkie again. "We're gonna hang, right?"

He stepped forward, all serious. He wrapped his pinkie around mine and nodded. "Hell yeah, we're gonna hang."

"Hunter!" his mom said.

But he just laughed. I laughed back, and it was all good.

1

CHEYENNE

I was lit, weak, and horny.

That was not a good combination for me. Usually my willpower was strong, like industrial-strength super-latexed condom strong, but not tonight. Tonight, the combination of the booze and cocktails had melded together and taken down my last holdouts of willpower. I was gonzo and then I got this text.

Dean: Mustang party! Now! Where r u???

Dean was my colleague, but let's forget about why he would be texting me because we are not 'texting' colleagues. Kansas City Mustangs. That was the important part of that text, and it was getting all of my attention.

Dear God. I could hear the whistle of the impending bomb right before it hit.

That was the professional hockey team that *he* played on.

Party.

Did I mention the *he* that was him? He, as in the only rookie drafted for Kansas City's newer team? He signed his contract after he had one year at Silvard.

The *he* that the team's owners were hoping could be grown into one of the NHL's newest stars, but that'd been a three-year plan. Nope. *He* had different ideas because once he hit the ice in their first debut game, he scored a hat trick in the first period. First. Period. Playing against five to ten-year veterans, and that had not gone unnoticed. By everyone. After that *he* exploded into the NHL scene and in a big fucking way.

They started calling him Reaper Ryder after that.

It was the same *he* that I perved on during a brief stint in high school, and then again during that one year in college before he got whisked away to superstardom. Though, he didn't know any of that 411 about my perving habits.

The second text from Dean gave us the address where to go, and the whistle got louder, target hit...direct implosion.

It was two blocks away.

He was two blocks away, and there went my restraint because I'd kept away from him for the last four years when I moved to the same city he was living in—of course he didn't know that— but this city was totally amazeballs by the way.

I was doomed. I might as well start digging my own bunker at this rate because I was already downtown partaking in some cele-bratory boozetails, so here we were. Here I was, well *we* because I wasn't alone. My main girl since Silvard days, Sasha, was on my right, and Melanie on my left. Melanie came after Silvard, but that didn't matter. She was one of my girls. The three of us. We were awesomesauce, and we were walking into this building that looked like a downtown loft, one that was probably the humble abode to someone not so humble, but someone with old-money wealth who enjoyed partaking in their own boozetails as well.

I already felt a whole kemosabe camaraderie with whoever owned this joint.

"This place is *fucking* awesome."

That was Melanie. She enjoyed coffee, girls, and she was an amazing barista at Dino's Beans.

"Girl."

That was Sasha. She owned a strip club, told everyone she

was an angry Russian, even though there wasn't one Russian strand of DNA in her body, and she enjoyed using one word for everything. That's not to say she didn't speak more than one-word answers, but those were her go-to for speaking.

"Whoa." That was me.

Melanie had jet-black hair. Sasha had ice-queen white hair, and me—I was the in between. My hair was usually a dusty blonde color, but today it looked a bit more brown than dusty blonde. I still enjoyed it, and I also had super chill ice-blue eyes. The other two both had dark eyes so I figured I was still the 'in between' for the eyes, too.

When we entered that party, all eyes turned to us, and not one of us was fazed. We were used to it. Where we went, we got attention. Guys loved us (sometimes), girls hated us (usually), and we didn't care (ever). We weren't going to tone down our awesomeness because of their insecurities.

But we were all works in progress, or at least I was.

I was known to have entire conversations and whole other worlds and every version of apocalypses in my head. That was just me. You'll understand the more you get to know me, but trust me when I say that I'm a lot better than I used to be. Meds, therapy, and a dead junkie mother will do that to you.

But enough about me.

Melanie was the shit, and she really loved the word 'fuck.' A-*fucking*-lot.

Then there was Sasha, she'd been my roommate from college, and here we were, three years out of graduation (well, four for me since I graduated early, and don't ask me how that happened because it still shocked the hell out of me) and going strong. But we were on a mission.

That mission was more boozetails.

There were people everywhere. Stuffy people. One woman who had a tiara on her head. There were guys in suits, some in hella expensive suits, and tuxedos, too.

Whoa.

This wasn't just a party party. This was like a whole shindig party.

Fake Stanley Cups were placed all around with mucho dinero inside.

Crap.

I started to mentally shift through the emails—easier said than done when one was halfway to boozeopolis—that I liked to avoid and I was remembering some of the subject lines of those that I had skipped. There'd been a bunch from Dean lately, though, and one was about some 'Celebrity PR for Come Our Way' and I needed to double down on the crapattitude because I had a feeling we just waltzed into a fundraiser.

"Cheyenne!"

Dean rushed over to us, holding a boozetail in one hand, and his eyes glazed over. He was medium height with a more squat build that he easily could buff up more, but I didn't think Dean went to the gym. He was always at work and because of that, I usually saw him with his hair all messed up. That's how it was now, and his eyes glazed over.

My dude coworker was lit.

I started smiling, but then no. Not good. What corporate espionage was he up to by telling me to come here?

"Where's the bar, Deano?" Melanie.

I was impressed she hadn't used her favorite word.

"There." Directions from Sasha and like that, both my buds moved away.

I settled back, knowing they'd have my back. They'd be bringing the boozetails to me—even better—so I had the time to grin at Dean. "What's happening, hot stuff?"

He never got my quotes. Or jokes.

He didn't react and he grabbed my arm. "Have you read my emails?" Then he looked at me, his head moving back an inch. "What are you wearing?"

Nothing appropriate for a work event, that's for sure.

But I only upped my grin wattage. "I was going for a Daenerys theme. Felt like wanting to tame some dragons tonight." Except I took my own liberty with the outfit. Instead of her flowing robes and dresses, I was wearing a leather, almost corset-like top, one that wrapped around my neck and hung off one of my shoulders. The bottom was more Daenerys theme, a chiffon skirt with a slit up one thigh. And high heels strapped to my feet.

It shouldn't work, but it did. It so totally did, and I had woven colored threads in my hair so they were swinging free, free and lit.

He took another step back, looking me up and down again.

"You are," a pause, "something."

I scowled. "Dude. Insulting."

He had to blink a few times because he hadn't realized I spoke again, then he refocused. "Wait. You're downtown. There's no way you could've gotten here this fast, even if you were at the shelter, but I know you weren't at the shelter. And your place is an hour out."

Case in point, my outfit.

He was right.

Come Our Way. The name of our kitchen had been a marketing and genius ploy, one put in place by Deano himself, because while I wrote the grant that got us five million (not a common thing to happen for a start-up) and got us going, his job was actually to work on marketing and promotions to keep the money, spotlight, and volunteers streaming to our little kitchen. I maintained our grant, and I helped with literally everything else. I was the final say-so on all executive decisions, except for matters that we needed the board to oversee. We had another full-time staff member, but she liked to Netflix and chill (and really Netflix and chill with wine, not the other Netflix and chill) on her evenings. But all three of us manned our little kitchen that fed a lot of the downtown homeless in our corner in Kansas City.

And Dean knew I wasn't known for one to partake in alcoholic libations, but we were here, and I was thirsty.

It was my last day on my medication vacation. I was taking advantage of it.

It was a thing that happened to help cut down on build-up immunity. Sometimes I enjoyed it, but it was usually a whole struggle to get back on and make sure everything was smooth running.

But that wasn't something I was going to think about tonight, though my brain was already starting to go there. Tomorrow I'd go back to living almost like a saint.

Where were my girls with my drinkaloo?

Also, I was firmly not letting myself think of the *he* and that took mundo restraint because he had been a big major part of my daydreams since my junior year in high school through now—especially now since I've been living in the city where he was hockey royalty.

I didn't answer Dean, but spying another Stanley Cup filled with cash, I asked instead, "What's the funding for?"

"Oh!" He perked up, throwing his head back and finishing his drink. A waitress walked by with a tray loaded with fully filled champagne flutes. He snagged two, for himself. "That's why I'm here. I got the final acceptance that the Mustangs are going to dedicate an entire two days to Come Our Way. Two days, Cheyenne. Two days? Can you believe that?" He leaned in, excited, and I could smell how excited he was.

Booze breath. It's a thing.

I edged back a step. "Totally."

So not totally.

"That's awesome."

Really so not awesome.

It was a great PR day for the kitchen and for the team, I was sure that's why they agreed to do it. It wasn't uncommon for Come Our Way to have local celebrities pop in for a day or an hour to volunteer, but the media that followed them was always too much for me. I either stayed in the back kitchen, or I took a personal day. Media days were something *extra* extra. Flashing cameras. Razor-sharp reporters. Sometimes you got a good one who just wanted to spread good news about our mission, but sometimes you got the reporters who wanted to swing things to a more controversial article for the click-baits.

I wasn't down for that poundage.

Plus, the extra buzz in the entire building was like hay fever for my meds. I couldn't handle it, and therapy had taught me to avoid those types of situations, so hence why I usually disappeared—and if the entire team was coming for two days, it'd be insane. I was already not looking forward to it, and yes, I wasn't letting myself think of *him* being in my place of business. At all.

I thought he'd known me in high school, but that turned out to be a result of some slight delusions from my undiagnosed hyper disorder, so that was embarrassing, and then when college rolled around, I intentionally stayed in the background. But if he was going to be at my place for two days—forty-eight hours— there's no way he wouldn't see me, and that information was already bumbling through my head like an intoxicated bee hooked on coke and champagne. It just didn't know what to do or where to sting. Super painful.

Dean was still talking. "...and that's why I'm here. They reciprocated with an invite here, and by the way, it's so on-the-downlow that there's no security outside. Did you see that? To even get in here, you had to know about it."

That made no sense.

Dean didn't care. "And I've already met half the team. Oh!" His eyes were bouncing around just like my intoxicated inner bee. "I got tickets to their game on Sunday. They rocked preseason, did you see?" He kept edging closer and closer to me the more he talked, something that was so un-Dean-like that I was having a hard time processing all this newness of what was happening around me.

Dean was around the same age as me, a few years older. Coming straight from grad school with a masters in reinvigorating the world to give a fuck about homeless and runaways, he had an axe to grind and an agenda to save the world. He liked to cut loose. You had to in our profession because burn-out had the highest success rate, but seeing him this tricked out had that bee flying sideways. He didn't know if he was in my bonnet or my hair braids.

Then I remembered; Dean was a hockey fan.

I was, too, but I kept my undying adoration on the down-low like a lot of things.

Not Dean. He was out of the closet and loud and proud about his love for the Kansas City Mustangs. He also turned traitor and was a Cans fan, as well as the Polars (boo, hiss), but both those teams weren't in this current building or city. So yeah, it made sense now. He was geeking out on the full freak-out reader.

That, and I was wondering how much champagne he had already consumed because he just downed both those two flutes in front of me. He was so drunk that my own lit meter was heading down into the empty zone. Not cool. Not cool, indeed, and where were my girls?

Just then, I saw one of them.

And my lit meter skyrocketed right into the red zone.

The crowd parted. I had a clear view right smack to the bar, and there she was. And she wasn't alone.

Sasha had her sultry and seductive pose out, clearly liking what she saw, gazing up at *him*.

2

CUT

This chick was saying she was Russian.

She wasn't Russian. I knew this because one: she was seriously faking the worst accent in the world. It sounded more like she was trying to sound Australian mixed with a German flavor to it, and two: if she thought I didn't remember her from college, she was fucking loco. I knew she went to Silvard, the same college I came from because she hooked up with my best friend in the year that I was there.

He told me all about a certain one-nighter he had that he wished could've been a whole one-monther, but he wouldn't go into specifics about why she couldn't have her 'deadline' extended. That was his thing. He gave his girls 'deadlines' about how long he'd stay with them. They never knew, but I did.

I never wanted to know.

He just whined about her, a lot, and complained about all the fun he could've had with the wannabe-Russian. He said she had no accent back then, so that was new. I was tempted to text him, let him know his one-nighter was back if he wanted another go? Whatever reasons had to have expired by now since we're what?

Four years after college? Hell. Longer. He said he bagged her our freshman year, but since that was the only time he and I were at Silvard together, I never thought to ask him about an update on his Russian one-nighter.

Me, because I obviously got drafted the next year to Kansas City. And him, because he followed me and attended Kansas University, going into their business program. He was a club promoter now, which was perfect for him since my boy liked to party. A lot.

Her hand started rubbing up and down over my bicep.

Totally texting my boy.

I was pulling my phone out when another person hit our group, stopping and smiling at the Not-Russian chick, holding his drink and taking a sip. "Well, hello there."

Franklin. He was first line with me, and his eyes shifted to mine, knowing I wasn't going to be tapping this ass. My tastes ran more toward girls who wouldn't be likely to try to knife me after the condom was pulled off. I avoided the crazy at all costs.

I grinned back and nodded just the slightest, giving him my go-ahead.

His grin turned into a smile and he shifted, putting his drink on the bar between us, insinuating himself more between her and me.

I moved back, just fine with this turn of events.

Cut: Your Russian ass from Silvard is here.

Chad: Where?

I sent him the address and put my phone away. If he didn't believe me, he'd still come. Chad didn't turn down any event. It was perfect networking for him, especially at these events. A lot of high-rollers were here who enjoyed being photographed with the players. This one was more off-the-books, so the liquor had loosened most everyone up, including myself. I had a two-drink rule, but we kicked ass at our pre-season games, so I was feeling the celebrations tonight.

"What's your name?" That was Franklin, doing his thing.

"I'm Sasha."

I could hear that she was pissed. She knew she got handed off.

I moved farther back, taking my drink with me.

"What's going on over there?"

Hendrix moved to the bar beside me, nodding to Franklin.

I turned, my back going to the room. "Frank's doing his thing."

"Thought you were taking her number."

"Nah. I know her from college."

"What?"

I grinned at him, signaling the bartender for another fill. "She hooked up with my boy."

"Is he coming?"

Hendrix and Franklin both started the team with me, so they knew Chad well. Unless you were brand new to the team, which was only two guys this year, they all knew my best friend. I was usually more disciplined with partying, meaning that I might attend parties, but I didn't partake in the activities that much. Chad was the opposite. He partook—and partook a lot. He made up for me missing three more years of college frat parties, and that was fine with me. I'd cut loose at the house if I was feeling it, but generally during the season (which was long and brutal) I stuck close to my workout and eating regimen.

"She came in with two other chicks."

"What?"

"She came in with others." He moved to scan the room.

I took note of the interest in his tone. "They're hot?"

He didn't answer. He was still scanning.

Yeah. They were definitely hot.

Then, he said, "Everyone noticed, dude. You would've, too, if you hadn't been bagging off those two society girls before that one saw you."

I grinned. He wasn't wrong.

It came with the job. Sometimes I enjoyed it. Other times I didn't. Most times I tried to avoid it, but since Hendrix was making a point of mentioning them, I turned, too.

"There's one." He pointed with his drink. "Black hair."

I saw her, and I watched as she was moving in on Cassie, one of our physical therapy staff.

Hendrix realized it the same time I did. He straightened. "Damn."

I started laughing. "You'd have more luck moving on Cassie, I think."

Cassie was bisexual, so I wasn't wrong in my statement, but Cassie had made it known she wasn't interested in anyone on the team, or anyone in the whole organization. She lived by the mantra, 'don't shit where you work.'

Hendrix groaned. "Where's the other one? She was hot, too." A second later, another groan. "Damn. She's worked all up in that guy. Who is he?"

I was looking. I wasn't seeing anyone. "You need to be more specific. Who am I looking—" I was looking, scanning, and bam. I saw her.

Hol—holy fuck.

Like, seriously holy fuck.

It was like I was being slammed into the glass by five guys all at once, and they were giving me enough space as they were moving off of me. When suddenly, the rest of their team, one by one, all started checking me. Bam. Bam. Bam!

That's how it felt, because ho-lee fuuuuck.

This girl was seriously hot. Not like hot hot. She was hawt *hot*.

Long legs that you could tell were toned and shaped under whatever the fuck kind of skirt that was, and her top—I had to take a second to compose myself. I stopped breathing for a minute. I had no clue what kind of twisted top she was wearing, but all I knew was that it was black leather and it wrapped around her torso in a way that caused my dick to weep. I wanted to be that fucking leather. I wanted to peel it off her, and watch her spin around as I uncovered each layer, and discover whatever secret shit she was wearing underneath. A bodysuit? A thong? Nothing? I wanted to see her nipples. I wanted to sink three fingers inside of her as my hello, then push her back against the wall and drop my mouth over hers. That's exactly how I wanted to introduce myself to her. Then maybe I'd tell her my name before asking hers.

Guy.

Hendrix said she was talking to a guy.

What fucking guy?

I was already growling, wanting to tear his head off, whoever it was.

"Dude."

That was Hendrix again, and his voice sounded like it was coming from a distance.

A part of my brain finally clicked in. I knew he was still beside me, but I was in the middle of having a reaction like one I'd never had before in my entire life. This was me and I wasn't giving a damn.

That girl was mine. Everyone else just needed to learn it. And fast.

I was normally a very chill guy.

I came from good parents. My dad was a rare breed—smart with money, but also not an asshole at home. Good father. Good husband. My mom was and still is a stay-at-home parent and crazy supportive. She ran an Etsy shop—one that she didn't like to let anyone know about, and she was super low-maintenance. Liked to joke with us, share a beer and watch a football game. My two little brothers were the same. I mean, they had attitudes. What teenager didn't? They were both good athletes, good-look-

ing, and they got their fair share of party invites and DMs from
girls their age, sometimes older.

But their successes never went to their head.

That was a testament to our parents.

Our mom and dad kept all of us grounded, so because of that,
I was grounded. Humble. The most baggage I ever had to deal
with came from my best friend, because while my family wasn't
messed up, his was. His family was seriously fucked up, though
his little brother was super fucking rad.

But all that said, general life stuff, I was a laid-back, easygoing
guy.

Except with hockey.

Everything went out the window when it came to hockey.

On the ice, I killed. I was a fucking animal once my skates hit
the ice, and the same competitive nature was in my family, too. At
a soccer game, my mom was quiet and cheering just like everyone
else. At my rink, my mom led the cheers in, "YOU FUCKING
KILLLLLL HIM, CUT! WE DIDN'T NAME YOU CUT FOR
SHITS AND GIGGLES! YOU FUCKING MAKE YOUR NAME-
SAKE PROUD, CUTLER RYDER!"

The whole team loved her, but there was always, *literally*
always, a stunned response from the fans when Hockey Mama
Alice Ryder came out. That part of my mom was what I inherited
and what was coming to the surface now and as *my girl* shifted...
that's when I saw the guy.

I wanted to take his head off, now. Right *fucking* now.

"Hey. Oh. Wow. Whoa. Okay."

I started forward, but Hendrix hopped in front of me. He was
blinking, a bewildered look on his face. His drink was gone.
Where'd that go? So was mine. I didn't care, but his hands were
up and he kept shaking his head.

"I can't believe I'm doing this, never seen you act like this, but
get yourself under control. You get the same look when you're

trying to piss off an enforcer. Now. Calm down before you head over there—"

I didn't let him finish whatever the fuck he was about to say. I was gone.

Loved Hendrix, but I was outta there.

The guy was standing by my girl. She'd learn. So would he. Everyone in the room would learn. I was about to claim her in a big fucking way.

I was almost there.

The guy—what the fuck was he wearing?

He was drunk. Could see that right off the bat. His face was flushed, sweaty. His eyes were dilated. He was waving his hand around, an emptied glass in his grasp, and he was moving in on her with each step he was taking. His eyes were shifting all over the place.

I eased back, just a bit.

Her head was down, locked in place. I could see her side profile, and she was biting her lip.

Not the lip. That was mine to bite, not hers.

Those were thoughts I'd have to express later because now was not a socially acceptable time to broadcast my intentions, and I had plenty. A shit-ton of intentions when it came to her, her body, her pussy, her mouth, her breasts, her legs. Her. Just her.

I wasn't dumb. I was reacting from some inner emotions that I'd never tapped into before. I'd never had a reaction like this, and I'd seen—and been with—some seriously hot women. Came with the job when we partied with supermodels at times or were asked to pose for photo shoots to raise awareness for a cause.

But this woman, this reaction wasn't just physical, though I didn't need to pour more gasoline on that flame. It was blazing and about to take down the entire building, so I needed a fucking second.

I took it.

I stopped, reaching for water from Alex, another teammate

who had also noticed me. His eyebrows were sky high, and his eyes shot past me. I knew Hendrix was there, and when I kept moving, I knew Alex had fallen in line behind me. They were there to keep me from getting handcuffs slapped on my wrists because they both knew I had a temper inside of me, and when it was switched, I never cared about the devastation I was about to lay out.

Then I was at their little gathering...and she wasn't looking at me.

I was here. Right beside her. No way in hell she didn't know I was here. I saw her face get tighter, her body more rigid, as I came over. She kept biting her lip and I kept aching to touch my hand there, wipe my finger over her bottom lip and dislodge its hold.

She suppressed a shiver.

I saw that and *good*. She wasn't as unaffected by me as she tried to appear.

I saw the shiver travel down her spine, and she gulped, still studiously avoiding my gaze.

"Hey!"

The guy, on the other hand, was having the opposite reaction.

Mouth open. Eyes bugging out. He almost dropped his empty glass that he'd been waving around moments before.

Alex moved around the group, chuckling, as he reached out and took it from the guy's slack fingers. The guy didn't notice. He was riveted by me.

"You—you're—whoooooooaaa. It's Cut Ryder, Shy. Cut The Reaper Ryder."

I stifled an inward groan. There was a reason I'd been given the team's mascot name as my nickname...all because of a certain game where I'd let this same anger out on a few opposing players. Like, five of them. The only one who hadn't gotten it from me had been the goalie, and that was because I'd been hauled off to the box by then.

He thrust a hand out. "I'm a big, big, big fan of yours. Well, the whole team, actually." He was still holding his hand out. I had no intention of shaking it, not because I was being rude or because he was in my girl's space, but because it was sweaty and I could tell just from eyeing it. He gestured to her with his other hand. "I was just telling Cheyenne that I can't wait for your guys' game on Sunday. Your whole team is coming to where I work for a couple days soon. Cheyenne works with me." He noticed Alex and jolted. "Whoa!" Then Hendrix. "Double whoa. Cheyenne, are you seeing these guys?" He whispered the last question, and by this time, I was locked in.

Fully.

Cheyenne. Her name was Cheyenne.

The guy ceased to exist for me, but she didn't. She was fighting the pull between us.

I could see the fight on her face. A bunch of emotions were shifting there.

Fear—like a gut punch to my chest.

Amazement right after. Pride on my end at seeing that.

Then, fear again. I was being checked in the glass all over again, and I had no back-up.

"Babe," that word whispered from me before I could stop myself.

Her head turned in my direction, but her eyes didn't. They were laser-focused somewhere lower on my face. She wouldn't meet my gaze. What the fuck?

I heard the guys fall silent, all hearing what I just laid out in that one word.

Then, Alex was pulling the other guy away, for his safety if he was smart, and I closed in, reaching out.

I touched her arm, and she was paralyzed as I felt a tremor rush through her.

"No, not like that." I moved in even closer, bending my head. Her front was almost brushing my front and I could feel her trembling. I lowered my voice. "Is that because of me? You're scared of me?"

I had to be smart.

I didn't want to scare her away.

She shook her head, just the slightest bit.

I moved my hand to her shoulder, but I kept my other one free. I didn't want her to feel like I was trapping her, but hell. I wanted to. So bad. I wanted to tug her out of here, take her home, and lay claim so she'd never want to feel another guy inside her.

"You know who I am?"

Another nod, but nothing else. Her throat was working, moving up and down. Whatever was going on with her, she couldn't speak.

"You okay with this?" My voice was soft now, so fucking soft. I moved my hand up, cupping the back of her neck.

I felt her tense at my hold, then she dipped her head again. Another nod.

Some of the tension was lifting. I wasn't scaring her. Thank Christ.

Then, I was not a guy who messed around. I asked, "You want to get out of here?"

Her eyes lifted all the way to mine with that question. My God, her eyes.

It clicked. Right in that moment.

They were like ice. They were glacial.

Whatever it was, something fell in place and this girl was really mine. She saw it now, too. Past lives, maybe? I didn't know, but it felt right and I should've been weirded out about how right it felt, but I wasn't. I couldn't bring myself to feel that way.

But I had to make sure. "You drunk? You know what you're agreeing to? And if you don't want to, that's fine. We can find a corner, have a talk—" Her hand shot to my chest, and she put her entire palm there. She could feel my heart beating a mile a minute, too. I was just as affected as she was.

Then, another moment, as words wrung from her. "Take me home."

A growl came from me. "*Fuck* yeah."

I was primed.

I took her hand.

FROM: CHEYCHEY
TO: KOALA BOY
SUBJECT: I'M IN TROUBLE.

3

CHEYENNE

He looked good.

He looked *damn* good.

I felt him in the party. Like, the whole time. I'd been horrified, then relieved when I saw him hand Sasha off to his other teammate, and by the way, I knew every single one of them. Season tickets and all, not that anyone knew I had season tickets, but so be it. It was my thing.

And him. He was definitely my thing.

I couldn't get over how good he looked.

I saw him on the posters and gigantic murals. I saw his picture on ESPN, and YouTube, and any and all places where local celebrity athletes had their pictures posted, but in person... Yeah, it wasn't the same. Cut was always pretty.

He'd not been built in high school. He'd been a lean guy, and that made him fast on the ice. But he had pretty eyes, high cheekbones (though still boyish), and his hair was a dirty blond back then. Watching him in college, then throughout the NHL, he had morphed. He was all man now.

He was still fast on the ice, one of the fastest in the league, but he was definitely not the same boy anymore. He was standing there and he was virile. The air felt like it was rippling off of him.

Smoldering dark eyes. His hair was cut short and a little darker now, but his jawline was filled out. Square. Those cheekbones, there was nothing boyish about them anymore. He was all man. Lush everything on him. Lush lips. I wanted to burrow in his shoulders, his chest, that glorious chest and I'd gotten glimpses of the valley road on his chest and stomach and there was a reason he was heavily talked about on all media platforms. The sports shows, but also the gossip ones, not that the gossip sites had much to talk about. Cut was private, hella private, and it drove them nuts.

I had felt him when he noticed me, and it was like my lungs were inflated balloons and someone took a needle to them, unable to take in air. As he prowled over to me, I'd been unable to do anything.

He walked over to me like a predator, but I was willing prey. I was freaking out because no way was this real life.

This was just all too much.

Too fast. Too much.

But no, not at all.

I'd been in love with Cut Ryder since high school, but he had no clue. Not one. What I did know was that he didn't remember me because I knew I didn't look the same. I mean, my eyes were the same. Who could forget my eyes? Well, someone who never noticed them before. And come to think about it, there was only one time he looked at me. One time that I know about.

It was all weird, but damn.

Damn!

He came over and he called me 'babe' and that would normally sketch me out, but it was the opposite reaction with him. And he asked if I wanted to leave, and now he was holding my hand and we were leaving—I was seriously trying not to hyperventilate trying to wrap my head around everything coming at me all at once.

There'd been a driver service for the players, so we got one of those, and the whole drive to his place, a whole thirty minutes, and that was because of traffic, we had our eyes on each other. I even knew where we were going, how laughable was that? He thought I had no idea. He thought he was taking me somewhere unknown?

I could've given the driver directions.

I should tell him.

No.

What was I thinking?

One night.

That's all.

One night.

After he found out, and I knew he *would* find out. He'd find out in the morning, for sure, and that was if everything happened how I thought it was going to happen, but one night. One *freaking* night. After that he wouldn't want anything to do with me because of who I was.

But I couldn't walk away now, even if someone was holding a gun to my head.

I couldn't tell him. That would be the same as walking away.

Okay. Yeah. One night. I could handle this for one night.

There were no words exchanged on the ride. I mean, what could we say that wasn't already said with our eyes and our intentions back at the party. We sat in the back, apart. He was against one side. I was at the other. The driver driving, and then we were at his place. Well, Chad's place, too. I knew they were roommates.

Not creepy, right?

We were exiting the car now.

Just breathe, Cheyenne.

He was leading me up the walkway.

Even in the dark, I could see all the brick, but then we were inside.

And—oomph!

He pushed me against the door, reaching down and locking it.

He moved in, almost touching me.

Nope. He was touching me.

His hand was on my hip and it slid up to my stomach, moving under my shirt. He bent in, his lips grazing my shoulder and I was already melting. I reached out, both my hands to his waist, just holding him there. I needed to anchor myself to him in some way.

"Are you sure you want to do this?"

Even the question, said against my neck, was making me want to jump him. I didn't need any more ammunition.

"What?" A slight hitch in my throat. My pulse was skipping all over the place, too.

He grazed his nose up my jawline, moving over until his lips were lingering just over mine. Not touching. But there.

"You didn't say a word in the car. Are you having second thoughts?"

I had to bite my lip to keep a half-hysterical laugh from bubbling out. If only he knew. But I shook my head, still biting my lip, not trusting myself to say much else, all I could muster was, "Nope. I'm good."

His hand moved to my neck, palming my head and tilting me to look up at him. He drew his head back, his eyes watching me from the full moon shining through the window. "You sure?"

I nodded, my eyes lost as I moved over his face, falling to his own mouth. I just wanted that on me, anywhere, everywhere. I'd been wanting that for ten years.

"Good."

His hand moved.

I thought he would kiss me.

He didn't. He so didn't.

His other hand moved south, bypassing my skirt, pushing my thong aside, and he found my opening in point two seconds. And oooooh!

I gasped as he slid in two fingers right off the bat, sliding all the way in and up and up and up. He was almost lifting me off the ground because of how deep he was, and I wasn't mad at all. His mouth dipped to my throat, he was already panting, and a second later, as I was breathing loud, a third finger joined in, but he didn't kiss me. Not on the lips.

Those fingers were working me.

In. Out.

Sliding. Thrusting.

Thumbing.

Tweaking me.

Caressing me.

I was going blind.

I was going mad.

I was going to scream and then he grated out, "Up."

I jumped and he caught me, so easily, as if I weighed nothing. My legs went around his waist, and he held me against the door, still pumping into me.

My head hit the back of the door, but I wasn't feeling it. I wasn't feeling anything except him, except those fingers inside of me as they continued to move in and out. Pleasuring me first.

He was working me like a professional.

Good God.

I was going to combust.

It was coming.

Rising.

Building.

A scream left me and I arched against him, feeling his mouth on my throat again as I surged over the edge.

There'd been no help from me, it was all him, all his fingers as he literally held me in place.

Holy shit.

I was so out of my comfort zone.

I wasn't even thinking normally.

I was like a regular person. That's how scrambled he'd made my brain.

Then a soft chuckle as he held me in his arms, and I trembled as I came down from a volcano.

"Good. Now we got that out of the way." He lifted his head, leaning me and trapping me against the door with his hips. His free hand went to my chin and he tipped me back so I could see those eyes of his blazing at me.

Like diamonds.

"Dude," I whispered, a ball unfolding inside of me.

He narrowed his eyes. "Dude?"

"You made me think normal." No one did that. Ever. Like ever ever, but I was me again. I was back and he was about to get a glimpse of how weirdo Cheyenne I could be. "Dude. It's a rightio dealio with me. It's stupendous. I was normal."

He frowned at me, stiffening.

He mouthed my words back to me. Rightio dealio. Stupendous. Then asked, "Normal?"

I grinned at him, slow and sated because I saw stars. I was still seeing stars. "Junkie mom. Dead now. Messed up all my life. That means I don't think or talk like regular bros and hoes. I'm a different calendar." But I could pull it together, like for meetings at work or grant writing. I was an ace typist. "Stars. You made me meet them."

I was still seeing them. His eyes. So smoldering.

He continued to stare at me, as if seeing me for the first time.

I tensed.

Maybe he was regretting this? Was my one-night stand a one-night finger bang instead?

I tried to stem the disappointment, but... Okay.

A girl had coping mechanisms. I could pull mine up, if I needed to.

I was hoping I didn't need to. I didn't know how I'd handle that either.

Then he must've made his decision.

He readjusted his hold on me, standing back from the door and his mouth twitched. "One rule."

"Yeah?"

I was about to see stars again.

"Don't call me dude again."

Dude. But I grinned. "Deal."

4

CHEYENNE

I woke, and the night flooded back over me as if I were watching an erotic sci-fi film backwards. By the end of it, alarms were blaring in my head and all I could think about was retreat, retreat, retreat...so I did the first thing I thought of.

Now, as I'm completing this roll, one might think I'm crazy.

I am, kinda.

One might also think this is ridiculous. I've loved Cut since I saw him in high school, but that was in high school. High school was a long time ago. It's been four years since I graduated. Four years since college. And add in another two years of high school, one of which I was only around him for a few months and he was only at Silvard for one year.

For a girl like me, this was all a bit much.

Like a lot of a much.

Like a lot a lot a lot, and I'm digressing.

When my body says retreat, I've learned to listen. I'll usually figure out why later, but until then—I grabbed my phone on the way and I army-crawled to the bathroom.

I didn't know a lot of things at that moment.

I didn't look at my phone. One would also think I should look at my screen, but nope. My brain wasn't hardwired to be thinking logically that morning, or well... Digressing. Once more.

I called Sasha, not knowing the day, the time, if I was alone or not, but I pulled myself over the heated (nice!) tile floor, and then Sasha picked up from the other end.

"What is it?" Her voice was groggy still.

I'd woken her up.

"Sasha," I whispered and hissed at the same time, but maneuvered around, my stomach still on the floor, and toed the door shut with a soft click. (I was so proud of myself.) I jackknifed up to hit the lights, then scooted back against whatever was behind me. I had no clue.

My phone was glued to my face. "I need help."

I'd heard her grumbling before that, and then total silence.

A second later, "What do you need?"

There's my girl.

She was alert, calm, and locked in. She may run a strip club, but I was sure she'd been a secret agent at one point in her life. Maybe that's where her Russian persona came from.

"I need an extraction. I need my clothes. And I'm pretty sure I need ice for the vajajay."

There was rustling on her end and then, "Dear God, not the vag."

"The vag."

"No, not the vag."

I repeated, "The vag."

More rustling. She was moving and talking at the same time. Atta girl. "Was it good, at least? Tell me it was good?"

"The vag needs icing. If it was bad, I'd be calling the cops."

Dead silence again. Then, "So, it was good?"

"It was fucking phenomenal."

"*Fuck*ing phenomenal?" She was awed. I took Melanie's word.

"Fucking phenomenal."

"Wow."

"I know."

"*Wow.*"

"I *know.*"

Another pause. We both digested that, then back to business.

"But you need an extraction?"

"Affirmative."

"I'm moving. Don't think I'm questioning you, but I'm curious. Why the extraction?"

I had to pause at how to answer that one.

Too fast? Too much? Too scared?

All the above.

I went with, "I don't remember his name."

It was lame.

She called me on it. "You're lying."

"I'm lying."

"You're scared."

She so got me. I nodded to no one in the bathroom. "If I was on the toilet, I'd be pissing." Though that was redundant. If I was on the toilet, I'd be doing that anyways. Who wouldn't?

"Why are you scared?"

I shrugged, to no one again. "It's..." What could I say? "I need to regroup for a bit."

"Got it." She was whispering now, "And I'm on my way. Text me your location."

I whispered back, just for the hell of it, "On it and I love you."

"Love you back."

I heard a man's voice before she hung up.

Who was that?!

I pulled up the GPS on my phone and sent her my location. We were in the suburbs of Kansas City, actually a bit outside the suburbs. And now I needed to perform some high-end assassin moves.

I went to the bathroom. (Not an assassin move.) I washed my hands. (Also not an assassin move.) I cleaned up, the quietness of

it all was an assassin move, though. I took stock of his bathroom.
He kept it clean, and there was a stack of clothes on the counter.

I fingered through them. Mostly shirts. A couple sweatpants.
Why did he have these here? For him? For guests? Was I one of
many guests? Was he a Boy Scout when it came to protected sex
and one-night stands, and he was always prepared? I didn't know.

I wasn't sure I wanted to know.

But fuck it.

I was so totally *that* girl.

I pulled on one of the shirts, and I had somehow slept in my
underwear and bra. Why the bra, I didn't know. I didn't think I'd
ever know. It would remain one of the world's mysteries, like
where did the socks keep disappearing to? I didn't think I'd ever
know the answer to it, and after that, I eased open the door.

I was assassin quiet.

He was there.

He was in the bed.

But, hold breath, hold breath—he was still sleeping.

Gah. He looked so good. The bedsheets slipped down so I
could see his back and his sculpted shoulders and those very very
broad shoulders. I was still on the shoulders. Moving down. The
curve of his spine, how his back was so contoured and itching for
me to touch it—nope.

Assassin mode back on. I was fully *not* paying attention to
anything in the *feelings* department.

Spying my purse (I didn't even remember bringing it with
me), the rest of my clothes, and my sandals, I nabbed all of them.

I tiptoed out of the door, still being my assassin badass self,
and once in the hallway, once I had pulled the door shut, I moved
down the hall a little bit. I shimmied up my skirt, toed on my
sandals, and was ready to roll.

I was not waiting around, so I reached for the door, and the
alarm panel caught my eye at the same time I had the door open.

An ear-splitting alarm pierced through the house, and I had a split-second decision to make.

Stay or bail?

I bailed. And awkwardly fast.

So *not* an assassin move.

My sandals were kicked off. I bent down, grabbing them and then I was running barefoot down the driveway. I turned down the sidewalk just as I heard the front door being wrenched open behind me, and I immediately went into stealth-mode.

I mean, not really.

There was actually a line of tall privacy hedges blocking his house, so I'd only managed to get behind the hedges. If he came out to the road, he'd see me. Because of that, I hotfooted it down the block. Seeing a tree big enough to shield me, I stepped on the other side of it.

Then, I called Sasha and gave her my new location.

I WAS WALKING down the block, on the other side of the road when Sasha found me.

I'd told her that I was going to be on the move.

A short toot on the horn and her minivan pulled up next to me.

It's an unspoken rule that no one is to ask Sasha why she has a minivan. It's been asked before, and the person who asked the question was never seen again. (That was a bit dramatic, but for real, I never saw the girl again who asked. I'm sure she lives in New Jersey, now married with two kids, but I learned to respect that rule.) I never asked why she drove a minivan. She just did. It was now Matilda, our home-mobile. Or that's what Melanie called it. Sasha didn't have a name for it.

The back had been converted into a small bed, so some mornings, it was the miracle van and not a minivan. Which was amazing if Sasha was picking us up on hangover-mornings.

I climbed up, strapped in, and turned.

She had my coffee waiting for me in hand. I took it, and there was a breakfast sandwich perched on top.

I so loved my girl.

"Thank you," I moaned from how good the coffee smelled.

She gave me a cocky grin before pulling forward and turning at the next street. "So, you ran, huh?"

I groaned, closing my eyes. "I hid."

"You hid?"

"Behind a tree."

She choked. "A tree?" She groaned. "Girl."

"I know." I groaned again.

"And your reason being?"

I was already shaking my head, knowing she was going to ask. "I have no idea."

Bleak. I was so bleak.

She let out a sigh, hitting the turn signal and pulling over. "I should take you back."

"No!"

Christ. My heart stopped just at the thought of that.

"You don't think I don't know how you felt about him in college?"

Oh. Crap. Where was Melanie with the toilet jokes when I needed her?

"College?"

I was still so bleak here.

I knew this was a serious talk because Sasha was not sticking to her one-word commentary. She was being real. And her voice was gentle as she said, "And since college. He's best friends with your brother—"

"Stepbrother, and he's not family anymore. Deek and Natalie divorced."

"Still. You guys share a brother. That connects you, and he's connected to your hockey hottie in a big way. Why do you think I was hitting on him last night?"

Blood rushed to my face. I was hot, like red in the face hot.

I didn't think she knew, so I thought it'd been a 'miss' kind of thing.

I eyed her, biting my lip. "You knew?"

She laughed. "You go to every home game. I know you work a lot, but *gurl*, I am not stupid."

"You're at the strip club."

She snorted. "Like I don't keep tabs on my girls. You included."

See. Total secret agent.

Pressure was building in my head. I knew I should have her take me back, but there'd been dreams and delusions. All that got steamed over when my own stepbrother took one look at me in college, in my own living room, and gave me such a look of disdain and condemnation that was burned in my head to this day.

Sasha and Chad had had a night, and that's how he ran into me for the first time at Silvard. He knew I was there. I knew he was there, but we'd successfully avoided each other up until then. I came into their lives for a brief stint before going away again, but his mom and my dad had been married during that time. They had still been married when the college plans were put in motion, meaning that Deek wanted me to get to know my stepbrother. That'd been the entire reason I went to Silvard.

Funny how everything turned out, and not in a good way.

Deek and Natalie divorced that first year we were at college.

Cut got drafted the next year. He left, and Chad followed him.

I was the only one who stayed at Silvard, but it worked in my favor.

I hadn't seen Chad since that day in the dorm.

"I'm not ready." I was talking about talking to Cut.

It was weak. I knew it, and so not like my usual awesome badassness confidence, but he had the power to shatter me. A girl like me, we took that seriously. He could send me right back to who I'd been when I had an entire delusional relationship with him in my head.

I felt safer gawking from a distance than being live and in person in his presence.

"Okay. Well, I have something to distract you with."

I looked over.

She cringed, before pulling back to the road. "I slept with your stepbrother last night."

"No way!"

She grunted. "Way."

We were back to the one-word responses.

FROM: KOALA BOY
TO: CHEYCHEY
SUBJECT: THAT DOESN'T SOUND GOOD.

FROM: CHEYCHEY
TO: KOALA BOY
SUBJECT: CRISIS AVERTED. HOW ARE YOU? MISS YOU SO MUCH

FROM: KOALA BOY
TO: CHEYCHEY
SUBJECT: SETTLE, JEEZ.

5

CUT

I woke up to an empty bed, and I was in a fuck mood ever since.

She ran.

It wasn't that she left. It was that she *ran*. The girl freaking sprinted from this house, because when that alarm goes off, you shit your pants and she wasn't anywhere near the door shitting her pants. That means she took off.

So, yeah.

Fuck day.

Saturday was supposed to be my rest day, but then Chad showed up.

He stalked inside, slamming his door shut on his end of the house we owned.

We technically owned two houses, one on each lot, but since it was the two of us, we merged them together. The bigger house was mine. The smaller one was his. The pool was behind my side of the house, but when Chad had parties, it was both of our houses. (Which meant he used my side of the house.) It was a cool project we did together, but I was getting tired of a few things.

"Hey."

He stalked through the room, to the fridge and yanked it open.

Okay.

"Not a good night?"

He grunted, taking out some day-old pizza and he tossed the box on the oven. The top was flung open. The slices were dumped on a plate. The microwave door was shut harder than it needed to be.

My roommate/best friend/brother was in a mood.

"Did you go to the event?"

A second grunt. This time he turned with a glare. "You weren't there."

"I took off."

"The guys told me."

Right. I hadn't texted him, but we were guys. We didn't do that.

"Did you see your girl?"

A third grunt. "She kicked me out of bed." The microwave beeped, and he hit the button. The door swung open and he had a whole slice stuffed in his mouth before he shut the microwave door on the back-swing.

He came over and sat at the table where I was.

"The Not-Russian?"

A fourth grunt as he stuffed a second slice in his mouth.

Then he was up, going to the fridge, and he pulled out a beer.

He opened it as he came back, and catching my look, he shook his head. "Don't start."

So, I didn't start, not that I ever did.

"Wanna go skating today?"

"Fuck yeah."

That was my Saturday.

❄

I BENT over to lace up my skates just as Hendrix dropped down to the bench beside me.

"Yo." He was doing the same thing, his head turned my way. "What happened with that girl from the gala on Friday?"

It was Sunday and we had a game today. I'd tried not to fixate on her, but damn. It was hard. Best I'd ever had. I was riled up and claiming her, because apparently that was a thing with me. I had no clue until her that I could possess such strong feelings... but now, I wanted to punch someone for just being asked about her.

"Nothing."

"What?" He straightened up, checking his skate. "You were all gung-ho on her that night."

"Yeah, but the next morning was a different story."

I stood, not wanting to talk anymore. Not about her.

Grabbing my stick, I headed out. We'd be going out to warm up soon.

Nodding at each of my teammates, we lined up in the tunnel.

Hendrix was coming right behind me, and he was giving me that look. I could feel it. I knew what that look meant.

I was full of shit.

He knew I was full of shit.

I didn't want to be full of shit, but I was full of shit.

That girl. Damn.

Cheyenne.

We never exchanged numbers.

We'd gone faster than that.

There'd not been a lot of talking once we got to my house.

Six fucking times. Six. Fucking. Times.

I'd never had that with another girl, not in a matter of a few hours. Maybe a whole day, but Christ. And when I woke, I was aching for her all over again. But she was gone. The alarm was blaring, and I looked out the door. Nothing. She must've just left, so I didn't know if she got a ride or what, but she was outta there.

Fuck, man.

Fuck.

I don't indulge in one-night stands. You never knew what you'd get if you did that. I preferred casual relationships, keeping with the same few girls who knew the score. They lived their lives but were open if I called on them. One recently got engaged, so she called to end our arrangement. I don't know. Maybe I'd been a little sore on that?

I didn't think so. I'd been genuinely happy for her when she told me that, but Cheyenne-No-Last-Name was under my skin.

I hated it.

It's a groin kick to the ego, having a girl dash from your bed and disappear like what we'd just done meant nothing. And it's not like I won't see her. We were signed up to volunteer at their homeless kitchen. She'd be there, or I was assuming. I remembered from being briefed on the venture that it was mostly run by volunteers, but they did have a few full-timers. She was probably one of them.

Alex. Hendrix. Frank. I caught a couple side looks, so I was figuring they all knew.

I wanted to get on the ice.

I wanted to get the game going, and I wanted to destroy the Riders.

They were in our city. It was our ice. It'd be our win.

6

CHEYENNE

My upbringing wasn't normal, and that statement was an understatement.

Nothing had been normal about where I grew up, how I grew up, and how I ended up out here in Kansas City. I loved this city. I loved the Midwest. It was different than the west coast. There were different values here, and sometimes I didn't like them, but it felt simpler at times, too.

Things were calmer for me, for my head, and that was my biggest relationship in my life. But actually seeing Cut, having Cut see me, talk to me, and what else that happened, I was shook. For real. Shook.

I didn't want to say that I followed Cut out here after college, but when an opportunity came to move here, I jumped at the chance.

Cut had already been here.

He left Silvard after the first year, taking Chad with him so I had a whole three more years stepbrother-free, but also Cut-free and I hadn't enjoyed that last part. It was probably for the best. I concentrated harder on my head, on my schooling, and being able to open up Come Our Way had been one of those benefits.

But Cut was connected to other people from my life, and it was those that were giving me the bigger headache.

Cut was connected to Chad.

Chad was connected to Natalie and her new husband.

They were all connected to Hunter, Koala Boy.

Koala Boy was connected to Deek.

Deek and Hunter were connected to me, but Koala Boy more than Deek.

Everyone had moved here. Not all at the same time, but the migration was connected in some ways.

Cut came first. Chad went with him.

Three years later, I came. No one knew I was here.

Then two years ago, Natalie's new husband got a job transfer here. I knew this because I liked to cyberstalk my little brother. And a year ago, Deek came because Hunter was here.

So, everyone left Pine Valley except (from what else my cyberstalking had uncovered) Cut's family. They remained back in Oregon.

I didn't have thoughts or feelings about Natalie, Deek, or Chad. I truly didn't, but Hunter. My little brother was a different story. The problem was Natalie. Well, the problem was all of them, but mostly Natalie. She never approved of Donna, and that cloud of judgment extended to me.

Once my head got clear, I thought long and hard about when I lived with them, and after Donna died. It took a bit to understand it, but it was hard to explain it. Sasha got it. She met Chad, who ditched her after finding out that I was her roommate. I was the one who had to break that to her, and it hadn't been pretty. She was hurting because of him, but she also wanted to rip his head off because of me. I loved my girl, but back to the whole shitbag of Natalie and Deek.

It was when I was trying to explain it to Melanie one night that I was starting to piece it together myself.

"Melanie. I lived on the streets."

She'd been tipsy that night. It was martini night and she swung her martini to the left, her eyes rolling to the right. "So?"

"So." We were talking about our families and she didn't understand how I couldn't have one.

Because I didn't.

Donna told me her parents were dead. She had no siblings. She never talked about aunts or uncles. And well, with Deek...

"Your dad just abandoned you? He brought you in and then what? Paid for your college and you never talked to him again? That makes no sense."

"Well." From Sasha.

Melanie lifted her pinkie finger at her. "Don't start with the one-word explanations. I've had way too many martinis to even start thinking that game is fun."

"Fine."

"Thank you."

And Melanie swung her head back to me. "Your dad's rich. Why aren't you rolling in dough yourself?"

Because that would make sense to Melanie, who came from a family where everyone shared everything. She moved to Kansas for school and fell in love with the city. She stayed so we got Melanie, but she lost her family life. They all lived in Texas, though they came up six times a year.

We were heading into winter so the next time they'd come up would be end of spring.

Their family was Italian so when her family visited, there were carbs. Lots and lots of carbs, and my stomach was shifting, growling, because apparently I needed some carbs today.

But I kept digressing and that was a normal thing for me, because well; because it's me.

It's how I'm programmed.

But back to Melanie who didn't understand that sometimes people you share blood with could be strangers and I was trying to explain that. Sasha gave up long ago, but her family situation wasn't much better. No. It was, but that was a whole other ordeal itself. Her family lived in Jersey and her mom did nails and her dad ran a pool hall.

Finally, I broke it down. "You know those assholes who look down on homeless people?"

Melanie took a sip of her martini. "Yeah?" Her eyes were narrowed. She knew I was going somewhere with this.

I did. "Natalie was one of those people. Me coming into her house didn't change anything. As far as she figured, she was just housing a street teenager."

Of course, I never considered myself someone who lived on the streets. It's just where I hung out when Donna was on a bender or when she locked me out. And sometimes those times lasted longer than a day, or a week, or a month, but to someone like me, and how I was, I was just giving my mother space while she sorted her latest drug habit.

"That's..." Melanie made a face, her cheeks stretching tight. She put her martini down. "...awful."

That was my life. I wasn't one to dwell, so I didn't.

I moved on, like focusing on Cut Ryder.

But fast-forward to today and my mind was going in circles and my stomach was in my chest. My heart was beating through my bladder.

I didn't dwell on my family, but coming to Cut's hockey game and I couldn't help but start dwelling.

I didn't like to dwell.

It never led me anywhere good.

But I was here. At his game.

Maybe I shouldn't have come?

Maybe so, but I was here. My season seats were a few rows above where the players came out. Normally I never worried about them looking up, which they did on occasion. But none of them knew who I was. At least not before Friday night. There was no reason for me to even care in the past. The only person I would've hid from was Chad, and he wasn't on the team. So no worries then, but it was a bit different this game.

I beat myself up all day yesterday, going back and forth if I did the right thing.

I still didn't know.

Ever been so scared that you were paralyzed? Where your mind and heart were conflicted? One saying stay and hide, be safe, and the other saying don't be a weasel and grow a pair? I was both, but hockey was my thing. I loved the game ever since learning Cut was its star, so I was here, just like all the times before. It had become my tradition to come to their games, some of the few hours I stepped away from the kitchen no matter what time the games were. This time, I knew Dean was here. I didn't know if he was in the stands or in the suites, but it didn't matter.

My usual seatmates were starting to arrive, and I settled back because the players were coming out for warm-ups.

"OH, DEARIE." Maisie leaned over to me, nudging me with her elbow and a nod to the ice. "Your boy is in a mood today, isn't he?"

Maisie, Otis, and JJ were the other 'regular' ticket holders who sat with me.

They fully knew I had a long-standing crush on Cut Ryder.

Maisie and Otis were married, a retired couple, and they were as religious about coming to these games as I was. JJ was younger than them, but older than me. She wasn't as regular as we were, but she was a strong second runner-up.

"I know." He hadn't looked up when they came out to the ice, and I'd been worried. I didn't know why. They never looked up, or rarely did. On occasion, if someone called out and it happened to be timed just right where the music and the announcer wasn't as loud, they'd look up, but again, that was such a rarity.

But Maisie wasn't wrong.

Cut was checking more forceful than other times. He was cutting across the ice. He was skating around the others in circles and doing it in a way that was almost humiliating to the other team. The enforcer had come out a few times against him, but it didn't seem to bother Cut. He rushed right back at the enforcer, heading to the box, double his normal speed.

His mood was also working for him.

He scored three times by himself, weaving in and out and not needing an assist from any teammate. Cut's mood had infected his team, and now all of them were on the edge, a bit more aggressive than normal. The crowd was loving it. Me, not so much. Games like this ended with someone's blood on the ice. Blood had already been spilled, but I knew there'd be more. A full team fight was in the making, and Cut was leading the charge.

Otis leaned around his wife, his face grizzled and his beard with patches of white and black. "You know him the best. What do you think's the reason?"

I did, but no way was I copping to that with them. Not these people. I adored them.

"I don't know."

Otis frowned, his wrinkles clearly defined. When I first met Otis, I'd been fanstruck thinking he was someone else. I couldn't speak. He could've been Otis Taylor's twin, a famous black musician, but they shared the first name. I'd seen recent images of Otis Taylor, and my Otis had half his hair, though both had the same blue eyes. Maisie was almost the exact opposite. Otis came to the games in a hoodie and a ball cap. Both were always torn up and shredded on the ends.

Maisie had carrot-like hair, a bright orange and red. A spray of freckles over her round cheeks. They were the couple that while Otis was gripping the team's program to shreds during every game, Maisie pulled out her latest crocheting project. She'd done five blankets so far, and she was working on a pair of gloves for their granddaughter now. I loved these people, even though the only thing we shared in common was a love of hockey.

JJ sat behind us, and she held the two seats beside her. Sometimes she came alone, sometimes she brought friends. Today was a day she brought friends, and they were annoying me. JJ was probably ten years older than I was. Mid to upper-thirties or even younger forties. I'd never had the courage to ask, but she kept her hair gray. I overheard Maisie ask her one time if she dyed it that color, and JJ responded, "Nah. I went gray early, and I'm too cheap to keep buying hair product for it. I don't mind the color. I kinda like it." And that was that, but JJ spent her money on other items. She and Maisie had a full conversation about the best places to vacation in the Ozarks. From what JJ was saying, she had a big house there already. I didn't know what JJ did for a living, but she obviously did well for herself.

She always wore the same outfit. Jeans. A Cut jersey. (I didn't hold it against her. His was the most-sold jersey.) And a red ball cap for the local football team, too.

"Girl."

That always made me smile. Reminded me of Sasha and Melanie.

JJ leaned down, adding as she cupped her hand to mask her words from her friends, "That boy could be my son and I'm up here about to climax. Jay-sus, you know?" She winked, lightly touching her fist to my shoulder before leaning back.

Maisie half-turned in her seat. She beckoned.

JJ responded, leaning back down.

Maisie's eyes shifted to JJ's friends. "Who do you have with you today?"

JJ's eyes turned sly and she crouched down between the seats, lowering her voice. Her breath was hot and beer-y. "I mentor the one girl, and she asked if her friend could come."

I could feel Maisie's excitement, but she was refraining. Or trying. She jerked in her seat, her eyes getting big, and then she let loose in a rushed breath. "What do you do? What kind of mentoring?"

"I'm an entrepreneur, and the one is opening an online, personalized styling service. We met through a business networking venture. I'm also seeing if I want to invest or not, but so far, I'm thinking no just because she's starting to annoy me. She and her friend are more interested in trying to find where Cut Ryder hangs out after games than trying to sell me on why her business is a good investment for me."

He hangs out at home.

I knew the answer.

I also knew he liked his downtime after games, and then he'd have a few friends over for a beer in the evening. Or he'd go to a close friend's place for the same. Beer and chill. One beer. That was it. And now that I was thinking about it, I wasn't any better than those girls because I knew that fact because I'd cyberstalked my stepbrother.

Chad wasn't my brother anymore, but still.

Stepbrother that wasn't a step, but we were extended half-siblings? We were both half-siblings with Koala Man, Hunter. So yeah. That's how I knew about his routine and all.

Super proud moment here.

Not really.

Maisie and JJ kept whispering about the two girls, but I tuned back into the game. First line was back out, and Cut was doing his thing.

Bam.

He checked a guy.

Another guy was rolling up.

The enforcer.

My stomach dropped because I knew what was coming next, and yep. It was happening as I was internally narrating.

Enforcer guy skated in, grabbed Cut's pads and pulled him

away from the boards. Words were exchanged. The crowd was standing. They were going nuts.

Fight. Fight. Fight.

A chant was starting.

And fists were up.

They were off—going back and forth.

I hated this part.

I knew the culture of the sport, knew this was part of it, knew people loved it, fed off of the physicality, but I hated it. Loathed it, and even more blood was spilled. Not the enforcer's, Cut's, and just like I knew it would happen, his teammates got in on the fight. The other team rushed in. Then the benches cleared. The refs were skating back to the chaos.

This wasn't normal. The crowd was *eating* it up.

Normally at the time, they'd be wading in to restore order, but nope. They were looking up. The clock was done anyways, and we were at the end of the third period. Game was over. Mustangs won three to one.

Otis leaned around Maisie, who was still turned toward JJ, and caught my eye.

I leaned over.

"We're going to grab a drink at The Way Station. Would you like to join?"

The Way Station was a popular bar that everyone knew the team sometimes stopped in. I say sometimes because only one or two had been spotted in there, and that wasn't too common. I sort of thought that was a rumor the team liked to put out there so they could go to their actual spot, or that they just let the bar run with it while everyone went home to their wives and girlfriends, if they had them.

Either way, it wasn't the first time I'd gone with Otis and Maisie, and today was a day I didn't want to head home and be by myself. Home would be where I would be alone with my thoughts and those thoughts, as was inevitable, would go to where I didn't want them to go to: a certain hockey player. I'd come a long way from years of therapy and meds, but my brain still wandered, and no amount of medication or techniques could control that all the time.

So, because of that, I nodded, and because I was nodding at Otis, I didn't realize what was about to happen. And what was about to happen was a loud screech from behind me.

"CUT, WE WANT YOUR PHONE NUMBER!"

I cringed, shooting both of JJ's seatmates a glare, but then icy dread settled in my bones because I knew what I was about to be confronted with.

I turned, in slow motion, and he was heading into the tunnel, just below us. His gaze was up. He had stopped, holding a helmet in one hand and his stick in the other, and he was looking up at us.

At me.

Correction. Me. *All* me.

His gaze was solidly on mine, and as our eyes connected, his got bigger a fraction of an inch at the same time I wished I could've shrunk into my seat.

Damn.

Damn!

He was all sweaty and dirty, and fierce.

I felt punched in the windpipes, just looking at him looking at me—and the way he was looking at me. As if he was seeing me naked. Well, he had, but he was seeing so much of me in that moment, all of my truths, that I shifted and ducked my head down.

His gaze narrowed, switching to something beside me, and then he went into the tunnel.

Maisie and JJ were fully staring at me.

JJ's seatmates? They were going crazy.

"He was looking at me!"

The friend. "No way. Me. I just jizzed in my pants." A beat. "Sorry, old man."

Both cracked up, and Otis turned to stare at them.

JJ cursed under her breath. "Respect."

They both quieted, and I was going out on a limb and guessing that that comment cemented the fact that JJ was not going to invest in that girl's business venture.

The game was done.

People were standing up, getting ready to leave. Some were chatting. Some were sprinting for the bathrooms. Most of the players were off the ice. The last of the coaches were bringing up the rear. All the while, I didn't move.

Neither did JJ. Neither did Maisie. Neither did Otis.

All three were staring right at me.

I couldn't take it anymore. "What?"

JJ raised an eyebrow, a curl of gray hair falling over her face. She let it be. "You know, Girl."

Maisie's face was flushed, and she was gripping those crocheted gloves to her chest. "You have something to tell us?" She said it in a hushed voice, a voice that told me she was also speechless.

Otis's eyes were narrowed, and he tilted his head to the side, but he didn't add his two cents. I think he knew that nothing needed to be said.

It was then that I noticed a familiar figure breaking from the crowd. At first, I didn't think anything of it. Of him, but he kept drawing closer. His head was down. He was in jeans and a nice sweatshirt, one of Cut's. He was wearing a ball cap, too. His phone was out, in hand, and he was looking at the seats, then back to his phone. He kept doing this, bringing him closer and closer.

Now I really froze in place.

He was standing on the top row, just five rows from where we were sitting. JJ's seatmates had left, I'm sure they were one of the sprinters for the bathroom, so he had a clear line of eyesight when he saw our group.

He saw Otis. Nothing.

He saw Maisie. Nothing.

He saw JJ. Nothing.

Then, his gaze tracked from his phone. He frowned. And lifted—he found me.

It was Chad.

Dread filled me, weighing all of my limbs down because I knew what had happened.

Cut must've sent a text to Chad, told him my seat number, and sent Chad to find me.

There was a brief flare of hope. Maybe he wouldn't recog— recognition dawned and he staggered back.

Yep. He actually staggered back. Blood drained from his face, and he'd just put my vagina together with the correct dick and got the right sexual position.

Me and Cut.

Then his eyes glittered. Anger flared. His jaw firmed.

He put his phone away, turned, shoved his hands into his pockets, and stalked off.

Well. Then.

Now I really needed The Way Station.

FROM: KOALA BOY
TO: CHEYCHEY
SUBJECT: I THINK I LIKE SOMEONE.

FROM: CHEYCHEY
TO: KOALA BOY
SUBJECT: IS THAT GOOD? WHAT'S HER NAME? I'LL CYBERSTALK HER.

FROM: KOALA BOY
TO: CHEYCHEY
SUBJECT: OMG, YOU'RE ALMOST AS BAD AS MOM. HER NAME IS MONICA.

FROM: CHEYCHEY
TO: KOALA BOY
SUBJECT: THE CYBERSTALKING HAS COMMENCED.

7

CHEYENNE

Unknown: It's true?

The first text woke me.

I checked the time. It was just past midnight.

A second text buzzed in as I was sitting up.

Unknown: You're Chad's stepsister? Cheyenne.

I was going out on a limb here...

Me: This is Cut?

Unknown: Yes. I saw you, sent him to grab your digits for me. He recognized you.

Cut: You're Chad's sister?

Me: Technically, no. Deek and his mom divorced.

Cut: Same thing. Both Hunter's siblings.

I sighed.

Me: Yes.

Cut: That's why you ditched?

I paused. If I said yes, I'd be lying. I didn't like liars.

Gah. Another sigh.

Me: No.

He didn't text again that night.

THE TEXT CAME the next day, at nine in the morning.

Cut: Why then?

I'd just pulled into Come Our Way's parking lot and turned the engine off. Grabbing my phone, I almost oversipped my coffee at the same time. Crap. I usually sipped with caution. My favorite coffee place liked to overheat the heat, you know? It burned my throat, but I read his text and felt a different sort of burning.

Regret.

And need. Sexual need.

Not heart need, because I was still clamping down on the feelings department there. And go me because that took effort. A lot of effort.

Six times, folks. Six. Times.

I sat back and typed.

Me: I don't like liars.

Cut: I'm not a liar.

Me: No. I know you aren't. I'm setting the parameters.

Cut: What parameters? I want to know why you ditched.

Me: And I'm trying to explain my response ahead of time.

A pause.

Cut: The fuck?

I grinned at that.

Me: I don't want to tell you why.

Cut: Why?

A third sigh from these text messages.

Me: Just...I can't explain.

I waited.

And waited.

I sat in my car and I gripped my phone, and I kept waiting because this time I wanted him to respond.

I needed him to respond.

He didn't respond.

HIS RESPONSE CAME at six that evening.

Cut: Dinner.

I was serving dinner to those at the shelter, felt my phone buzz, and stepped away from the line. There was a volunteer helping out, so I headed for my office and read his text.

Me: ?

Cut: Explain over dinner.

I didn't respond. I didn't know what to say, but I was feeling things. I was doing all sorts of feeling. My heart was starting to pound in my chest. My hands got clammy.

He wanted to still see me?

I didn't know how I felt. A wave of relief, but nerves all jumbled together.

Cut: You are the one who rolled out of my bed.

A fourth sigh.

Me: Fine. When for dinner?

Cut: Thursday night. We're away, then volunteer at your place Wednesday and Thursday. I can do that night and I'm on the road again this weekend.

My stomach started doing somersaults because whoa. I'd get to see him three times this week. A group of them were volunteering for the brunch shift, and they had a home game on Thursday.

Cut: After the game that night.

Then that would most likely be drinks, not dinner. I guess he ate late, probably needing the calories after his game.

I already knew what I was going to say, hence the sweaty palms and the hitch that turned into a wheeze in my breathing, and I could've pulled my own hair out from the nerves. So. Many.

Feelings! It was almost too much and this was just over texting. Hence, why I rolled and ran that morning.

Me: Fine.

Cut: You'll be at the game? Or that last game was a fluke?

Me: Yes. I'll be there. Same seats.

Cut: Get a ride there. I'll drive us after.

Just like that, I had a date.

My hands were now shaking and sweaty.

8

CUT

I had something extra in me at our away game.

Feeling the chill from the ice, how it felt fucking flying over it, easing in and around my opponents, all of that and more. There was just more happening tonight.

The smack talk wasn't affecting me one bit. I was in a zone.

My stick was a part of me. The puck too.

Hendrix lined up, but I knew his read. It was in our play, and I skated up into place. His wrist moved. The puck came to me, and I was there, ready for it, and it flicked past two opponents, past the goalie, and swish. I went Top Shelf. The puck hit the net.

This shit never got old. Ever.

I completed the turn, rounding past the goalie, and Hendrix was on the other side to meet me.

One done.

More to go.

This would not be a one and done. Not for damn sure.

Then, the call came, and we switched up. Second line was out, and we were on the bench. I got some pats on my pads, my helmet. The coach gave me a nod, and Franklin banged against the box. He was still doing some time. We'd all been there before, it was just part of the play.

Sitting, taking a breather, I got a water and towel handed to me. That felt good, but I wanted back out there.

"Your family came tonight?"

It took a second for the question from Hendrix to penetrate.

We weren't far from where I first grew up.

"Yeah. My brothers too. We're doing dinner after. You want to come?"

He nodded. "You know it. I like Mama Alice."

I smirked. Everyone liked Mama Alice, and all hockey fans *loved* Killer Mama Alice at our games.

"Ryder."

I looked at Coach. He motioned to the ice. "Get out there."

It wasn't unusual to switch up the lines, but hell yeah, I was ready.

We waited, then made the switch. Alex skated in and I jumped off, moving into position.

I pushed forward, meeting up against the other team's defender, and it was then that I got it. He was fast. I knew he was fast. Everyone knew he was fast, but going against him, Alex wasn't as fast.

Thirty seconds later, Hendrix moved next to me.

We changed lines.

Changed again.

It was the end of the first period when we got the puck back, when I fainted at shooting, gave it to Hendrix, and he got it in.

Lines changed up. I got a breather, and like last time, Coach sent me out for Alex once more.

This guy on the other team was good. He was winding up, but I moved in.

He slapped it to his teammate. Franklin was moving in. He intersected and we weaved around each other, then back into position.

We were holding it.

The other team was good. They'd held us off for most of the first period, but we had two goals in.

I should've been ready. A part of me was ready, but Franklin hit the puck to me.

I got it and *bam!*

I was shoved down, blindsided and looking up—their fucking enforcer.

His check was legal, barely, and he flew past me with a smirk on his face. "Two more to go, Ryder."

I glared, feeling a spike in my blood. The magical spell of the game had been interrupted, but I knew that was why he was targeting me. He wanted in my head. Well, welcome to the shit-show and walk your ass right in. Enforcers didn't work on me how they worked on most players. They brought an edge to the game, knowing you're targeted, and I welcomed that edge. I used that edge to up my speed, up my adrenaline, up everything, and the more aggressive he got against me, the more aggressive I got against his teammates.

He just didn't know that yet.

IT WAS in the second period when he made his move.

He swung in.

I saw him coming, moved the puck to Franklin, and I turned to meet him.

Okay, asshole.

He read me and veered back.

He was bluffing, but I read him right and I nodded to Franklin.

I pushed forward, veering right past their enforcer as he was swinging back around. He wasn't ready for that. Franklin shot to me and I moved forward with the puck, Franklin swung in against their enforcer. No contact was made, but Hendrix was skating with me.

I passed to Hendrix.

Hendrix passed to Franklin.

Franklin moved in, got cut off, and the puck came back to me.

I lined up, did a tight circle, and tapped it to Hendrix.

Hendrix got it in.

Goal three.

Then their enforcer came at me.

There was no bluffing this time.

TWO GAMES IN A ROW.

Fuck.

My jaw hurt. My hands hurt. Everything hurt.

I was tired.

The mind games had me tired by the end of this game.

We were up three to one. Alex let one in, and I was hurting, so Coach kept me for my breather.

He signaled the line change, but I was held back.

Alex stayed on.

Another thirty seconds.

The third line went out.

Alex came back in and his gaze found mine. I read the apology there and dipped my head. There was nothing else to say. This was the game.

"You good?" From the assistant coach.

I nodded. I wasn't but I gritted my teeth. That was all strategy from their team. Their defender was better than Alex. I was out there. I had the stamina to meet him, best him at times, and then they sent their head-fuck guy in and it worked. I fought him off, but that beast was raging in me, simmering underneath. He wanted out to play.

I hit the ice, felt that 'home' feeling, and I smiled.

I was letting the beast out.

There was no way they'd see him coming.

AT THE END of our last period, I heard from the stands, "WAY TO KILL 'EM, CUT! I NAMED YOU THAT FOR A REASON!"

There was a roar from the stands.

Yeah. Everyone loved Killer Mama Alice.

9

CUT

The team headed for the hotel, but I had it worked out to stay the night with my family. It was on my dime to fly back the next day, not with the team. It was worth it, especially now walking out from the arena, my entire body tired from our post-game workout and my mom was waiting for me.

"Hey, big guy."

Same greeting after every game, with a wide smile, and she held her tiny arms out for me.

I bent down, hugging her back and she embraced me, squeezing tight. Another reminder never to underestimate Killer Mama Alice. She had the grip of a bear, and once she was done hugging me, she let me go and patted my arms. "You're looking dapper."

I raised an eyebrow.

Dapper.

The Killer part of her name was gone since the game was done.

"Hey, Mom."

Her face softened, and she pulled me back in for another hug. "Oh, man. I have missed you."

I glanced around, but no one else was with her. "Where are the others?"

"Your dad went to get the vehicle, and you know Dylan and Jamison. They said to text them when you showed and they'd meet us at the door."

I did know my brothers. "They're off flirting with girls?"

She grinned, patting me on the arm as I started for the arena's door for the players and family. "You know it." She was pulling her phone out when one of the attendants came over.

"Mr. Ryder, a driver is out front saying he's your father."

I nodded.

Alice snorted. "Can we tell them he's not your father?"

"Mom."

She laughed. "What? It wouldn't last, but it'd be fun to see what he would do."

Her phone was buzzing and I noted, watching her as she read the messages, "He'd just park and then call you to have us walk out to him."

"True. It's not worth it." She was punching buttons on her phone, frowning and biting her lip. "Your brothers. Do they really think we're going to let them go to a nightclub with some girls they just met tonight?" A pause. A ding from her phone, and she laughed. "And I don't care to see these girls' Instagram accounts. The amount of skin these girls are showing does not help their case." She was narrating as she typed, "No. You cannot go out with these girls. We're here to see your brother. Period. Get back. Now."

We were nearing the door. "You told them, Mom."

"Damn right, I did." She was still frowning, still talking to the phone.

Another ding.

She groaned, then hit a button and put the phone to her ear. A second later, she said in her 'mom' voice, "I do not care how nice these girls seem like. I'm sure it has nothing to do with the size of their breasts, but we came here to see your brother. Your brother who has just played a game and I'm sure is tired and under-hydrated and you are his brothers and you're holding us up! Get here now." A break. "The family doors. The same ones we've exited many times before because this is not the first time we've left with your brother after his away game."

She'd raised her voice, and was garnering attention.

I was just enjoying it. Same Dylan and Jamison.

She rolled her eyes. "You've got two minutes or you can pay for your own Uber to the restaurant. Got it?" She didn't wait for their response. She hung up and turned, a bright smile for me as she linked her arm around mine. "Your brothers are excited to see you. They love you very much."

I barked out a laugh now, and lifted my arm to circle my mom's shoulders. I pulled her in and leaned down, giving her a kiss on the forehead. "I love you, Mom. And I was a boy, too. I know what my brothers are loving more right now than me."

Some of her annoyance eased and she relaxed. "They're good boys."

Dylan was a junior and Jamison was a sophomore.

Both were good-looking, and both played sports. Jamison followed me into hockey while Dylan kept with football and baseball, but both were athletic, popular, and they had their fair amount of girls hitting up their DMs.

The family SUV was parked by the curb, two parking attendants were standing by the driver's door and as we neared, I wasn't surprised to hear my dad talking about the game.

"Oh yeah! I know. And did you see that cheap shot at the end? I wanted to head to the ice myself."

Both attendants were nodding, agreeing, and then Alice opened the front door.

"Cut! Yo!"

Dylan and Jamison were heading down the sidewalk, coming around the back end of the arena and both were walking fast.

Their voices carried. The attendants looked through the SUV and I heard them starting to talk, but I stepped back to meet my brothers.

Alice reached over, taking my bag from me.

She was Supermom Extraordinaire, and she was putting it away for me as both my brothers got to me.

They looked good.

Each wrapped me up in their arms, giving me tight hugs.

Dylan. Jeez. I hadn't seen in a while. "You've gotten even bigger."

He smirked, raking a hand through his dark curls. "Yeah, well. Gotta keep up with our superstar brother." He pounded me on the arm, then turned for the SUV.

Jamison wasn't as cocky, but he was just as tall as Dylan.

I whistled, shaking my head at him. "Fuck. That's gotta piss D off that you're as tall."

A cocky smirk showed now and he ducked his head down, shrugging one shoulder up. "He's so scared I'll go out for football next year."

I laughed. "Right. He'll be a senior."

"His big year."

Jamison took after our mom, his hair was blonder. Dylan had Dad's dark hair, and I was the mix. But Dylan had our dad's extrovert attitude while Jamison was shyer. Mom again, except at my hockey games, which had me wondering...

I followed Jamison inside and asked, "What's Mom like at your games?"

Both groaned.

Dylan rolled his eyes.

Jamison pretended to hit his own forehead. "You think she's bad at your games?"

Dylan looked at me. "She's worse at our games."

Alice turned around from the front seat. "I am not. I'm the same volume, but it's not my fault the fans are quieter at your games. They shouldn't be. High school sports need loud supporters."

"You're obnoxious sometimes, Mom." From Jamison.

Dylan added, "You're not Killer Mama Alice at our games. She's Serial Killer Mama Alice at our games."

Alice turned back around, as our dad had said goodbye to the attendants and he was starting to pull forward. "I just have to tell the world how much I love you boys."

It was then when we were pausing in line, and David turned around. "Hey, Cut! I was getting out to hug my oldest when you all piled in like we were late for the NASCAR race."

Dylan and Jamison both groaned at the same time, leaning their heads back. "Dad. Seriously. Stop with the NASCAR references. We've had enough."

Jamison said to me, "Dad met a NASCAR driver on the golf course two weeks ago, and guess what's his favorite sport now to watch? It's not hockey anymore."

"It'll always be hockey. You don't listen to your brothers. I'm just intrigued. That Case Triven seems like a nice guy."

"Case Triven is a professional dirt bike rider. You met his brother, *Ace* Triven."

"That's right. Case is the more famous one, right?"

Dylan couldn't stop rolling his eyes. "They're both famous, Dad, and that's why you started talking to them because of Cutler."

"That's right. It's like you guys were both there."

Dylan and Jamison said at the same time, both so over it, too, "We were."

"Right."

I chuckled, seeing my dad wink at me through the rearview mirror.

Dad. David.

Mom. Alice.

It didn't matter how old I was going to get. I had missed my family, and I had missed this, our tradition.

They picked me up after the game.

We would go to the same restaurant that we'd been going to for four years. We'd sit in the back room, eating and laughing for the next three hours. And even though Pine Valley wasn't a far drive, my family opted to stay close to cut down on the time driving. We'd been going to the same hotel for the same four years. We'd all stay in the presidential penthouse suite, with two rooms attached on both sides. And even though I'd try to pay for the rooms, Alice would blackmail the front desk clerks to make sure she paid for the ensuite and all the rooms attached and not me.

In the morning, we'd have breakfast on the hotel suite's balcony.

After breakfast, we'd lounge around and do whatever until my flight later in the day.

The team would have flown back in the morning.

My family would pack up from the hotel, give me a ride to the airport, and I'd fly back home later.

All this to spend a few extra hours with my family.

Always worth it.

IT WAS THE NEXT MORNING.

Dylan and Jamison went to get coffee from the coffee place around the corner. The hotel was exclusive so they wouldn't be hitting the coffee place in the hotel lobby. Not enough girls their age there, so yeah. They'd be gone for an hour because I've seen that line. It was always the same, out the door.

I was sitting on the patio with my mom.

David had gone to the gym, which Alice said was really code for the spa.

It was then when I asked, "You remember in high school

when Chad came to stay with us?"

She was thumbing through a paperback, but lifted her head, frowning at me. "Yeah. Why?"

"What did they say was the reason for him coming over and staying so long?"

"Uh." She put her book down and tilted her head up, her forehead marring. "It was because Deek needed to house his daughter for a bit. Something about her mother was going on. Why are you asking? Is everything okay with Chad?"

I didn't answer that question. "They ever say anything about the daughter? Any specific reason Chad had to not be at the house when she was there?"

She was chewing on the inside of her lip, staring at me. Studying me. Another dip of her eyebrows, and she answered, but she answered slowly, "Well. I think they were just being cautious. Natalie was concerned about the boys because the girl's mother wasn't a good influence. I'd be cautious, too, to be honest. If a kid's coming from a bad environment, you never know what behaviors might be coming into your home."

Right.

That made sense, except I couldn't see Cheyenne being like that.

"What's going on, Cut? It's not like you to ask a question like that out of the blue."

I shook my head. "It's nothing. I just don't remember hearing about Deek's daughter, that's all."

"You know, I don't remember Chad mentioning her much. He spent a lot of time at our house anyway. It might've just felt normal for him. Something come up with Deek's daughter now? Now, Deek and Natalie divorced so she wouldn't be any relation to Chad anymore, would she? Well. Wait again. There's Hunter..."

It wasn't sitting with me right. None of it was.

"It's too bad that Natalie moved out there. I mean, not for Chad's sake. He gets to see his mom and brother, but I suppose

I'm talking out of order here. I always thought Hunter and Jamison would be best friends like you and Chad. Didn't turn out that way, though."

She yawned before standing up. "I can't wait for those boys to get back with our coffee. I'm going to make a pot in the room. You want a cup?"

"Nah. I'm good. I've got my water."

"Yes. You keep hydrated. I know those games are so hard on you players." She moved around me, patting my shoulder as she went inside.

I pulled out my phone, pulling up the old text conversation I had with Chad.

CHAD: The fuck? That chick you banged is Deek's daughter.

Me: What?

Chad: Cheyenne, right? Did she use the right name? What alias did she say to you?

Me: She didn't. We didn't exchange names, but what are you talking about?

Chad: You sent me to those seats because you wanted to grab the number from your Friday bang. It's Deek's daughter. You remember. She's vile, man. Stay away from her. There's a reason I basically lived with you guys our junior year. It was her. She was at my house instead. Mom and Deek didn't want us around her, she's that bad. Just stay away from her. Trust me.

I NEVER RESPONDED to his last text, and I deleted the whole conversation now.

It didn't feel right having that in my phone.

Actually, none of this felt right.

10

CHEYENNE

Cut wanted to do dinner on Thursday.

Cut wanted an explanation.

Cut was going to look at me like I was crazy, because well...technically speaking, I was. And boy, that was going to be a depressing conversation, so yeah. Not looking forward to dinner or the date, but I really was—but wasn't at the same time.

I went to work the next day and I was a ball of nerves. That was *really* not a good thing for me.

"Yo!"

"Heehaw!"

That was my go-to startled reaction/scream. Do not make fun of me for it, and I rounded on Dean, giving him the stink eye because I hadn't even taken two steps inside Come Our Way before he popped out of his office.

He was used to my heehaw by now, and he frowned for a split second before his entire body joined him in the hallway. It'd just been his head, and now I was the one frowning at his tie. He was wearing a Mustangs logo tie with his little hockey sticks cufflinks.

I made no comment, because this was the adorable five-year-old side of Dean. He truly was a fanboy of the team.

"So, we're down a volunteer."

I sighed. Dean was carrying a whole file of paperwork. And he was waiting for me, that meant he was going to follow me into my office, sit there, and not move until we'd talked about everything he needed us to talk about.

I changed courses, heading into the kitchen first. I was going to need coffee for this, a lot of coffee.

"Cheyenne-the-eye-of-the-tiger!" came from behind the grill, and our main chef lifted up one of his beefy hands, booming his normal greeting to me. He told us to call him Boomer, and well, judging by his greeting, you can see why. He kicked his head back and flashed me some pearly whites. "How's it hanging with my especially fabulous-looking girl today?"

I gave him a smile back, but I didn't try to keep anything from Boomer. He had the inherent ability of seeing everything, and I mean everything. If you had been anxious about something three days ago, he'd ask how that was going. Boomer and I shared something that Dean never would. We had both shared time on the streets, and there was a vibe we got from the other.

I thought those days were long behind me, like way, way behind me, but one look from Boomer and he understood. I wish I could look at him and know what he was feeling, but Boomer liked to remind everyone that he was our All-Knowing, All-Wise, All-Black Maestro. His words. I overheard him introduce himself that way to the new volunteer last week, and even she seemed transfixed with him.

"Boom, I need—"

He turned back to the cutting board but pointed to the coffee area. "Already got you covered."

"Thank you, thank you, thank you." I breezed past him, grabbing a mug asap.

I hoped Dean would step back, give me a breather for a minute.

Nope.

I got my coffee, turned back, and there he was. Still waiting, readjusting his Mustangs' tie. Those cufflinks flashed again, and for some reason, that settled me. I grinned at him. "You going to get through the next dos dias? Need a fresca? A bebida?"

He frowned, twisting his tie the other way. "I don't know what any of that means." He lifted up the papers. "But I want to hash all this out before the first Mustangs get here." His gaze dropped to my coffee where I was still pouring creamer into it.

I was a cream type of girl.

"You done yet? Want some coffee with your creamer?"

My grin spread, all slow like. "And there you are, thinking you can write the manual for office sexual harassment. You go, boy. You lead from example."

He blinked at me. "Huh?"

"Never mind." The moment was gone. I led the way to my office, and once inside, my purse was dropped on the floor. Coffee set on the desk. I dug out my phone and booted up my computer. First things first, right?

I grabbed for my coffee, and leaned back, taking a big whiff. This was my porn.

"Okay, Deano. Let's do this."

He just rolled his eyes at his nickname and pulled out the first sheet. "Cut Ryder was taken off the volunteer schedule for today. He might get in tomorrow, but they're not sure."

Well, there went that porn-inspired coffee-creamer mood.

I tried to ignore the shrinking on the stomach lining. "Why? I mean, did they say how come?"

He shook his head. "Said something about PT, but since they're sending the entire team, I think we can still use them for our social media marketing. And if he doesn't come tomorrow, I'll reach out and see if we can get him to come alone on another time. This might work in our benefit." Second sheet was pulled out. "And we need to talk about changing our distributors—"

I mentally checked out.

I was trying not to think about Cut, about what PT he'd need, about everything that had nothing to do with Come Our Way. I was still looking at Dean, and he thought I was paying attention. I could tell because I was simultaneously monitoring his word efficiency, speed, tone, and volume frequency.

But I was thinking about Cut.

He was in PT.

Probably because of his fight. He'd had two in two games.

And he was being used to cover two lines.

He was fatigued by the end, and I'd wanted to text him, ask if he was all right, but I was also more of a chickenshit at the same time.

Dean's speech hadn't changed. He thought I was paying attention...but there was Cut.

He wasn't coming today.

That was good.

Right?

Maybe it wasn't.

No, no. It was good.

Even if he came tomorrow, it was business. And I'd be hiding in the office, and that made me remember—"Wait, I'm not coming in tomorrow."

Dean stopped, his mouth open and in mid-sentence. "What?"

"I have a thing tomorrow."

"A thing? We need you. It's our biggest social media day."

I shook my head at the same time my mind was buzzing, so was my blood. I was whirling. Winding up. He had no clue what he was asking of me, but nada. I couldn't do it. "No comprendo."

"That means you don't understand." Dean huffed. "I had a photo op planned for tomorrow, especially if Cut Ryder is coming. We need you—"

"No, you don't." *Blood, calm down. Mind, pause. One thing at a time.*

Thoughts... I was mentally watching them. They were wheezing by. I could almost feel the breeze from them.

Slow. Down.

They slowed.

I turned the thoughts into words. Words I could read.

I read one at a time. One word at a time, and as I did this, knowing Dean was now focused on talking me into coming tomorrow, it was working. I was calming down.

I could tune in, pick up what he was saying, and he was saying, "—I never know what Boomer is going to make if you're not here. He loves you. Worships you. He'll make everything great and something worthy of a magazine spread, but if you're not here, he gets all adventurous, starts thinking our budget is ostrich egg and lamb chops, and we don't ever have the budget for that."

He was right. Our grant was good, but not that good. We allocated most of it to education, recruiting, and general resources for everyone. Not to mention, the food. Food was expensive, but we tried to maintain a healthy standard, and it helped land us in multiple magazines, even a television show interviewed us, including Boomer.

Boomer got a kick out of Dean getting a kick out of that.

Me. I hated it. That'd been an extra bad day on paying attention. The reporter had been *extra* extra on everything. Extra smiles. Extra flirting with Dean. Extra perfume. Extra makeup. Extra loudness in her voice. Extra jewelry. All that went away the second the camera came on, and that whole segment showed me sucking in air like I'd been dying in a desert.

Not my best moment, but really, there was a whole long list of them, and maybe that wasn't too bad after all.

"Cheyenne!"

Crap.

He got me.

I'd been slipping and I was saying something. I had no clue. I recognized my voice and my own tone. Okay. That was convincing. Dean would be convinced I was paying attention, but I had to be adamant. "I'm not coming tomorrow. You know I don't always come to these days. And I can't. Sasha needs me."

He snorted. "What does Sasha need you for? Writing a grant for new stripper poles or something."

I frowned. Could I do that? Was there a grant for that?

"Stop." He leaned forward, planting his hand on the desk. "I can tell you're struggling right now."

I thought I'd been so sly. Crappers.

He kept on, "You think I can't tell, but I can. And like right now," he raised his tone, "You're starting to drift—"

"This is why I can't be here tomorrow! It's too much. I just can't—" Dean didn't know about my history, or my medical file, or any of it. He didn't even know I'd been homeless at times. "Dean. Do not push me on this."

Cold sweat was forming on my forehead, and I felt it on my top lip, but my words were spoken quietly, and slow, and that meant they'd come across as clear and articulate to him. But also beseeching, almost begging, and who could say no to that?

Well. Most people, but Dean had a soft spot for me. I wrote the magic and he knew it. I knew it.

He was quiet.

Now was my chance, and I shoved all the distracting background thoughts and noise to the far reaches of my mind and I pounced. "Boomer can bring Gail." He was quiet again, pensive. I recognized that look on his face and added, "You know that everyone loves Gail, and everyone adores Boomer and his wife being the duo they are in the kitchen."

He mashed his mouth together. "We don't know if Gail can do it—" *Score!* Because that meant he was open to that idea. "—and I still think you should be here tomorrow."

I was so not needed, and I was gone again.

I was doing cartwheels. I mean, I was sitting, but the inside of my body was fully doing somersaults, and I was a gymnast and flying in the air, and none of this would make sense to a normal person.

Sigh.

Because I wasn't normal.

I tuned back in for the rest of what Dean needed to talk about, and we only agreed on one out of the eight items, but all the while I started replying to emails. Dean was used to this. It was how I worked. He knew I needed to do two things, sometimes three if I was really distracted, in order to actually pay attention. A while back he asked me what was wrong, why I always had to be busy, and I just answered, "I have a really hungry brain."

I knew it wouldn't make any sense to him, but I'd long given up hope that some people would understand.

Some did. Most didn't.

11

CHEYENNE

Sasha called when I was getting off work, said she was heading to Melanie's for a pit stop, so I went to meet her. Dino's Beans was a cute hipster coffee bar downtown that Melanie worked at not far from where Come Our Way was. Because of this, it wasn't uncommon for me to see a few of the same guys there who came for meals at Come Our Way. Some of them had enough coinage to grab a coffee. Some didn't and knew Melanie had a soft heart, and she gave it out for free, but only if they came in with a good attitude and had recently showered. The ones who hadn't, she still didn't refuse them and had them sit outside with their coffee.

I wasn't surprised when I saw a couple of our regulars.

Petey. Moira. Dwayne. All saw me. All raised their hands. All sent me mumbled greetings, but they knew this was my friend's place, so they didn't come over to talk any more than that.

Sasha was already sitting down when I got to the counter. Melanie was watching her, standing behind the counter with her hands on her hips and her head tilted to the side. Her hair was pulled high and wound in a tight bun on top of her head, like right on top of her head. Red lipstick. Dangling earrings. Her

shirt was pressed and the collar was folded over, cinched in with
a pearl button.

My girl was dressed to work.

Without looking in my direction, she knew it was me and
lifted her chin up toward Sasha. "She's down."

I looked over.

Sasha was sitting in a booth, thumbing through a magazine
and her own lips were pressed together. She seemed almost
bored, but then I caught how she closed her eyes for longer than
a blink. It was brief, but she closed them, and her chest bent
down in a sigh at the same time.

Mels was right. Sasha was down, but she was here, and she'd
called me, so that was giving us the clues that she needed us to
pick her up. I looked back, met Melanie's gaze, and both of us
raised up an eyebrow at the same time.

"Hmmm-mmm," she hmmmed right back at me, though I
hadn't said a word. She was on the mental wave train right
with me.

I asked, "Bar?"

She shook her head. "I'm thinking club judging by the way
she's dressed."

I looked back and gave it some thought.

Sasha was wearing a black tank top that was tied around her
neck, and when she shifted in her seat, I saw it was backless. It
only covered her front, from high on her neck to her stomach, but
the back was held together by two more strings, both looking as if
they were tied together. One time a drunk guy thought he could
slip the knot and that the top would fall free enough for him to
see some boobs. Little did he know, the knots in the back were
merely for decorations. They were sturdy motherfuckers, and the
guy instead caused Sasha to swing at him with a firm right-hand
hook. When the cops showed up, they weren't sure who to haul
off because the guy's entire face was busted up. Sasha hadn't

stopped with that one punch. There'd been a left, another right, and maybe a knee.

Yeah, she was serious about whatever was going on with that top on.

Then her jeans.

They weren't jeans at all.

She had slicked-on leather pants.

Oh yes. Club it was, but I said to Melanie, "We need to go hardcore tonight."

"Got it." Succinct and to the point. We were on a mission.

Her coworker walked out from the back at that point.

"Hey, Chey—"

When Melanie decided something, she moved fast. She interrupted, "My girl needs a girls' night. Can you cover for me the rest of the night?"

Her coworker braked, opened her mouth, stopped and took both of us in. We both had full game-on expressions... we were set and determined to go. Consider these expressions our warpaint. And she closed her mouth. "Okie-dokie."

Melanie pulled her barista apron off, closed out the till, and grabbed her purse. We were off.

"Have fun tonight."

Melanie's response was a grunt, her laser eyes never moving from Sasha.

I gave a smile and wave, but never missed a beat.

Sasha knew something was up when she saw us coming, noting Melanie's purse, and my empty hand. "No coffee?"

No words were needed.

I grabbed Sasha's purse and Melanie grabbed Sasha. Or, she took her hand, and pulled her from the booth. "Let's go." And Melanie was off, leading this charge.

Sasha looked over her shoulder at me, her eyebrows raised, but I just gave her a stern look. She knew better.

As if reading my mind, she sighed again, the first time in deep thought at the table all alone, but this time in surrender.

She knew what we were doing.

"Thanks, guys."

Melanie's hand tightened over Sasha's and I dipped my head down to hers.

We were always here for the other, no matter what.

MELANIE WAS NOT FUCKING AROUND, her words when we asked where we were going.

We went to Bresko's.

No one knew who owned Bresko. Rumors were that the mob owned it. Others said the cartel, but weren't they really the mob, too? I never understood the difference. Still, other rumors said big time CEOs of Fortune 500 tech companies had their hand in it. A few rumors were that relatives of Marilyn Monroe's owned it. I was thinking that last one was far-fetched, but whoever owned it was making a killing.

It wasn't even in Kansas City. It was the outskirts, like, in the middle of nowhere. For real. There was nothing around it for miles, and when you approached you had to get your car approved to go through a gate. A long, winding, gravel driveway was next, and it always felt like a full mile you had to travel before you came to a parking lot. If they were really busy, and you were in your own car, you got a pager from a guy at the front of the lot. Then you were directed to a parking spot, and you waited for an indeterminate amount of time. When your pager lit up, you got the green light to go to the waiting line.

But this place was always busy, so when we stopped at the pager guy, no one was shocked when he gave us one and indicated where to go for our parking spot.

I didn't go to Bresko's on a regular basis, like maybe four times in three years.

We never had to wait long once we got to the waiting line outside, thankfully.

And I knew once Melanie parked, she was going to pounce.

She did.

She turned the engine off and twisted in her seat to face Sasha, who was in the front passenger seat. "What gives. We're here for you. You know we're your girls, but we gotta know the basic layout of what we're working with here."

I loved when Melanie was like this. I had to do nothing except slip into Happy Cheyenne-Land, and right now, I was so down for that.

Melanie's eyes were hawk-like on Sasha. "Spill it, honey. We need to know."

Sasha flicked her eyes to the ceiling, but groaned, reaching up and rubbing at her forehead. "I don't want to." She slumped down in her chair. "It's embarrassing and stupid."

Now my interest was really piqued. I leaned forward, a hand curved around her seat. "Whoa. What's going on?" Wait. I frowned. "Is this about my brother?"

"Bro—" Melanie did a double-take, her frown landing on both of us if that were even possible. "Brother?! What?"

I answered at the same time as Sasha.

"He's not really my brother. His mom is my dad's ex-wife."

"Fine. I slept with him in college, and again last Friday night."

Melanie's eyebrows both skyrocketed. "What?!"

And me again, "But Chad and I have a half-brother in common, so we're kind of, but not really like, siblings. I don't think it's a thing. I'm not tight with anyone in my family, so it doesn't bother me."

Sasha groaned again. "That's why it's a problem. I feel like a traitor to you."

Me?

She looked up from her spot to me, tipping her head upward. "Do you hate me? I slept with him again last night. And maybe the night before."

My eyes bugged, but they really bugged out after the second time. "Two nights?" I whispered. "In a row?"

Melanie's mouth was clamped shut, but she squeaked out, "So this is serious?"

We both shot her a look.

"What?"

"No—"

"I hope not."

I twisted back to Sasha. "Really?" Because the way she said that, it was like it could be. And whoa. I was expecting a fly-by from my brother. He had demolished her in college. Sasha didn't like talking about it, then or now, and I'd been quiet. I'd been waiting knowing what happened, but hearing they slept together twice... I was hoping I didn't need to pick up the pieces again.

Sasha clamped her mouth tight, but she mumbled, and that was so not a Sasha thing to do, "Ireallymightlikehimand..." She groaned again, swearing under her breath before sitting upright in her seat. "Fuck it." She moved to face me. "Chad wants to keep seeing me. I want to keep seeing him, but you're my girl. If you say no, the dude's gone. I will never lose my friendship with you over some dick."

Well.

Then.

I loved my girl.

I was almost crying here. "Date him. Love him," I was gushing. "Marry him. Have his babies. But if he hurts you, I will let Melanie run him over with a car."

I gave her a look. I remembered how he hurt her in college.

She saw the look and read it right, a resigned look coming over her as she nodded. "I gotcha."

Melanie laughed. "You okay, Shy?"

Oh yes. I nodded. I was finding my Zen place tonight. I'd need it for Bresko's. The place was hard on me, so I was reinforcing my Happy Walls.

Sasha grinned, shooting her a look. "She's in Happy Cheyenne-Land. Don't you see it?"

I was. I almost held up my hands and touched my fingers to my thumbs in a whole Zen-pose.

Nothing was getting to me tonight. I wasn't going to let it happen. These were our roles. If one was hurting, one of us was stern and took on the mama-bear role. The other brought out the happy and laughter. Melanie was dressed for stern mama, so I had no choice but to go this route.

Honestly, though, I was usually this role.

"Girl's checked out."

I wasn't checked out. I was so checked in, so much so that it looked like I was checked out. Both knew me. Both understood, and Melanie went back to asking, "How much do you need to talk about it?"

"None now that I know our girl is fine that I'm boning her Not-Brother."

A cheeky grin and a thumbs up from me. Everyone deserved to be boned. Now, when I saw Chad—and I would see Chad whether he wanted to see me or not—he and I would have a different type of relationship.

Melanie's eyes were knowing as she murmured, "You really like him, huh?"

Sasha sighed again, glancing out her window. "He's grumpy. He can be a dick, but I want that dick so bad, and I have no clue why." She looked at me. "I'll toss him once I stop thirsting for his dick. I promise. But I've been thirsty since that night back in college, so..."

Melanie didn't know all the details about their history in college.

I'd be filling her in on that later because that was the real gauge of how much she was in love right now.

Melanie was grinning, watching me. "So, who's at the Cum Palace tomorrow?"

I'd stopped snorting at Melanie's own title for our kitchen long ago. "The second half of the Mustangs' hockey team."

Sasha whirled around in her seat, her eyes big and now fully knowing at me. She knew.

"Is their PT girl going to be there?"

Sasha was distracted at that, looking back at Melanie. Her eyebrows twitched, morphing into a pinch, but they cleared when she turned back to me. Yeah, Sasha was all good now.

"Was he there today?"

I coughed.

Melanie didn't know about *him*.

Melanie asked, "He?"

See.

She turned to me. "Who is he?"

Sasha answered, and apparently she had no problem throwing me under the bus. Fine with me. I was going to do the same with her about Chad from college, too. She said, "Cut Ryder."

"The dude you slept with Friday night?" She shared that frown with both of us. "You both got fucking lucky that night. Where the hell was I? We were all at the same damn party. I got a number, and we've hung out a bit, but not what you two did. I want more."

And immediately, both Sasha and I raised our hands in the air, palms and fingers spread out in cheer-mode. The 'fuck' word had entered the night. It'd be in every third sentence from Melanie after this.

She scowled. "Fuck's sake."

See again.

Sasha and I started laughing.

"You two are fucking annoying."

Full-out laughter now.

Melanie growled, but the pager lit up, and she grabbed for it. "About time, when you both start cheering me on with my fucking language after I have to about rail you both to get one fucking word about your sex lives. You both got boned and left me high and fucking dry, literally." She was getting out of the vehicle, muttering to herself.

Sasha and I got out on the other side, and we heard her grumbling as the doors were shut, locked, and she met us around the back. She pointed the flashing pager at us. "And don't you two fucks think I don't know that there's more to both your stories. I'm not stupid, you morons." After that, she marched to Bresko's entrance.

Sasha walked with me, and after her third sigh for the night, she linked our elbows and drew next to me. Her hip bumped mine, but she held me tight. She inclined her head. "Are you sure you're sure?"

I patted her hand holding my arm and whispered, leaning my own head to touch her forehead, "I'm sure I'm sure."

Her hand tightened.

I patted again.

We shared a smile and walked the rest of the way.

I was totally fine with her and Chad.

And we didn't talk about Chad or Cut the rest of the night.

FROM: KOALA BOY
TO: CHEYCHEY
SUBJECT: DID YOU FIND OUT ANYTHING?

FROM: CHEYCHEY
TO: KOALA BOY

SUBJECT: THAT YOU'RE AWESOME! NOT KIDDING. SHE LIKES YOU.

FROM: KOALA BOY
TO: CHEYCHEY
SUBJECT: WHY DO WE ONLY USE THE SUBJECT LINE?

FROM: CHEYCHEY
TO: KOALA BOY
SUBJECT: BECAUSE YOU'RE AWESOME!

12

CUT

Having a messed up elbow sucked, but it sucked more that I was missing Come Our Way.

I got called in for extra physical therapy and Cassie had me going through a whole rotation today.

PT was amazing. PT was magical, but some days, PT sucked ass. Today it was sucking ass in the way that for once I didn't want to be here today.

But, my elbow needed it.

Cassie stepped back from me, nodding to my elbow. "It's still sore, but you should be fine. I think they were smart to pull you in yesterday and today. Just do a lot of soaks today, or as much as you think is needed. You know your limit."

She was our physical therapy worker. To some, she was the younger sister, and to others, the big sister. She was more a friend to me, and I nodded. "Sounds good. Thanks."

"So..." She grabbed a towel, pausing before heading back to her office. We were in the back PT room, and a few of the other guys had come in early as well.

I waited. She had something to say.

"You know that girl from Friday night?"

Jesus. Did *everyone* know?

She kept on, "I saw her again last night. She and her friends. They were at Bresko's." Another pause. She was eyeing me, her head cocking downwards at a tilt. "I think one of her friends was the one you took home that night, too."

It took a second, then—Cheyenne.

And she wasn't talking about my girl at first. Her girl.

"Wait. What? You saw Cheyenne last night?"

"Yeah. She's nice, too."

Fucking fuck. I was jealous of my PT friend.

That was a nice kick to the dick.

"Yeah?"

She was still eyeing me, and at that, they went flat. "You don't want to talk about her?"

I did.

But I wanted to be able to participate in the conversation, and I couldn't, and my PT friend could, and that was making my balls clench up.

"No. I'm good. So, you had fun last night?" Wait. "You said Bresko's?"

She nodded, giving me a duh look. "You don't think anyone knows, but we all know."

Goddamn.

This team gossiped worse than high schoolers.

"You have a new girl in rotation."

I frowned. "What?"

Her head inclined toward me, her hands going to her hips. "You don't do the randoms, but you don't have a girlfriend, and we know you have a few girls you keep in rotation. I might've saw an engagement post by one of them, and then..." She lifted up a shoulder. "You took that new girl home with you, so you have a new girl in rotation?" Her voice rose, becoming clearer, a bit more professional. "I'm just letting you know because I might be hanging out with her friend, and I know you're big on privacy. Now you know."

Goddamn again. I had no clue how to process any of that shit.

"You're hanging out with the friend? What does hanging out mean?"

Cassie blushed, her head dipping down again. "It's just, I don't know." She lifted once more, her cheeks all pink. "I go slow, if you didn't know that by now."

"So you're not actually hanging out. You're like, dating, but slow dating?"

"Uh..." She began edging backwards, grabbing another towel and flicking it over her shoulder. "Consider you have been given the heads-up and I'm off to my next client. Good luck tonight if I don't see you before you pad up."

"Thanks, Cassie."

She gave me a small smile before heading out, disappearing into the hallway.

Hendrix was coming in as she left. They both said their hellos, then he turned my way.

"Hey." He came over, hopping up on the seat next to me. "They checked you over?"

I stretched my arm out. She was right. My elbow was still tight, but it'd be fine. I knew that already this morning when they called, said I should head in here instead of the community outreach project with Come Our Way. I'd been hoping to see Cheyenne, see her in her element, but no go, and I glanced at Hendrix.

He'd been there yesterday.

He also knew what else went down, and I hadn't been in the mood to talk about her.

He'd get a fucking kick out of it, but fuck it. "How was the thing yesterday?"

Hendrix had been stretching his arm over his chest, and I

didn't miss the quick, shit-eating grin before he looked over. "Curious, eh?"

"Shut up." I scowled. "Just tell me how it was."

"How it was or how she was?" He switched arms. "Frank texted. She's not there today."

I was supposed to be there today.

Maybe I should walk? She didn't show the day I was supposed to. She ran from my place, then this? The girl was trying to tell me something, and yeah...fucking battery acid was what I was eating right now.

"What's that look about?"

"What?"

Hendrix lifted his chin toward me. "You look like you saw your grandma's saggy tits just now. You gone on this girl or something?"

Was I? I thought I was.

I wanted to fuck her again. I knew that much.

I rolled a shoulder. "Not sure."

His grin was too knowing, but he said, "She's cool if you are. Whole place was cool. Their chef had lots of personality, but he doted on her. He's probably fifty, and his wife showed up. She kept snarking on him, had all of us laughing so much we didn't notice the time was done."

"What about the suit?"

"Nah. He's nothing. Fanboy, most likely. He kept trying to ask your girl questions, and she kept dodging him. That was fun to watch, too." He got serious. "I kinda wanted to go again. I might do my own thing after this. You didn't go at all?"

I shook my head. "They wanted me in here today."

He nodded, rubbing over his jaw before yawning and leaning back to start raising his leg up. "Makes sense. You got worked over the last game. You good for tonight?"

I flashed him a look.

And he grinned. "That's what I figure. These guys are aggressive."

I grunted, knowing that, too. But they didn't have the speedster the last team did. I'd be able to keep to only my line. "We'll get 'em."

"I know."

But his grin wasn't cocky, because no matter what, all these teams were good. All had solid guys on them, and it seemed they just kept getting sharper and sharper each season.

"We're gonna kick their ass tonight."

He nodded back, and I slid off my table to go and soak.

13

CHEYENNE

C ut: You still coming tonight?
My phone buzzed and I tried to quench the entire heart-jump in my chest. It didn't work. I reached for my phone on the coffee table next to me.

Melanie was sitting across from me, lounging back on one of Sasha's couches. Her leg was hanging over the side and she raised her head up, frowning at me, or more specifically frowning at my reaction. A little overkill here, but yeah. I'd been waiting, my stomach in knots the whole day, and when I swiped over and read his text, my tongue tangled around itself. I had one doozy of a knot.

"Who the fuck is texting you to get that reaction?"

I flushed and slid down in my own couch, trying to hide my head behind a pillow.

She was off her couch in a second, and my pillow was ripped from me. Her mouth was hanging open as she took me in, me holding my phone, me almost dropping my phone because I was shaking, before she retreated back to her couch. She felt behind her, not looking, and lowered herself to safety. "W.T.F., Shy. W.T.F."

Sasha came out of her bedroom, heading down the hallway. She paused at the opening to the living room and kitchen area, taking us both in. "Did I hear a phone go off? Was that mine?"

A squawk from me.

I didn't like this.

I was all blushing, and nervous, and rattled. Me rattled wasn't good. Ever.

But I focused back on responding because I knew Melanie would demand the 411 from Sasha, which she did when she pointed at me. "I've never seen Cheyenne act like this, ever. Who is this guy? He's not just a one-nighter. There's no way, and Cheyenne doesn't do one-nighters, so there's more to this story."

I looked up, feeling Sasha's eyes on me, and I read the unspoken question.

I nodded.

She sighed, coming over to perch on my couch's arm. "Put it simply, he was a daydream since before I knew her. Not at all her reality—" She looked at me because she knew I'd been about to protest. "—he wasn't. You didn't know him. You never talked to him. You were in a shitty situation, and he was an idea you clung onto to get you through it. He didn't even know you until," I closed my mouth and she focused back on Melanie. "Friday night. Our hockey stud got one good look at Cheyenne, and you know what happened. He felt the sex sparks from across the room, and the hockey beast came out claiming and swinging. He wants in her pants again, *bad*."

Melanie snorted. "Who doesn't?"

I caught her teasing grin, but she coughed. "I'm getting a feeling there's more to it than just that."

Sasha stood back up, and we shared a look. I *so* got that she kept the other guy out of the equation, and her mouth twitched. "Imagine thinking you're all in love with someone, then you get a night with them, but the idea of them had been what held you together for so long? What happens when you finally got 'em, or worse? If they didn't want you in the morning?"

Damn.

Damn.

Damn!

She hit it right on the mark. She was right.

Was she? I didn't know anymore, but I had walls up and issues to deal with, and we'd not even touched on the amount of therapy it would take to blow them down.

But I'd been through harder shit in my life, so I could do this.

I managed a text back.

Me: Planning on it, yes.

I put the phone back. Sasha was still eyeing me. Melanie just looked like she was bugging out, absorbing all the drama, before her face cleared and she snapped her head toward Sasha. "You have work?"

"Yeah." She glanced at the clock. "I should already be there."

The fact that we got Sasha for this long at all last night and today was huge. She almost lived at Tiyts. Fancy spelling, but the name was basic and memorable. The Y was silent. So...Tits.

Also self-explanatory.

"Okay. It's decided." Melanie stood up, stretching her long legs, with a yawn that no one believed. She was up to something. "You and me." Her eyes found me. "We're going to that hockey game."

Yep. Definitely up to something.

Also, I didn't have a plus one with my seat.

Sasha said, "Those tickets are already sold out. They sell out fast."

"Pretty sure I can get myself in."

She pulled out her phone and Sasha frowned at me. "You'll be okay?"

I nodded. "I'll be fine. Really."

The worry lines never moved, but she touched my shoulder

as she started to head back to the bathroom. "Call if you need anything."

"Yo." Melanie's head popped up. "Cassie said she can get us in. Three seats. You sure you can't come, Sash?"

Sasha had already started back for the bathroom. "No. I gotta go check on my girls. Come to Tits tonight afterwards. It always fills up with guys after the games."

Melanie's head tilted sideways, her eyebrows pinched together, and she was biting the inside of her lip again. "When are you and this 'ideal guy' getting together?"

"He's not my 'ideal' guy." Though, a younger version of Cheyenne was whispering to me that he was, that I'd fallen in love with him when I first saw him, and why was I trying to lie to myself. Logic was telling me to agree with Sasha, but the totally illogical side was whispering, 'who the fuck cares? Just give in to the unicorn utopia.'

I felt like I was getting trounced by those unicorns right now. Hooves all over my chest, a few making sure to stomp on my forehead in the process.

I was nervous. Really nervous.

But I said to Melanie, "We're doing something after the game."

"Something?" Another lip twitch from Melanie.

"He said dinner."

"The main entree is pussy."

Sasha barked out a laugh all the way from her bathroom, and that was past two bedrooms. Her hearing was on point today.

"Come on." Melanie went to get her purse.

I stood. "Where are we going?"

"We're going to a hockey game. I'm hoping at least one of us gets laid tonight. So that means we need to pick out the best clothes." She raised a hand, hollering out, "We're heading out. Bye, Sash."

"Bring your girl to Tits tonight!"

Melanie pulled out her keys, heading for the door. "Will do!"
I followed her outside.

She said over her shoulder, "I know you're nervous. You don't have to be. This guy is already panting to lick your clit, but I need my girl with me. We're going to get manis and pedis right now." She moved to the side, linking her elbow with mine, and it was just the right thing to say to me.

I bumped my hips to hers. "Only if we get mimosas."

Her smile was almost blinding. "Done."

I WAS NERVOUS.

I was fully nervous.

I was palms sweating, heart pounding, and edges of my vision blurring. That type of nervous. Maybe I shouldn't have been. Melanie read me right and switched all conversation to her and Cassie. The PT girl who had met us at Bresko's, and who was gorgeous, and who Melanie was totally vibing with. She really liked her, but Melanie more loved the chase than the actual falling in love part. Correction: she enjoyed the chase and the sex, but she never lied about either.

And when we took an Uber to the hockey arena, I was feeling all of the nerves.

Literally.

All. The. Nerves.

I was about to see Cut again.

He hadn't texted, neither had I. I felt as if we were both locked in, knowing there'd be a talk tonight, and there was no way I telling him the truth. That I fell in love with him the moment I saw him. I was going to hedge my bets and go with everything else that caused me to run, like my mom, like my upbringing, like —okay. That'd be too much. It was too much for *me* at times, and I'd lived it.

I'd figure it out, probably on the spot, and until then I'd be freaking.

"Hey." Melanie nudged my elbow. Her tone was quiet but concerned. "Did you take your meds today?"

Meds.

What meds?

Oh yes.

Those meds.

Wait.

Shit.

Shit!

My meds.

I wasn't panicking.

Nope.

I'd been good.

I didn't drink last night.

I didn't partake in the mimosas today.

And why was that? Because of my meds, because I was off my vacation from my meds and... I was thinking, remembering, and I was coming up blank.

There's no way I forgot to take them, or start them back up again. No way.

But there was a way.

I'd been distracted.

Very distracted.

Very very distracted, and I pulled out the container, looked for my day's slots and shit—I hadn't. *Shit, shit, shit.* I was fully hyperventilating now because this wasn't good.

She saw, and I heard her quick curse under her breath. "Okay. No problem." We were walking up to the side entrance that Cassie told us to head toward, but Melanie reached in her purse and pulled out a small water bottle. "Take 'em now."

I could, but it took a long time for them to even start getting into my system.

I was fucked for the night and how could I have forgotten them?! By now this should've been like breathing. I just do it, but I'd never had such a distraction like Cut before. And now I was panicking thinking about how I was fucked and I was setting off my own panic attack here. I could feel it rising up.

The room was already buzzing right along with me, and we'd just gotten to the back of the stadium.

Nope. No way. I'd be okay. I'd have to be okay.

I popped a pill, putting the bottle back in my purse. "I'm good."

Her eyebrows pulled together. "Cheyenne."

I forgot.

It was starting.

I was thinking back over the last week, and the first day I forgot them was Saturday morning. I woke up at Cut's. Sunday. Monday, I remembered. Tuesday, I forgot. Wednesday. Thursday, today. I'd forgotten almost the whole week.

Fuck.

The heat wafted in from a nearby food vendor.

A door opened, and I felt the chill of the ice slide in, too.

I could hear people talking outside in the seating area. I heard people coming in behind us. We'd used the staff entrance, and a security guy was coming toward us. He had a radio in hand, a frown on his face, and he was skimming over Melanie and me like we were groupies.

I had a routine down, and I was so far gone from my routine this whole week.

"Ben!" A woman was coming from a side door, her hand raised.

The security guy looked over.

She indicated us. "They're with me."

His head moved up. "Got it. You need—" He stopped talking, seeing her hand and the two lanyards she was holding. "You got 'em already."

Then Cassie was next to us. She and Melanie were greeting each other, a kiss to the cheek, a slight hug before Cassie turned toward me. Man. She was really beautiful, and warm. I'd seen her before, but it was different this time. There was a glow around her. Did Melanie not see it?

I was noticing all of this as if I was using one side of my brain. I had separated inside. One side of me was shut down. The other part of me was noticing everything else. It was a coping mechanism I'd been trained to use in counseling.

I needed an anchor, and I needed to let everything else move to the back of my head. I had to, but it was hard. It took work. I would be struggling—I needed another drink.

Cassie was moving to greet me, a hand to my shoulder.

She had sprayed perfume on herself that smelled like lilacs, and she pressed a chaste kiss to my cheek. The lilacs were a lot right now. She was saying something, but the buzz from everything else had deafened me. I couldn't hear her, but my eyes dropped to her lips, reading them.

"Hello, Cheyenne. It's so nice to see you again."

She squeezed my shoulder lightly, out of affection. She was happy.

And she turned back to Melanie.

She was happy Melanie was here, but there was more to her attention toward me. Something else, something with me, but I couldn't decipher it.

How could I have forgotten my meds for so many days in a row? Well, I'm me. There's that.

I drew in a breath, closing my eyes.

I needed to channel everything.

It wasn't staying in the back of my head.

I felt Melanie looking at me. She was worried, too.

I had those drinks earlier, and no wonder my anxiety was starting to take over.

I had to do something.

Be something…I was shifting.

My shirt felt like it was suffocating me.

I was cold and hot all at the same time.

More people were coming in behind us, and I squawked as I moved aside. They all gave me weird looks.

Everyone was looking.

They all knew.

Knew I was crazy. That I was insane.

I'd hear the whispers.

I'd be asked to leave.

I pressed my mouth shut so I didn't make any more sounds. This happened, too. Too much stimulus, and I couldn't read the right cues. I'd say something when I shouldn't, answer a question that was asked five questions ago, and the looks. More looks.

People didn't like what they couldn't understand.

It scared them.

They couldn't understand me.

I heard Melanie saying something to Cassie, and suddenly an arm wound around my shoulders.

I tensed, but it was Melanie, and she was pulling me against her.

She was my anchor.

My hand found hers, hiding between our bodies, and I clung hard.

She squeezed me back. "Head down, babe. We'll go somewhere you can handle. I'm sorry."

No, no. I wanted to tell her I had regular seats, that this would've happened there, too.

I should've taken my meds.

Why had I forgotten them?

I kept my head down a little bit. We were walking down a hallway, past people. The lights were overwhelming. A new person popped out of a room, and kept popping out, and popping out. They were all saying hi to Cassie.

She was loved here.

But now she was worried, too, casting a small frown over her shoulder at us.

Melanie was covering for me, her head almost ridiculously high to make up for my own. Her shoulders were as wide as she could make them, and she was holding me almost under her arm. Cold sweat was running down my back, but this wasn't my first rodeo.

I could fake it...and I was.

My mouth was pressed tight, but I was smiling and gave a small head dip to people who were turned toward us. Even if they didn't say a word, I gave them a small smile, just in case. And then we were through a back door and going up stairs.

The lights were darker.

Cement floors.

The echoes from Melanie's heels were like firecrackers being set off.

Cassie had sneakers on. Nice and comfortable and silent sneakers. And her clothing was quiet, too, except I could hear the soft rubbing of her sleeve against her Mustangs' jacket. Still, it wasn't as loud as Melanie's leather skirt or those heels.

She asked my opinion.

I told her then it was 'dead sexy,' and now I was rethinking my terminology.

No. It still looked sexy.

Cassie liked it. She was looking at it, but there were rings of worry around her mouth, too.

But then Melanie was talking to her. She must've told a joke. I'd probably hear it in thirty seconds when it caught up to the chaos in my head.

Cassie was laughing, and she relaxed.

Melanie was such a good friend, because she was shielding me as best she could, but Cassie wasn't detecting it.

Melanie was making Cassie think she had it under control, that her nutso friend would be fine.

Nutso.

Weirdo.

Street chick.

It's funny because those words were coming back to me now. I was an adult, but they were words I'd been called when I was in high school. They'd bounced off me then. Why were the simple memories of those words and phrases penetrating now?

We were through another door, on a higher floor, and things were muted, but I could still hear, see, feel, sense, taste, and again...why had I forgotten my damn meds? *Stop it, Cheyenne. Deal with it. It's not your first time here, and it won't be your last.*

Recognize the chaos.

Know there'll be chaos.

Look straight and try to find your tunnel.

"This will be a lot quieter, promise."

Cassie's words came from a distance.

Melanie was chuckling right into my ear, and then a door was being unlocked, opened, and we were inside.

I almost wept from relief. The floors were carpeted. That helped the intensity of everything so much.

There were leather couches. Leather chairs. A few high-top tables.

A bar in the corner, and Cassie was nodding to the guy standing there. They spoke to each other, their heads bent together, and he nodded before leaving.

I never knew about these boxes. And we were so high up, but I needed to pull myself together.

I stepped away from Melanie and she frowned at me.

I patted her arm. "Give me a bit. Go and flirt, have fun."

"You sure?"

I nodded, even though that sent everything spinning once again.

I needed a new anchor. It wasn't fair to put that on Melanie. "Go." I motioned, then threw a warm and fake grin to Cassie. "I'm going to sit for a spell."

I didn't know if Cassie was looking in our direction or not. The stimulus of looking back in her direction was too much, but I needed to cover my bases, and slipping away, I eased into a side room where there was no one.

Just me. Just four seats in the front with glass partitions keeping me from the people underneath us, and I sank into the seat in the far corner and bent over.

Forehead to knees.

Sometimes this helped. Just a bit. I needed a handle on it because I was having a slight panic attack, and I knew I'd been triggered at realizing I was off-schedule for my meds. But I could do this. I'd done it for years before, and now at least I had the coping mechanisms in place.

Head closed. Eyes bent forward.

I mean, switch those around, and a breath.

I recognized the sound of a door closing, and that had to be Melanie.

I didn't know who was supposed to be in this box with us —if they were going to come in here or not—but I knew whoever it was, Melanie wouldn't let them through. No way in hell. I was safe and I could relax and I needed to find a tunnel.

I needed to find a line.

I needed to focus on that line—and when some of the buzzing faded a bit, I looked up.

I ignored the people underneath.

They were a part of an ocean.

I was in a boat.

I was looking forward, at the surface of the water. That was the ice, and the guys were out there, already warming up.

I found Cut, he was zipping around. Shooting. He was

laughing with one of his teammates, and I was so damn tired. Exhausted already.

I should go home.

I'd be worthless by the end of the game, but no. I could do this. I just needed a small handle on it. The panic attack was easing. It would slide away and things would be easier after that.

It had to be, I'd waited so long for him to notice me.

CUT

Jesus. It was a barnburner.

I was wiped, but hyped by the end of the game. We won three to two.

Hendrix came up to me. "I can't believe Squatch. He came out of fucking nowhere, right?"

I was on a high. This was the best part of the game. Well, not the best. Part of the best. Playing. Fighting. Icing. All of it, being out there, going head to head, pulling out a win.

I fucking loved this game.

"Guys are heading to Bresko's. You in?" He held out a fist. "We'll use the back room."

"Uh." I met his fist with mine. "I'm not sure. I'm supposed to meet up with someone."

His grin turned cocky and knowing. "Nice. Bring her for a drink or two."

"Maybe." But no way, and not at Bresko's. We were all heading for the locker room, but I looked up. I looked up every time we left, and she wasn't there.

She said she would be, so what the fuck?

Everyone was happy. They all wanted to celebrate, and I was there with them, but I needed to get to my phone so I could see what was going on with Cheyenne.

"Cut."

Cassie popped in from one of the hallways. I gave her a chin-lift. "Hey, Cassie." And kept right on going.

"No, Cut..." She tugged at the corner of my sweater, indicating to a side room.

Already not liking this, I went with her. Cassie wasn't asking about my elbow, and she looked strung out, nervous almost. We stepped in, and she moved to the door so it was only open an inch. "Hey, um..." She tucked a strand of hair behind her ear, glancing back to the hallway we just left.

"What is it?"

Her shoulders rolled back, her head lifted higher, and she spoke, more sure, "I don't totally feel right doing this, but I also don't totally feel right not saying anything."

Fuck.

"What is it?" My teeth were starting to grind against each other.

"Melanie called before. She said you and Cheyenne were heading out after the game tonight."

"That's the plan."

"Well, they showed up and they'd been drinking."

Okay...

"Something's wrong with your girl."

"What?" I frowned. "She sick?"

"No, I mean, well, maybe. She was acting drunk, which was fine, but it wasn't the right kind of drunk. Melanie was holding her up, but not at the same time. It was all off. I took them to one of the VIP rooms, and she went in a side room. She was in there by herself most of the game until suddenly, Melanie got a text from her, and they hurried out of here."

"She left?"

"Yeah, but, Cut..." She moved closer, dropping her voice, and she was biting into her bottom lip. "I wasn't getting a good feeling about her. It's like she was on something. Drugs, maybe. And I know you're not like that, and you're definitely not into that with your girls."

"Drugs?"

Drugs? But Chad had been quiet about her, said shit was bad with the family, and I knew she was a part of the reason he stayed with us in school for a bit. But drugs?

But her mom had been a junkie.

I didn't like thinking that.

"I'm real sorry." She touched my hand, giving it a squeeze. Her phone was lighting up and she swiped to read a text. "That's Melanie now. She's offering to meet up."

"Without Cheyenne?"

She nodded, chewing at her lip again.

It was obvious she felt bad, but drugs? I don't know. That just didn't feel right.

I gave her a little nod. "Go out with your girl. Have fun."

She grinned, easing back. "I don't know how much fun we'll have. I feel like I have to tell Melanie what I told you—"

"No, you don't. You're looking out for a friend, but I'll take it from here. Don't worry about it. Just go, have fun, and do whatever you do."

She paused again. "You sure?"

"I'm sure. Go."

She did, after another moment of hesitation, but fucking fuck. Drugs?

Chad didn't like her, didn't want me around her, but... Fuck! Fuck.

Jaw hard, I moved forward, ripping open the door a little harder than necessary. Two guys in the hallway jumped, but I stalked past them for the locker room.

Fucking drugs.

No fucking way.

14

CHEYENNE

I hadn't been able to do it. There was no tunnel for me.

Midway through the second period, I was jumping at every roar and cheer and buzzer, and I felt like my skin was trying to rip off of me. I called it quits, but I tried to reassure Melanie I could cab it home alone. She didn't need to stay. And yeah, she never left my side until I was in my apartment. She still waited until the game was done, which we finished watching on television.

By the end of the third period, I was much more sane.

I hated using that terminology, but it was how I felt.

There's a reason for everything, not enough receptors or dopamine or neurotransmitters in the brain, but when a person felt the world was spinning around them, that was the general vibe of this. We were nuts. But I was home, and safe, and I knew what was happening, and that was most of the work. It allowed me to become grounded.

Melanie took off after the game, planning on meeting Cassie at Tits, so when she left, I shot Cut a text before turning off my phone.

Me: Feeling under the weather. Went home. I'll call you tomorrow? So sorry. Great win!

After that, I ran a bath, and by the time I was done with it, I felt a bit better. Almost normal. I was still rattled, the exhaustion was starting to seep in. It'd been there the whole time, but I'd been holding it at bay, which caused it to be even worse. When we got to the apartment, I didn't let myself crash. I held on, wanting to watch the rest of the game, but now...now I was almost stumbling, needing to head to bed.

That's when the doorbell rang and I froze.

Who—*pound, pound!*

"It's me, Cheyenne. Let me in."

I sucked in a breath. Oh, holy shitballs.

It was Cut. How'd he—I mean, Chad had no clue where I lived.

He spoke through the door, "Just let me in for a few minutes. I'll leave after. Promise."

A few minutes.

Pfft. Easy for him to say. He wasn't the one feeling his skin trying to jump off his bones.

But, still. I glanced down at me. I was in a soft tank top, my sleeper shorts, and whatever. My hair was a mess, but my toes and fingernails at least looked good. That made me feel better, and with another sigh, trying to ignore all the butterflies and tickling caterpillars in my stomach, I unlocked the door and stepped back.

I crossed my arms over me, hugging myself, warding him off, at the same time as he opened the door.

God. He looked so good.

He was wearing a ball cap pulled low, a t-shirt, and jeans, and the way all of that fit his body...Good Lord...six times. Six times. I was trying not to remember how he worked magic with those fingers of his as a warm-up and I stepped back, swallowing a knot.

"Hey." That was him.

Gah. Seriously? He was speaking all soft-like to me.

I wanted him to be an asshole, then this would be done with and I'd figure my shit out afterwards. But nooo. He had to be looking at me all kind-like, and sweet, and tender, and his tone sounded like soft caramel and he smelled of fresh shampoo, and I loved his fresh shampoo smell.

"Hi." A bullfrog had taken over my throat. It was speaking for me.

He cracked a grin. "Can I, uh, can I come in?"

I scurried backwards and he moved inside, his hands going into his pockets.

That made his shoulders look even better.

Okay.

Here we were.

I let out a breath.

He heard me, frowning. "Are you okay? You said you were sick."

"I was. I am. I mean, it wasn't..." Were we doing this? Already? I felt like upheaving. "We haven't even had a first date."

He raised an eyebrow. "I know. That was supposed to be tonight."

Right again.

"No. No. You wanted to know why I left the next morning, and I said I didn't want to lie. That was supposed to be for tonight, but you're here, and I'm now realizing that's a serious, *serious* topic, and that's too early. We had sex, and before that you—" OH DAMN! I'd been about to tell him.

I clamped my mouth shut.

He inclined his head. "I what?"

"Nothing."

He frowned, cocking his head to the side. "You what? You were going to say something."

"I wasn't."

"You were."

"Was not."

His head moved back, lifting, and surprise flared in his gaze. The other side of his mouth tugged up. "Are we fighting about this?"

"We're not fighting."

"We're disagreeing. You were going to say something about me."

"No, I wasn't."

A full-out frown from him, and he edged back a step. He was reassessing me.

Great, now he was looking at me like a mental patient, but for the totally wrong reason.

A slight grin showed on his face. "Look, you're right." He scanned me from head to toe. "You seem okay now. Do you want to go somewhere for a drink?"

More drinking.

But, gah. I would need to go back on my meds tomorrow, and I couldn't take them when I was drinking, and last Friday was supposed to be my last day reprieve. But this, this whole week except one day of forgetting to take them, was why we couldn't take one-day reprieves. There was no vacation from what I suffered from, not unless it would morph and it would grow, and I would spin and I'd have a night like tonight.

But also, who was I kidding?

This was not going to work, and I might as well scare him away now.

"I can't do this."

He didn't respond.

That was fine.

It plunged the knife harder in my chest, but I had to do this. I had to do this for him.

I had to let that idea go because that was another reason I'd been spinning tonight. Sasha had been right. He wasn't real.

Getting a boyfriend in school was supposed to make things right? But it wasn't about getting a boyfriend, it was about someone loving me, even just liking me, because so many of them didn't like me. My mother. Chad. My father. My stepmother. Hunter had been super chill, and thinking about him made me destress, just a bit here.

I needed some Koala Man emailing, but back to the situation in my living room.

Cut was standing, still looking so fucking fine, and I tried to ignore that as I went to the dining table. No way could this conversation happen when I was sitting on my nice comfy couch. If I had to bolt or even ask him to leave, I'd be fighting with my cushions to stand up, and then the whole dramatic effect would be lost.

I sat down and Cut took a seat across from me.

His eyes.

So fierce, but also just knowing me. He was looking at me, like *at me* at me. How many people have looked at you and not really seen you? Not this guy. Straight fucking through me, and I was stalling. Big time.

Fine. Here we go.

"You know about my junkie mom."

He dipped his head down. "You mentioned her."

Right.

Gah.

Six. Times.

And why was I scaring this dude away again?

But I needed to, for him and for me. I couldn't grapple with the reality that he liked me. That just didn't make sense to me. Or even make sense to the universe.

"My mom was a junkie. She was a junkie before she had me, while she had me, and most certainly after she had me."

I waited, because this was the moment when people generally got a different look. Like an, 'oh, holy shit' look, like 'oh, she came from that type of background.' I'd seen it enough and it never made sense to me because I might've come from that environment but that environment wasn't me. Most people didn't get that so they had a look.

Cut didn't have that look. He was watching me. He was listening to me, but I hadn't shocked him with that revelation. Yet.

I would.

Just wait.

I was just getting to the good stuff.

I kept on, "I was homeless on and off when I was a kid. Spent time with my uncle. Had a stint at my dad's, and I was so 'bad' that they shipped Chad and Hunter to live somewhere else." He knew about that. "I didn't even know I had a half-brother until they slipped and mentioned his name. I never did anything. I never stole. I thought the house was super chill because I could get water whenever I wanted, and they fed me. I didn't have to feel like I was stealing from my neighbors even though I now knew they put out water, sandwiches on purpose for me to take. I had problems. Big problems. Big enough problems that I was half-checked out of reality." I wasn't going to list the diagnoses I'd been given. Some were right, some weren't, and some disappeared over the years. Meds, therapy, but mostly having someone give a fuck was priceless.

I'd already said enough, and I was studying him. Gauging his reaction.

He didn't look scared.

Why didn't he look scared?

"Want to know what I was diagnosed with?"

He leaned forward, resting his elbows on the table. "What are you doing? Telling me all of this?"

I leaned forward, too. "Saving you." My eyes flicked to the door. "Leave. Run. Go away."

His eyes narrowed and he eased back, but he didn't move.

Why wasn't he moving?

"I saw you talking to that suit, and I hated him. You were mine." Still a soft tone, but his nostrils flared. His eyes flashed. "I don't know what that was, but I felt it—"

"I thought I was in love with you in school."

He stopped.

I didn't. "I thought you knew me. I thought you liked me back. I thought we had a whole relationship, in my head. I was delusional. You didn't have a clue who I was." I kept going. "I was in the car. Chad came out to talk to his mom, and you were with him. You waved at me."

His nostrils flared again.

"You said 'hey' to me in the hallway. Once." And he didn't remember.

"What's your point?"

"My point is that there's a reason you didn't remember me."

"No, there's not." He laughed.

He actually laughed.

He added, "All I cared about was hockey back then. I woke up, hockey. I went to the bathroom, hockey. Showered, hockey. Went to school, hockey. Everything was hockey for me. I liked girls. I liked getting sex whenever I wanted it back then because it was easy for me, but hockey was my life. I didn't remember you because I probably saw you and still only saw hockey. I don't remember any of the girls I fucked from back then, or in my one year at college. I see you now. I want you now. Why's that such an issue for you?" He leaned forward again. "Why are you so scared?"

Too fast.

Too overwhelming.

Too much to lose.

"I have issues."

"So? I have a busted elbow."

The room grew sweltering. "You do? Are you okay?"

"I'm fine, but I'm still not understanding your whole thing

here. You can't decide for me if I should want to fuck you again or not."

Heat seared through me, and a whole tingly thing was starting in my body. It was starting between my legs, where I was remembering what it felt like to have him there, feel him sliding inside of me, how he gripped my hips, how he used my body—but I had to stop.

My throat was starting to seize up.

And he knew.

I saw it.

A whole smirk and cocky knowing was there, and then his eyes turned and they were starting to smolder. Stop the smoldering.

Please.

I couldn't take the smolder.

I whispered, my voice cracking, "That's not fair."

"What's not fair?"

His voice was silk now.

"Chad doesn't like me."

"Chad doesn't know you."

"You don't know me."

"I would like to know you."

But why?

None of this made sense.

Sex, yes. I was hella hot, but anything beyond that? No. It just didn't happen. Who would want me?

I started shaking my head. "I have to take meds to pay attention. To focus. If I don't, it's a whole chain reaction. I can't focus because I'm noticing everything. I can't put up walls and filter things out, but it's not just that. I had a panic attack tonight, that's why I bailed, and it's embarrassing to have that. God knows what Cassie thought of me. You can't function. You can't read cues right. Basic things about when to laugh, when to speak quietly, when to read a room—I can't do any of those things when I'm having an attack, or *especially* when I'm having an attack. I look like I'm drunk, but inside I'm dying."

He didn't react to that.

He sat there, but his eyes looked down at the table.

I waited.

I didn't want to be waiting how I was, all tense-like, sitting on the edge of my seat, like I needed his approval or disapproval or his rejection, acceptance? Anything. I hated it, but it mattered. It mattered more than I wished it did and I was holding my breath.

"That's what happened tonight?"

There was a balloon in my chest, filling, filling, getting tighter and tighter at his question, at how his tone was so not judging, at how, just like that, the balloon started to deflate.

I nodded. "Yeah."

"What's it like? What do you feel?"

Like a herd of cattle are stampeding over me, and I can't ask for help or raise a hand for someone to grab. But I couldn't tell him that —wait. Why not? So, I did. I repeated every single word, and I waited again when I was done.

This is one of the worst parts. When someone is asking, when you've made yourself vulnerable to them, opened yourself up for judgment, and you then have to wait if they'll 'get it' or if they'll dismiss it because when they dismiss your truth, they dismiss you.

"Jesus. It's like you're being Kronewalled again and again and again."

The sympathy mixed with torture from him had me blinking back tears.

"Yeah. I guess, but I don't know if it's exactly like that." Because hello, being Kronewalled looked like it sucked. Getting hit that hard against the walls, I saw him do it and saw him get checked like that, and I was already cringing just imagining it.

But he got it. Kinda. Or he was trying.

That said everything.

"I'm sorry you go through that."

More tears. I was just blinking nonstop right now.

"Dude," I whispered.

He laughed, then grew fierce as he leaned forward, his eyes capturing and holding mine. "We've been over this. Don't ever 'dude' me."

"Dude." I laughed.

He grinned, then his eyes grew warm again, looking me over. "You were heading to bed?"

I nodded. "I was."

"Can I talk you into watching a movie? Or sports highlights? I mean, is it okay if I just hang out with you, that is, if you're feeling up to it now?"

More heat. More tingles, and I was beginning to throb. There was a whole blooming thing happening in my body. Like a blanket coating my insides and it was spreading, and it was delicious, and it made me feel a way that was dangerous for someone like me to feel.

But I found myself whispering back, "Yeah. That'd be rad."

He snorted. "Rad."

So, we did. On my couch. A blanket pulled over my lap. A movie on, and he took one look at me, at my blanket, and shook his head before reaching over, hooking an arm around my waist and hoisting me over him.

I squawked, which he laughed at as he positioned me so I was tucked in the corner of the couch. My legs and half my body were draped over him, his other arm behind my back, and he tugged me so my head fit into the corner of his arm and chest, and I burrowed in there.

I felt every inch of him for the rest of the night.

I had no clue what we watched.

FROM: CHEYCHEY
TO: KOALA BOY
SUBJECT: DUDE

FROM: KOALA BOY
TO: CHEYCHEY
SUBJECT: DUDE

FROM: CHEYCHEY
TO: KOALA BOY
SUBJECT: DUDE OF THE DUDEST! I LOVE YOU.

FROM: KOALA BOY
TO: CHEYCHEY
SUBJECT: DUUUUUUUUUUUUDE

Two away games later, I was pulling up to the house when I heard the music blaring from inside.

Chad was having a party.

The music wasn't my first clue.

The thirty vehicles parked in the driveway and down the road had been. We had bought two lots, joined the houses together so I was able to pull into my garage. Chad's was full, but the grand doors opened onto my side of the house, and I was tempted to sneak in through the back, go up those stairs and slip into my room. I could lock that shit down, and I was now thinking of a whole new design plan to turn my second floor into an apartment, with doors that could come down to close out the stairs. That'd be convenient right about now.

I didn't, because Chad knew I was coming home, and he knew I'd been avoiding him since Thursday night.

A few women were hanging out on the front porch when I parked, heading over.

"Cut! Hi."

"Hey, Cut. Sorry about your loss."

I grunted. "Yeah."

I was normally polite, but standoffish. These women, though...Chad had partied with before.

I nodded a hello, and kept moving around them.

They wanted me to stop. And I wanted to go to bed with Cheyenne. We all didn't get what we wanted.

Thankfully, it wasn't as packed as much as I thought it was going to be when I went inside.

A few guys in the foyer.

More in the living room.

I dipped into the kitchen, grabbing water, a few sports drinks, and food. There was a whole gathering in there, and Chad saw me. He was at the sink, his arm around a woman who wasn't the Not-Russian he'd been spending time with. He straightened, his arm falling from her, and he called out, "Hey, buddy! Great game last night."

We won the first game, lost last night.

I lifted my chin at him. "Thanks." I scanned the rest of the room. I realized I didn't know any of them, which made it easier for me to turn and move through the room that connected the kitchen to the living room. I could swing around, going up the back stairs, but as I did, I saw where the party was. Outside.

The giant patio doors were slid open. People were laughing. That was where the music was coming from, and lots of bikinis. Lots and lots of them.

"I'm planning on moving the party to Bresko's later if you wanted to join?" Chad spoke from right behind me.

I turned, catching his grin, but it was a masked grin.

"Nah, I'm good."

I started for the stairs.

"Hey." Chad got in front of me. "What's going on with us? You've been off for a week."

He wanted to know about Cheyenne. I told him about Cheyenne. Then *he* told me about Cheyenne, but I found out

Thursday night that I was thinking he didn't know a lot about the sister he didn't want me to see.

I stared at him. "You know what's going on."

He quieted, the grin slipped and he eased back a step. He was holding a beer and his hand tightened, gripping it. "You're still going to see her?"

I gestured in the direction of the kitchen with my head. "What about that bunny? I thought you were seeing Cheyenne's friend."

"She's not a bunny."

"You know what I mean."

He quieted, nodding. "Yeah. I do."

And there was silence.

Which I figured.

Chad liked that I was usually laid-back off the ice. Until now, because I wasn't anymore when it came to Cheyenne, and there were feelings involved. Those feelings came out of nowhere. And they were intense, and we were all playing catch up, including myself.

"I don't want you seeing her."

"That's your answer to my question about her friend? You quit seeing the friend, hoping that'd make me not see your sister? Yeah, that's not gonna happen."

"She's not my sister." His knuckles whitened around the beer before smoothing out again. "But you are? Seeing her?"

"I don't know. We don't even know."

"You've been gone. I mean, how would that work?"

I frowned. "Phone. Texting. I'd think the normal way."

His neck was getting red. "That's what you're doing? You're sexting with my sister?"

"Like you said, she's not really your sister."

He rolled his eyes. "Whatever, man, she's Hunter's sister."

"She doesn't seem to have a relationship with anyone in your family besides Hunter."

"That's because—"

I was waiting.

I hadn't cut him off. He stopped himself.

"Because?"

The red was crawling up. Chad was getting pissed. "She's a fucking mental case. You got no clue what she put my family through in high school—"

"She told me she had a crush on me in school. Did you know?"

He looked away.

So, he knew and he hadn't told me. I asked, "Did she ask you not to say anything to me?"

His eyes lit up, and he sneered. "Ask me? Fuck no. We never talked. Like never. I barely saw her myself. Mom wanted Hunter and me out of the house, and that was for a reason. Her mom—"

"Was a junkie."

His head reared back.

"She told me. She told me a lot, actually. She was trying to scare me off. Thought I'd bolt at the first red flag."

His eyebrows furrowed. "She did?"

"Chad, baby." The woman from his side in the kitchen came out, wrapping herself around him. She rested her head against his shoulder, smiling up at me. "Hey, Cut. How are you? You played great both nights."

I nodded, but didn't reply. I said to Chad, "I'll be upstairs."

"You coming out tonight?" It was the woman.

I looked her over, flicked my gaze to Chad and left.

I heard her pfft behind me, and I didn't care.

Christ.

I didn't know what was going on with Chad. He'd been my best friend for so long, we were brothers, but this side of him? It only came out when he talked about Cheyenne, and she'd been referred to as 'that girl' in the past.

My phone buzzed when I was putting my water and food on the desk.

Hendrix: Your boy texted, saying he's got a party going to Bresko's tonight. You going?

Me: No.

Hendrix: Want to come over here? Could watch the game.

Me: Let me check with someone quick.

And I texted to Cheyenne.

Me: You around tonight?

She didn't waste time getting back to me. My phone buzzed right away.

Cheyenne: Was planning on heading to Tits tonight. My friend runs it. You're back?

I grinned.

Me: Fucking love that you hang out at a strip club.

Cheyenne: Want to come? Hang out? I'll give you a private lap dance, just make sure you bring those dollar bills.

And my dick was hard.

I stifled a groan but typed back.

Me: We still need a first date. Let's save that for the second date.

Cheyenne: Deal.

Me: I'm going to go to a friend's, but I could swing by your place after? How long do you stay at the titty bar?

Cheyenne: I'll be there till about 9. You sure you don't want to come? How many girls have you dated that try to entice you to a strip club?

Me: None. I don't date.

I waited.

She didn't respond right away.

I waited a little bit more.

Then...

Cheyenne: Maybe the lap dance can be tonight at my place?

I was full-on smiling now, and I didn't care.

Me: I am holding you to that.

Me: Text more later?

Cheyenne: Sounds good. I'm heading to the gym now.

Me: Be safe.

We ended it there, and the same feeling I had over the last few days, between our texting and our phone calls, was the same. This was new to me, but it felt good. It felt right. And I'd never felt that before either.

The music went up a whole decibel level, and I was done.

I texted Hendrix.

Me: You at your place now?

Hendrix: Yep. Game's on.

I chuckled. If anything else, we were a predictable lot.

Me: Heading over now.

Hendrix: Pick up a pack, would you? I'm out.

I glanced at the food I grabbed, and none of it looked appeasing.

Me: Food?

Hendrix: I stocked up on the way home. Just bring the beer.

Me: On it.

16

CHEYENNE

A girl's ass was bouncing in my face.

And it was close enough that I could tell she put a strong dose of vanilla cupcake perfume right there. If I looked close enough, I could probably identify which self-tanner she used, and she preferred purple glitter rather than the regular all-color glitter.

Yep. Too close.

I focused on Sasha who was sitting next to me, lounging back in one of her booths, with an arm resting over the top of it, her hand dangling, and her other hand stroking her glass on the table.

"Why is Juna giving me a lap dance?" As I asked, the dancer in question turned and hooked one ankle around my neck, and her whole body fell backwards. "Oh! Whoa!"

"Don't touch her," came from Sasha, but she wasn't too upset. She wasn't even looking.

I looked down and past a thong that I did not want to see... there, in all her glory, I saw Juna looking up at me. She was laughing.

I asked, "You okay down there?"

She unhooked her ankle, sliding to the floor, and came back up to slide in on the other side of our booth. It was a round booth. It was Sasha's special booth. She used it when the club wasn't too full, and one of us was here.

"Yeah." Juna winced, rotating her arm in a circle. "I was trying a new move, but it didn't work. Everything else up to then was good, wasn't it?"

"You don't need the new move." Sasha was still not watching us, she was looking out somewhere else. I didn't think she was even seeing the main stage, or all the other booths that were spread out before us and below us. We were at the highest spot in the club. The rest was shitty seating, or really great private seating, depending on how you viewed it.

"You don't think?"

"No." Another monotone answer from Sasha.

Juna rubbed at her arm, frowning at her boss before looking at me. "What do you think?"

"I'm not a dance-expert, but the shows I've seen you do, I don't think it's needed either."

She sighed, standing. "Okay. Maybe I'll think about doing something else."

"You don't need anything new. Stick to what you do. It's already perfect."

"New tricks mean new tips."

"The regulars like what you're doing already."

Juna was walking away and heard this last comment, sending a last grin over her shoulder before a guy snagged her up. Warm smiles, and soon she was air-grinding on a dude in a corner.

Sasha noticed, watching. "She better not try the new move."

"But if she does, maybe she'll get better tips."

"She'll hurt herself and then there'll be *no* tips."

Sasha could be a hardass, but not usually like this.

I frowned. "What's going on with you?"

Not even a blink, she sent back, "What's going on with you?"

I raised an eyebrow. "Come again?"

"You and the NHL guy." She scowled. "You're seeing him?"

She knew I was. I'd called and told her what happened. "We've been texting. He's had away games."

"You think that's smart? He was your ideal in school and college. That gives him an edge over you. He could hurt you, ya know."

She was griping. Griping and Sasha went together like peas in a pod, but this was more. I gestured to my own face. "Right here."

"What?" A sharp snap from her.

I touched the corner of my mouth. "Right here is where you have this line that goes down."

She touched her own face, but her movements were jerky, impatient.

I shook my head. "That line just got worse."

I was trying to tell her this, and I was trying to lead her down the path, but there was a buzzing. It was in the background, and my meds had kicked back in, but it always took a little before they really helped center things away. Because of that, I was sitting here, and I was acting like normal, pretending to myself and to Sasha that I was normal, but I wasn't. The buzzing was building. It was in my blood, and it was rising, rising. If I let it overtake me, I'd be gone.

I couldn't do that again.

I liked Tits. I liked the darkness of the place. I liked that there was some grime in it, too. I liked the girls. Of course, I liked the boss. The security guards were like uncles and big brothers. There was an undertone that was settling to me, even all the glitter, too.

I was able to relax in Tits, but Sash was interrupting that flow.

I scowled at her now. "What is your problem? And don't turn it back on me. You're in a mood. What gives?"

Her scowl just deepened, but she studied me a moment and let it go. "You're jonesing."

"I'm not jonesing."

"You are. I thought you got back on your meds."

"I did, and it doesn't really matter where I'm at. You know how it is."

She quieted, because she did.

"What crab crawled up your claw?"

She snickered, shaking her head. "You."

"Me?"

"Well, your. Your brother."

Chad. My scowl just deepened. Fucking Chad.

"Again, he's not my brother, but what happened?"

"He'll always be your brother, because that's your relation with him, through your parents, through Hunter."

I grinned. Koala Dude. He could always make me smile.

But we needed to focus here. I couldn't get distracted. "What about Chad, though? What'd he do?"

"He dumped me."

Oh-kay. This now entered the terrain where I really had to focus. That meant sitting up, leaning forward, and turning toward her. All the background shit needed to be just that, background. "Say again?"

She had a faint grin, knowing what I just did, and I scooted closer as she said, "He dumped me. Said since you're seeing *his boy,* then he can't see me. It was an either/or situation. And I'm not pissed at you, because you're not the one choosing. He is." As an afterthought, she said, "He did."

Back to scowling. "Fucking Chad."

She sighed, all the sniping gone from her. "Fucking Chad."

"Let's go toilet paper his house."

"What?"

I grinned. "You heard me. I know where he lives."

"That's your boy's house, too."

I lifted up a shoulder. "They joined their houses so we can

toilet paper only Chad's side. And besides, Cut has money. He can pay for cleanup, no problem."

"This won't piss off your boy?"

"I'm not sure we're at the stage where he's 'my boy' yet."

"What stage are you at?"

"We're in pre-talks of the actual talk."

"That makes no sense."

I flashed her another grin. "He can say all he wants, but until he sees my crazy shit and is okay with it, he and I are only talking and," thinking about tonight, "doing other things. We're enjoying each other right now. That's our stage."

"The enjoyment stage?"

"The enjoyment stage."

"Holy cripes!"

That came from a booth in the back and we turned.

Juna was upside down on a guy's lap.

Sasha sighed. "She tried the move."

I nodded, seeing Juna flip over on the guy's lap, but she jumped to her feet. The guy was cradling his dick, glaring at her. "You fucking bit—"

Three bouncers rushed in, and Sasha was getting out of the booth. "I told her not to do the move. She did. I don't want to sit and hear her babble how she shouldn't have done the move. Let's go now."

My blood buzzing just picked up a whole notch because I knew what this meant.

It was toilet paper time.

17

CHEYENNE

There were so many different uses for toilet paper.

The obvious wiping your ass use. Toga use. Bridal party use. General party decoration use. Apocalypse panic-buying use. Then, you know, the whole rolling it and stuffing it somewhere and everyone's imaginations can fill in the blank for those places. Bulging penises. Bras. Maybe just the use of wiping sweat from under the boobs. But today, no, *tonight*. *Tonight* the toilet paper was being used to make a statement: to be a pain in someone's ass.

Chad's ass, to be specific. Fucking Chad.

The entire back of Matilda was filled with toilet paper. Some might think we went overboard, but no way. The TP would always be used if we didn't use it tonight. Pulling up, Sasha cut the lights and we frowned at the massive amounts of vehicles parked in both driveways and on the street.

"Did your boy say they were having a party?"

"The house is dark."

"They have a backyard?"

I glanced sideways at Sasha. "You've not been here?"

She shook her head, her face grim and focused on the house. "He came over to my place each time."

Right.

Fucking Chad.

"I think they have a big backyard."

Her mouth tightened. She swallowed. She tightened her hold on the steering wheel, she might've been trying to strangle it, pretending it was Chad's neck. She let it go in the next breath and unclasped her seatbelt. "Let's do this."

My heart started pounding.

My blood started searing, rippling, getting worked up.

We were in our older twenties. We were into our careers. We should know better, right? Well, we did. But I still loved doing stupid, immature stuff like this.

Made me feel normal.

Not that we didn't do this when we were in college, but I'd still been figuring things out. Half the shit I did, I didn't know what I was doing or why I was doing it, I was just in a craze. Now, though...now I could enjoy it. And my girl was hurting, and fucking Chad, but I was having fun this time.

I was just hoping no cops were called, because ... embarrassing.

Right now, we were both moving stealthily.

The secret agent and the assassin.

We were business-like.

We'd even gone to Sasha's and changed clothes. All black.

I wanted to wear a mask. I had a cool, skull-looking one at my place, but Sasha vetoed it, saying we'd for sure get cops called on us then. So, we were going no mask, but still all black, and though my heart was thumping out of my chest, both of us were the epitome of a Toilet Paper SEAL Team being called in.

It was effin' awesome.

Sasha lifted the back door. We each took an entire case of rolls and then we went to work.

Cut had told me once that Chad's side of the house was the smaller one, so that's where we went. We went over, stopped in the lawn, and perused the house. Then, exchanging a nod, we got to work.

The toilet paper cases were dropped on the lawn. Tore open. And the first roll was out, being cocked back, and we each let 'em loose. They flew through the air, the paper trailing behind it looking like a small, fluttering little kite tail. It was a sight to behold. Absolutely glorious.

I went back to Matilda and grabbed some earbuds from my purse.

A good bass and some rap beat were going to make this night epic.

An hour later, the entire front was covered.

We weren't thinking. We should've done the back first, but we had already committed. We couldn't back out now.

Sasha waved and yelled over my music, "I'm going to the side."

I nodded, trekking back to Matilda for my third case of toilet paper. This stuff was caked on in some places.

Then I headed to the backyard.

Two hours later, Eminem and the *8 Mile* soundtrack was blasting in my ears and most of the backyard was done.

Over the windows.

Tucked in between some of the siding.

Over, around, and through the hedges.

Under some of the rocks. Over the rocks.

I had made trails of toilet paper over and around the other

piles of toilet paper. I was considering the logistics of making a whole toilet paper igloo when I felt a tap on my shoulder.

Expecting Sasha, I was smiling, and knowing I looked a little drunk because that was the level I was on, I turned and it was not Sasha.

Not Sasha at all.

My Not-Brother was glowering at me.

He was *so not* happy.

Fucking Chad.

18

CHEYENNE

My Not-Brother reeked of cologne, perfume, sweat, and smoke.

He was also still not happy, even thirty minutes later. He first showed up with a whole entourage of people. When he tapped my shoulder, I saw him, saw Sasha behind him, and then saw everyone else behind her. The women were barely clothed, but with some seriously rad clothes. Sequins and glitter galore. I'd be in heaven if we were doing nightclub costume night. Their hair was all sleek, even late in the night, and their makeup was barely smudged.

I needed to find those women and ask for pointers. When I went dancing, my makeup was easily streaking off of me within an hour. I've been told that's the con of being in shape, you sweat easily—okay, I was getting off track.

Back on track.

But first, Sasha. She was pissed when Chad showed up.

Her arms were crossed. Her mouth tight. She wasn't talking to him, even when his glower faded when he looked at her. My Not-Brother was muscular, maybe around five eleven. He looked like a little body builder, but not to the extreme levels they were. A box-like jaw. His hair had reddish hints, but it was mostly brown now. I remembered those eyes. They'd been pretty in school, and his eyelashes were all long and curly. I didn't usually notice eyelashes on guys, but he'd been my brother back then, and I remember thinking that he got a mom, a little brother, and those eyelashes? Lucky ducker.

Even my brain was autocorrecting me now.

When he looked at me, he was all scowls. When he looked at Sasha, he was all regret. Could see it a million miles away, but Sash, she wouldn't look at him.

He'd sent his entourage away by now, and we were now inside the generously toiled-papered house. He raised a hand and gripped the back of his head. "Sasha—"

She turned away, for the thirtieth time.

I'm not exaggerating.

And I frowned. "Are you calling the cops?"

I couldn't remember if he told me. He probably did. My mind had been distracted by all the outfits behind him before he sent them away, and he let out an aggrieved sigh now.

I was sure he told me.

"I already told you—" See. "I didn't call them."

Sasha said, only looking at me, "He got an alert on his phone. We tripped the security when you went into the backyard."

My bad.

She kept on, "But it took him forty minutes to notice because he'd been getting two lap dances at Bresko's."

He went back to scowling. "I was not getting a lap dance. I was just dancing. That's it. There's nothing wrong with it."

"Correction, he was having non-penetrating sex with clothes on in a private venue, so it took him a long time before he pulled up the security footage." She threw him a nasty look. "Apparently that's something I should let my girls do at Tits."

"I've never said that, and that's not what was happening. I was just distracted. The music was loud." He rolled his eyes. "I still can't get over that you run that strip club."

"It's a private dance club."

He snorted, his hand dropping from behind his head. "Right. What she said."

I knew cops. I didn't want to deal with them. "So, no cops?"

Also, they were bickering because he'd been distracted from noticing the security alert. I was thinking Sasha wasn't realizing what side we currently were on. We were pro-distraction right now. She could be anti-distraction when we weren't the ones setting off the security alerts.

Both looked at me.

"No cops."

My Not-Brother added, "I was calling them when I recognized Sasha, so I hung up. It's all good."

I let out some air. Good. No cops.

I frowned again. "Then, why are we waiting? Did I miss that part, too?"

Not-Brother scowled again.

Sasha grinned. "He called your boy. He's on his way."

Oh, crap. I remembered our 'maybe later' date and scrambled for my phone. I'd missed two texts, and both were right when the rabbit rapper was trying to fix his car.

"She works with the police, ya know." Sasha was nodding in my direction.

My Not-Brother frowned, swinging his head back my way. "You do?"

"I work at a kitchen for the homeless. Our paths cross sometimes."

"Right." But he continued to frown, taking on a more distracted look, before his eyes paused looking at the window, and whatever he'd been thinking just then vanished. His eyebrows pinched together, and the sides of his mouth curved

down. "You guys have to clean that shit up. And why only one of
our houses—"

"Because it's yours." Both Sasha and I said that at the
same time.

Chad shut up before rolling his eyes. "I need a drink." He
started out of the room. "You guys want anything?"

Sasha, "Hell yes, all that rolling has me parched."

Me, "I'm on medication."

Chad's head came back. "What?"

Sasha started laughing.

"I'm on heavy, psychotropic medication. Do you know how
bad it would be if I had a drink? Know how *nuts* I would get?" My
voice took on a threatening tone.

I couldn't help myself.

Sasha knew what I was doing, and she looked away, biting
down on her lip.

Part of this was to get back at him, but he was remembering. I
saw the look, and he was remembering it all from high school.

I started for him, my head tilted to the side. "I was so bad that
you were sent away. Remember? That I was so nuts, that they
didn't tell me I had a little brother?" He winced at that one. Good.
I kept on, "That I was so dangerous, that when my mom died, I
couldn't be with my dad. Everyone feared it would fuck with your
hockey training. Remember that? I sure do. That's what Natalie
was worried about."

The air after I finished saying my peace was heavy.

My heart was beating, and fuck me, but I was suddenly
completely and totally focused on one person.

Chad looked like he wanted to throw up. His mouth pressed
in. White lines formed around his mouth, and then, behind us
all, came a gravelly voice.

"What the fuck are you talking about?"

I stiffened.

Chad swore.

Sasha purred. "Oh. This just got fun."

I looked, and standing just beyond the doorway to the large house, in the doorway that led to the living room where we were standing, was Cut. His jaw was clenched. His eyes smoldering, and he looked *fierce*.

Chad swore again. "It wasn't totally like that."

"It was totally like that."

He swung around to Sasha. "You weren't even there."

She shrugged, her chin raising up. "Doesn't matter. My girl doesn't lie, and she told me years ago how it went down. Her mom died, and instead of going to live with her *father*, she went back to her uncle's until she went off to college."

He started for her, his hand up. "She wanted to stay with her uncle."

She snorted, rolling her eyes this time.

He swung my way. "Didn't you? That's what I was told."

"It would've messed up your hockey training. My first time living there had already messed up enough."

His mouth hung open. "That's not what I was told."

No one said a word. There didn't seem to be much of a point at this time in our lives.

I didn't think it would hurt, but then again, I never thought about Chad, or thought I'd have this conversation with him. I guess all I focused on back then to get me through was being in love with Cut for so long, from so far away—it had taken on a whole fairytale feeling to me. Sasha was right. He was the knight in shining armor to me, and I had no idea why I put that image on him.

I glanced his way, his eyes were laser-focused on me. His gaze was piercing, and I winced, feeling him slide right inside, just like the first night at the charity gala. He saw me, and he claimed me, and he hadn't backed out. Yet.

He would, though. It was just a matter of time.

Fuck. Fuck! That hurt realizing that.

This was stupid. We shouldn't be here.

I shouldn't even be playing with the notion of him and me. It was all going to end in disaster. Every relationship in my life did, except Sash and Mel. Both of them had stayed so far.

"Shy," a soft call from Sasha.

I already knew.

Shit, that hurt.

I was swallowing knives. Pain sliced down my chest.

"Cheyenne, whatever you're thinking, stop."

"*Not* how my brain works," I gutted out.

"Well, stop it. Do your exercises. I can see you're thinking a whole lot of bad shit that's going to sabotage you, so stop it. Right now."

"What kind of things?" Cut.

And damn, his tone was soft, too.

Here it was. He was seeing the beginning of a freak-out. I'd be bouncing off the walls in two seconds, then he'd run. Then he'd be the one to call the police, not Chad.

It'd be done then. Once and for all.

Sasha ignored him, saying to me, "You drive your brain. Got it? Not the other way around."

She didn't get it. And if anyone got it, it was her, but she didn't get it. Her brain wasn't a total rollercoaster ride by itself, and now I was shaking because dammit, I was trying to do what she was saying.

The carpet was extra soft.

There was a lingering smell of tanning lotion in the room.

Some blinds in another room were rustling.

I was bouncing around.

"What's going on?"

That was Chad, but he sounded like he was running around me.

"She's overwhelmed."

"I thought she got back on her meds."

I jumped, but a hand touched my arm. Soft. Gentle. It was Cut, and he was there, right next to me.

I leaned into him, not even thinking.

Mess, mess, mess. Me.

He'd run.

I was a mess.

"She's sweating."

Sasha cursed. "Babe, what do you need?"

I was shaking my head. No wonder it was getting worse? I was working myself up, or not even that. It was like a bull always in my head, always ready to go and charge at a moment's notice, but sometimes I could corral him in. But this was me, letting him out myself and I had to stop it.

I kept seeing the pool outside. A few floaties were on the surface, lights underneath were now lit up, and I was moving for the back patio doors in the next instant. "I need to swim."

There were voices behind me.

The floor's texture was smooth, but there were a few pebbles under my feet. I could tell Cut how many different colors he had in just his living room. I could tell him there was a weird whirring sound from upstairs. I could tell him so much more, but then I was outside and I breathed in the air.

I was always better outside, and then two more steps and I was jumping in the air.

Then, *splash!*

Everything was doused. Dulled. Quieted. I stilled under the water, drowning out the raging bull inside.

I could think.

It was only me, the water, and my thoughts.

After that, I kicked off and I swam.

I needed to exhaust my brain.

❄

CUT

I HAD no idea how to help her.

I'd been watching her swim laps for thirty minutes, and she just kept going. This wasn't normal. I mean, I knew. She'd told me, but this was... This just was. I had nothing to back that up.

When Chad called me, I thought he was high. I'd been at Hendrix's and I'd sent her a couple of texts. No answer. I hadn't thought much about it. I knew where she was. Anyone sitting at a titty bar was either enamored or bored out of their minds. I figured since it's her friend's place, she was having a good time. Then, Chad sent me the footage, and holy shit. Mind fuck.

She was toilet papering our place. Not even the whole place. She was toilet papering Chad's side.

I cracked up, showing Hendrix the footage, and he cracked up, too.

But coming here, I hadn't been pissed off at all.

Chad was Chad. I figured he'd be pissy and throwing his weight around. He did that on a normal basis, but I knew it'd be more with Cheyenne and yeah, there was history there that I knew I still hadn't uncovered, but here we were. I mean, she warned me. I saw her getting worked up, and now she was doing laps in my swimming pool and I had no idea what I was going to say to her when she finished.

Chad took the other one home. Both of them had been drinking so they got an Uber, but I didn't expect him back until tomorrow at some point. Tension was high between those two, so we'd see what unfolded tomorrow. But back to my girl, because she was mine, even with the shit that went down here tonight.

My Cheyenne.

Was this fast? Yes. Hell yes.

Was there stuff I needed to unravel? Fuck yes.

Was I walking? Not a chance.

Then she stopped swimming, did a flip in the water, and

stood at the edge. She had tossed her clothes after two laps, so I'd watched her swim the entire time in only her bra and panties and my dick was hard the entire fucking time, but it wasn't the time for that. She stood, water dripping down from her, and she just stared at me. She didn't hide herself. Her hair was slicked back. Her hands went to her side as she rose out of the pool.

Still standing tall. Straight. Her hands never left her side. Her eyes didn't waver either.

She was waiting.

To see what my reaction would be, I suppose.

I stood up and Jesus, I had no fucking idea what I was going to do, but I said somehow, "Ready for bed?"

A tired smile appeared—or maybe that was relief—and her top lip lifted. "Yes."

19

CHEYENNE

I woke the next morning, and I froze.

I remembered everything. *Everything*. And holy Moses, I freaked yesterday. He actually saw it all, but on the Cheyenne Scale, that one hadn't been bad. Swimming it out of me helped, but I was tired, and my body ached. I hadn't swum in a really long time, and my body was revolting against the coping mechanism I'd chosen to calm the chaos.

A body shifted on the bed beside me, and I closed my eyes before turning over. Looking.

He was waiting for me. Head on his pillow, turned toward me, and he grinned. "Morning."

I wanted to die. "Morning."

His eyes softened. "How are you feeling?"

I shrugged. "It is what it is."

Those same eyes darkened. "What does that mean?"

I had to put an end to this. I sat up, swinging my feet down, and noticing my tank top, I grabbed for it. It'd been dried and was folded on a chair by the bed. My pants just underneath it. I had stripped everything off in the bathroom and tugged one of his shirts on.

He did my laundry for me.

Oh, man. That was really sweet of him.

Sweet. Fuck.

I *really* had to end this now. I would be doing him a favor in the long run.

I pulled my top on, and reached for my pants. When I had one leg inside, he said from behind me, "Why am I getting a weird feeling here?"

I almost scoffed.

Because he was intuitive?

I only murmured, putting my second leg in, "Because you're smart."

"What does that *mean*?" He'd dropped his tone a whole octave lower. I heard him standing, felt the bed move. "You need to tell me. You need to talk to me."

I stood, pulling my pants up and zipped them up, buttoning them. Shoes?

A strangled cough came from him, then, "They're on the bed."

I looked. He'd just put them there for me, straightening and standing back. His eyes were hooded. His face was granite.

That hurt. I knew it was me doing this, but he would thank me later.

"You're running? Only this time I'm awake and witnessing it."

He said it with such contempt, but he didn't get it. He did not get this.

I grabbed my sandals, letting them plop one by one on the floor as I put my feet into them. I owed him an explanation, he heard about my freak-outs, and he witnessed the beginning of one last night, but that look—I'll never forget how utterly help-less he looked when I was in the water.

He didn't think I saw him, but I did. He never moved from his spot, and the longer I swam, the longer he stayed. Some might start falling in love with that, if they hadn't been, or if they weren't freaking out about losing their mind.

Some.

Not me.

Because I was guarded.

Because I had to be guarded.

For him.

Not me.

I was doing this for him.

And again, I was not falling in love with him, or realizing I had always been, or—nope. That wasn't me. That wasn't this mental case.

"I'm not a charity case for you."

He actually flinched. "Who the fuck said you were?"

"I know guys. I know sometimes they want to save the girl, and you're looking at me. You're seeing how messed up I am, but I'm not just temporarily messed up, this isn't a once-a-month, hormonal thing." I pointed to my head. "All this is because I don't have the right neurotransmitters working up there. It's the same as someone getting cancer or arthritis. My brain is sick, and the problem with that shit is that I'm battling my own brain every day, every minute, every second, every fucking year of my life. This doesn't get magically fixed. They don't know enough about it to fix it. I can't have back surgery, and voila, I'm all good. It's not like that. You're thinking you're all in now, but you aren't. Trust me."

My chest was squeezing. A whole knot was sitting in my throat.

I was getting choked up, because, my God, he'd been the idea that got me through all the bad shit with my family. But that wasn't real. I was walking away from it. I had all these walls put in place. Those walls kept me going. They kept me enduring, and he'd been so many of the walls. Protecting me from the outside world. The idea of him had been the foundation holding those walls up, and now it was gone.

And shortly, so would he.

Because I knocked all of them over in one swift move.

I felt bereft, and a whole feeling of doom was settling in my chest. Pressing in, pressing down. It was spreading through me, and I was fucked. I was so fucked.

Grabbing my purse, checking that my phone was inside, I had to go.

I had to go now before I changed my mind.

I was at the door, my hand on the doorknob, when he said, "Never took you for a coward."

Oh. Oh no.

I swung around. "Don't even go there." My head was up, eyes wide, and I was breathing in fire. "Do not even go there, to that place where you think you can goad me for what? Running away? I live with this. You just got a visitor's pass, but trust me, you don't want a permanent residency. You train for your job but imagine if that same amount of work was what you needed every hour of every day just to keep breathing. Don't call me a coward, dude."

"Dude?!" His nostrils flared. His eyes turned smoldering, even more heated. "I hate that word from you."

"Yeah. Well." I so didn't care. "Don't call me a coward, and no, it doesn't compare."

I had to get out of there. It was *imperative*. I saw the fight rallying in him.

Seriously. My mouth was going dry just looking at him. His hair was all messed up, but it was in the hot, messy, sexed-up kind of way, and I know he hadn't done anything with it. That was all natural, and he'd pulled on some sweats. They rode low on his hips. That V on a hockey player. Damn. That V.

But it wasn't how he looked.

It was how he just was.

Because he was good, and kind, and he was humble. And he

didn't take shit from my Not-Brother. And he fought for me. And he sat by the pool for thirty minutes being terrified, but still stayed.

He stayed, and he was still standing here. He was still staying.

What was I doing?

I was walking away, feeling like I was ripping myself in half here, but it was needed. It was so needed.

"I have to go."

"Wait." It took him two steps.

I opened the door, he slammed it shut, then he was stepping up behind me. His body pressed against mine.

It felt right.

If this felt right why was I doing this? I'd asked myself that before and still didn't have an answer.

I wanted someone to love me.

My mother never had. I had no dad, then I had a dad, but I still didn't have a dad. I had no one, so I created him in my head. He got me through until I found Sasha, then we found Melanie and it's been us three since. Only us three.

But damn, I just wanted to be loved.

And he was here.

And he had stayed.

But I felt the ache low in my body because whether he knew it or not, he was out of his depth. They never knew, until they knew and then they wanted to be gone.

"Let me go, Cut."

He'd be just like them, but I would tear through him like a tornado and I'd only leave behind debris. I would damage him, and I couldn't do that because if I did love him after all, if I was falling in love, or always had been—it was enough not to do that to him.

His hand flexed against the door.

I felt how tense he was. It was bouncing off of him in waves, sucking me in, making the room stifling, but after a second flex, he stepped back. His hand lowered, but he said, his voice almost pinning me in place, "I heard what your friend said. I don't know what's in your head, what you're thinking, but whatever this is, you're going to regret it." He pressed up against me again, his head lowering.

I felt every inch of him.

And I shivered.

He felt that.

I couldn't suppress it, and his head dropped.

I felt his lips graze my shoulder.

Another shudder.

God.

I wanted to let him sweep me up in his arms.

I wanted him to carry me back to his bed. I wanted to feel him inside of me.

But it was that look. *That* look.

He would walk. They *always* walked.

I wouldn't live through it if it was him.

My mom. My dad. I survived them, but him—he would be different. I had needed the idea of him.

I reached for the door, tears blinding me, and I left.

But people like me never got what we wanted. We never could.

I'd learn how to not need him. I'd have to, and if I didn't?

Well, then...

CUT

WEEK ONE.
  The girl was a headcase.
  Fine.
Fuck it.
Fuck her.
Maybe this was better?

WEEK TWO.
 I didn't miss her.
 I wasn't thinking about her.
 She wasn't in my head.
 I wasn't the headcase.
 Fuck.
 I wanted to call her.

WEEK THREE.

She was still gone.

I had not called.

But I kept checking to see if she had called.

I kept opening the phone to text her.

Damn.

Dammit so bad.

I missed her.

WEEK FOUR.

Still fucking missing her.

Still wondering what the fuck I should do.

WEEK FIVE.

We were loading onto the plane, heading to Seattle for a game tomorrow night. I had my headphones in, music blaring, and I didn't want to deal with anyone right now.

I never thought of myself as a moody bitch, but that's what I had become. Cheyenne ran, and I'd been in a mood ever since.

My phone buzzed.

That wasn't hope in my chest. No—and then a real no because I saw who sent it. My whole fucking chest deflated. It'd been five weeks and I hadn't talked to Cheyenne, or Chad.

I wanted to talk to Cheyenne. I didn't want to talk to Chad.

Chad: Can we talk? You've been avoiding me. Good game the other night, by the way.

Right. The last game had gone past in a blur for me. I hit the ice and I wanted to kill. Crow was confused since he was the team's enforcer, but I'd been wanting to fight. Itching for one. Coach called me in, talked to me, wondering what was up, too. I hadn't said a word. We weren't like that. I wasn't like that, but hockey was my sanctuary. I hit that ice and that's all I could control so I did. I controlled everything, everyone.

I was attaching to it like it was a lifeline right now.

Fuck.

Maybe Cheyenne had been right?

I was already worked up, worked up this much over her, and I'd only seen her a few times.

She was right. I mean, I didn't know what the hell she actually went through.

Christ.

Swinging into my seat, I stuffed my bag under the seat in front of me and typed back.

Me: Let me call you when we land and I get to the hotel.

He'd been right. I had been avoiding him, but it wasn't hard. He never came home the next day after the whole toilet papering event, and after our home game, he was out partying. I went to the house. Woke. Went to the arena.

We'd been traveling almost ever since. This was my life during the season. Chad knew it. It wasn't uncommon that we went months without seeing each other. He was only saying something now because of Cheyenne.

Me: You back with the Russian?

Chad: She's not a Russian.

Me: She pretends she is.

Chad: Lol

Chad: You and Cheyenne?

Me: What about us?

Hendrix dropped into the seat next to me, and I could already hear the music blaring from his headphones. He got settled, then tugged his headphones off and nodded to my phone.

"Your woman?"

"Chad."

"Nice. I saw him at Bresko's the other night."

"Yeah?"

"Went there after one of our games with a few guys and he was there, in your box."

I frowned. It wasn't really my box, but I was a silent investor, and the owners kept a VIP section for us. Chad dropped my name, a lot. It was partly his job, but not for Bresko's. I knew he was never employed there to promote them. The club didn't need him, but Chad needed Bresko's. He used his connection there to build up the crowd that he could pull for other clubs.

"Who was he with?"

"Not as many as normal. A few people, no one I remembered."

I went back to my phone.

Me: Who'd you party with at Bresko's?

Chad: Huh? Why?

Me: Cuz if you're using my name, I want to know.

I was being a bitch. He always used my name, and he knew I knew it. This was just the first time I was saying something about it.

There was another long pause.

Chad: You don't want me to use your name?

Me: I want to know who you're taking to the VIP area and using my name.

Chad: WTF?

I scowled.

Me: Just tell me who you partied with.

Chad: Don't be a bitch because my sister took off on you.

A whole whoosh sensation went through me. This fucker.

I was scowling.

Me: Wow, first time you actually called her that.

Chad: What the hell is your problem?

Fuck's sake. I had to calm it down. He was right.

Then my phone started ringing. *Chad calling.*

I didn't trust myself to talk civil to him. I didn't know what I'd say to him over text either.

I hit decline and turned it on airplane mode.

Switching back to my music, I noticed Hendrix had been paying attention, but he didn't say a word. He stuck his headphones back in his ears and we flew to Seattle just like that.

21

CHEYENNE

I was doing a bunch of self-reflection lately.

I had my job, and I loved working at Come Our Way. I loved everything about it. The guys. The workers. The volunteers. The mission. And I had my girls. I saw them almost every day. We were family. That's how it was, but I hadn't thought about my love life. I hadn't had to, to be honest.

I was fulfilled.

Or I thought I had been, but with my stuff, a person goes through a situation where they really question things at a deeper level. Like, would it be fair to bring someone else in on the struggle you endure every day? If you did, was it fair to bring a child into the world who had a mother with the struggles I had? On the surface, she would seem to be just a mom who's distracted or disorganized.

But follow down the line, and it's a mom who's not listening to you. It's a mom who forgets to pick you up. It's a mom who forgot to pay your meal plan for a year, for the second year, for a third year. It's a mom who forgets to pick you up not once, but twice, three, four, five... The intent is there. The love is always there, but the struggles are there, and they are often greater than the whole, and they can chip away at a person, at a child, at a husband, at a wife. If something gets chipped away at enough, holes get created and those holes get bigger and bigger over the years.

Did I want to do that? God no.

But would I struggle at some point? Without a doubt.

I was still young. I wasn't a virgin. I hadn't been waiting for Cut, but I had been at the same time.

There were a few boyfriends, but no one serious. They never lasted long and again, never serious. These questions and self-doubts didn't come into play because those guys weren't my forever guy.

Cut was.

Cut could be.

Or, Cut could've been.

And now I was thinking myself into circles.

Actually, I was torturing myself into circles.

I was at work. There was a meeting going on. Dean's voice was droning on, and I was doodling. I could do that. Sometimes it helped me channel so I could focus better, but I had to be honest with myself.

I was hurting, and I wanted Cut. I missed Cut.

I didn't know what I was doing anymore, why I wasn't calling him, texting him. Then I'd have to remind myself and here we were again, once more around the pass about how I couldn't do to him what my mother had done to me. Not the same struggle, but a struggle nonetheless.

I was trying to justify all the reasons why I ran from him.

The reason was real. What I had, no one I loved should go through it with me. Sasha and Melanie were different. They had their own issues, and I was there for them. It was the same with me, but I also pulled back with them. They got it. They under-stood. I had my stuff, and I never wanted to burden anyone else with it, not too much. It's not their problem to deal with. It's mine.

I tried not to watch his away games. I hadn't lasted on that. The puck dropped and I was scrambling to turn my television on.

My chest was burning because they were playing at home tonight, and I was trying to tell myself that I wasn't going. But I was going. I already knew I was going. Why was I trying to lie to myself?

"—what do you think, Cheyenne?"

"Huh?" My pen dropped and I looked up.

Dean, Reba, and Boomer were all waiting for my answer.

I blinked, trying to remember. I had no clue. "What'd you say?"

Dean frowned, his eyebrows pinching together. "You okay?"

Reba grunted. "You get distracted at times, but you've been more the last few weeks."

Reba was our other full-time worker, the one who worked, and went home to actually Netflix and chill. She was built like a trucker (her words) with the curliest hair I'd ever seen on someone before. She had dark auburn hair, and her curls were the type that had curls within the curls themselves. Getting a comb through them with product must be a nightmare for Reba, so she let it flow. She came to work and her hair was bouncing every which way. I loved it. The freer, the better, but today she had it pulled back under a red bandana.

I was missing the usual fray wildness. I connected with it in my core. Her hair was like all the things going on inside my own head.

But Reba handled all of our ordinances. She was the glue in the shelter. Dean and I were almost like decorative props in the building. If we didn't have Reba, there would be no shelter. Sturdy and tough. I loved me some Reba, and if Reba was noticing my distraction and commenting on it, then I had to handle it because it was serious. Reba noticed a lot, but she didn't comment on anything that wasn't worth commenting on. She was a wise soul, and she never wasted her breath on something. It was her golden rule.

Boomer's mouth turned in and his head went down.

Reba didn't notice. "What is going on with you?" Her head twisted sideways, as if a new thought had just come to her. "You seeing someone? This seems like guy distraction."

Guy distraction.

Aptly put.

I opened my mouth, but Boomer lifted his head up and said, "Let's leave her alone. If she wanted us to know, she would've told us." He gave Dean a pointed look. "You sure about switching distributors on some of our foods?"

Dean was still frowning, but turned back to him. "Uh. Yeah. Yes. We need it for the budget, but speaking of our budget, I think we should plan a big charity gala event."

Oh no.

Call it a sixth sense, but I knew exactly where Dean was going with this. He'd been on his own buzzing level since the Mustangs were at Come Our Way.

He cleared his throat, sitting up straighter. "I have a meeting with the Mustangs' PR team tomorrow, and I wanted to clear it with everyone here."

"We already had them here."

Dean glanced to Reba. "I know, and it went amazing. Our social media push brought in a lot of new volunteers and contributions locally, but I'd like to plan a big, big event—"

"No."

All heads swung my way.

I never vetoed anything. I might ask not to be around for an event, but I never outright did what I just did.

Boomer's gaze was speculative, so was Reba's. Dean's was just big and bulging. He hissed, "Let me finish before you just say no—"

"No." I stood, gathering all my papers.

"Cheyenne." Dean stood with me.

I saw the determination on his face. His jaw was set.

He wanted a big to-do. He wanted to invite all the hoity-toity rich, and nope. Not going to happen. Because he wouldn't stop there. He'd ask the players, obviously, but he'd ask the players' friends and families. That meant Cut. That meant Chad. That meant others, like Cut's relatives, because he had a supportive family. They would fly in for that, but there would still be others.

Deek was here.

Natalie was here.

They were all here.

The entire group had been here for a full year and the only reason I knew was because of Hunter. No one reached out so I knew their priorities. So far, their world had not crossed mine. I did not want that to happen and Dean's ambition was putting us on a collision course. So, I was going to do what I needed to do. I was going to stop it.

I pushed my chair back, gave Dean a firm look, and stood my ground. "I said no. You have to have a unanimous vote for any big event, so it's not going to happen."

"But—"

I left. I didn't care.

And fuck it. I was going to go to the hockey game.

I could only say no to so much today.

22

CHEYENNE

Otis, Maisie, and JJ were all giving me looks.

It was understandable. The Mustangs were on an away phase, but there'd been a few home games sprinkled in and I'd not been here for any of them. So they were giving me the looks.

I could feel them. I didn't even need to see them, but I felt singed from them.

My normal seat. My normal seat companions. Our normal section.

Everything was normal. Except me.

The season seat group knew something was *up*.

The team came out on the ice, and it felt right again. Just right. All right.

He didn't look up here, not once. And he skated wonderfully, but he had been all season so far. He had more of an edge, like right now as he was skating up with Hendrix and Franklin. Hendrix was in the middle, skating forward. The defensive line was on them, reaching in, trying to dislodge the puck or make them trip up.

Hendrix shot to Franklin.

Franklin danced between two linemen, hitting the puck forward with his skate, his stick lifting up and over their heads. The puck went past, right to Cut, and he skated around the last defensive end. The goalie was there, he was expecting it. Cut read him, and shot the puck back to Hendrix.

Everyone had forgotten Hendrix was there.

Hendrix reached forward and shot it up and inside.

Everyone was on their feet. Screaming. Shouting. Clapping.

Adrenaline was high, but adrenaline was always high for the games, win or lose. It was part of it.

All the guys circled around Hendrix, patting his helmet and shoulders. Cut swept in, and Hendrix wrapped his arms around Cut. The entire arena was wailing, hitting the ice barriers. Rags were being circled in the air, and it was overwhelming, but I was good. I was right with them. The stimulus was a lot, but I was on my meds and I had now added a full hour of hard cardio to my regimen in the mornings. It was the best way to keep my head as clear as could be, and I was so glad.

My chest was full.

I could do it this way.

Be here. Watch as a fan. Support. Enjoy. But only from a distance. I had to do the distance thing.

I made a point of going to the bathroom when the first period ended, and when they were heading off the ice. I made a point of heading to the concessions when they came back and stayed away until they began playing. It was a repeat for the end of the second period and the beginning of the third.

They'd lost one of their away games, and in the beginning of the third period, the opposing team tied up the score. Everyone was on edge. They needed a win, especially a home win.

There was another line change.

Cut went off.

The teams were trading the puck back and forth. No one was moving it forward or backward. It was an even exchange. No.

There was a break, the opposing team. No, no, no. Then, Dorchak came out of nowhere. He was one of the rookies this season. He swung in, dislodging their breakaway. The puck was back in Mustang territory. They kicked it back. The goalie had it.

Line change.

It was supposed to be the third line, but Cut dropped in. He skated across the ice. The goalie shot the puck to him.

Franklin and Hendrix were with him.

There was only two minutes left.

They could do a couple more line changes, but the way Cut was moving, they were staying in. I felt it, and he was pushing forward at a fast pace. Two guys moved forward, meeting him. They swung their sticks in front of him.

He moved the puck around, keeping control.

Past the one player, around the second. He veered between them.

Another was coming at him, coming hard, and Cut hit the puck sideways, almost dropping backwards to miss the hit. The player kept going, clotheslining into one of his other teammates.

The crowd was back on their feet.

Cut skated in a tight circle, grabbing the puck back up and he reached far. The goalie went with him.

Cut tapped the puck the other way, and he moved his foot forward, his stick tapping the puck in between his feet. It sailed just under the goalie's leg.

GOAL!

The sirens lit up, and everyone was screaming.

That'd been the theme for this game.

They had a minute and thirty-two to hold them.

Cut and his line stayed.

A minute and twenty-five.

The other team made a push, slapping the puck back and forth. Franklin moved in, but he was too late. The puck was pushed forward. He was going in hard, but then Cut was there and he was intersecting him. Thank goodness. If he had hit him illegally, he would've gone to the box, and it would've been a power play for the other team. They could've scored, probably would've, and it'd be overtime.

One of the other players swung in, words were being shared.

Franklin surged forward, but Cut was holding him back. He was reaching for the guy, trying to get free.

Cut held him back until he turned himself, but he just moved the other player away. Two more players moved in, helping to separate a potential fight. Hendrix was pulling Franklin away, but both were watching, making sure to cover Cut's back if they were needed.

A ref blew the whistle and I could've sagged from the tension.

They started playing, but the Mustangs held them off. They won two to one.

I was so exhilarated from the win, from the tension that I forgot my early pee break.

When I looked down, Cut was still on the ice, but now he was staring right at me.

Maisie clamped onto my arm. "You're going to The Way Station with us."

It was after the team filed away, and after the crowd was starting to dispense. I'd been frozen in place seeing him seeing me, because every fiber in my being wanted to go to him.

He reached inside of me, grabbed everything inside of me, and he was pulling me to him. That's how it felt. Even the fucking air had been surging me toward him, and I'd been sweating trying to hold back, trying to remember what I was doing again?

What *was* I doing?

Confusing, right? This was what it was like in my head sometimes. Or most times. Or—I was on a runaway train once more.

No tracks. No engine conductor. Just me. The train and I were free falling all over the place.

Then Maisie reached for me, and I was pulled out of my mind. Thank God.

Her face was set. Otis was right behind her. JJ dropped down the aisle, so she was standing behind Otis. All three were determined.

I sighed. "I can't drink, but I'll come."

Otis harrumphed a nod. "Good. I'll drink for the both of us."

Maisie's smile turned sweet, and she linked her elbows with mine. Bumping next to me, she whispered, "He really will. We took a cab here."

When we got there, I made sure to ask if we could sit in a back booth. None of my companions knew about my struggles, so I wanted to contain it the best I could. When we were led to a back booth, I made sure to sit on the edge and with my back to the wall. This way, I could decipher what noise was coming from where, and it wouldn't give me a migraine later on.

And Otis hadn't been joking. He ordered two beers for himself.

I ordered a water.

JJ ordered a mojito.

Maisie ordered a Long Island Iced Tea.

Once the waitress left, all three turned to me.

"Now." Maisie put her palms on the table, her shoulders forward and her head lowered a little. She was taking on a whole earnest tone, but it was gentle. "Sweetie."

Oh, ho! We were going with the 'sweetie' talk. I was done for. I might as well roll over and bare my belly. I'd overheard Maisie use this voice at other times and start her talks with her kids over the phone when she wanted something. They always gave in, no matter how long they protested.

From the knowing looks on the faces of both Otis and JJ, they'd all talked about this.

"You're the spokesperson?" I asked her.

That didn't faze her. "Cheyenne, sweetheart. I know sometimes you think we don't notice things about you, but we do. We've been seat companions for a long time—"

"A long time." Otis's head bobbed up and down.

"—and we care about you—"

JJ interrupted, "Cut the shit. Did you sleep with Cut Ryder?"

And apparently Maisie was taking too long for JJ.

"Sweetie. Cheyenne, dear."

Why was I even fighting this?

I told them. I didn't tell them everything, but they got the first night, my roll and run tactic, and the whole Not-Brother situation. I'd been vague about everything else.

Otis was squinting at me, he was two beers in by now, and had two more coming. "So, you ended things?"

Yeah. I hadn't told them the reason. I was going with the whole brother aspect being the issue.

I nodded. "Yeah."

Maisie stared at me.

JJ was frowning at me.

Maisie's the one who burst out, "That's total and complete bullshit! Who does your Nut-Brother think he is? He can't demand shit. If he were my son, I'd have a good talk with him. I'd sit him down and educate him on how we're lucky to have anyone considered family in our lives. Anyone. And you. Oh, my poor dear. I had no idea about your mother."

I blinked at her a few times. Shit. I'd forgotten that I went that deep with my family tree.

Also, no way in hell was I correcting her 'nut-brother.' I loved it. I was going to share with everyone.

I reached for my water. My throat was parched. "I mean, it all worked out okay."

"No, it did *not*."

That was JJ, and she slammed her fist on the table. The force had her drink sloshing over the rim, as well as Maisie's, who picked up her drink. If I were foretelling the future, I'd guess Otis and Maisie would be making some happy love tonight, either that or the snoring would wake the neighbors. Either way, fun.

"I had no idea. None."

I was waiting, but that was it. JJ stopped talking, her head tilted down.

Maisie was watching her, too, grabbing her straw and taking a long drag from her drink.

Otis was staring hard at me. "You know what you should do? You should write a letter to your brother, tell him how he's got no right to make an issue. And it's Cut Ryder! Cut The Reaper Ryder. He is a Mustang personification." He sat back, crossing his arms over his chest, and he was shaking his head.

I had a feeling Otis was just settling in.

"I just love the guy. He rose up out of nowhere. No one was watching for him, and bam, he's on the new start-up team, and bam, he's damn near doing figure eights like an ice skater. He's just a joy to watch, a total joy. Yeah." He burped. The waitress dropped off two more beers, and he reached for one, but settled back again. "A total joy. I'd love to shake his hand one day. But you know what I'd tell him? I'd tell him he shouldn't let you get away. You, my dear, are a one in a million. One in a million, and so's my daughter." He remembered Maisie was sitting next to him. "Both of our daughters. Rosie and Callie are one in a million, too. Maybe we could set them up with Cut Ryder?"

Maisie patted his arm. "Callie's engaged, honey."

"That's right. I don't like that guy."

"That's why we don't bring our kids with us to the games. You start speaking truthfully. It never ends well."

The two were having their own conversation.

Otis grinned at her, the lines around his mouth soft and his eyes a little glazed. "I do, don't I?"

"You do. That's why I love you. One of the many."

He leaned closer to his wife and whispered loudly, "You're one in a million, too, sweetie."

She patted his arm again, beaming back. "I know. You are, too."

He burped again. "I am, aren't I?" He finished his beer in one gulp. Putting it back on the table, he blinked a few times. "I gotta piss. Excuse me, ladies."

Maisie giggled, her face almost beet red from the drinks by now. She slid out and gave her husband a pat on the ass as he bypassed her. He threw her a grin backwards, his hand grazing against hers as he went. They shared another look before Maisie sighed and slid back in the booth. "I'm so lucky that I got to marry that man."

JJ and I shared a look.

It was sweet, but I knew that wasn't something I would ever have.

JJ's look was a little wry as she picked up her second mojito. "That's not for me. I had a husband. It didn't work out. I love my corporate world, thank you very much."

"And you do that. You do what makes you happy."

As if they were one person, both looked at me.

Maisie's the one who spoke. "Cheyenne, sweetie. Does Cut make you happy?"

My tongue was heavy.

My stomach was all twisting on the insides.

I had made my decision. Sitting here with them, seeing the love between Maisie and Otis, seeing that JJ was happy being single—I wanted to do what would make me happy, but they didn't know. They couldn't understand. Sometimes staying away was simply for them, not yourself.

But it was too hard to explain that, especially in a bar when JJ and Maisie were both two drinks in.

I just grinned, reaching for my water. "Yes, he does."

Maisie's eyes got big. "Then go and be with him. Text him. Right now."

I felt JJ shifting. And I reached down, grabbing my phone just as she was going for it.

It came alive in that instant.

Cut calling.

I swore, at the same time JJ shouted, "The universe just spoke!" She snatched the phone from me, hitting accept, and had the phone to her ear in a split second. "Hi! This is Cheyenne's friend." Annnnd she was off and babbling to him. "We sit with her at every game, and we're at The Way Station right now. Come and get your girl. Right now." Then she hung up and put my phone in her pocket. "Sorry, dear, but I can read you better than you think. I know it's an invasion of privacy, but I care about you. We've been watching hockey games with you for a long time, and you tried to feed us both some bullshit. The guy called you at the perfect time. If you believe in the Almighty, maybe believe there was a reason for that timing. I'll give you your phone back when he shows up. Can't have you calling him to back out or have you running away again now, can we?"

Otis chose that moment to come back. He stood at the end of the table, a rosy glow on his cheeks, and he held his hands up. "What'd I miss?"

23

CUT

We were asked to do random 'pop ins' at The Way Station throughout the season. Management had a deal worked out. We got free catering at events. In exchange, we showed up at the bar every now and then. Never long, but enough to be seen. Enough to have our pictures taken.

Because of that rumor, it was always the place for the hockey fans to go after the home games. And because of that, I was surprised Cheyenne would be here, but I donned a baseball cap and headed inside. After the game we had, I knew there was no hope of getting in there (even through the back) and not get recognized so I wasn't surprised when the first guy did a double-take after I stepped through the door.

"Whaaaat is happening? That's Cut Ryder!"

He came forward, shook my hand, asked for a selfie.

He was the first in line.

Five minutes in, and there was a good enough crowd that the night manager came to my side. "Cut." He shook my hand and leaned in. "We didn't know you'd be coming tonight, or we could've been more on top of that."

I said, leaning close, "I got a friend here. I'm trying to find her."

He nodded, clapping my back. "Can we help?"

I gave him the description of Cheyenne, and who her seat-mates were, or what I remembered about how they looked, and he headed off. "We'll find her. We'll get it set up. You want to stay a bit or head out?"

I had no intention of leaving without Cheyenne, but I also had no faith in her either. "Can stay a bit. Maybe in the back?"

"We'll get it taken care of. Just wait. I'll put you upstairs? You want to be seen or total privacy?"

"Privacy would be nice."

"Got it." He gave me a nod and a thumbs-up. "Be right back. You keep doing your thing."

I signed napkins, a few arms, a forehead, a couple hats. Some shirts. A woman wanted me to sign her bra strap. It was a few minutes later when the manager reappeared and tapped my back. He motioned for me to follow him, and we headed through the bar, around to the stairs and up. It was roped off, with a bouncer standing by the side. He was talking to a few women, but gave me a nod as we went past.

Once upstairs, I saw we were totally alone.

"Here you go." He held his hand out toward one of the back booths. The upstairs was sort of a loft with some tables set near the railing. There was a line of booths behind them, and another row of booths behind those. He indicated the second row. "I'll send Dee to take care of you guys."

He headed back down, and I went to the second row.

She was sitting in the farthest corner booth, also the biggest, and I had to smile for a second.

Cheyenne looked up at me. "What?"

I shook my head, sliding in to sit across from her. The table was big enough that I almost could've laid out on it. "We could pull another table over to add to this one. Would that make you feel more comfortable?"

Her eyes latched onto mine, staring, and then her mouth twerked. "I just wanted privacy."

I nodded, glancing around. We could hear the sounds below, but they were muted from how far back we were. "This is definitely that."

We heard footsteps, and Dee came over. Two napkins were placed in front of us, and she put waters on both. Giving us a professional smile, she never reacted at the space between Cheyenne and myself. "Can I start you off with appetizers?"

I knew Dee. She'd worked at The Way Station for a long time. She was a worker at Bresko's as well, and she knew I was an investor there.

"Hey, Dee."

"Heya, Cut. Good game tonight. I caught it on the TV." But Dee knew if I was sticking around, I didn't want to chit-chat with her. She turned back to Cheyenne right away. "How about you, sweetie? I talked to your server downstairs. She said it was mostly water for you. Want anything else? Coffee? Or—"

"Coffee. I'll do coffee." Cheyenne gave me a little look.

Her meds. She wasn't drinking because she was on them.

"I'll just do water. Maybe some lettuce wraps?"

She nodded. "I can do that, but Oscar was mentioning you might want a board he can put together. Healthy snacks for the athletes when they come in."

"How about both?"

"Will do." She knocked on the booth. "Give me a holler if you need anything else?"

Once she was gone, I focused back on Cheyenne.

She was looking at me, but looking around at the same time, and she had her hands in her lap. Outward appearance, she seemed fine. Inward feeling, she was skittish as hell. Or that's what I was getting from her.

"You glad you came to the game tonight?"

Her eyes danced back to mine. She swallowed, reaching for her water. Her hand shook a tiny bit. "Yeah, I'm always glad to be at the games."

This sucked.

All of it.

I was remembering the first time I saw her. Damn. I had wanted her so bad. I still felt that way, but she was the scared one.

She admitted, "I couldn't stay away."

That felt good, though I knew it was more about hockey. Not about me.

But I was going to pretend it was about me.

"You played really well tonight."

I nodded. "Hockey's been my outlet in life. No matter what's going on off the ice, that's where I'm in control. Some guys, if they've got shit going down in their personal lives, they get distracted. Head's not in the game. Not me. It's like the ice is the only place that makes sense to me." I gave her a rueful grin. "But I pushed a little too hard. Got too aggressive, I guess. Coach called me in, asked what the fuck was going on with me."

"Really?"

"Yeah." It hadn't felt good going through that talk. "I gotta scale shit back a bit."

She nodded again, and we stared at each other.

I wanted to touch her. I wanted to hold her. Hell. I really wanted to pull her on my lap and have her grind on me. But I did none of that, forcing myself to sit here and stare back at her like we were just friends.

Fuck that. I was jumping back in. "Chad's fucking your friend again."

Her hand jerked in reaction, shaking her water a little. "What?"

I grinned. "Or he did that night. And the nights I've been home, he hasn't. He and I got into it before my Seattle game."

"You did?"

I was trying to read her, but I couldn't. I had no clue what she thought about that.

I said, "Called me out, that I was avoiding him."

"Were you?"

I shrugged. "Kinda, but not at the same time. He was gone when I went home, and then I was traveling with the team. I was going to call him from my hotel in Seattle, have it out, but now he's blocked me."

Her eyes got so big. "What?"

I laughed. "Chad's been my boy for a long time. Don't worry about it. We'll get through it."

Her head bent again, and she started running her thumb up and down her glass. She was doing it, not knowing she was doing it, and I was having a hard time not picturing that was my dick.

Christ. I shifted in my seat, knowing I was already hard.

"Did you mean it?"

She looked back up, and I winced, seeing some sadness in those eyes.

I said softly, "That first night at your place when you told me that you used to love me. Did you actually mean it?"

Her lips parted.

I knew I was still in the learning stages of getting to know this girl, but I felt like I already did. I felt it deep in my core. It was the weirdest sensation.

She sighed, her hand falling from her drink. "I thought I did. I mean, yes. I wasn't... Back then, I had an altered state of mind. I formed a coping mechanism. It sounds weird, but it's like my brain couldn't handle everything coming at me, so I was thinking things that weren't true to help me get through it."

"But that night when we went to my place? That first night. You felt it then, too?"

She swallowed, her lips flattening for a second. "I... The idea of you became my foundation. You were my goal, but it was a lofty and far-off goal and I never thought it'd happen. I mean, I didn't know that at the time. I didn't know that until the next morning when I ran. It just got too real, too fast and I freaked out."

"But I know now. You told me and I'm still here. I still—fuck! I've never had to ask a girl to let me in. Like ever." Which was sad, in a way. "I don't know how to handle this. I called you tonight because you were up there, and I couldn't not call. I tried. I feel like giving your friend a trip to Tahiti."

And yeah, even saying that to her was a humbling moment here.

I didn't even know what else to say. I was here. I wanted her, but what can you say when they've already said no? You keep pushing it and you're the asshole.

"So, you and Chad are fighting?"

"Yeah, but it's not about you."

She bit down on her lip. "It feels like it is."

I shook my head, reaching for my water. "It's not. I've let things go for too long, and I think you were just the catalyst. There's some things he needs to stop doing. He knows it. We'll be fine." I already told her, but she looked worried. "Really. He and I haven't *fought* fought in a long time. This was due." And that made me wonder, "I know Natalie moved here a couple years back. Chad mentioned that Deek moved here, too. A year ago? You ever see him?"

Her shoulders seemed to shrink in size right before me.

She shook her head. "I—no. Hunter and I email, but that's it."

"That's it? Fuck. Hunter's what? He's in high school by now."

"He's a junior." Her grin was proud, but also sad. "He's playing hockey. You're his idol."

"I'm his what? Chad never said a word."

She looked away.

I leaned forward. "Hey."

She turned back.

I sighed. How could someone look so fierce, so proud, so stubborn, and so sad at the same time? How could someone reach inside you and yank out all these emotions that you didn't know existed? She did that, and this wasn't going away.

I said instead, pushing all that shit to the side, "I didn't know what was going on in high school. You said your mom was a junkie?"

We heard footsteps, and we looked.

Dee was bringing the appetizers over. "Here you guys go." She glanced at the drinks. "You need anything else?"

I was making an executive decision. Reaching inside my wallet, I handed over my card. "Can you just ring us up?"

"Oh." She took the card. Her gaze was more assessing now. She was taking in how stiff Cheyenne's shoulders were, and I didn't want to think what she saw when she took me in. "Maybe some to-go boxes?"

"That'd be great. Thank you."

She nodded, another pat on the booth, but this time it was softer.

As soon as she was out of earshot, I said, "I want to see you. I'm sorry. I know you've ran from me twice now, but—" I groaned. "You don't get to make the decision for me. I get to make that decision. You can't push people away for the rest of your life."

Cheyenne wasn't looking at me.

"Cheyenne. Please."

"This is so hard."

Agreed. "Let me give you a ride home. Can we talk while I give you a ride home?" A different thought came to mind. "How are you handling being here? And the games? Is it too much for you?"

She looked up, the bags under her eyes more pronounced, but she shook her head. "I'm good. Or, I'm as good as I normally am. You, you bring more stress, and that wears on me. It's like I have walls set up from the meds, and you break them back down.

But now I'm doing extra cardio in the morning. It all helps. I'll do meditation tonight, too."

Meditation. Meds. Cardio. She couldn't drink. Her life was close to mine.

"I've never tried meditation before."

She grinned, a slight one, but it was there. "It really helps."

Dee was coming back with a box and the bill. She handed both to me. "Thank you both." She paused on me. "Do you...?"

I shook my head. "I got my truck here." I signed the bill and handed it back, but my gaze was on Cheyenne. "I'm hoping to give this one a ride home?"

Cheyenne sighed, closing her eyes a beat. When she opened them, there was a new light there. She nodded, though it was tentative at first. "A ride would be nice."

A ride. We'd still never had that first date, so I'd start there.

24

CHEYENNE

We left down the stairs.

Cut walked half in front of me, with an arm behind me, resting on the small of my back. Little touches like that, and I was dissolving into a puddle. I wasn't paying attention to everyone paying attention to us, and it was him. It wasn't the meds. It wasn't my condition. It was just, straight up, him.

We stepped outside.

I glanced back, but I hadn't been able to see Otis, Maisie, or JJ. They practically pushed me out of the booth when the staff first came over, and I knew they'd expect a full report at the next home game. But now we were walking down the sidewalk, and Cut kept glancing over at me, a teasing little grin on his face.

He focused me.

I realized it now.

Or, he focused me tonight.

I wasn't going to question it. It was nice. A small reprieve, and tonight, a small voice was whispering in my head. Tonight. Enjoy tonight. Tomorrow I would be responsible. Tomorrow I would wake myself up from this dream, pull away all over again. Tomorrow.

That meant we had tonight.

And unable to help myself, feeling a pull on my hand, I reached out for his and he clasped mine tight. We got to his truck, and this was nice, too.

We were halfway to my apartment when his phone started ringing. He had it connected to his truck and we both saw on the radio's screen, *Chad calling*. A small frown, but Cut reached over and disconnected the call. Guess he'd been unblocked. He hit another button, and I saw that he was sending him a message instead.

Then, ten seconds later, my phone started ringing.

Melanie calling.

He saw my screen. "She was with Cassie tonight."

I sighed, knowing this wasn't a coincidence, and I hit the answer button. Loud music blared first, but I still asked, "What's up?"

"We have a problem." Melanie was tense, but calm.

Dread lined my spine. That was not good, so not good.

I tightened my hold on the phone. "What's going on?"

"We're at Bresko's. Cassie invited us out, said she knew some people who'd be here. I called Sash, not knowing who the 'some people' were. She's here and she's going nuts on your Not-Brother."

At hearing her, because her voice traveled, "What do you mean, she's going nuts?"

Cut hit his turn signal and veered to the left. We hit a light, but it was green at that second and he whipped us around in a U-turn.

"I mean, she's upset. We came here, saw Not-Brother grinding on a girl, and Sash went over and started pinching him."

"Pinching him?" Had I heard that right?

"Yeah. Legit pinching. Took him by the ears, and he crumbled like a twelve-year-old. Fell down. Then she started pinching his other ear. The chick he was with took off. Sash is in rare form tonight."

Oh, boy. I knew what that meant.

I shared a look with Cut. His whole face was rigid, but his shoulders were shaking. The guy was trying not to laugh. I said into the phone, "We're on our way. Be there in twenty minutes."

"Who is we?"

"Cut and me."

She was quiet. As I knew she would be.

"You're with Cut?" Her tone was somber.

I sighed. "Yeah."

"Babe."

She knew my decision. So did Sasha. They didn't agree with it, but I shared with both of them the day I left his house for a second time. And now, here I was, going back on that very decision.

"Okay. We're here. Cassie is dying. She thinks this is the funniest thing she's ever seen."

And speaking of, Melanie had been quiet lately about her and the PT lady. "Mel."

"Yeah?"

"We need to have a chit chat."

She sighed now. "I know. I was just thinking the same thing. But hurry up, because I gotta go and shit as soon as you're here."

And we were back to the normal Melanie.

Just needed to hear that one word.

She added, "Like right fucking now, babe."

There it was.

"We're on our way."

As soon as I hung up, Cut said, "I need to tell you something."

My stomach took a nosedive. "What?"

"I'm an investor at Bresko's."

I frowned. "What do you mean?"

"I mean, I knew the owner a while back. He asked for an investment, and I gave him money."

"That place must rake in ..."

Cut grinned. "It does well, yeah."

Holy. Crap.

He was a local god, a national hockey celebrity, and now he was saying he was an investor at Bresko's? Why in the hell was he interested in me?

"What other investments do you have?"

"A few others."

"Like?"

He glanced at me from the corner of his eyes. "Like, is this a problem for you?"

You know, at this point it was like fuck it. I'd run from him. I already told him most of my bad secrets. He saw a freak-out, and I tried to end it a second time. I didn't have anything to lose here by being honest.

"You just keep getting bigger and bigger to me."

"What?"

I was back there, with my mom, leaving food outside her bedroom door hoping she'd eat. "I was homeless, and I didn't really know it."

"Wait. Back up. What are we talking about?"

Riding in a car at night was soothing to me. The lines became a constant blur. The feel of the vehicle moving under you. And the best feeling was when you felt safe.

I felt safe with him.

I couldn't remember ever feeling safe with anyone.

But in here, with Cut driving, it felt soothing, and then to find out about his investments? Maybe a normal woman would be thinking she had won the jackpot, but that wasn't me. People always left, investments or no investments. Pain sliced through me at the stark differences between us.

"I was homeless, Cut."

"Yeah. You said that before."

"You don't get it." And he never would, but he was lucky in that regard. "When you're homeless, there's a desperation you feel. And if you get so used to it, you become a different animal entirely. You've never felt that in your life. The older I get, the further I get from that girl, the more I realize how different we are. You're already a celebrity and now Bresko's? And you don't want to tell me about the rest. We're just so different."

"Why's that bad?"

"It's not. I think a younger me would've been even more insecure because how could I matter to you? What do I have that I could give you? But now, I'm just having a moment. I've come so far from that girl, but I'm still struggling. That's what this stuff does to you. You struggle no matter what. Every day. Every minute. You are fighting your own mind. And people don't get it, people don't want to get it."

"I do. I mean, I want to get it."

I looked him over, watching the lights and shadows dance over his face. I felt that safe feeling again, but there was a lull around him. He did that. He lulled the edges that used to pull at me, distract me, ingrain inside of me until I couldn't focus on anything.

"But you never will, and I think that's what the luckiest thing is for someone like you. You won't get it."

I'd gone back and forth so much, but right here, right now, I was coming to a decision. It made my heart pound. It made my chest tighten. It stretched every nerve ending in my body, and I couldn't believe I was going to make it, but I was.

I was going to try with him.

If I didn't, I felt like I was back on those streets. I felt open to the elements. I'd always be fighting, feeling the desperate edge because I couldn't go back to where I was when my mom died. I couldn't, but he soothed the outside around me. He helped me

focus. It was like he was a home for me, opening a door and beck-
oning me to come inside.

If he pushed me out, then I'd have to deal.

I closed my eyes. I really enjoyed this feeling.

It was warming to someone who'd only ever been cold.

I hadn't known anything other than the cold until the first
time he touched me.

25

CUT

Since the first event, I'd gotten so many different looks from Cheyenne. Perplexion. Vulnerability. Hilarity. Sexiness. Freeing. But this one was different again. She felt serene, almost peaceful. I'd never seen her like this, and I wanted to help in any way I could.

I had to help, it was just what I was going to be feeling with her.

I was not that guy. Never had been. I let Chad use me, but that's because I loved him. He was my brother, but even Chad never brought this reaction out of me. My family, my own brothers, none of them. It was different with Cheyenne. It was all different, and I was starting to realize that I wasn't just seeing her in a different light, I was starting to see everything in a different light. Not better. Not worse. Just different. There was more texture, more colors, more depth.

Also, I needed to be real with myself. This was rocking me to my core a bit.

"Oh, wow."

Cheyenne sat up, seeing how far the line to get into Bresko's was. It extended at least a full mile, if not more.

I drove past. The line was in a third lane that we got special approval to get put out here.

I said, "I was in on some of the planning." I gestured around us because Bresko's was in the middle of nowhere for a reason. "We own all of this land. Did this on purpose because we knew the parking lot wait would be a lot."

"Why do that, though? So people have to wait in their vehicles."

"Makes it more exclusive. That was the thinking behind it. Also, if you're driving to the club with friends, there's the idea that you're already having a pre-game in your vehicle before you even get to the club. We wanted to build on that."

She was listening, her eyes thoughtful. "It's just different. People can't come off the streets or hop out of a cab to enjoy what this place offers."

"Exactly. If they're coming to Beksso's, they're committed for a full night, or they've got some serious cash, or they're determined enough to get inside. There's also some serious poker games in the basement going on. Those last till the mornings, usually. And there's some VIP rooms that are always booked. They're full every night."

"For celebrities like you?"

My mouth twitched at that. I knew I was a celebrity, but I never felt like one. "You'd be surprised how many celebrities have a house in the area."

We were coming to the turn off and I hit the signal, but eased to a stop. One of the parking attendants approached the vehicle.

"Mr. Ryder. I didn't know that was you."

"Hey, George. How's the night so far?"

"It's good. It's good, sir." He lifted his radio. "I'll call you up."

"Sounds good. Thanks, man."

"Of course, sir." The attendant moved his head to see Cheyenne. "Miss."

I raised the window again, and Cheyenne laughed. "Miss. I thought I was going to be a 'ma'am'."

We eased forward. We still had two lanes to head up, but one lane was taken up by those waiting in line to get inside. We had it looped so two lanes went up, around, and we had two lanes heading out. The two ways never crossed over each other. When people left Bresko's, they headed to the east. People had to come from the west to get into Bresko's. It helped cut down on the traffic and smoothed out the overall experience.

George called ahead for us, so when I pulled up, we wouldn't have to go through another attendant. (Which was the situation for everyone as there were three main checkpoints along the way.) We'd get clocked, then waved through, and there'd be a slot right at the door ready for us.

"Is that usual for an investor to know a worker's name?"

I shook my head, going into the first roundabout. "No, but the owners give a fuck about who works for them. They wanted loyal workers, so they treat them right, and the hope is that the workers will be loyal back. It was a mission I liked and why I bought in. George has been with Bresko's since the beginning."

I felt her gaze on me the rest of the way, and then wheeled into the slot that was left open for us.

"Mr. Ryder."

I nodded to Juan this time and started around the truck. Henry and Penny were on the sidewalk as Cheyenne was getting out. Henry at the door, and Penny waiting with a drink in hand already. I didn't greet them by name, but they knew I knew them, and each gave me a smile and nod.

Cheyenne bypassed the drink but gave both a smile.

"She's a water girl."

Penny's eyes lit up in understanding. As we headed inside, I knew she'd be radioing ahead. Cheyenne would have a water at her disposal the rest of the evening, whether she knew it or not.

Cary met us inside. I took Cheyenne's hand, but glanced back to read how she was handling the inside.

Her eyes were squinty, but she was looking around for her friends.

Her hand seemed good, strong. Her head was up and steady, too.

Maybe it helped that she'd been here before. I didn't know for sure, but she seemed good.

I was suddenly grateful that the owners purposefully kept the inside of Bresko's dark and low on stimulus. They didn't want customers to get overwhelmed when coming in, but instead feel more like they were being eased into paradise. The interior opened to a small front room. A bar was set up. Clean and simple lines. Only two staff stood inside. Cary glanced at Cheyenne, but stepped back as I walked toward her. She fell in step with me as we walked through a back hallway. "Mr. Miller is in your usual box. He had some guests join him. Are you here because of the situation?"

I nodded. "The new guests are her friends. One of them called."

Cary glanced to Cheyenne, but swung back to me. "Do you want any extra assistance?"

She was asking if I wanted her there, or security, or anything really. I was always low-key the few times I came here, so I appreciated her asking. I liked to slip in unnoticed and quietly. "We'll be fine." I indicated to Cheyenne again. "This is a close friend."

Cheyenne frowned, but didn't say anything.

Cary nodded immediately. She knew what I was saying. The only other 'friend' I had was Chad. If the other players came, they came in on their own celebrity. Chad was given special treatment because of me. Cheyenne would now receive special treatment as well.

"I'll leave you two here then."

Cary gave us both a smile and a wave as she headed down a

hallway toward her office. Her hand was already up in her ear, and she was sending the notice about Cheyenne to the rest of the staff.

Since we were alone, I pulled Cheyenne to the side and squeezed her hand. "You doing okay?"

A look of wonder was on her face as she looked up at me. Her eyes were a little dilated. "It's never been like this for me."

"Like what?"

She went back to looking around, though everything in the hallway was dark except a trail of lights on the floor by the walls. It was similar to a movie theater feel.

"I've gone to Bresko's before, but there's always this grating feeling. It's in the background, and if my walls are thin, I can't stay long. Or I needed something to dull the edges, but tonight it's different. It's all different. I actually feel like I might enjoy being here tonight rather than just getting through it, you know?"

I winced on the inside. I didn't, but I was glad I was the reason for it.

I was starting to think that I'd never understand what she goes through.

A whole surge of needing to protect her, care for her, swelled up in me. I cupped the side of her face, tilting her up to look at me. "What can I do to help you?"

Her hand went to my chest and pressed there. "You already are. You're being you."

I had no idea what that meant, but I'd go with it. I gave her a small smile, my thumb running by her mouth. "I'd like to take you home after this."

Her eyes caught and held mine.

We'd go in there. Her friends were in there. They'd sweep her up. I was realizing that's the inclination you got when you knew Cheyenne, and when you cared for Cheyenne. It was just her, but I wanted this night. With her. There was a feeling in me, like I'd only get tonight, or like this night was different and I needed to take advantage of it as much as possible. Whatever it was, I couldn't let go.

She nodded. "I'd like that, too."

A small bit of tension eased in my chest, so I dropped my hand back to hers, laced our fingers, and headed forward.

26

CHEYENNE

The calmness I felt standing in that hallway with Cut was gone the second we entered his private box.

I heard the yelling, then a wave of everything else hit me. And it hit me hard. The smells of the club rose up swiftly. The techno music, the hard bass, the neon lights flashing flooded me. Sweat. Grime. Beer. Perfume. Cologne. And other smells that I didn't want to identify. It was jarring, and I sucked in my breath, remembering to fortify my walls.

It was a whole imagery-coping mechanism I learned. Sometimes it helped, other times it didn't.

I took a moment, imagining all the music in a bubble, then I moved it aside. I did the same with the smells. After that I could focus a bit better. Sasha's voice carried to me, along with Melanie's and Cassie's. The last two were sitting on one side of the box, giggling and wrapped around each other. I looked around, and Sasha and Chad were on the other side. Sasha was standing, arms crossed, head tilted up and away from Chad.

My Not-Brother was standing in front of her, his arms out and his head down. He was speaking to her.

"Come on, Sasha. Be reasonable."

I sucked my breath in at that one. Not the right words to use with Sasha.

Melanie's head lifted, her laugh fading, but then she saw me, and her smile came back. "Shy!" She was up and heading for me when Sasha heard and turned, too.

I stepped free from Cut, and the three of us merged in the middle. We'd done this so many times. Our arms came up around each other, our foreheads next to each other, and we formed our own huddle.

"Hey." Me.

"Heya." Sasha.

"Holla." Melanie.

And squeeze. We all moved in, closer together. That was just the greeting.

"Sash," from me. "What do you need?"

"You came with Cut?" Her eyes were big, ignoring my question.

Melanie's grin turned secretive. "I already knew."

"And you didn't tell me?"

"You were fighting with Not-Brother. I wasn't going to interrupt that."

"Nice. I could've used the distraction."

I told them what Maisie called Chad.

Melanie's smile was almost off her face. "I want to meet this woman and I want to kiss her feet. Not literally, though. The feet. I'd like to meet her."

I asked Sasha, "Distraction enough?"

She closed her eyes, a soft smile there and she nodded. "Yes. Thank you."

Melanie snorted. "Nut-Brother. That's awesome."

Sasha released us and pressed into her forehead, rubbing her temples. "He makes me so crazy." She dropped her hands, found her place around our shoulders again and said to me, "We're on and off, and I haven't said anything because every time, I swear, every time I promise myself that I won't let him in. And then he calls or texts and he's all nice and charming, and the next hour I'm pretending to do Juna's ankle-slide move on him."

"Didn't need that information."

Sasha ignored Melanie. "And tonight, we came and he was dancing with another girl. That's fine and all, but he was blowing smoke up my ass just last week. Saying that he wanted to be with me, and maybe he was wrong about you, saying maybe he didn't know you after all, and blah, blah, blah. It's been weeks. I don't understand his revelation now."

Melanie grunted. "Dumbass. He just needs to see her and know whatever stories his mom said to him was all bullshit."

I missed Hunter, but there were no hang-ups about any of that stuff for me. "That's all in the past."

"Not for me. Not for Chad. He goes back and forth, remembering what his mom said, and then saying maybe he needs to get to know you. And now this other chick. I can't keep up."

"What happened to the other chick?"

Melanie grunted again, a cocky grin on her face. "She took off. Saw Pinchy Sasha, and her eyes got all panicky. Cassie was just walking inside the VIP area and the girl almost bowled her over."

"Was Cassie okay?"

"Oh yeah. It was a close clash, but nothing happened. I bet you anything that chick is still here, just somewhere else in the club."

Sasha's gaze skimmed over our heads. "I really liked coming here, too. Now that's all ruined. Stupid Not-Brother put a bad taste in my mouth."

Melanie just started laughing. "Nut-Brother."

Sasha rolled her eyes. "Stop."

Melanie met my gaze. We were getting back to normal Sasha, the one who used one-word statements. Chad really had knocked her off balance.

"Fuck." Melanie.

I frowned. "Wait. Didn't you have to go to the bathroom?"

"What?"

Melanie answered me, "I did. Sash calmed down a little, and Cassie was here. You don't mess with PT people. They know things about your body you don't want to know they know, you know?"

"No."

She shrugged. "It's all good. I got my dump done."

Sasha was shaking her head. "Girls."

Right. Another one-word answer.

For a moment, Sasha almost looked like a normal girl, using full sentences and talking about her feelings. She closed her eyes, took a deep breath, and opened them. "Thanks." She looked from Melanie to me.

We got her drift. She was back to being our Sasha.

I nodded.

Melanie nodded.

We were all good to go. The emergency to get here was settled.

One more last group squeeze and release. We dropped our arms and turned, facing Chad who was talking to Cut now. Cassie was still sitting in their booth, a half-smile on her face, looking at us as if we were a new entity to her. Her mouth was parted in that half-smile, too.

Cut first looked at me. "You good?"

I nodded. I was good.

Both Melanie and Sasha took note of that question, sharing a look before glancing to me.

"Sasha, let's talk about this. Please." Chad stepped forward.

Sasha moved back, and her eyes got cold. "No." She inclined her head toward me. "Home?"

I shook my head. "Cut's going to take me. You want a ride from us?"

Cassie had come over to join our group. Melanie shifted, standing closer to her, but they weren't touching. Melanie said, "We got her!" She sidled up, linking her elbows with Sasha and bumping her hip against hers.

Sasha looked like she needed to take the dump now.

Melanie gave Chad a dirty look, but she didn't say anything.

He was taking all of us in, including Cassie who had joined our ranks. With a groan, he raked his hand through his hair, grabbed his drink, and said, "I'm out of here." He jerked his chin up at Cut. "See you at home." He spared us all one last look before he left the box.

Cassie said to Cut, "It's nice seeing you out and about."

He laughed. "Right."

"It's a rest day for you tomorrow, so I'll see you at eleven for a soak."

He dipped his head down again. "Got it."

She raised her eyebrows, but she was grinning as she did it. "Okay, then. Looks like all is well now. Ready, babe?" She reached for Melanie's hand, and all three of them gave a wave before heading out. Melanie and Sasha both stepped close for one more half-hug.

Mel whispered, "Have fun! You look good with him."

Sasha added her one cent, "Happy." Then she narrowed her eyes before stepping back and following the other two.

Cut frowned at me. "I'm now wondering what the emergency was?"

"Sasha would've gone nuclear on him if he hadn't stopped. That's the reason for the call. Mel relaxed because she knew once I walked in here, Sasha would calm down, and she also knew Chad would leave. Which all happened."

Cut winced. "What a great endorsement for Chad."

Yeah...

My chest felt a little heavy now. Some of the background was seeping back in.

"I'm sorry."

He shook his head, his arm coming around me as he pulled me to him. I stepped in, touching his chest, and then his head came down to rest against mine. "Chad's got some good. It's just that some of his bad is showing right now. He's like a brother for a reason. He'll come around."

Maybe. Maybe not.

"I don't care about Nut-Brother. I want you to know that."

"Nut-Broth—you know? I don't want to know." He frowned down at me. "But your dad, and Hunter—"

"I'm not like that. I'm not built that way. What happened was kind of shitty, and I thought it was really cool that Deek took me in when he did. My baggage isn't him, or Natalie, or Chad. I didn't do anything wrong when I was a kid, but they acted like I was going to rob them blind. I came in from the streets and that's how they viewed me. Some people have those thoughts and they can't get rid of them. It's like fostering a teenager, I'm sure. Some are scared to do it, but I had no control over my life at that age. Only one who didn't judge me was Hunter, and that's all I kinda care about. It'd be cool to see Hunter, but we email and I'll see him more once he's older. My baggage is just my head." I tapped my head. "It's in here. This is enough to deal with. Everything else is cosmetic. Surface shit. It doesn't matter."

"Family doesn't matter?"

"They aren't family. Sasha. Melanie. Hunter. They're my family."

His grin turned crooked, and it was adorable on him. "You simplify things."

I shrugged, stepping closer because I couldn't help myself. There was that pull from him again, and I was remembering high school. I was remembering when I first saw him, how I felt it then, too.

"I'm saying this stuff so you don't take any of it on. Whatever's between you and Chad, I don't want you taking on my stuff. I don't harbor any feelings toward Chad. If I did, it'd be on behalf of Sasha. Me and Chad, there isn't a me and Chad thing. I'm okay with it."

"I reserve the right to feel a certain way, just like you said you could feel a certain way on behalf of your girl. It's the same thing for me."

I opened my mouth. I was going to say it wasn't the same thing, but ... it was.

It was because he cared about me, and I was really starting to feel that. He'd said it before, but hearing someone cares about you and actually believing someone cares about you are two different things.

A whole warm feeling was spreading through me. It went to my toes and fingers, and I was starting to tingle. "Okay, but I don't want you to worry about what I'm feeling about him. That make sense?"

He nodded. "It does." And his hands slid down my sides, rounding to my back, and he pulled me flush up against him. "Since we're here and we're alone, wanna stay a bit?"

I'd almost forgotten we were in a nightclub. That said volumes right there.

"Yeah."

He pulled me over and we sat in the back booth. As if they'd been watching, giving us privacy, a staff member came in then to check on us. She brought us waters. As soon as she left, he lifted me up so I was on his lap.

We sat like that, not talking.

There weren't words for how good this felt.

I wasn't just stepping inside from the cold here. I was inside and there was a fire, and I was getting handed hot chocolate with marshmallows. It was that kind of feeling, and sometime later, I relaxed so much against him that he was cradling me in his arms. My back was to his chest. I was watching the play of lights on the ceiling, and my legs had fallen to the side of his.

I felt like I was in a trance, like where you inhale happiness and contentment, and it filled you up from the inside out. I was so calm that I was breathing out peace and tranquility. It was a trip, the whole thing, and I knew then that I was fucked.

I just didn't have it in me to care.

FROM: KOALA BOY
TO: CHEYCHEY
SUBJECT: I BROKE UP WITH MONICA.

FROM: CHEYCHEY
TO: KOALA BOY
SUBJECT: NEED ME TO HURT HER? I KNOW A HERB WHO HAS A VICIOUS DOG.

FROM: KOALA BOY
TO: CHEYCHEY
SUBJECT: YOU'RE JOKING, RIGHT?

FROM: CHEYCHEY
TO: KOALA BOY
SUBJECT: DUDE.

27

CUT

Two days later, I was leaving the locker room when Cassie popped out from the PT room. "Margo wants to see you."

I frowned. Margo was the Mustangs' owner, one of them. She and her husband owned the team together, but Marcus was usually off doing business around the world. Margo stayed put to oversee the team, or just be on hand. She was involved with the program every day, and she never called me to her office.

"You know what about?"

She shook her head, her ponytail swishing from side to side.

I shrugged, taking my bag with me in the opposite direction.

As I passed her, Cassie shifted. Her hand came up to rest against the doorframe and she asked, "Hey, uh…"

I paused.

"Did you have fun the other night? At Bresko's?"

It'd been a game changer for Cheyenne and me. I took her home, and she took my hand, leading me to bed with her. We slept and cuddled, but it felt good to wake up with her next to me. Last night was a repeat. I knew we needed to have a conversation about the change, but it was like she came to a different decision.

She was letting me in. I was somewhat going with the flow, uneasy to upset the balance either way.

"Yeah. You and your girl looked good. You looked happy."

She lifted up her shoulder. "I like her. We're having fun so far."

"Fun is good."

"Um..."

I started to head out, but held back again.

She was biting down on her lip, her head looking down. She shifted forward, her heel lifting behind her, and she moved it back and forth in a distracted way. Then, she stopped and looked back up. "I was wrong about Cheyenne."

"I know."

She grinned. "Mel mentioned something about a group get-together this weekend, Sunday."

"Yeah?"

"Is that something you'd be interested in doing?"

"What? Like you and your girl, me and Cheyenne, and ..."

Cassie opened her mouth, then stopped. "I have no idea."

"Yeah."

She laughed. "How'd it end with those two?"

I didn't have a clue. Chad hadn't texted or called. I'd only been to the house to go in, get something, and I headed back out. "Who the fuck knows with those two."

"Yeah?"

She was fishing, and as long as I'd known Cassie, I didn't know her as a gossiper. That was telling me she was fishing for someone else. Didn't need a hunch to know who it was, and that meant that not only the Not-Brother wasn't sharing, but the Not-Russian must not be sharing either.

And I was starting to think in Cheyenne speak.

"I'm going to head up, find out what the boss wants."

"Okay. Don't forget your ice soak."

"I won't." Fuck, I hated those.

Margo was in her office when I stopped in. Her door was left open, and I could hear her on the phone. I waited outside, hearing, "...I'll run it by him, see if he's willing or not. Okay... Okay. Sounds good. Yes. Talk to you later."

I knocked on the door right as she looked up.

"Cutler." Margo was one of the few who called me by my full name. She was a no-nonsense owner, and I liked that for some reason. "Come in. Can you shut the door behind you?"

I did, moving to take one of the seats across from her. "I don't think you've ever called me up here. What's going on?"

She pointed to the phone. "Got a call earlier today. You know Deek Fausten?"

I frowned. "He used to be my best friend's stepdad. You know him?"

No way in hell was Deek calling about Cheyenne. Or I was hoping not, because if that were the case, if this trail was going to lead to where she'd get fucked over, my relationship with Deek would change from being civil to a whole different level.

She nodded, her eyes narrowing. "Kind of. He's new, and he's working some of our business accounts. He's got some friends in high places, personal friends of mine. That's the only reason any of this is coming from me. We got a request yesterday to do a funding event for that kitchen downtown. Come Our Way. The two connect because I got a call that this Fausten was invited. He reached out to me because of you. Said there might be a conflict of interest." She paused, her head tilting to the side. "You know anything about that?"

That fuck.

And fucking Chad, because I knew where all this was going, and fuck everyone. Except Cheyenne.

She kept on, "—he explained that you would know what he's referring to."

That *fucker*.

"The thing is, is that I'm confused why we're getting a call and why he's not directing his issue straight to Come Our Way. From what I was told, the place is legit. Good staff there. Good morale. They're doing good work, not corrupt or being greedy. Not scraping by, but their hearts are in the right place. Now, as he explained to me, is that his issue isn't with you. He's not saying you can't be there, which also has me scratching my head about why that'd even be an issue in the first place." Her eyebrows were fully pinched together. "You want to explain to me what all this is about here?"

This dick of a father was putting me in a position where I'd have to get on the phone and reach out to him, see what the fuck his problem was.

Fuck. Him.

My jaw was granite, I was sure. My whole body felt like one big rock of cement, but I shook my head, a hard clip to the side. "As far as I know, he's good with Chad, but I can ask him about it."

"That's what this is about? Your best friend?"

"At this point, who knows. I'm as confused as you."

"Conflict of interest indicated he doesn't want someone there. I know Chad frequents the team's social gatherings, but I've never heard of something like this."

"Me either."

It was unprofessional. It was messy, and it put me in a messed-up, awkward position. I was starting to climb on board Cheyenne's whole motto that she didn't care about Deek Fausten.

I admitted, "I always thought he was a decent guy."

"But Chad. He's a bit of a partier, isn't he?"

"That's what he does for a living."

"Yeah?"

I dipped my head up and down. "Clubs hire him, and he shows up with a whole group of beautiful people ready to party."

"That's actually a job?"

I gave her a look. "Come on. You know it is."

She only gave me a little wink. "Maybe. Maybe not, but okay. You can squash whatever's the issue?"

Like fuck I would, but I gave her another nod.

She stood, so did I, and she held out her hand. "You've been playing amazing this season. You usually do, but you're sticking out even more. I know you've got a contract renewal coming up in the next couple years. I'm telling you now that we aren't letting you go anywhere. You got that?"

This was typical business stuff.

She'd say this to smooth over any feelings and as a way to stroke my ego. Some players soaked it up. Not me. My contract would be renewed if I played the same, and if my terms and their terms were all copacetic. I loved this game. I breathed this game, but underneath it all, this game was a business.

I knew that.

I also knew that Deek Fausten coming to a charity event, one that I didn't even know about, and seeing his daughter there wouldn't have anything to do with that contract.

But because I was still feeling it, fuuuuck him.

28

CHEYENNE

Cut was coming over, and I was trying not to freak out about it.

But I was. Because I could. And I was happy, and my mind was racing, my pulse was racing, and my sweat glands were racing. I almost wished I had some wine here, but then the buzzer sounded, and a weird, calming sensation came over me.

Cut was here.

I hit the button, unlocked the door, and I was still standing there when it swung open.

He stood in the doorway, fresh from practice, and he not only had flowers in one hand, but he had dinner in the other hand. He raised up the bags. "Z-man sandwiches."

My mouth was watering. "Yes, please."

He moved in, putting the bags on the table, and I went around, grabbing for the other one. "Did you get—"

"I did."

The seasoned fries were in there.

Wait.

I grabbed him, standing up, and I pressed a kiss to his mouth. "Thank you, and hi, how are you?"

He laughed, but his hand snaked around the back of my head and he held me still. "Wait."

"Hmm?"

He pulled back, still holding me. "Are we to the kissing part yet? I mean, I think we're moving fa—"

"Shut up." I was laughing, but then I pulled him back down.

His mouth fit over mine, and I could've sighed from contentment.

Lust and pleasure, and warmth, and my toes were curling, and I was sagging in his arms. Or I felt like sagging, because my knees were getting weak and that's such a cliché response, but it was true. Heart palpitations. Well, I already had my heart racing from before, but it was more now. It was for a whole different reason, and I couldn't remember why I tried walking away from him...

Except I could, and a voice started to whisper in my head—I hushed her. She needed to shut up.

Then Cut's mouth was opening over mine, his tongue moving inside, and all thoughts were silenced.

This was like the first night.

He was claiming me.

I could taste him, and I wanted him to taste me, and then I was climbing up his body. His hands went around my ass, he was palming me, and he lifted his head. "Are you—"

"Yes." No more talking.

I squeezed my legs, starting to move against him, and he cursed into my mouth. "Fuck."

"*Yes.*"

"Babe."

He turned me, sitting me on the table. The food was shoved to the side.

I wound my legs around him, burning up from the inside out.

I made my decision at Bresko's, before Bresko's even. I was in. I had to be in. I had to try.

I had to let him choose, and he chose me, and he was moving down my throat, his hands moving down to my hips.

An inferno was lit inside of me.

Forget my brain.

Forget my fear.

Forget everything.

Just forget.

I *wanted* to forget.

I slid my fingers through his hair, grabbing ahold—BUZZ!

He stiffened.

"No," I groaned.

BUZZ!

BUZZ!

BUZZZZZ!

His head lifted, and those eyes...those adorable eyes were filled with lust, and my heart jumped in my chest, because that'd been for me. I reached down, my thumb grazing his lip.

Simple things like that.

I could do that.

I could touch him like that.

That took my breath away.

BUZZZZZ!

"Jesus Christ." He tore from me, stalking to the door.

I flicked my eyes upward.

Then he was hitting the button. "Who is it?"

A crackle, and then, "Melanie."

I tensed because that wasn't happy and fun-fucking-and-shitting Melanie. Her voice was trembling.

Cut looked back at me.

We sighed at the same time.

I started to slide from the table as he hit the button to let her in.

He raked a hand through his hair. "You okay?"

I nodded, dumbstruck from all the sensations still flooding

me. My throat was full, for some reason, and a second later, we both heard Melanie hurrying down the hallway.

"I'm going to make myself sparse for a bit."

He was going down the hallway, and he stepped inside the bedroom just as my door swung open.

Melanie burst into the room, and I could smell the booze in her backdraft. "You're fucked. I'm fucked. We're all fucked."

I opened my mouth... and nothing. I had nothing.

I closed it and waited.

Melanie went to my fridge, opened it, and stared for thirty full seconds. "You have no booze."

She rotated, her head turning to stare at me. Her fingers were curled over the top of the fridge door. "Why don't you have any booze?"

"I went back on my meds, remember?"

"Right." She closed the door and went to my sugar container. Lifting the lid, she pulled out a container of tequila.

My mouth dropped. "You had that there this whole time?"

She snorted, going back to the fridge and pulling out a container of orange juice. "You don't eat sugar. It's my own personal stash."

I watched, feeling like I should be dumbfounded, but not being dumbfounded at all. I was more impressed, as she poured a hefty amount of tequila into a glass. The OJ was next, and she swished it before popping some ice in the glass. Once done, she turned, hitched her hip to the counter and gave me a head tilt.

"I was just dumped, and your dad's a dickhead."

The dumping part got my attention first. "Wait. What? You were dumped? What happened?"

"Cassie and I were having dinner tonight when she brought up your dad."

"My dad?"

I was not following this conversation, at all.

She snorted, cursing at the same time. "Your fucking dad,

whom I want to drop a shit on because he's a major fucking asshole. You remember mentioning that Dean proposed a charity gala at Come Our Way?"

Vaguely, because I felt bad nixing it so quick.

That was days ago.

Wait— "He didn't?!"

"He did." The drink was swirled around once, and she took a long drag. "And I know this because Cassie asked me about Deek Fausten. Ask me how Cassie knew about your dad. Do it. Ask me."

I didn't want to. So, I didn't.

Melanie didn't need the extra prompting. Her eyes were almost feral by now, and she was showing me her teeth. "That fucker had the balls to call the Mustangs. Cassie informed me that she'd been asked why Deek Fausten, who apparently has some connections to the Mustangs' owners, why he'd think going to a charity event for Come Our Way would be a conflict of interest and why that had anything to do with Cut?"

I—was staggered.

It took a beat, and my brain never needed to take a beat, but it did this time.

Deek. My dad.

Mustangs.

Come Our Way.

Conflict of interest.

Oh, no.

No, no, no.

No.

Everything good that I'd been feeling, from Cut coming over, from Cut being here, from kissing Cut, from being able to touch him and knowing he wanted me to touch him, from all of it—was wiped clean because my mind caught up.

My stomach churned.

I wanted to throw up.

Vomit rose up in my throat, and I clamped it down.

My dad.

Not even.

I didn't think of him as my dad, not back when I was a kid, not when I was a guest in his home, not when he came to my mom's funeral, and not even when he paid for college.

My mom overdosed and I stayed away.

The truth was that I'd been fine with that, but Deek never fought for me.

He hadn't wanted me. It made sense to me now as an adult. It hadn't back then.

Natalie hadn't wanted me either. She didn't want me in the same house as her sons, breathing their same air. Me. The homeless kid. The crazy kid. The kid with the coked-out mother who decided she was done going to rehab, and never went again until she overdosed.

A stigma was put on me, and it was still there. I felt it.

Dean went ahead with the charity gala, without our say-so, and he approached all those 'high-end' folks whom he said he was going to approach. That meant the Mustangs' team. That meant my father, I guess.

I hadn't known.

And though their names hadn't been brought up, I knew who else would be invited to that party. Natalie and her husband. Dean would approach her husband because he was a lawyer for a local big-name firm. And he'd approach because he would do his homework, and he would learn who was connected to the Mustangs, and Chad was connected, and then he'd go from there.

Damn Dean.

Damn him so much.

Melanie had been talking, but she fell silent until now. "Cheyenne?"

A door opened from down the hallway.

A muted footstep on the carpet, and I lifted my head.

Cut stood there. He had heard everything.

I asked, "Did you know?"

He nodded. "Yeah, just today."

Another pang, this time it cut straight down my middle.

They asked him. The guy I thought I had loved since I first saw him. The guy whom I actually did love since I first saw him.

I asked, my voice cracking, "What'd you say?"

His eyes grew fierce. His jaw hardened. "I lied. I told my boss that it must be because of Chad."

Melanie gaped at him, a gargled sound ripping from her throat, one that sounded like it was half of a laugh. And a pleased laugh.

"You said what?"

His jaw clenched before he said, "I knew what that fucker was trying to do, but fuck him. I put it on Chad."

I almost swayed from the surprise.

He hadn't turned on me...I'd been expecting it. A pocket deep inside, one reserved for all those people who weren't supposed to turn on you, but they did—that pocket had been making room for one more.

It stopped.

"I might be into guys," Melanie whispered, her eyes big and gaping on Cut. Then, she flinched. "No. I can't even joke about that, but honestly, fuck girls right now, too." She glanced at me. "You know what I mean."

A nod from me. I did. Forget Deek right now. "Let's go to the park, pick up old dog poop, and put it on Cassie's car."

Melanie's eyes started shining from unshed tears. "You'd do that for me?"

I frowned. "Of course. And if Sash was here, you know she'd already be grabbing her tools to break into Cassie's car so she could take a dump herself in the front seat."

Melanie pressed her lips together, a small laugh slipping out. "She would, too."

I nodded.

"That's why I came here first."

I nodded again.

Melanie's gaze flashed again, her mouth curving down. "Cassie asked me about Fausten because she couldn't figure out the connection with Come Our Way. Said it had something to do with Cut. They must've asked her before asking Cut." She glanced at him. "I got upset because, you know, what a douche your dad is being. Cassie got upset at me because she said he was going to be doing business with the Mustangs and I needed to respect her employers. Before I knew it, she was saying we were moving too fast and she couldn't risk her career since you and I are so close."

Cut remarked, "She's real particular about her dating life not touching her career."

My friend was hurting.

I was going to take any of my pain from Fausten, and I was going to wrap it up. I was going to put a bow on it and shove it out of my mind because he didn't matter to me. Melanie did, and she was hurting. So because of that, I knew two options could happen here. Cassie might've really meant what she said to Melanie, or she didn't. She said it in haste, and she'd want her back. I know in both situations, Cassie would regret it because it was Melanie. And thinking back on how I had watched both of them hold hands, sneak kisses, cuddle, hug each other, whisper to each other, and how there'd been times if Melanie was upset and Cassie reached for her, I had a feeling I knew which option would happen.

"Cassie's going to come around and she's going to apologize for what she said."

Melanie wiped a tear away. "You think?"

"I know so, so don't let those words sink in any further. They're not going to stay long, and don't let them have any more power. That's done." And because I knew how to cheer her up. "Let's go have banana split sundaes at Tits."

"How do you know that's what Cassie will do, Shy?"

Because she loved her. I could already tell, but I only said, "Because you're one fucking amazing catch."

That made her smile, and that's when I moved in, wrapping my arms around her. I pulled her in close, my head going to her shoulder as her forehead went to mine. A second later, her arms circled me, and we both knew the real tragedy of the night.

There'd be no poop surprises for anyone.

CUT: I was going to tell you about Deek later tonight. Just got distracted.

Me: I know. I enjoyed the distraction.

Cut: You okay?

Me: Juna is still trying to perfect her upside-down shimmy, so how could I not with a glittery thong in my face?

Cut: I don't know how to respond to that.

Me: Thanks for being okay with letting us have a girls' night.

Cut: Yeah. I get it, though Hendrix got excited when I told him you guys were at Tits.

Me: Who wouldn't?

Cut: True.

Cut: For the record, what Deek did was shitty, but he's your dad. If you'd like me not to say something, I won't, but I'm hoping you'll let me handle him. I'd like to handle Deek.

Me: What would you say?

Cut: Let me handle him.

Me: Okay. Go for it. Should I thank you for this?

Cut: No. It's going to be all my pleasure.

Me: How are things with you and Nut-Brother?

Cut: Different, but he and I will be fine. We're like you and your girls, but we just take longer because guys don't like to talk about shit, ya know.

Me: I think I'm a dude then.

Cut: Would make sense why you keep saying dude.

Me: I gotta go. Juna is now jumping up and down on her heels. Sash is yelling at her to stop jumping.

Me: She just did something to her ankle.

Me: She's fine. She declared it.

Cut: I'm at a loss on how to respond again.

Me: That makes two of us

Cut: Hey. Can you do me a favor for later? Text me when u get home, no matter how late.

Me: No prob, Bob.

Cut. No dude, and no Bob.

Me: Okey-dokey.

29

CUT

I hit the house, and either unlucky or lucky for Chad, he was home.

My girl was at a strip club so my boy was going to hear some words from me. Going inside, Chad was in the kitchen and he froze, seeing me. "Hey."

Then, he saw me, *saw* me and he unfroze. His back went to the counter, his hands beside him, and he nodded. "Okay. Let's do this."

"Your stepdad's a piece of work."

I dropped my bag, my keys, my wallet.

I was tired. I was grumpy. And I was still pissed about being pulled into Margo's office.

Chad frowned. "Jon?"

I grunted. "Deek."

"Deek? Deek's not my stepdad anymore."

"He was, and he's a piece of shit."

Chad's frown just deepened. "I'm not following this conversation."

He and I still hadn't had it out from before, but this took priority.

So I told him. I told him everything.

Margo.

Me throwing him under the bus, which he snorted/laughed at.

Me going to Cheyenne's and not getting into it with her because I was getting *into* it. And I ended it with Cassie, and Melanie showing up at Cheyenne's, and Chad was grinning by the end.

"So, you throw me under the bus—"

"—because you're an asswipe and you deserve it." And he'd show up at the party anyway, and Margo would be gone by the time he did.

He inclined his head slowly at that one, "—and my Not-Sister—"

I'd shared with him how the girls referred to him, the Not-Brother. I hadn't shared about the Nut-Brother.

"—goes to Sasha's job to cheer up her friend?" His smile just widened. "I'm thinking you're right."

I frowned. "What?"

"You're right. My mom's a piece of work, something I've always known and never took into account, and you're right about Deek. That was shitty what he did, and like a fucking bitch. And you're also right about Cheyenne. I'm seeing that I'm going to have to get to know her because of you, but also, she seems kinda cool."

Knots I hadn't known in my shoulders just unclenched. "She's fucking amazing."

"Yeah. I'm starting to get that." He was nodding, and suddenly his eyes closed, and his head fell down. "I've been an asshole."

This talk was turning out easier than I thought. Chad was doing most of the work.

He kept on, "And I know you're about to lay down some rules, but you don't have to. I mean it. I get it. It's uncool that I drop your name at Bresko's as much as I do. And at Robbins, and at Hank

Hamburgers, and well, at a ton of other places that you don't know about and we should probably not get into that."

Of course.

But I was now tired.

I was shaking my head. "I've missed you."

"I'm a dick."

"Yep."

"I'll work at not being a dick."

"That'd be good."

He waited a little bit, assessing me. "Can we talk about Sasha, because I'm all sorts of fucked up about her. She's got my head spinning, and man." He let out a breath, giving me a rueful look. "I don't know if it's morning or night and I've no clue how to handle this shit."

I was even more tired now. All the shit that'd been building up was gone after this one conversation. Chad would work at not being a dick, and I got my best friend back in one go. Took fucking long enough.

"We got a game tomorrow."

"Right." He straightened from the counter, his hands falling down and he was looking around the kitchen.

"So, just one beer for me."

His head popped back up. A wide smile spread over his face, and he nodded slowly. "Right. Just one."

We shared a grin.

It was good to have my boy back.

30

CHEYENNE

Melanie liked Juna, a lot. Or she liked Juna's boobs.

She kept trying to talk to them, but she was talking about how much she loved Cassie. How sad she was about Cassie. How she already missed Cassie. How she hadn't known how much she cared about Cassie until their 'tiff' that night.

I was saying 'tiff.' Melanie kept saying 'tits.'

Juna's boobs didn't care either way.

And Juna sat on Melanie's lap, commiserating with her, and it was more of a friend consoling another friend, except for the whole thing where Juna's boobs were out.

Sasha was frowning at them, then just shook her head. We were in Sasha's special booth, and Sash was doing paperwork while we both listened to Melanie. Our duties weren't so needed tonight, since Juna was taking care of it for us, but we were here. We needed to be here. After closing, Melanie was drunk off her ass. She and Juna had moved to a different booth next to us.

Melanie's eyes were closed, and her head was back.

She was talking all about Cassie while Juna was smoothing out her hair.

"Oh, that's so sad."

Three more dancers joined them. All sitting, listening to Melanie talking about Cassie, and a couple of the girls were brushing away tears.

Yeah. We were so not needed tonight.

Sasha was looking at them, too, and she snorted before closing up her paperwork. She reached for her brandy, then turned to me. "Tell me about your man."

"I never asked you about Chad."

She snorted. "Bullshit, you did. You called the other day and we had a three-hour conversation about your Nut-Brother."

Right. I was deflecting here.

"Talk."

She'd returned to the one-word statements. So I had to talk.

"Three nights ago I decided to try with him."

"Why?"

"Because... I *do* love him." Crap, crap, crap.

Just, crap.

I whispered, "It wasn't just an idea back then."

The music had cut out so she could hear me, and her eyes turned sad.

She grabbed her drink in one hand and took my hand in her other. She squeezed.

I felt it.

I clung to her hand with my other and we sat there like that for a second.

Gah. All these emotions. They were rising up and choking me.

"Girl." A soft sigh from Sasha.

I felt that in my gut. "Right."

One of the bouncers headed our way, and he stopped at our booth, taking us in. He saw the brandy in Sasha's hand, her hand between both of mine, how we were both lounging back, and how neither of us were talking.

"Chicks." He shook his head and headed out.

The girls said their goodbyes, and one by one, they all started heading out, too.

Melanie's booth was emptied out. Each of them came over, said a goodbye, and slipped out through their dressing room. Juna brought Melanie back to our booth and stood, staring at us much how the bouncer just had.

She was frowning heavily at Melanie, whose eyes never opened, and as soon as she hit the booth, she turned into whoever was next to her. That was me, and her arms wrapped around one of mine. Her head went down and was resting into my side. She was snuggling into me.

"She's pretty sad tonight."

A loud snore ripped from Melanie in that moment.

No one reacted.

Sasha just nodded. "Thanks for taking care of her. Did she tip you at all?"

Juna shook her head, lifting up a shoulder. "Seemed more of a humane thing to do tonight, you know?" She shrugged again, then a brighter smile came back. "Okay. I'm out. I'm off tomorrow." She said to me, "Tell your man good luck on his game."

Cut. My man.

The little thrills were there.

I liked feeling those thrills.

"I'll tell him."

She waved again before heading out, disappearing into their back dressing room.

Sasha put her brandy back down and lifted her hand. She was reaching into a bag on her other side, and when one of the last of the bouncers came over, she took out a big envelope. Tossing it on the table toward him, she said, "Divide that up. Eighty percent to Juna. Break the last twenty between the other three who listened to my girl the last hour."

He dipped his head down, took the envelope and headed toward the dressing room.

I'd seen Sasha do that before. All of those girls would come back with an envelope stuffed inside their lockers, and the thing was that none of them expected cash for listening to Melanie. To them, that wasn't part of their job that night.

"You're a good boss."

Sasha grunted, picking up her brandy once again.

Melanie just snored.

ME: It's 4 am. Taco Bell is amazing. I'm home.

Cut: Good. How's Melanie?

Me: She'll be okay, I think.

Cut: How are you?

Me: Easy peasy. I got Taco Belly tonight, so all is right with the worldy.

Cut: You know what I mean.

A pause.

Me: I really liked the distraction tonight.

Cut: Me too.

Me: I didn't know I'd wake you up. I'm sorry. Go to bed so I can enjoy my fiesta potatoes guilt-free.

Cut: Will do.

Cut: Cheyenne?

Me: Still here. I'm eyeing the chicken quesadilla instead.

Cut: Your whole 'idea' thing? I hope it wasn't just an idea.

Me: Damn. I'm going for the cinnamon twists instead now.

Me: You're making me a girl.

Me: I'm really looking forward to some Cut Reaper Ryder tomorrow night. Sorry. Tonight.

Cut: Lol. Okay. Night.

An hour later,
Me: It wasn't just an idea.

31

CUT

Hendrix sat next to me and bent over to finish tying up his skates.

It was before the game, we were heading out to start warm-ups. This was our normal thing. Hendrix and I were close, and we were close enough that when he glanced sideways at me, still tying up his skates, I knew I wouldn't like whatever was coming my way.

"Heard we're heading back to your girl's Come place."

"Shut up." But that was funny. "And don't say it that way either."

He finished tying and sat back up. "Like what?"

"You know. Don't be a douche."

He broke, laughing. "Right. But we're heading back for some party thing next week. After we get back from our away game." He pulled on his shin guards, then reached for his tape. "How's that going to go?"

"What do you mean?"

"You know. Come Our Way. You. Your girl. The guy who wants to get in her pants."

I was thinking, remembering. That first night flashed in my mind. "He works with her? That guy?"

Hendrix's grin was slow and smug. "He does. He's the one setting everything up."

Of course.

Jesus Christ.

Of course.

I shook my head.

I didn't need another problem on hand, but it was good to know. "Thanks."

He dipped his head down.

We finished suiting up, and by unspoken agreement, both stood and headed out for warm-ups.

It was game-mode time now.

32

CHEYENNE

I woke up with a gnawing in my stomach. I didn't like it.

Bones are supposed to be gnawed on, not my stomach. I figure I had that feeling for a reason, so I was about to do something. I didn't want to do this at Come Our Way. The weekend staff was on, and they were mostly college kids looking to do good. I didn't want them to feel the same 'not good' feeling I was having, and I knew Dean was a hockey fanboy, so here we were.

I was waiting for him on the side street before heading down to the arena. Dean was supposed to be coming since he was going to the game after this.

I heard a car door shut. A beep. And I turned, there he was. Just finishing locking up his car, and he waved, jogging around and over to me. Eyeing his sweater, he didn't have a right to wear Cut's number, but I kept that fact to myself.

Dean had no idea about Cut. He had no idea about anything except his job and wanting to get the word out as much as possible, and getting as much funding in as he could get. Those were both good goals, but he went about it the wrong way this time.

"Hey, Cheyenne." The wind picked up, blowing some of his

hair around and he raised a hand up, smoothing it down before putting both his hands in his pockets. "What's up?"

"You had no authority to send out those invites for a charity gala."

Straight to business. We had a hockey game to get to.

He blinked a few times. "Whoa. Okay. I didn't think you'd actually care that much. I just figured it was a one-time—"

"You sent those invites out and you opened up a hornet's nest for me. No authority. None. You fucked up."

This was always my favorite time.

Someone did something wrong, and now was when they either owned up to it or ...

He scowled. "Are you kidding me? You can't come at me—"

I stopped listening.

I knew what path he'd chosen.

He chose wrong, but he didn't want to feel the bad for making a bad call. Therefore, he was now going to either deflect, attack, or say some excuse. The excuses were the best because the ingenuity was the genius. If an excuse was given, somehow it'd lead back to the person wronged and how everything was actually their fault.

Somehow him not getting my approval for the event would be my fault.

Him sending out those invites would be my fault.

Newsflash. None of this was my fault.

I interrupted whatever he was saying. "Company policy is that you needed a unanimous decision. I am one of those voices. I never gave approval. You violated a company policy."

He started talking again. I tuned in, hearing, "If you'd just—"

I tuned out again. He was now attacking.

Me again. "No matter how you spin this where I'm at fault, you know I'm not. You fucked up. You."

He stopped, his face all red and puffy, and he clamped his mouth shut.

He was seeing me, seeing I didn't give a fuck what he was going to say, and then he growled. "If you had explained why—"

"No. This is where you don't get the floor. I will be bringing you in front of the board."

"What?! You can't—"

"I can. Now." I gave him my ticket. "Enjoy the hockey game."

I was going, but I wasn't sitting in my seats. Sasha and Melanie were pulling ranks. They wanted to enjoy the game with me, so after Dean looked down, frowning at my ticket, he crumpled it up and stalked off. Sasha and Melanie stepped out from around the corner.

Melanie frowned at me. "You gave him your ticket?"

I nodded.

Sasha was frowning, too. "Why?"

"I told him to come down, that he could go to the game if he wanted. He said yes, but he didn't know that I was going to ambush him."

"Cassie told me that you have season tickets. That seat is going to be better than any seat we all get together."

I shrugged.

Sasha was giving me a harder look, her eyebrows pulled together. "You're setting him up."

Melanie glanced at her, then to me. "Huh?"

I only shrugged again, but I was.

I would lose if I brought this to the board. They wouldn't be happy Dean didn't get my approval, but they would deem his cause was worth it. I didn't want that precedent. And after Dean found out my family connections next Saturday, I didn't want him doing something like this again, because he would. He would find out about myself and Cut, and that'd make it so much worse.

I was doing this to get in his head.

I wanted him to feel bad.

I wanted him to feel indebted to me.

I also wanted it to look on paper that if I was actually upset with him, why would I give him my season tickets, because at some point down the line, this could be a him versus me sort of thing, and even though I wrote the grant to get Come Our Way so much money in the first place, it was Dean who continued to bring in more money. The board for Come Our Way liked Dean, a lot, and they should.

But I didn't like how he went over my head. There'd be consequences.

"Let's go to the game."

"Wait." Melanie grasped both our arms, stopping us. "What if Cassie sees me?"

I frowned.

Sasha inclined her head. "That was the point."

"I know, but..." Melanie flushed, glancing away. "I'm just really nervous to see her."

Sasha took her hand from her arm and held it a second. "You'll be fine. Cassie will see you and know she's made a dumb mistake."

"You're right." Her head lifted a bit higher and she squeezed my arm before letting it go. "Let's go."

Turns out, that's not what happened.

33

CHEYENNE

T he game was insane.

They were tied at one to one. The Bravado were pushing hard back at the Mustangs. Cut's line was tired. The second line was tired. The third. Fourth. All of them. There were so many shots on goal, too, so I could only imagine how tired the goalies were.

I was tired just from the stress of the game, but we were in the third period. Just starting. There'd been no Cassie sightings. I saw Cut looking for me in my normal seats, then skate past when he saw Dean there instead. He had crumpled up my ticket, but I knew he'd still use it.

As seats went, we didn't get too bad considered we got them the day of the game. With each game that passed, with how well they were doing, this wouldn't be a thing that could happen soon. Each game would be sold out days, if not weeks, before the game. That's just how it was. I knew the box seats were gone the first day any opened up, and that was if they weren't already bought from a years-hold which happened. A lot.

Either way, it was fun to sit and cheer with Melanie and Sasha.

Sasha informed us that she did not want to talk about Chad. Nut-Brother was a douchebag of epic proportions, so we were in the one-word zone during the game.

I asked now, "I'm going to hit the bathroom before things get super nuts. I'm walking by the concessions. Want anything?"

"Beer."

I looked at Melanie. She shook her head. "I'm good. Just hurry back."

"Will do." I pushed out our row and headed up the stairs for the hallway.

It was after the bathroom, after I went to get beer for Sasha, when I was turning back to head for my seat.

Cup in hand, I was walking past a wall.

I didn't think anything of it, not at first.

It was a transparent wall, more of a boundary for crowd control. People walked one way if they were leaving the seats and returned on the side where I was.

A man and a teenager were heading from their seats, and I wasn't paying attention. Or with me being on my meds, I was enjoying that I wasn't paying attention. I could do that now, but then the teenager ground to a halt.

I noticed that. It was odd, but nothing out of the ordinary.

I kept going.

The man stopped, turned back. I heard, "Hunter?"

And *that*, that had me paying attention.

My head whipped back. The teenager was staring at me, mouth hanging open, and he was gaping at me. He was on the other side of the wall, maybe ten feet away, and I was slammed back from a force inside of me.

It was Hunter.

It was my brother.

Then, a third male was coming after that.

I tagged him from my periphery, and I noticed his walk first. I knew that walk, but I didn't know it enough. It was teasing me, nagging at me, but back to the teenager.

Holy—I was taking him in. Looking at everything.

His eyes.

His hair. Brownish with blond streaks.

His little nose.

How clear his skin was. Youthful. Young.

He had an athlete's build.

He was wearing Cut's number.

This was my brother, but he was older. He was a teenager now.

He wasn't the ten-year-old I remembered, the kid I squatted down to brush knuckles with at my mom's funeral.

The back of my mind already identified the man—and the other guy coming toward us—Chad. And my father. That's what made sense, but I didn't care about them. I was busy taking in my brother when the other two stopped, took in what was going on, and closed ranks.

Literally.

Chad and Deek stepped in front of Hunter, and a growl came from me. It was automatic. I didn't know I was going to growl until I heard it, and then I wanted to growl again. I swung my gaze to Chad and stepped toward the wall. "Move!"

He blanched, then shook his head. "Can't, Cheyenne."

I surged toward the wall, my heart surging with me, and I slammed my hand against it. Palm flat. One hard pound. Not a slap, a pound. This was the street side of me. This was the part that was still inside of me. I growled again, "Move."

His eyes went wide, but he took a deep breath and held firm. "I can't."

But it didn't matter.

Hunter had moved to the side, around his dad. "Cheyenne."

I grimaced, shoving the street in me back down, and I went over to him. "Hey. Hey there."

We'd exchanged pictures. I didn't have social media accounts, but I used Come Our Way's Instagram page to follow his. I'd seen him grow up over the years, but it'd been too long. Way too long.

"You got big."

"Hunter." His dad moved in, throwing me a sideways look, but his tone was half hushed and half cautious. I didn't spare Deek a look, and he knew why. Before his call to the Mustangs, I might've been welcoming, but he made his choice.

"Dad, stop! She's your kid, too."

Deek threw me another look, but he ducked his head and moved back a step.

Chad came up. He took in Hunter, me, and sighed. He put his arm around Deek's shoulders. "Come on. Let's grab this little punk a beer, because apparently he thinks he's an adult."

Hunter rolled his eyes up. "Har har. Don't be sour because she actually wants to talk to me."

Chad laughed, pulling Deek with him.

Hunter laughed, too.

They exchanged lighthearted punches to their arms, but then Chad was heading away. Deek was stiff next to him, and Chad glanced over his shoulder at me. Hunter had already turned back, so only I saw the very real and very serious warning in those eyes.

He didn't trust me.

I hadn't thought much about Chad before. What I said to Cut had been the truth, but now I was doubly grateful because if I had cared, that look would've filleted me. As it was, I turned to the only one standing in front of me that could hurt me, but I knew he wouldn't.

"You're the Koala Man now."

Hunter laughed, ducking his head down. He ran a hand over the back of his head, giving his hair a little shake before dropping it back down. His head went back up and he shifted on his legs.

Feet apart. He was giving me the cocky athlete stance. "I play hockey, too."

"Yeah?"

"I'm like Cut. First line."

He was damn proud of it. I could tell.

I hadn't gone to any of his games, obviously. I knew what school he went to. He'd told me over email. I knew of two girls he was interested in. I knew his friends' names. I knew he liked his school, but he missed where he had been. I knew he had two best friends there whom he really missed, and one was a girl, and that girl was someone he thought he could have feelings for. I also knew that he was shutting it down because he was here, not there.

And I couldn't help but wonder how much of that did Deek know? Did Natalie know?

I was betting not that much.

"You're liking it?"

Some of the cockiness faded, and his hands came out of his pockets. He nodded. "Yeah." He started eyeing the wall between us. "I'd say you should sit with us so we could catch up, but knowing—" He nodded to the side where Chad and Deek were still in line for beer. "—I bet they'd actually shit their pants, huh?"

Melanie would like him.

I grinned. "Yeah, but imagine how smelly their shits would be if you gave them the slip and sat with me instead?"

Hunter laughed a little louder, his shoulders eased a bit more, too. "That would be almost worth it." He got somber, his smile fading. "I don't get their problem. They act like—"

I knew.

They acted like I was my mother.

I changed the subject on purpose. "Do you get to see Deek a lot?"

He shrugged, and his face closed up. "Every now and then"

So he was saying he didn't. Which was interesting since Deek moved out here because of Hunter.

"How's your mom doing?"

His face opened back up a little, a small grin showing. "She's good. I mean, as good as can be. It's Mom, you know." His face shuddered. "Or, I mean, no. She's not your mom. She's Natalie. Chad would understand."

I was nodding, going with it. "I'm sure he would. I bet he'd have a whole joke to insert. I don't. I'm sorry." Gah. I wasn't trying to make him feel bad. "I just don't know Natalie that well, you know?"

His eyes grew fierce. "You would if she gave you a chance. Fucking Nata—"

"Hey!"

He stopped, his eyes widening at my sharp tone.

I eased it back, a little. "Sorry. Just...she's your mom. Appreciate her."

We never went serious in our emails. Everything was light and joking, and it hadn't been a hardship. Seeing him now, though; seeing the changes, seeing what I missed out on, it was a little harder to remain all surface-level here.

I was swallowing some bitterness, and I didn't usually feel that.

"You, uh, you look good. You seem different, too." He inched forward toward the wall, dropping his tone. "It's not right that I didn't see you all those years. I've talked to Dad and Mom about it, but I don't care what they say. It's not right. We should've..."

"Hey." I tapped the wall.

He was blaming himself. He shouldn't do that.

"Hey."

He paused, frowning at me, but I saw the fight still there. He was torn.

"Your parents had reasons for keeping me away."

He snorted. "Maybe in the beginning, because they were

worried about your mom's influence, but not later. You were in college and I was..." He trailed off because he was still growing up.

I flattened my palm against the wall. "Listen to me. It is what it is. You cannot look back on 'what ifs' and 'should'ves.' Trust me. You were a kid. You're still a kid, and I was getting my head together. We're here now. That's the great thing. Now...you walking down the same time I was walking in, that was meant to be. I believe in that shit. Believe in that. Okay? No look-backs. Got it?"

He didn't at first, but then jerked his head down in a nod. "Yeah. Fine. I got it."

Good.

Good.

I saw Deek and Chad heading back, beer in hand and it looked as if they were heading to fight a Marvel supervillain. All scowls, and I had to flinch because one of those guys was the reason I'd been born.

"Super Scowls are returning."

Hunter grinned, but stepped back from the wall.

I let my hand fall back. "Let's text instead? Or call, even? I'll email you my digits."

He nodded. "Sounds good."

Then Chad was near us and he had his head tipped up in a challenging way.

I considered pointing out that there was no fight to be alpha between us, though; let's be realistic. It's hard to out-street someone from the streets. Chad might scoff at that, but someone else from the streets would get me. They'd be on the same wavy train.

"I looked at your seats, but you weren't there tonight."

I almost laughed at that. "Because you cared or because you needed to know which route to take to the concessions stand to avoid me?"

He winced at the last suggestion.

Right.

So lovely.

I let out a sigh. "I'm going to ignore the blatant disrespect you've shown me over and over again. I'm going to ignore a whole lot of things right now, but how about instead we could focus on what I should say when I go back to the seats I am sitting in tonight?"

He frowned. He had no clue what I was talking about.

This guy. Honestly. No deep thought?

"I'm about to head back where I'm sitting with Sasha and Melanie."

At Sasha's name, his eyes bulged and he lost a little blood in his face. He had a whole 'oh shit' look going on.

Yeah. That's what I'd been referencing.

"And so what do I say? Because you know she's my family and she'd be pissed off that I didn't tell her how you just treated me."

Chad swallowed and went back to scowling. "What do you mean how I treated you? I treated..."

"Dude. You didn't." This was from Hunter, and he was shaking his head. "Like, at all. You treated her like she was a criminal."

I made sure to give Deek a pointed look, and as soon as I did, I regretted it.

He looked like me.

And Hunter.

And damn.

I told Cut a while back that I didn't have feelings for Deek or Chad, and to an extent I didn't. But staring back at someone who was an older and male version of me, I was seeing someone I could've had in my life.

And then the 'ifs' started, and I couldn't stop them.

If he'd been different.

If my mom had been different.

If I'd not been screwed up.

If Natalie had been more kind and loving.

If. If. If.

I had to stop. No one wins in that situation. It happened how it happened.

Right?

Yes.

I was swallowing tree bark, but yes. I had to accept that.

Nothing could be changed, so it didn't matter.

Damn, it hurt to swallow that.

And Chad hadn't answered me.

His mouth was tight, and his Adam's apple kept going up and down, but then he let loose with a string of expletives.

"Hunter," Deek barked, his own voice tight. Grim. "Go back to your seat."

"But I—"

"Now!"

"I have to piss, Dad." Hunter shot me a look before he swung around Chad and Deek, marching off in the direction of their seats, and his entire back was rigid.

"I've come to realize that things are different—"

"Deek," Chad cut him off, then softened immediately. "Let me, you know. Let me handle this."

Handle this.

I was refraining from commenting on that.

He took two steps away before I called after him, "Hey, Deek."

He stopped, half-turning back.

He didn't say anything.

I wasn't surprised.

I did, though. "You do know that I'm not the bad guy in this story, right?"

He flinched.

He got the message.

It was kind of a shady thing to do, but he was my dad. Yes,

there was no relationship. Yes, I was okay with it. Yes, at some point he had tried until for whatever reason, he decided to stop trying. Then, I remembered that he had paid for my college.

I yelled out, "Just kidding. Thanks for the college tuition."

Oops.

Chad didn't comment on that, but he was hella frowning still. "Can you not say anything to Sasha about this?"

"Uh. No. Sasha would be pissed if I didn't."

He grimaced, saying under his breath, "Shit."

Cut told me Chad was going to try.

This wasn't him trying.

"Let me tell her."

That seemed to take so much effort from him. He said it through gritted teeth.

"What did I ever do to you?"

His head popped up at my question.

"I've done nothing, nothing that I can think of. Did I push you out of your house? That wasn't my call. You know that, right? I've not said anything bad about you to Cut or Sasha. I've said nothing negative about anyone, except for that dig I just said to Deek, but do you blame me?"

He edged backwards a step, looking like he was biting the inside of his mouth. He was looking every which way, but at me.

I caught sight of the clock on the wall. Half the third period was over.

Now I was the one who wanted to swear.

Nut-Brother still hadn't answered, and I was losing patience. "Forget it. I apologize for whatever I did, and I won't say anything to Sasha except that there was an exchange, and she needs to hear it from you first."

After that, I was out.

Once I hit my chair, I pulled my phone out and checked our emails. There was an email with his number so I sent him a text back.

Me: Koala Sister here. It was nice seeing you. Missed you. The emails are great, but you know.

A minute later.

Koala Boy: Koala Brother here now. I missed you too. And I know.

That. Right there. That was everything worth Deek or Chad. Everything.

THIRTY SECONDS to the end of the game, the sirens lit up.

The Bravado scored.

Mustangs lost.

34

CUT

Hendrix dropped his towel on the bench beside me.

I didn't look up. Everyone was pissed. Hendrix was pissed. I was pissed. Alex. Crow. Everyone. Coaching staff. Margo swept through the locker room with a scowl of her own. We lost games. That was part of the job, but it wasn't a good part. Every game counted because we wanted the Cup this year. Bad.

Pulling on his pants, Hendrix dropped down, snagging a shirt on the way. He raised it up over his head, before yanking it down to cover him. "Talked to some of the guys. They're up for heading to Bresko's. Want to forget this game for the night." He eyed me. "You in?"

Cheyenne was here, but checking my phone I saw that Chad, Deek, and Hunter were also here.

I frowned. "Uh... maybe."

He smirked. "Got to run it by your woman first?"

I shot him a smirk back. "Spoken by someone who'd love to have a woman that he runs things by."

Hendrix's laugh was quick and slightly abrupt. He stood back up. "Right. Maybe, if the right one comes along." He reached for his shoes, starting to pull them on, but frowned at me again. "That Not-Russian friend of your girl's, maybe you should invite her tonight, too."

I rubbed at my forehead, enjoying what I was about to say. "She owns Tits, you know."

His eyebrows shot up. "The strip club?"

I nodded.

"No shit?"

Another nod. I was right. I was enjoying this.

He whistled under his breath. "Now I'm really intrigued."

"Heads up, though. She's somewhat involved with Chad."

"Your boy Chad?"

I nodded.

Hendrix got all serious. "Good to know, but Bresko's though?"

"Maybe." I was in the mood for some dark corner, sitting in a booth, holding Cheyenne and forgetting this game. I grabbed my bag up, giving Hendrix a nod. "Heading out. I'll let you know about the club."

"Sounds good. Bring her with you. I forgot to add that. That was a given."

I assumed.

Going through the door, my bag over my shoulder, I took two steps before my phone starting ringing.

Chad calling.

"Hey, man." A bunch of people were coming down the hallway.

They saw me, and a few raised their hands in hello. A couple stood back, waiting for me to pass. I had to lift my bag up and over a little kid, and his eyes were bugging out. I grinned down at him. "Hey, kid."

His mouth fell open.

I kept going.

"Hey..."

Everything tensed inside of me.

That wasn't an easygoing-ready-to-down-some-beers Chad. That was his I-have-to-tell-you-something-you're-not-going-to-like voice.

My mood was going to take a nosedive. I felt it coming. "What happened?"

He took a breath, and I could hear some voices behind him. Male voices. One sounded younger.

"Who's with you? That Hunter?"

"I have to tell you something and you're not going to like it."

I was just turning the corner for the parking lot, and there, standing just inside the door was Cheyenne. She was with her girls, Cassie included. The other three were talking, but Cheyenne was staring right at me. I took all that in, and I didn't like what I was seeing or hearing.

Cheyenne had a knowing look in her gaze.

Chad was about to tell me something not good.

I bit into the phone, "What the fuck did you do?"

"I, uh...I got protective of Hunter, and Deek was there, and yeah. Not the proudest moment of my life."

"Chad." Another growl from me.

Cheyenne broke off from her group.

I was getting attention, but she was ignoring it.

I was ignoring it, though; I knew I couldn't ignore it all. Sometimes shit that got overheard got spun and sold to websites and there was a whole section of click-bait hungry people out there, so I had to keep this neutral...for now.

Cheyenne had made her way to me.

I lifted my arm and she moved in, her arms sliding around me and her face touched my chest. I adjusted, putting the phone between my face and shoulder and cupped the back of her head with my hand.

"Hi." She looked up, a whisper from her.

I smiled back at her, but I was tense. She felt it, and stepped back, a small frown showing. "Cut—"

"Where are you going after the game tonight? I need to explain things. And I think I need to grovel to Cheyenne, too."

I ignored Chad and asked Cheyenne, "Why would Chad need to grovel to you?"

She stepped back so quick, it was as if she was snatched away.

"She's there?" Chad in my ear, sounding slightly panicked.

My eyes on Cheyenne, I responded to him, "She's here."

He cursed at the same time Cheyenne looked away.

"Hey."

She looked back, and I was looking. I was searching.

Something happened, that was obvious.

I asked, "Why am I getting a really bad feeling here?" That was to her. To Chad, I clipped out, "We'll be at Bresko's as long as Cheyenne can handle it. You want to grovel, get your ass there. And fast."

I hit the end button and held my phone.

"I don't trust myself to be at the house with him right now. Can you handle Bresko's?"

She nodded, too quick for my liking. "I was going to ask you, actually. Cassie said a bunch of the guys are going and Melanie wants to go. Those two made up."

I didn't give a fuck, but I reached out, and pulled Cheyenne back to me. I just needed to hold her.

I sent Hendrix a text.

Me: In for Bresko's.

Hendrix. Awesome! See you there. Bring your girl's friends too.

I showed Cheyenne the text and she nodded.

"Wait a second." She touched my chest, heading back to her friends.

Cassie was standing next to Melanie, and she tipped her head back.

Cassie was smart. She could read people and she was reading me.

She said something to the others, and it wasn't long after when Cheyenne was giving each of them a hug and breaking off to head my way.

She got to my side. "Cassie offered to drive the girls."

Thank you, Cassie.

I put my phone in my pocket, shifted my bag, and reached for Cheyenne's hand.

Our fingers were laced and we headed out into the masses that way.

35

CHEYENNE

I was with Cut, in his truck, heading to Bresko's, and I just finished updating him on Melassie.

Cassie saw us at the game, came over. She and Melanie talked to the side for a bit. There was crying. There were hugs. Cassie apologized for being wrong, but I didn't know what she was talking about. In the end, all was good.

"I'm not saying this to come off as an asshole, but I don't give a flying fuck about Melanie and Cassie." He glanced sideways to me, his hand tightening on the steering wheel. "Can we fast-track this conversation to where it's about you and Chad?"

Oh.

Yes.

That.

I'd been avoiding it, because who wouldn't? The whole situation sucked. So, I told him. I told him everything. What I said. What Hunter said. What Chad said. What Deek said.

At the end, he cursed.

"Fuck."

It started off soft, then he cursed again.

"Fuck!"

Louder.

"Fuck him!" Even louder.

"That godd—" Lots of expletives here. And he finished it with, "Fuck Deek. Fuck Chad. Fuck both of them, but also fuck Natalie. I didn't know you back then, but fuck her."

Lots of fucks given here. It was almost like I was in the same vehicle with Melanie.

"Babe." I reached over, grabbing his hand. "Chad said he needed to do some groveling. Let's give him the chance?"

He shook his head, a long and deep sigh leaving him. "That's the thing. It's too late. He had time to deal with it, whatever is the issue. He doubled down with how he treated you tonight. He had an opportunity to make it right, and he didn't. Now he's going to come and he's going to apologize, but for how long? Until Deek shows up at your shelter's gala?" He glanced over.

His eyes were bleak, and my heart stopped.

This was costing him his friendship.

I reached out, tightening my hold on his hand. "Chad was your brother."

"Was." He looked back, staring out the window. "How do I make that right inside? That someone who was my best friend, my brother, is treating someone I care about like what? What's even the word, Cheyenne? What you said was right. They're treating you like you're a criminal, and you did nothing wrong. Nothing. You were a product of the environment you grew up in, and instead of becoming just like your mom, you made something of yourself, something good, someone who betters the world."

Oh, man.

This was rocking me, in a bad way.

I fell back, my hand loosening over his.

I said, "Back then, I was used to being treated how I was, and it wasn't just them. There were others. Social workers over time. Teachers. Teacher aides. I got used to it, but I never let 'em in.

Never. Because I knew how they viewed me wasn't what I was on the inside. I was so strong inside that they never made a dent. I don't want Chad to make a dent. You know I'm not bothered by how he's treating me."

"I don't understand—"

"It's narrow-minded bullshit." Point blank. Period. The end. "That's it. My mom was a junkie, and I got looked at the same way. Don't mean a thing that I never touched drugs. That I was never like her, ever. They looked at me like I was her or I was going to be like her, and they're wrong. That's their issue."

"Yes, and that's my best friend."

Shit.

The dent just got made.

I was bleeding for *him*.

"I'm sorry."

We were reaching the outskirts of town, and he turned onto the interstate. It'd be more smooth driving now, and he glanced over as soon as we merged. "If he asks, how can he make this right?"

I shook my head. "He doesn't have to do a thing for me."

"Cheyenne."

"No, Cut. Listen. It's not me he's wronged. Not in this situation. It's you. He's doing you wrong because you care, because you asked him, because he said he would be better. He didn't do better, for you. You have to answer that, not me. I'm hurting for you, not for me. I'm never going to let them hurt me, so you need to understand that. I'm only hurting because they're hurting you and in the process, they're hurting Hunter."

"Jesus." He shook his head. "When I think I'm starting to get you figured out, then you say things and I'm now looking back at myself and being humbled."

I grinned. "You're good. It's Chad and Deek who are the assholes."

He grinned back, there was still sorrow there.

My heart ached, an invisible hand squeezing it together, but I couldn't do anything there except have a word with Nut-Brother myself. But even then, Chad was going to do what Chad was going to do.

"He's hurt Sasha, too, by all this."

Cut was quiet, turning off on our exit.

I added, shifting to start seeing the line of cars waiting to get into Bresko's, "He's hurting you and her. Two people who care about him the most. She won't tell me what he says, but I know they go back and forth. I also know that I'm the reason."

"Cheyenne."

I corrected, "He's the reason, but you know what I mean. His thoughts, or whatever."

"I still don't like it."

Which was fair.

I didn't know what else to say, but then Cut asked, "So, you finally saw Hunter, huh?"

That was it. Now I *totally* knew what to say and I didn't stop talking until we were pulling up to Bresko's.

OUR TREATMENT WAS a lot of the same when we headed inside.

A water was handed instantly to me.

Cut held my hand the whole time. The difference between our arrival tonight, versus our arrival the other night, was that it seemed there were more people around. Then again, it was Saturday night. I suppose that was bound to happen. I'd been talking about Hunter so much, I hadn't paid attention to how many people were waiting in their cars, but I did remember that there was a larger-than-normal crowd waiting outside the doors.

And as soon as Cut stepped out of his vehicle, word went through them real quick.

I heard Cut's name a lot. The phones went up and the flashes started.

A few people were still in the entryway, and seeing Cut, they came over for autographs.

He glanced at me, but I nodded and slipped away. I was okay with this.

I got it. I really did.

His eyes darkened and his mouth tightened, but that was his only reaction.

They didn't last long.

It seemed the staff was on point.

The autographs were signed. A couple selfies were taken, and they were whisked away by staff. The manager, the same one as the other night, showed us to the box. The exception this time was that a man was waiting inside.

He was standing at the edge, watching the dancers with a drink in hand. The other hand was in his pocket. Dress pants. A white buttoned shirt, that was unbuttoned at the top, and the ends were loosely tucked inside his pants.

"Tanner." Cut strode forward, his hand already out.

"Cut. Hey." The guy turned, and I was greeted with a startling beautiful face. Shaggy blond hair. Dark eyes. He had a whole rakish feel to him, and he was checking me out while skirting between Cut and myself. He indicated me with the drink. "This yours?"

Cut laughed, stepping back. "She is. This is Cheyenne. Cheyenne, this is Tanner. He owns Bresko's."

Oh. Wow.

This guy looked not even a day over thirty and he owned this place?

"Hi. Hello. I'm Cheyenne."

Tanner's mouth twitched. "It's nice to meet you." He said to Cut, "I was in town. Cary told me about your game, that a few of your teammates might be coming out. Thought I'd stick around, see if you were one of them." He nodded to me. "And to meet your woman, it's a double pleasure."

Cut turned to me. "I met Tanner a few years ago."

Tanner took a sip from his drink, his eyes looking me over before his mouth did another twitch. "Cut's being very gratuitous. He met my brother, and I inherited Bresko's through my brother. But," his gaze swept past us and narrowed as he took another sip of his drink. There was a restless vibe to him now, and it crawled up my spine. I wasn't sure if it was in a good way or not. "It's nice that you pretend it's been me this whole time."

"Tanner."

Danger, danger, danger was blaring in my head, but I didn't feel it was in a bad way. That was confusing, but I still moved forward and curled a hand around Cut's arm. I pulled him back, toward me.

Tanner noted the motion. "See. Your woman has good instincts. Listen to her." Then, he looked back over the dance floor, and his eyes seemed to catch on something—or someone. He tossed the rest of his drink back. "It was nice seeing you again, Cut. It was lovely meeting your better half, and now that I've done my owner's duty, there's a certain someone I'm off to go and see." He held his hand out, shaking Cut's, and then moving in and brushing a soft kiss to my cheek. He stepped back. "Enjoy tonight and forget about the game."

He was gone after that.

"Tanner is..." Cut let out another sigh. "Tanner enjoys being a silent owner, like I enjoy being a silent investor." We went to one of the booths and settled in. He turned to me, raking me over. "Chad's on his way, and I need to know how you want me to handle him."

I started to repeat the same, but he held a hand up.

"I know you're going to say he did me wrong, not you, but that's not the truth." But he quieted, studying me, and I felt as if he decided a big decision. He nodded. "Okay. I know what to do."

I needed to say this, put it out there so he knew.

"Most people have walls. That's how they cope in life, and I don't know why they're up. I can only guess, but people like me, there's an openness inside of us. And I know you might be questioning me about Deek and Chad, but those aren't walls that I have for them. It's like inside, I'm flat. I'm open. I have my struggles, and I love my struggles because they make me normal in a way. But I'm just not the same as you or Chad. I don't operate the same. I have certain anchors in my life. Sasha and Melanie are anchors for me. Hunter. Come Our Way and the mission we have, is another for me. It's like a continuous river inside of me, and I'm good to just keep floating along. Most people, home people like you, have walls. In my world, instead of just being on the river, you got a boat and a dock, and you have a home that's off the river. You want to see the river, enjoy the river, but only when you're protected. People like me, we're in the river. And the river is wild, so I guess we're wild, too. There's also freedom there, but you got the danger that goes hand in hand with the freedom. Being safe, that's what 'home' people are. They're safe, but they're boxed in. People like me, we want to be one with the river. Though, every now and then, I'll come up to one of my anchors and I grab hold and I stay there for a bit. I don't slip away because of my anchors. You're one of them. You've almost dammed up my river and I really like that."

There.

If that didn't scare him away...

He looked at me, and his head cocked to the side. It was like he was now seeing me in a different way.

Like he was finally seeing me.

"What does that mean?"

What did that all mean? I had no clue.

Then, I thought about it.

"I think I'm willing to give up the river for you."

His eyes took on a tender and loving look. He softened, and

he leaned toward me. "If you're saying what I think you're saying, then... me too."

I laughed lightly, almost laughing into his mouth because he was right there. "Although, in your world, your river is probably frozen over and you're out there, skating away, playing hockey to your heart's content."

"Cheyenne."

"Hmm?"

"Shut up."

His mouth settled over mine, and I shut up.

36

CUT

Hendrix was eyeing Sasha. And that was not making Chad happy.

My box was next to the one that the Mustangs' players used. I got my own because of my investment so when Chad showed up, I knew things would kick off with a bang tonight. And they had.

Hendrix cozied up to Cassie as soon as he showed up. Cassie had Melanie there, and whatever they'd been sharing with him, he had a whole different look when it came to Sasha.

Sasha, on the other hand, had barely left the booth where she was sitting with Cheyenne and myself.

I left, though.

I left to talk to Hendrix. I left to talk to the others. I left because it seemed that Sasha needed Cheyenne, so I was giving them some time. That's when Chad walked in, and then Hendrix's eyes lit up.

I recognized that look.

It was the same one he got when we had an opponent he really wanted to destroy. Of the other guys from the team, only Crow and Alex came out tonight. They were the single ones, and both were in a far booth with five girls hanging around them. Two to each, and a third going between them. Totally in their element.

Chad headed my way at the same time Hendrix decided to make his move.

He slid into my emptied spot, but I know he did that so Sasha would have to see his face. When I would return, Hendrix would apologize, get up, and sit right next to Sasha instead. He'd make sure his arm was brushing against hers, but he'd wait to see if she was into it. If she wasn't, he'd cut his losses and leave. I'd seen him do it a thousand times.

"Hey." Chad approached, but he was swinging a frown in Sasha's direction right away.

Hendrix lifted his drink to us in a salute, before doing exactly what I thought he would do. He sat in my seat and leaned forward, making sure Sasha had to see him to respond.

"What the hell?"

"How about you and me have our conversation before you head over for that one?"

His gaze swung back to me, and he nodded. "Yeah. You want Cheyenne involved?"

I shook my head. "Cheyenne's made it clear that this is between you and me more than her."

He frowned.

Yeah. It confused me, too, until I thought about what she'd said. Then it made sense and it also made me feel a certain way about her, even more.

Hendrix and the others had joined my box once we got here, so theirs was now empty.

Chad and I had our drinks and headed over. There was a booth overlooking the dance floor, but some of the sound was more muted there. I slid in.

Chad slid across from me, and then he leaned forward, resting his elbows on the table.

I started it. "How about you tell me what went down."

"Didn't Cheyenne?"

"I want to hear your version."

He nodded, his head down before he spoke. "Deek reached out. Thought it'd be fun to catch a game with Hunter and myself. Personally, I think he wanted to talk about Cheyenne and get a feel for what all was going on. He knows things have changed, that you're seeing her now. I mentioned it when I went over to hang out one night with Hunter. But, yeah. He and Hunter were heading for concessions tonight. I came up behind and saw Cheyenne hassling them. I felt a certain way and got in there. I—"

"Hassling?"

Chad quieted. "That's what Deek said. Hunter looked uncomfortable."

"Deek said that? Her father said that?"

"If he said it, I don't know. I've never not believed him."

What the fuck was Deek's problem?

"He's supposed to be her dad, too."

"If she doesn't want him around, he can't force his way in there. You know?"

"What the fuck, Chad? What the actual fuck?"

He quieted again, frowning. He was looking to the right, to the left, up, down. He grabbed his drink, drank all of it in one go, and held it up, motioning for a refill.

He was stalling.

Fine. I'd let him.

For now.

But still, what the fuck?

When the server brought over another one, she slid it over with a smile and included me with that. "You want another, too?"

I shook my head. I'd barely touched my drink.

As soon as she was gone, it was my turn.

"Okay. Let's go over this timeline. Cheyenne's mom goes to rehab."

Chad nodded. "Correct."

"You had any interaction with her before that?"

"Not a one."

"She comes into the house, you're shipped out."

"Hunter too. Mom was worried about..." He trailed off, then added, his eyes darting down, "Cheyenne had a history of shoplifting."

"Shoplifting from stores?"

He frowned, thinking, and then shook his head. "No. The neighbors, I think."

"So, food and water that the neighbors put out for Cheyenne, but she thought she was stealing?"

He opened his mouth, had nothing to say, and shut it.

That's what I thought.

I kept on, "According to Cheyenne, she was never told about Hunter. She found out his name in a meeting with her social worker."

"Really?"

Everything in me went flat. How'd he not know any of this shit? "Thinking about my own brothers, if they existed and I was never told, I'd be going Reaper on someone. That would not fly with me."

He swallowed, reaching for his second drink. "Yeah. I can see what you mean."

Moving forward. "Her mom dies and she stays with her uncle. That ever hit you weird?"

His mouth opened, again.

His mouth shut, again.

He had nothing to say, *again*.

Except, "What are you getting at, Cut? You want me to light up the torches or something? I'm not going to do that. Deek's not my bio dad, but I gotta say, he's way better than the dad I did have.

That guy was an asshole, and I love my mom. She did the best she could for us. If you're trying to insinuate things a certain way, then back up because you're wrong."

I was out of patience. "Cheyenne doesn't hassle. Ever. She runs. She hides. She doesn't hassle. You spend more than two minutes around her, and not fucking glaring at her, you'd wake the fuck up. You're dead wrong about her, and I don't know what Deek and Natalie were thinking when—"

He shot up in his seat. "They were scared of her, okay?! Scared. I would be, too. I heard them talking to her social worker. They never knew I did, but I overheard the whole thing. Her file, she was crazy, and she spent more time on the streets than in an actual loving home. Think on that. Think about what that type of environment will produce. You want that coming into your house? No, thank you. I get where Deek and my mom are coming from. They were worried about their family. They just wanted to protect us. There's nothing wrong with that."

I had to take a beat, because I couldn't believe what I was hearing.

Their family.

Protect 'us.'

Crazy.

Streets.

'You want *that* coming into your house?'

That. Not her.

He was set in stone.

He'd never get it right.

Deek and Natalie were so ingrained in him.

This was the same guy who helped check fuckers on the ice for me. He slept at my house. Ate at my parents' table. He wrestled with my brothers. Played video games with us. I got drunk with this guy. Knew all about the girls he liked and the girls who liked him, and now I was staring at him and wondering where'd that guy go?

But he was the same. There was just this other side in him, one that wasn't meshing with me.

"You're quiet." That was Chad speak for 'what are you thinking?'

"Yeah. I am." That was code for 'I'm not liking what I'm hearing.'

His face twisted up in anger, and he jerked forward, hitting the table. He didn't notice. Both his drink and mine spilled over. He didn't notice that either.

"I don't understand our issue here. What's your problem? You want me to be nice to Cheyenne? Fine. I'll be fucking perfect to her. Polite. I'll open the door for her. Want me to bow to her?"

I was shaking my head, because Cheyenne's words were coming back to me, and she was right.

"She knew."

He stopped, a whole half-sneer showing. "She knew what?"

"She told me that you weren't hurting her."

He started to scoff, looking out over the club.

I added, "You're hurting me."

He looked back, the scoff disappearing.

"You're hurting Hunter."

His Adam's apple bobbed up and down.

"And you're hurting Sasha."

A scowl started. "I don't get this. I've fucked chicks you didn't like—"

"It's not about that. It's not about you not liking Cheyenne. It's about you being totally wrong about someone all of us care about. You like Sasha. I can tell."

"Yeah, but—"

"No buts. You do. You say you do, then you say you don't, then you're breaking up with her, and then you're screwing her brains out."

"Nice, Cut."

"That's my point. You care enough, you care about how I'm

talking about her. And I'm not even on the same level as how you're talking about Cheyenne. 'That.' You called her 'that.'"

He flinched.

I added, "You know the difference between how my family would've handled Cheyenne versus how yours did? My mom wouldn't have looked at Cheyenne as a potential threat coming into the house. She would've seen a girl whose mom hadn't been there for her, and she would've cried for her. Welcome fucking arms, man. Instead, Natalie probably hid the silverware. Two different drastic ways, and I can see that you're *still* not getting it."

"I—"

But he wasn't. A whole blankness came over him when I was trying to explain it.

"What do you want from me?" He threw his hand in the air.

"Nothing. You can't change your thoughts or your behaviors, and that's what I'd need from you." I started to stand up.

"Wait, wait, wait." Chad did, too, hurrying to block me from walking away. An edge of panic came over his face. He held his hands up. "Tell me what to do and I'll do it."

"You're a hundred percent wrong about Cheyenne, but *you* need to realize it. And it's not about you liking the girl I'm falling in love with."

His eyebrows shot all the way up, and he rocked backwards.

"She's Hunter's sister. Don't hurt him because you're wrong in the head. And fuck's sake, that's her father whose saying this shit about her. Think on that. Her father. If your dad said that shit about you—"

Chad blinked a few times. "My dad is an asshole, though. He's said and done worse."

"Was he right about what he said about you?"

A whole new beast came over Chad. A new scowl, but this one had more heat to it. "Fuck no, he wasn't."

"That's Deek and Cheyenne, and man, Deek is so far wrong

about her, that it's not even sad. It's just wrong. And you're wrong for taking up his side."

"Deek's been there for me."

"So have empathy for the kid he hasn't been there for, and you know what? If you can't see the similarities between your dickhead dad and how Deek is being regarding Cheyenne, then I don't know what to say or do."

"Does she want him to grovel or something? He paid for her college."

I stilled, giving him a whole new look because was he actually being this stupid on purpose.

I said, going with him on this one, "You're right. I mean, he bought her off in a way. What right does she have to push for a relationship with her brother? Her college got paid off. How dare she?"

"Exactly!"

I stared at him. Hard.

Chad frowned, and I could see the thoughts going on in his head.

He said a second later, "You don't actually believe that."

"Not a *fucking* chance in hell." My blood was boiling.

I never wanted to put hands on my best friend, but I did tonight.

"My parents paid for my college, too. They'd never think of using that as a string to control me."

"Well, Deek isn't—"

"It doesn't matter. Maybe he had a moment of conscience when Donna was in rehab? Maybe that's why he let her move into the house? Maybe he decided against it later? I don't know. I'm just looking at a guy I thought was like a brother to me, refer-ring to someone I'm falling in love with as '*that*,' and he's got no clue why I'm not down for it."

He closed his eyes, his body weaving backwards a little before he opened them again.

"Cut," a raspy whisper from him. "I'm thinking I might have gotten a few things wrong over the years."

I leaned in, done with this conversation. "No. Shit. Me too."

I headed back to my box and over to the booth where Cheyenne was sitting. Her gaze found mine instantly, and her eyebrows pulled together. She looked behind me, then back to mine.

I turned, too, but the box was empty.

The door was just closing.

Chad had bounced.

I went over, thinking what a shittastic ending it was to this whole day, but Hendrix got up. He held out his fist to mine, a drunk smile on his face, and I met it with mine before he did what I thought he would. He moved in and he was all in Sasha's area.

But she was for it, judging from how she snuggled into his side.

I slid in and Cheyenne moved over to me. "You okay?"

I didn't respond. Too much shit was upside down, and I didn't care who saw us. I lifted her up, sitting her on my lap, and she leaned back against me.

This made the shittastic day a helluva lot better.

37

CHEYENNE

I was feeling all warm and toasty, and that was because of Cut.

We stayed at Bresko's for two hours, and he held me the whole time.

Warm. Toasty. So Cut.

Sasha had been flirting with Hendrix all night, and there was some sadness in her eyes. I dubbed them 'Chad eyes' because she only looked that way when he was around or when he was supposed to be around. By the end of the night, I was noticing her 'Hendrix eyes' were a whole lot happier. She was giggling, and Sasha never giggled.

Ever.

This was secret agent-like Sasha. Strip club, no-nonsense business owner Sasha. Giggling was not in her list of abilities until tonight. And she blushed. I *never* saw that. Melanie blushed. I got flushed sometimes, but that was the extent. Russian-like Sasha, no blush.

The world was officially tipped upside down.

But then there was Melanie.

After the tense talk between Cassie and Melanie, the two were good. They were holding hands, sneaking kisses, and they were laughing at whatever Hendrix was saying.

It was a good night. For me. Not for Cut.

I waited until we got to his house, and we decided on his house because we were already outside the city limits. A quick swing around and we were closer to his place than going into downtown for my apartment. I was also secretly planning on stealing another one of his hockey shirts, and by stealing, I meant to say that I would ask which one I could have because keeping a boyfriend's shirt—*especially* a pro-hockey player's shirt—was every girl's age-old tradition. That or a never used pair of his boxers.

Heading inside, he waited until I went past to put in the alarm code.

"You want a water or anything?"

I shook my head, biding my time.

His jaw was clenched.

He had held me most of the night, but he was tense, so I knew something was up.

Letting out a sigh, he took my hand and led me upstairs. We went to his second floor, and once in the room, he let go of my hand and went into his closet.

I went to the bathroom, taking my time to do my business and wash up.

When I opened the door, he had a shirt on the bed. "If you wanted to wear that to bed?"

I took it, seeing it was one of his muscle shirts and squeaked on the inside. *Of course* I'd wear this to bed.

I took off my clothes, leaving my underwear on and pulled on the shirt.

He came back out of the closet, and his eyes darkened when he saw me. "I, uh...I bought a toothbrush for you. It was in the bathroom."

"I saw it, figured it was for me."

"Good." He was only wearing some sweatpants, and they were of the softest material. I'd seen him wear them before, and my hands itched to feel them every time since. I was also itching to feel them because I wanted to take them off of him.

He was standing in the room, half-torn between his thoughts and whatever he was about to do now.

No shirt.

Barefoot.

His hair all sticking up and messy.

And those pants riding low over his V...my mouth was watering.

He was so not only an idea to get me through life. Not because of his outsides, but I was just enjoying those right now. A lot.

I really did love Cut at first sight. I'd just been too young to know what to do about it.

"Cut."

"Hmmm?" He blinked, refocusing on me, and those eyes fell to my legs. "God, you're gorgeous."

Warm. Toasty. Again.

But I had to focus. He'd been tense for a reason.

"What happened tonight?"

"We lost a game."

"Cut."

He sat on the edge of the bed, and I moved up behind him. My legs went around him, and I wrapped my arms around his shoulders, looping over the front of him. I propped my chin on his shoulder. "I saw Chad show up. I saw you guys going to the other box for a talk, and he didn't come back with you."

His head lowered, resting on my arm, and he reached up to lace his fingers with mine. His thumb started rubbing back and forth over my palm.

"Can we just leave it how it is?"

"You know anything he said won't hurt me."

He drew in another breath of air, going rigid.

I moved my legs so they were completely around him, and he hunched forward. I was fully plastered against his back, and his other hand went to my legs. He began running his finger up and down on the underside of my thigh.

Tingles were following in his trail, but I was holding my response back.

I knew that he needed to get this out, whatever it was.

"Cut."

Another sigh. "I might be losing my best friend."

My eyes closed.

Sadness billowed through me, and I rested my cheek against the back of his shoulder blades. "I'm sorry."

"I know." He squeezed my hand a little. "But that's on him, not you and not me. And honestly, this could've come out later down the line."

"This?"

"Whatever kind of thought process he's got inside of him where he couldn't see you were a fucking person."

"Oh. That."

"Yeah. That."

Damn.

I didn't want Chad to hurt anyone I cared about because of me, but it was happening.

"I'm sorry again."

His hand stopped and then flexed over my thigh. "It's nothing for you to be sorry about. It's Chad."

"You can't make him think a certain way."

"It's a bit more than that. He needs to see you as a person, and he doesn't. I don't understand why he doesn't."

"I know people think certain ways about people who come from my beginnings, but I can't explain the reason why they think like that."

"Yeah." His back rose and fell again, and he went back to rubbing the inside of my palm against his chest. "We'll just deal with it, whatever happens."

There were no words because I couldn't take away his pain, like he couldn't take away how I was raised. But I could do other things and I could say other words to maybe replace the hurt. My cheek against his back, I whispered, "You weren't an idea for me."

Saying it in person was a whole lot different than saying it over text. He needed to hear me say it tonight.

He sucked in his breath, his hand holding mine in an almost cement grip.

I kept on, "I think I did love you when I saw you."

I didn't think. I knew. I know.

"Are you telling me you love me now?"

My hand flexed under his now, and I went rigid, my thighs gripping him hard. And then, my eyes closing as I said it. "Yes."

Please don't leave me now.

Please don't— He twisted, his hands went under my arms and he lifted me clear. He stood, but he was moving us back on the bed. His eyes were hooded and dark, and he didn't want any more words.

I was laid down. He came down on top, his mouth was on mine, and he was hungry.

He was commanding.

He was demanding.

Oh yes, I definitely didn't think he was going to leave.

Then, I answered him back.

His tongue swept in, and my toes curled.

There were no words to process this.

None at all.

He was touching me. He was kissing me. Loving me. And it felt like, finally.

Finally we were one.

Finally we were whole.

Finally I was with who I'd been waiting for all my life.

Finally.

I was lost in every touch, caress, whisper, every sensation. All of it. As the clothes were removed. As he moved over me. As I felt his arms, his chest, his hands. As I felt him slide a finger inside of me.

Our gazes were locked as he thrust inside, out, back in, and he moved his finger around. A second finger. I wanted him, but I was also helpless against the sensations he was building inside of me, and it was only after I climaxed that he repositioned and reaching down, I caught his hands.

I laced our fingers and he pushed inside.

I moaned, my head falling back. My throat was exposed and as he began moving in and out, his lips fell there and he was kissing me, tasting me all over again.

Every move, we were together.

My legs were wound around his waist.

Our hands stayed together, and he pinned them next to my head.

As he lifted himself up, going for a deeper angle, going harder, my eyes opened again. He was right there, staring into me. He was seeing me, all of me.

I was splayed out for him, for him to take, freely and willingly, and his eyes darkened as he began moving harder, faster.

It was building. Building.

Priming.

I was right there.

Then, he held a second, and I cried out.

Another thrust, slower and farther than he'd been and I was pushed over. I fell over the edge, my entire body exploding in his arms. The edges of my eyes blurred, but I kept seeing him. Watching him. He held my gaze as he waited for me, then he moved in and out until he groaned, his head falling to my shoulder as he was coming with me.

I couldn't move.

I didn't want to.

We were in a cocoon and it was perfect.

Then I heard against my neck, his breath tickling me, "I love you, too."

38

CHEYENNE

I wasn't a snack person, but I woke up with racing thoughts a couple hours later and I knew I was done for. I had to get up, eat some sugar, and head back to bed. Sometimes it was the only thing that worked. Cut's arm was laying over me, so I slid out, felt around for my phone and found the rest of my clothes.

I'd learned that Cut didn't usually sleep hard, but he always did after a game. I wasn't too worried about waking him up as I slipped into some clothes and padded barefoot across the room.

A few steps creaked and the door squeaked a tiny bit, but I waited, and he didn't wake up.

I was good to go, and speaking of that, I had no clue where to go. I thought he kept a kitchenette on his floor, but I wasn't sure. I didn't want to go searching around with my phone lit up, feeling like the criminal my father and Nut-Brother thought of me. I headed downstairs to the actual kitchen.

Flipping on the lights once I was in there, I knew I was far enough away so I wouldn't wake Cut up. After that, it was snack time.

They had pizza.

Chips. Old nachos—gross.

Then there was a ton of salad, green vegetables. Yogurt. Chicken. Lots of chicken. Some seafood in the freezer. Lots of fruit. Protein powder on the counter.

A container of old sloppy joe.

I was sensing a theme, and I was pretty sure I could identify which was Chad's, and which food was Cut's.

Finding some whole wheat bread, and some natural peanut butter and honey, I was making myself a sandwich when a car pulled up outside Chad's side of the house.

A car door slammed shut.

A stifled shout, and then the car backed up and headed back where it came from.

I sighed.

That was Chad, and he'd had to get a ride home.

That meant Drunk Chad was coming inside.

The door opened. I heard a series of beeps and then a long beep.

The lights switched on after that, flooding the hallway that connected the two homes.

I heard some keys being tossed somewhere.

A yawn that grew louder as he came down to the kitchen.

His hand was in his hair as he stopped, and he had to blink a few times. His whole body swayed back and forth from the effort.

He scowled. "You."

I scowled back. "You."

He frowned, blinking a few times. He rubbed at his eyes. "Are you real?"

Oh...kay. This was too good not to play along.

"No. Are you?"

"What?"

"What?" Me.

"You're Cheyenne."

"You're lying."

Another frown, and he shook his head. "Wait. What?"

"What?"

He looked around. "What's going on here?"

"What's happening here?"

He pointed at me. "You're fucking with me. Stop fucking with me."

"You're fucking with *me*."

Another frown, this one deeper and he rubbed at his eyes. "I'm so confused. What's going on here? Why are you here? Wait. You're banging my best friend. That's why you're here." He lumbered over, walking like he was an overgrown zombie, and he threw open the fridge. He stared inside, and spotting the pizza, he grabbed the whole container.

Then, we had another moment.

He stared at me, him still holding the pizza, and he didn't know what to do.

I could see the confusion on his face.

Giving in, I took the container and motioned to the table. "Go and sit. I'll heat this up."

"I don't heat up my pizza."

"You eat it cold?"

He scowled again. "What? No. Who said that?"

So drunk. I motioned to the table again. "Go. Sit. I'll take care of you."

"Why would you do that?"

But he sat and I didn't answer. No way I was going to have a talk with him at this hour of night, and when he was this wasted.

"You took my best friend from me."

Apparently, he wanted to have this conversation.

Ignoring him, I put his pizza on a plate and put it in the microwave. A good fifty seconds would heat it up, but not too hot for him. After that, I spotted a canned coffee in the fridge and poured it into a glass. Taking that, along with a bottle of water, I put both in front of him.

He scowled at those, too. "I don't want those."

"There's alcohol in them."

"Oh." He grabbed the coffee first.

The microwave beeped, so I grabbed the pizza next and put it beside the bottled water.

He was finishing the coffee, all in one go, and put the can in the middle of the table. He motioned to it. "Those are my favorites."

I stood there, uncertain what to do.

He paused, stared at me, then looked back at the kitchen. "Go get your samich. Sit wid me."

I did, more because I wanted to see what else he'd say. I wasn't sitting here because I cared about Chad. Because I didn't.

I didn't care. At all.

I was just curious. That's it.

I barely touched my samich, I was so engrossed in what he was going to do.

He picked up a slice of pizza and took a bite. "Damn. That's good." He scowled at me. "You werrright. The pizzaisbedder-headdup."

Uh-huh. I had no idea what he just said.

But I took a bite of my samich.

They'd forever be samiches in my mind now. I'd share that with Chad someday, probably on his deathbed.

He went back to scowling at me. "Why'd you take my best friend away? He was mine. Not yours."

I sighed. He was a confrontational drunk.

"Arend you gonna answer me back?"

I narrowed my eyes at him. "You know who else liked to have drunk conversations? When she wasn't passed out from drugs, I mean." I barely paused. "My mother."

He flinched, then started rubbing at his forehead. "Donna."

"Her drink of choice was vodka. What's yours?"

Another frown. Another flinch. He kept rubbing at his forehead. "I'm not an alcoholic. Is that what you're saying?"

"Not at all."

"You're implying it."

"Are you?"

"Am I what?"

"Are you implying it?"

It was taking such effort for him to enunciate his words clearly.

I was enjoying his struggle.

"What?"

"I'm confused." That was me. I was playing again.

He shook his head all around, wiping his hand down the side of his face. "You're messing with me because I've been drinking."

"I couldn't tell." A straight face on me.

He stared at me, his eyes narrowed. He couldn't tell either.

He rolled his eyes. "If you're trying to ingratia—ingradia—ingracia—if you're trying to make me like you, it's not working. I can tell you're making fun of me."

Still a straight face. "I would never do that."

He paused, studying me, and his shoulders rose and fell back down. He reached for another piece of pizza. He'd forgotten his first one. "I'm going to give you some hard truths. Cut will never love you. Never ever. He'll always look at you, and think, 'she's the bitch who made me lose my best friend.' And you know what? It's going to happen. He thinks we're done being friends because of me, but it's you. It's all you. It's your fault, and you want to know why?"

He was a mean drunk.

Still deadpan. "No." I leaned forward. "Tell me. Please."

"Because you're nothing. *You're* nothing. You come from *nothing.* Your mom was a junkie whore, and that's who you come from. Everything comes around, and when you're old and alone, you'll be back on the streets. You'll be the one with a needle in her arm, and you'll be spreading your legs for your ex-husband's newest stepson like your mother did for me—"

"Shut the fuck up," a snarl ripped through the room.

I couldn't move.

Up until then, I'd been impassive, not taking anything Chad said to heart, but then he said that.

That.

And...

I—

Cut was furious. I felt his anger slapping against me from the room. It was rolling off of him in waves, but then my mind went blank.

SOMEONE WAS SHOUTING.

There was a scream, a primal scream.

A TUGGING AT MY HANDS.

"Let him go, Cheyenne. Let him go."

Cut's voice sounded like he was submerged in water.

Why did he sound so far away? He was standing right next to me.

I WAS RIPPED AWAY from someone.

Something? I didn't know.

My hands were bleeding. I recognized the feel of warm blood.

I saw it, too, lifting up my hands.

Blood trickled down. It was coming from my fingers. My nails.

Why were my nails—? One had been ripped off.

That didn't make sense.

"You're not going to say a thing."

Cut was angry. He was back to snarling, and he was sounding barely restrained.

"Are you kidding me? That bitch tore chunks out of my throat."

"You're not going to say a damned thing."

"Cut!"

"I mean it, Chad. You talk, and you're not going to enjoy what happens next for you."

I blinked, focusing back in again.

They were huddled together across the room.

I was shaking. Why was I shaking?

Cut looked over at me, cursing under his breath.

He started for me.

"Is that a threat?" Chad rose up from where he'd either been leaning or sitting. I couldn't tell.

Cut never spared him a look, but he said, "You're damn right it is."

"Babe."

We were in his bathroom.

I was on the counter. He was standing between my legs.

A dab.

I hissed, feeling the burn.

He was cleaning my wounds.

It started to come back to me then.

I looked up as he was holding my hand, and our eyes met.

I asked, "I attacked him?"

Cut never answered me. He didn't need to.

I knew.

39

CUT

C had told me an hour after I got Cheyenne to bed.

I went back down, sat across from him, and said, "You talk or I call my lawyer tonight to start the ball rolling on how to make you sell your half of the house to me."

He stared at me, long and hard.

There were red marks around his neck. Scratches from Cheyenne. Blood seeped out over the dried blood already, and his entire neck would be black and blue tomorrow.

Fuck.

I grimaced because he could take pictures, if he hadn't already, and I couldn't promise Cheyenne would be protected.

He let out, shaking his head, "You're going to regret choosing her. She's got a wild side to her, and she'll never not have that in her. It was how she grew up. She had to be wild to survive, but that gets in them people, and that's just how they are the rest of their lives."

"You should stop talking about Cheyenne...seriously...and tell me about her mother instead."

He looked to argue.

"Now."

There was nothing to argue with me. He talked or I left.

Another beat where he studied me, as if he were gauging me, but then he gave in. He told me the story.

It was after Cheyenne had stayed with him. Deek wanted him to run over to their house, check on Cheyenne. Deek never told him why he wanted him to do that, but he did. He went after one of our hockey practices, and instead of Cheyenne, he found Donna.

She wanted a fix, so she needed money.

He said, "She offered to sleep with me for cash."

"And you did that?"

"I was in high school. I was young and horny, and Donna was hot. Yeah. I did, and I've hated myself for it ever since."

Jesus.

"Did you give her money?"

"It wasn't like I paid for sex, but I felt bad and she was asking. Said she didn't have anything for food for her and Cheyenne. I gave her what I had in my wallet. Fifty bucks."

"She'd been sober before that?"

"Yeah. It was after her rehab stint. She was really going nuts for a hit."

Christ.

"How soon was it before she overdosed?"

I waited, hoping...

Then, a soft, "Fuck."

I stood, moving my chair back.

Chad looked up at me. "What are you going to do?"

I didn't know, but I took his phone. He had no camera, and he was clueless how to use a computer.

"Why are you taking that?"

"So you don't do anything stupid with it, stupid that you and I both will regret later on."

"Oh."

I shoved his phone in my pocket and turned.

"Cut?"

I'd been heading for the stairs. "What?"

"What's going to happen with you and me?"

This was what he wanted to ask now? I gave him the only answer I could.

"I don't know."

40

CHEYENNE

I woke up tasting peanut butter and regret.

I'd like to say the peanut butter was the strongest taste, but it wasn't.

"Hey."

I looked over.

Cut was sitting on the edge of the bed, dressed in his sweats and shirt. He'd showered and he was eyeing my hands as he asked, "How are your hands?"

I flexed them, and hissed. "They hurt."

I wanted to pretend that I didn't know the reason they hurt, but I couldn't. My brain thought of everything and remembered everything, and I just wanted it to shut up. Today would be the best day for that miracle to happen.

"I asked Chad to leave."

"What?"

"Correction." He reached for a coffee mug on his nightstand and handed it to me. As I sat and took it, he added, "I packed a bag for him, woke him up, and shipped him out of here. He should be on the plane and heading for Vancouver as we speak."

I swallowed over a knot. Damn. "You sent him to Vancouver?"

"The team has a timeshare there and I wanted him gone for a while."

He sent him out of the country, and then I spied the phone on the nightstand beside his phone. "Whose is that?"

He gave me a dark look. "I packed a cheap throw-away phone in his bag. He'll find out when he gets there that it's not his phone I said I packed."

"You lied?"

Another dark look, and if possible, this last one was even darker. "I know Chad. He won't be motivated to buy a camera. He won't even think about buying one, and if he tries to take pictures of his neck with his phone, then he's an idiot. The quality will be shit."

Oh. Whoa. He did that all for me.

Yes. He was so not an idea.

I was fully and completely in love with this man.

I murmured, "Thank you."

He nodded. "What do you need to help you today? I don't want you thinking about what happened last night."

That was an easy answer. "My girls. And work."

"Work?"

I nodded. "I'll work the line. I do that sometimes. Boomer knows if I need to quiet my mind, I'll do whatever he needs, and I'll listen to music. I'll put headphones on. And after work, I'll go to Sasha's. They'll take care of me."

He nodded, some of the tension leaving him then. "Good. You have good friends."

"I have the best friends."

"Yeah…"

Crap. "Sorry. Bad choice of words."

"Can you handle being around him?"

I frowned at how startled and abrupt his voice came out with that question. "What?"

"He's like a brother to me. I hate what he did. I loathe it, and I loathe him, but I've never been good at throwing people to the side. So, if I didn't? Could you handle being around him? Knowing what he did?"

Oooh. He was talking about my mom, not about what I did to his best friend.

I was already nodding as I scooted over to him, holding the coffee steady. "Of course. I don't like the words that are usually used, but my mom—she did sleep around. A lot. She did it for drugs. She did it because she liked sex. And yeah, I know she did it for money. I'm assuming that's what happened. He showed up, looking for me or something? It's the only thing that makes sense, unless she went looking for an easy score, but I don't see her doing that. She liked to stay to our neighborhood and had her regulars. I'm guessing he knocked or walked in, she wanted drugs, and it's obvious that Chad had money. And I know my mom was good-looking. She had a lot of boyfriends, some bad, but some not so bad. She was beautiful. I'm not upset at Chad for sleeping with my mom. I reacted last night because of how he talked about her, and how he was saying I was the same. It's a trigger for me. Always was, but I haven't gotten in a fight over her for a long time." I laughed, uneasily. "I should be more ashamed that I'm in my older twenties and I got in a physical fight, but I'm not. Not really."

His head dropped a whole inch as he was staring at me. "Are you serious? You're not even bothered by what happened last night?"

I laughed, sipping the coffee. It was good, really good. "You don't know what life is like with a junkie. That would've been a tame night for us."

"What would be a bad night?"

I shrugged. Another sip of coffee. "Me being taken away. Someone in jail. Someone in the hospital where it's a multi-day stay. Or waking up and being told you gotta run from a local drug dealer because they're going to kill you. Those would be considered bad nights."

"Holy shit, Cheyenne."

I shrugged. A third sip. This was so good. "It is what it is."

"So, me sending Chad away—"

"Probably for the best, because you're right. He would've taken pictures of his neck or called someone, and they would've wanted to know what happened, and I'd be arrested. Not good."

"You agree I was right to send him away?"

"You were right, and being smart, and ..." Damn. He did that for me. I was so in love with him that I was becoming mushy. My voice cut out as I said, "Only people who've ever done something like that for me have been Sasha and Melanie."

His eyes held mine, darkening and softening. "Come here."

I clambered over to him.

He swept up the coffee, placing it on the nightstand, and in the next second, I was airborne. I landed with him on top of me and his mouth was on mine, and this was the *best* way to turn my brain off.

41

CHEYENNE

There'd been talk of a group picnic. That obviously didn't happen.

Instead, I headed home for some Zen time. I did a hemp facial mask, saged the crap out of my apartment (because that made sense to me), and did yoga with some meditation. Melanie came over ready for some yoga, too, so why not? I did another session, but yeah; the second round of yoga was hella hard. I was more into the meditation that round, and because it seemed to fit the theme, we hit Sasha's afterwards.

Juna was happy to see Melanie happy. There was no upside down shimmy this time.

Cassie came later in the evening, but only to pick Melanie up. They headed off after a drink.

My phone buzzed later on.

Cut: How are you?

Me: Good. Surprisingly. At Sasha's.

Cut: Girl time tonight?

I was down for how he didn't seem to mind how much time I spent with my girls.

Me: Yeah. You?

Cut: I've got some business I can do, then head back to the arena tomorrow.

Sasha asked, "That your man?"

I gave her a look. It was more of a twisted-crooked grin.

She grunted. "Still weird to think of him like that?"

"We spent the day apart. Do I offer to go there? Do I ask him to come to my place? I don't know how to do this."

"You guys are new. Do you want to see him tonight?"

But my phone buzzed again.

Cut: Did you drive to Sasha's?

Me: Yes.

Cut: Let me know when you're leaving. I can follow you back to your place? Or do you want to stay at my place?

Even with 'the Chad thing' last night, I liked his place. It was peaceful.

Me: Yours, but I'll be fine. If you're worried about safety, I can get one of the guys to walk me to my car and I'll head home, get a bag and head to your place.

Cut: You sure?

I liked that he was caring about me. I liked it a lot.

Me: Yes.

Cut: Text me when you're leaving the club, tho.

Me: Will do. I'll go in an hour, I think. I want to talk to Sasha a bit.

Cut: Have you told her what happened last night?

Me: Not yet.

Cut: Text if you need anything, okay? Chad didn't open up about him and Sasha, so I don't know what's going on with them. I do know it bothered him to see her liking Hendrix.

Me: Good!

Sasha picked up her glass. It was brandy tonight and swirled it around before gesturing to me. "You seem happy, though."

I nodded. "I am, which scares me."

A soft chuckle from her. "I hear you."

"Okay. We need to talk about The Chad."

An instant sneer from her, but she was trying not to laugh. "Fucking Chad."

"Fucking Chad."

We both laughed, but then it was serious time.

She was eyeing me, as she sipped more of her brandy. "Why don't I have a good hunch about this conversation?"

"Because... because you're probably not going to enjoy it."

She raised an eyebrow, but other than that, there was no reaction from her. Just a simple eyebrow raise, and another sip of her drink, and she was so cool. Like ice.

"What's going on with you guys?" We had talked before about him. There'd been a three-hour phone call, but I needed the most updated update.

Her face shuddered now. It was brief and slight, but I saw it. She was putting up the guards, and I ached that she even had to do that.

"Sash."

She clipped her head to the side. "No. Not for that asshole." She drained her drink and shoved the empty glass to the end of the table. A beat later, it was swept up by one of her bouncers. Another one would be coming to replace it. It was the system she had down pat. A hard look came over her eyes, but she blinked, focused on me, and she softened. "Great sex. I thought I might've loved him, but he's not the guy, Shy."

I was aching again.

She was my girl. She deserved the best fucking guy there was for her.

"There's not much more to it. He'd reach out. We'd have sex. He'd say that it was a mistake—" Oh, that dickwipe! "—then he'd reach out again, said he made a mistake, and it was just a repeat. The longest we lasted was two days, but same thing." She closed her eyes, and when they opened, there was a haunted look that she masked quickly. Same Sash. "It is what it is. I'm done with him."

I waited a beat.

Her gaze lifted to mine. "You can say whatever you'd like. If you two made up and he realized he's the biggest douche in the world and now wants to be your brother, then you've got my blessings. But him and me, we're six feet under, Babe. I'm sorry. There's no going back for either of us."

Some of the tension I'd been holding lifted.

That was going to make this a bit easier. And there was no easy way to smooth into this, so I just ripped off the Band-Aid.

"I found out that he slept with my mother all those years ago and I attacked him, but now I'm thinking about it, and that would've made my mom a sex offender."

Oh. Crap.

There was so much there to grimace about.

Sasha's eyebrows pulled together. "*What?*"

"Yeah." My gaze fell to the table. That really was making my stomach do figure-eights, and not in the happy way.

"Chad and your *mom*?"

"The Chad."

She grunted. "Fucking Chad."

I snickered because I couldn't help myself. "That just took on a whole different meaning."

A third grunt from her. "Am I supposed to feel bad for him?"

"I don't think so? I mean, he gave her money afterwards so she could get a fix."

"Gross. Fucking Chad."

Yeah. "Fucking Chad."

"I feel bad for all other Chads out there in the world now."

"Me too."

Her new brandy came over and she reached for it. Settling back in, she cocked her head to the side. "Wait. When did this happen?"

"Last night."

"At your guy's house?"

"I got up for a snack. Chad came in drunk. You know the side where usually people are lovey-dovey when they're drunk and they're just assholes when they're sober?"

She cocked up an eyebrow, her arm resting on the back of the booth and she was turned toward me.

"Not for Chad. Turns out he's nicer when he's sober."

"Damn."

"Yep."

"Did Cut hear any of it?"

"Well..." This was the part where I told her what really went down, on the whole me going for his jugular. And then I waited because it was complete silence at the table afterwards.

She took a breath, blinked a few times, and then drained her second brandy. "Damn again."

"Yep. Again."

"He's gone?"

I nodded.

Her eyes slid sideways to me. "And you have his phone?"

I met her gaze, also sideways. "I mean, it's at Cut's house."

"You're saying that we can get to it?"

"Why?"

"Because I might know his passcode."

My mouth dropped.

I had no words. I didn't know if I should be excited or wary.

Forget that.

Excitement. All day every day.

"What do you want to do?"

"What do you think?" Sasha just gave me a knowing grin.

Oh yeah. We were about to get into some trouble.

"Are we too old to do stuff like this?" I said this as I was sliding out of the booth.

Sasha was right behind me. She snorted. "Two words: toilet paper. Let's fuck this guy's life up a bit."

ME: You at your place right now?
   Cut: I headed to Hendrix's. You done already?
   Me: Nope. I think it might be a late night.
   Cut: Okay. Have fun.

WE WERE IN MATILDA'S, and I put my phone back in my purse just as the light turned green.

I was driving this time, and I glanced at Sasha. "I feel like I should tell Cut what we're going to do."

"Plausible deniability."

Right. That was a good way to think of it.

I added, "I'll tell him later."

Sasha's head bobbed up and down. "Later."

Like next year later, maybe.

"You know the code to get in?"

My stomach dipped. "Yes. And I know where they keep the extra key."

A smile from her. "Excellent." A beat later, "Plausible deniability."

"Plausible deniability."

KOALA SISTER: Um.
   Koala Brother: Um what?
   Koala Sister: Um um.
   Koala Brother: OMG, Cheyenne. Just say it.

Koala Sister: Nothing. Love you. Miss you. How are you?

Koala Brother: Dude.

Koala Sister: DUDE!

Koala Brother: Same, by the way.

Koala Sister: Dude.

42

CUT

"That was your girl?" Hendrix asked, coming back with a beer in hand.

He handed it over, sitting down on his couch.

I took it. "She's doing a girls' night."

Hendrix frowned, taking a sip of his beer. "I had a buddy who always thought 'girls' night' was code for 'I'm going out drinking with my girls and I'm going to cheat on you.'"

"I don't think that's what this is. Cheyenne's not like that."

"Still." Another sip and he shrugged. "He found out after they broke up that his girl had been cheating on him the whole time. Screwed him up for life."

"That's a seriously depressing story."

Another sip. Another shrug. "Just saying it how it is."

"Girls' night for them is at Sasha's club. Where other girls dance."

He grinned. "That's awesome. You got a cool chick."

"Speaking of—"

"Nope." Beer in hand, he pointed at me, shaking his head. "Don't go there."

"Where?"

"I'm into the Not-Russian, but we're not those guys. We don't talk about chicks with each other, or our feelings about them."

"I was going to ask if you wanted to go down to Come Our Way on Friday for a volunteer day. We're back then and have a half-day. You mentioned doing an extra day."

"Don't I feel like a dumbass now."

I grinned. "I never did it the first round. Thought it'd be cool to go before the charity event."

"That's Saturday night, isn't it?"

"Yeah."

His eyes narrowed and he took a slow sip from his beer. "I'm in." Then, he eyed me. "Be honest, dude. You're going to check out that Dean guy, aren't you?"

I never answered him. It wasn't that I didn't trust Cheyenne. I did, but he was there and he worked with her and ... I'd be checking this guy out.

He laughed. I didn't have to answer him.

We went over to the hockey setup he had in his apartment.

I went first, hitting the puck into the net and the sirens lit up.

43

CHEYENNE

The mission was set.

Get inside the house, get Chad's phone, and fuck up his life. Those were more Sasha's words, but I was along for the ride. I was an eager accomplice. We pulled up to the house. The lights were off. Everything seemed easy enough, right?

Wrong.

As we were heading inside, a pair of headlights swept over us and we both froze.

A second later, the car parked and the lights went out.

I was sweating out my own piss because I'd have to lie to Cut, and I didn't want to lie to him. But two car doors shut, and we saw two slender figures heading our way.

"What the hell? You're doing a Possible Mission without me?!"

I relaxed. It was Melanie.

Then, I stiffened. It was Melanie and someone else.

"Who's with you?"

Possible Mission was the name we used for missions just like this, and we had a strict three-person attendance rule. Sasha.

Melanie. Myself. No one else was allowed on a Possible Mission. We also had a *Fight Club* rule where we didn't talk about Possible Missions outside of the three of us. Our toilet paper mission hadn't been classified as a Possible Mission because Melanie wasn't there. Same as tonight.

"Heya, Cheyenne." It was Cassie.

And dammit. She sounded all sweet, and she gave me a little wave like I just made her feel bad.

"WTF, Mel?"

I took Possible Mission rules serious. Straight to the heart.

Melanie flinched.

She knew how serious I took them.

"Sorry. I wasn't thinking. She's one of us."

Both Sasha and I gasped.

Sasha had been bent over the doorknob. It might've seemed from the outlook that she was trying to pick the lock, but we had a key. Both of us forgot our phones in the car, so we had no light. She was fumbling to get the key in when Melanie and Cassie showed up.

"No, she is not!" I was also a bit passionate on this subject, too.

Another grimace from Cassie, and I could see because both of them had their phones out and pointed toward us. Melanie knew better. This wasn't our first near-criminal mission. Cassie, bless her heart.

I softened my tone. "Sorry. I didn't mean that how it came out."

Melanie helped me out here, turning to her girlfriend. "You're an 'other.' You're not in the triad. That's me, Shy, and Sash. That's all she means."

I added, "Other means significant other, not other as in an outsider. That's a key point."

The hurt look faded from Cassie and her shoulders bounced back up. "Oh. I got ya. I understand. I have some friends like that."

The door opened, and the alarm beeping commenced.

Sasha straightened. "Entrance."

I scooted around her, putting in the code.

At the time I heard Melanie ask behind me, "You do?"

I could almost hear Cassie's shrug. "Just some friends from college."

"Are they straight friends?"

Sasha grunted. "She's with you, Mel, about to do a breaking-and-entering. Stop with the jealousy shit."

"What? I'm just asking."

Another grunt from Sasha as she swept past me, hitting the light switches. The front main rooms all flooded with lights, and I made a note to ask how she even knew those were there. I had no clue, and I thought I'd been here the most.

Apparently not.

"Check your insecurity," I told Melanie as both came inside.

Cassie's gaze went to the floor, and Melanie's eyes widened at me.

I was normally not this forthcoming, but again, I took these missions seriously. Though, we were not in an official Possible Mission because Cassie was here. We were now in Prankland Territory. The rules for that were as followed, not a Possible Mission. That was it. Those were the rules.

When Sash and I toilet papered Chad's side of the house, Prankland.

If Melanie had joined us: Possible Mission.

Melanie started to say something and I held up a hand, shutting the door at the same time. "Not the time and place."

She shut up. Everything was off-limits when we were committing these acts.

Sasha came back from looking around. "Where's the phone?"

It was in Cut's room. "Stay here. I'll grab it."

I took off as I heard Cassie asking, "If you guys were all about the breaking-and-entering, why turn on all the lights on the inside?"

Melanie was the one who answered. "Because we don't actually like to break the law. We just like to pretend we're breaking the law."

"Oh." Cassie totally didn't understand it.

This was why she wasn't included for the Possible Missions.

I grabbed Chad's phone from Cut's nightstand, and headed back out. Though, we were pretending to be thieves here. I couldn't help myself and snagged one of his hockey shirts like I meant to do earlier. It had his name and his number on it. Not an official jersey or anything, just a t-shirt.

Now it was mine.

Grabbing it, I went back downstairs.

Melanie and Cassie were sitting at the kitchen's island. Sasha was mixing drinks for everyone.

I loved my friends.

I slid the phone down the island toward Sasha, and then pulled Cut's shirt over my other shirt. Cassie and Melanie just looked at me.

"What?" I said to both.

"Nothing."

"Nada."

Sasha picked up the phone. "Nice." She put in the passcode and showed us the screen.

We were in.

Time to get fucking.

Chad didn't know this, but when he got his phone back, he'd have to learn Hebrew. (Who really knew that language anymore? Besides priests and seminary students.) Everything would be password protected. I was pretty certain Sasha would be changing all his passwords to his social media, and from there, who knew how long she'd keep those accounts before letting him back in.

That was the tip of the iceberg of what Sasha was going to do.

I only hoped she didn't post something to get Chad put on the FBI's watch list, because I knew that was real.

And something she'd do.

44

CUT

Three hours later.

Four women were twerking in my kitchen when I walked inside.

I stopped in the entryway and glanced back. I had the right house, right?

Then, I started recognizing them.

Cheyenne was the one wearing the hockey pads with my Mustangs' t-shirt underneath. She had a black ski-mask pulled down over her face, and her body I'd recognize under anything.

The blonde hair poking out from under a hockey helmet must've been the Not-Russian.

The black hair coming from underneath a goalie hockey helmet that a girl gifted me one time because she had no clue what position I played was Melanie.

The last one was a puzzle, until she did a flip and I recognized those arms. Cassie. She dug those elbows into my body on a regular basis.

Of course. I should've guessed immediately.

It took me a minute because she was wearing a gorilla mask. Where the fuck did they find a gorilla mask?

I shut the door, and all four gasped, whirling toward me.

I raised an eyebrow. "I'm surprised you heard, considering I could hear your music turning onto the block." I lived at the end of my block. There were a lot of houses between here and there.

"OH MY GOD!"

Cheyenne pulled off her ski mask and looked ready to faint. She took a step backwards. "I completely lost track of time." She glanced at the rest. "And I'm the sober one."

As if they'd practiced, the other three all started laughing.

The vodka had been pulled out. The rum was next to it. Someone was drinking whisky, and a bunch of mixers were scattered over the kitchen island. The whole kitchen rank of booze.

"Hi, hi, hi." Cheyenne came over, reaching up and giving me a kiss. "It was...uh..."

"Cheyenne." The regular helmet was scowling.

The goalie helmet added, "Learn to lie, woman. It's a good goal to have in life."

"I know how to lie," she hissed at them, her hands curling into my shirt. (The one I was wearing.) She looked back at them, then me, back at them, and swung right to me. She was chewing her lip as she did.

"What are you guys doing here?" I gave pity, asking instead.

"Oh, fuck." Sasha stepped forward, pulling her helmet off. "We came over to mess with Chad's phone."

I let that sink in for a bit.

Then, looked down at Cheyenne, who waved. "Hi."

Hi, my ass.

"Did you tell?"

"Only Sasha."

Through the goalie helmet, "Uh, but now that I know there's something to be told, she's going to be telling me, too."

I cut my gaze to Cassie, who had pulled off the gorilla mask. Her hair stuck up, frizzing. Her eyes were wide and she shook her head. "I won't even ask. How about that?"

Jesus.

I bent my head down, my forehead resting against the side of Cheyenne's head. "I sent him away for you."

She turned more into me and whispered to my chest, "They won't tell. I promise."

Christ.

"That was for *you*."

"I know, and I really appreciate it." She lifted those eyes up to mine. A whole wave of something strong rushed through me. Then she added, "They're my family."

Fuck.

I groaned. "I'm going to regret this."

"No, you won't. I promise that, too."

Still. I just sent someone out of the country whom I considered family, so my confidence was a little shaky on that front.

I hugged her, hard, because I needed that. "Okay. Trusting you."

"Are you going to ask what we did with his phone?"

I didn't know who asked that question, and I didn't look up as I shook my head. "No way in hell."

Someone whispered, "Plausible deniability."

45

CHEYENNE

C ut was leaving for an away game today, and waking up, I didn't want to move from the bed. My bladder did, but my heart was holding firm.

I rolled over, and Cut was staring right at me. "Hi."

"Hi." Then, I grinned. "Not so long ago, I might've rolled to the floor and army-crawled to the bathroom before running and hiding behind the tree hedges on the sidewalk."

His eyebrows went up. "That's what you did that morning?"

I nodded. "Not my finest decisions."

He grunted, then softened. "It worked out."

"It did."

I stretched, smiling at him, and I was feeling all these mushy feelings. Someone like me didn't get these feelings, and if we did, we lost 'em right away. They were taken from us. It was the rule of the universe, but damn. I'd fallen so hard for him.

No. I'd already been there, just had to let myself remember those feelings.

"What's wrong? I can see it on you."

As always, Cut saw me. Well, except for those times in high school when he had no clue who I was.

And that reminded me. "I went to a hockey party at Silvard, when you were there."

"Really?" He sat up, sitting against the backboard.

I nodded, rising up to sit back on my knees. My ass was on my heels. "You didn't go to a lot of the parties, so I only went to the big ones."

He sighed, leaning his head back. "Like I told you, I was all about hockey." His gaze fell down to the opening between my breasts. The cleavage was loose and open with this tank. I considered sleeping in his shirt, but Cut gets hot in bed. And he cuddles. Hence the tank instead of a full-on shirt. I was happy I picked this one now.

His eyes narrowed as he tilted his head to the side. "I missed out on a lot."

"But you're doing your dream."

"I am. Yeah."

I narrowed my eyes now back at him, my head cocking to reflect his. "Are you not happy with where you're at?"

He picked up my hand, but he didn't tug me toward him. He played with my fingers, running his up and down and around my palm.

I was trying to ignore the tickling that was mixing with the sensual sensations. Both were zipping through me.

He murmured, lifting my palm to fit against his, our fingers flat, "I would've wanted you back then."

"No, you wouldn't have."

"I would've."

"You saw me in high school, and you didn't."

"Once." He gave me an admonishing grin, holding up a finger.

I reached for it, and he laughed, catching my hand instead, and this time he tugged me onto his lap.

I fitted over him, straddling him, and I leaned back. Our faces were inches away from each other. We stared at each other.

His eyes roamed over my face, falling to my lips. "I remember you in high school."

"You're lying."

"No. I remember you. It took a beat. I didn't remember right away, but you were leaving here the other morning and you looked back. You said, "Hey." And I remembered you. I remembered liking you, too, but then one of the girls asked me about my hockey game, and when I looked back, you were gone."

"Are you serious?"

He nodded, his hands falling to my hips and he started kneading me there. His thumbs slipped under my underwear. "I looked for you later, too, but I never saw you again. I thought one time I did, but by the time I caught up to you, it wasn't you. It was some other girl."

"I was in the car when Chad had to come out to talk to Natalie."

My heart pounded. I had no idea why it mattered. It shouldn't. It was so long, so trivial, so minute, but... it did. It mattered.

"I couldn't see you. And he told me that his mom had to give some girl a ride home." He lifted up a hand to my chest, pressing it flat between my breasts. He felt how hard it was pounding. "I don't believe in love at first sight. Never have, but I know it exists for some people. I also don't believe that you and I aren't going to work out if I hadn't remembered you in school. People are people. Boys are generally stupid at that age, and usually only thinking about sex. I was thinking about sex and hockey, mostly hockey. But I'm not lying about when I remembered you and I remembered noticing you."

I had no voice, not for a second.

He had noticed me.

There was this sadness flooding me, but that didn't make sense. I couldn't understand that either, but I choked out, "I developed a way of thinking and talking that overrode what my senses were telling me. I got so overwhelmed by them, that it was a reverse way of handling the world. Or that's what the psychologists told me, but they told me I was crazy."

"They used that word?"

"It's a word and it's mine to use, about me. No one else can use it about me. It's my word to own." Another nod. Another knot in my throat. "One did. A couple did. And nurses. A counselor. I've had a lot of counselors."

He let out another deep pocket of air, his hand moving to cup the back of my head. "I'm sorry."

I looked up, meeting and holding his gaze, and for one heartbeat, we were one. Just one. He got me.

His eyes darkened.

I couldn't help myself. I whispered, "Please don't love me and then throw me away." I couldn't look at him when I said that.

He didn't answer.

I shouldn't have said that.

Why did I do these things? Say these things? Always at the wrong time.

I was always so inappropriate.

I couldn't read the room.

That meant I couldn't even read him right, and I was sitting on his lap.

My stress was rising.

My panic.

The air was stifling me, pressing down, and I could smell everything.

I could feel everything.

I was noticing everything.

Oh God.

Why wasn't he answering?

I was frozen, still on his lap, and there was just silence from him.

"Cheyenne," he whispered.

I felt him now. He was moving, but he was getting closer.

I looked up, and he was right there. My nose brushed against his and his hand moved to touch the side of my face. He whispered back, "Never."

I WAS STILL in bed an hour later when his phone buzzed.

"Can you grab that for me?" Cut called from the shower.

Unknown number: I'm bored af. Coming back. I'll make things right. I promise.

"Who's it from?"

My tongue was so heavy in my mouth, but I looked over. I blinked a few times, barely noticing how he had water dripping down his body and he was holding a towel only in front of his dick. And I could usually obsess over his dick, so my shock was saying a lot here.

"Nut-Brother."

A wall slammed down over his face.

I swallowed over a boulder inside. "He's coming back."

He swore under his breath but went back in the bathroom.

46

CHEYENNE

I met Otis, JJ, and Maisie at The Way Station to watch Cut's away game. Melanie joined us, and she became fast friends with all of them, so she worked her magic and my seat companions joined us going to Tits afterwards. Cut's team won, which I knew that would've made him happy.

He was planning on seeing his family since their away game wasn't too far from where we grew up.

I sent him a couple texts congratulating him and then asking him how the family was doing.

He didn't reply right away so I tucked my phone away when we got to Tits.

Otis was bouncing off the wall. "I can't believe you guys hang out here—" His words choked on themselves when he saw Sasha walking toward us.

It looked straight out of a movie.

Her hair was low, and long, so she must've added extensions. It touched the tops of her thighs, and she was wearing a black leather bodysuit.

Melanie and I shared a look.

Sasha was in her 'secret agent' mood.

Chad must've reached out. I had shared with both that he was coming back, but word's been quiet on The Chad front. I had zero expectations he would reach out to me, but he cared about Sasha and Cut. I wasn't surprised at seeing the secret agent back in place.

She came over, grunting her one-word answers, and we all morphed into our usual personalities. I was using 'dude' and 'rad' and 'rightio' every third sentence. Melanie was 'fuck' this and 'fuck' that, and lots of references to shitting.

Otis, JJ, and Maisie loved it. All of it.

Maisie was whispering, "Awesome," under her breath when one of the bouncers brought over her drink. She couldn't get over that, but there were enough guys milling around for security, so whoever was free brought Sasha's drinks over. Sasha's and her guests'. That was usually the guys, so it made sense to us. And they wanted to hear about Cut, but I had put them off at the bar, saying there were too many prying ears. And there had been. That same server from before had been there, so I just used her as an excuse, then apologized to her later by giving her an extra tip. She had no clue it was for throwing her under the bus, but my soul knew. My soul needed to make it right.

It was later, after Melanie crashed on my couch and I was getting ready for bed, that I saw Cut had texted back.

Cut: Thanks. It was a tough game. They're a good team.

Cut: You around? Could do with a phone call with you.

Cut: Okay. Assuming you're out with the girls. Miss you.

Cut: And I did notice you.

I was smiling so wide and so big when I texted back.

Me: Have fun with your fam tomorrow.

I GOT up for the bathroom a couple hours later and checked my phone when I crawled back in bed.

Cut: Always. Missing you. Have a good day.

My heart flipped over. I was tired, the sun was just starting to peek out. I had another hour and a half to sleep, but I grabbed my phone.

Me: Always. Missing you. Have a good day too.

Cut: Smartass. Go back to sleep.

Me: You too.

Cut: Already on it.

Me: Overachiever.

Cut: Ha!

Cut: Miss sleeping with you.

Another heart flip.

Me: Me too.

47

CHEYENNE

I did yoga and ran five miles this morning.

To quote Melanie, 'Fuck yes.' I was doing it.

I had my shit under control. Wrapped up tight.

All the wrapping...and I had an extra bounce in my step as I was going into Come Our Way.

Hard cardio in the mornings.

Eight hours of sleep... that was really more like four since Cut and I had been talking on the phone, and then my brain had a hard time shutting down after. But not a big deal.

I was eating healthy. Like, super fucking healthy.

I was drinking so much water that I was over-hydrated.

My brain was working. The cylinders weren't overfiring.

No booze. My only stimulant was caffeine.

Meditation.

Medication ...

I stopped in mid-step.

Medication.

Shit.

I'd forgotten to take my meds this morning. And I was thinking, remembering...

I couldn't remember the last time I took them.

Backup.

I thought my cylinders weren't overfiring, but maybe I was wrong.

I'd forgotten my meds, and feeling rising panic, I hurried to my office. Dean was coming out of his office, his coffee raised in greeting to me, but I muttered a quick reply and went around him. I was scrambling by now. My heart was trying to pound its way out of my chest.

I sat down, dug into my purse and pulled out my bottle. We weren't supposed to travel with them, but shit, sometimes I had to, and I was running down the days and the numbers of pills I was counting out.

I was five extra.

Five days.

Five, that meant I forgot on Sunday.

Where had I been on Saturday? At Cut's. I slept over, and the morning had been fantastic, and that's why I forgot. Monday I was at his place again. Tuesday...I watched the game and I'd been out and about. Melanie crashed over that night.

I just forgot. Every day.

Shit, shit, shit.

This wasn't good.

Last time this happened, I spiraled. You forget one thing this day, another thing the next day. Your mind is moving a little bit faster, clearer, and you go with it, but you're forgetting and you're forgetting that you're even forgetting. So you don't remember what you're supposed to be remembering. Made sense, right?

No. It doesn't.

It makes no sense, because your fucking brain doesn't stop and add in stress. Add in one thing you forgot from a perfect recipe where you have to follow anything to have a semblance of a normal day for someone else, and you're exhausted from just trying to be normal that you forget one fucking thing.

The whole pile falls over.

Down.

You're fucked and you don't realize you're fucked until you're so fucked that it's currently happening. And you're beyond fixing anything because meds take time to get in your blood circulation. Everything takes time.

Time. Time. Time.

You don't have time sometimes when you're trying so hard to be normal, and—yep, I was spinning. Right now. Right here. In my office, and I had a staff meeting, and they'd know because I was recognizing the speed of my own thoughts.

Racing.

Speeding.

I was no longer driving the bus.

The bus was getting out from under me. I was more on the side of the bus.

I'd be a passenger in the bus, and that was always bad.

There goes the camper that my bus was pulling. The fucking mental struggles I had, all in that camper, all behind me, and I was pulling them along, but pretending we were all copacetic together. There it is. It's unhitched and it's passing me and we're all in a busy city intersection and that shit is going to crash into someone else's car, and I have no control over any of it, because if I wanted to keep in control, I needed to not forget my fucking pills five days ago!

The room was starting to go around me.

My blood pressure was steaming.

Sweat trickled down my spine.

My hands were clammy.

My chest was getting tight.

Oh great. Hello, panic attack. This was a great time for you to join this sad and pathetic party.

A knock on my door.

"Who is it?" I cringed, not knowing if my voice even sounded normal anymore.

"Hey." It opened and it was Reba. She was frowning, but to be honest, I was more paying attention to the three people at the coffee machine, and the smell of whatever Boomer was cooking, and—what did she just say?

She was looking at me.

She'd already said it.

Crap.

"I'm sorry. What'd you say?"

I had to concentrate this time. Harder. The hardest. The hardiest of the hard...and I missed it again.

She was frowning, and then a bulb clicked on and she came inside.

Oh, that helped. A little.

But I could hear the voices outside, and the clatter of pots and pans, and was there a larger than usual amount of people here today?

I must've asked Reba that, and she was looking at me all concerned. Shit. She knew. I walked inside with an extra bounce in my step, thinking I'd been slaying this dragon, and now I was in full-fledged panic attack mode even before the worst of the worse got to me.

"Cheyenne."

She was speaking calm, and low, and she totally knew.

"Yeah?"

"Are you off your meds?"

An unhinged laugh came out of me, and before I knew it, I was laughing like a banshee. Head bent over my desk and I couldn't stop. Full freak-out here I come.

It wasn't usually this bad, or so soon. The panic hysteria was extra because Cut was coming back today. This morning. He might already be here.

I think he was, actually.

He said something about a meeting downtown, too. Or was

that tomorrow?

I should've texted him.

Had I already?

Had he not texted me back?

Was he getting sick of me already?

But no. I was remembering that we had texted last night and there'd been a good morning text from him when I woke up, but he was on the plane. They did come back super early today.

I couldn't remember the reason, but there'd been a reason.

Wait. Was that today? Tomorrow?

I was losing time now, too.

The charity event was tomorrow night, and last time I handled it by jumping into his pool and swimming for thirty minutes. This time, I didn't know what to do. More running? I already ran five miles. I already did yoga.

I was already eating healthy.

I was already doing meditation.

I was already trying so hard to be so fucking perfect and no one got it.

"Hey, hey."

Another knock on my door. This one was rough and abrupt, and the door opened. Dean came in, not looking, not waiting for permission. He took a step inside, not even looking over, already saying, "We have a surprise for you."

Oh God.

I closed my eyes and let my head hit the desk, cradled by my arms.

Let me hide now, please world.

"Get out!"

"What? What's going on? Cheyenne?"

"No. Out. Now. You knock and then wait for permission to come in. What if she'd been changing clothes, huh? What if she'd been on a private call? What if she just found out her grandmother was dead?"

"What? I'm confused. Her grandmother passed away?" He dropped his voice. "She never talks about family. I had no clue."

Reba made a gargling frustrated growl. "Out. Now. And while we're at it, meeting's postponed till tomorrow."

"What?! I have to finalize everything for tomorrow. I need to loop you guys in on everything."

"Oh, why do you care now? You didn't care when you made the decision to move forward with the event, and you're the one who decided the invite list. This is your thing. You handle it on your own."

"We have celebrities coming today to help serve. I wanted to tell Cheyenne who they were. What's going on? Is there something going on I need to know about?"

"Out. Now." Reba was firm, and she *really* needed to do more than watch Netflix every night. I had a feeling she'd be a trip in Prankland Territory.

I needed to gather myself, and I could do it.

I was freaking out on the inside, but faking and forcing was another motto I enforced. I was enforcing it now, and lifting my head, I made out that Reba was standing in front of Dean. She'd actually gotten him back outside the door and he couldn't see past her.

I loved Reba. I really loved Reba.

The rest of the room was swimming and blurring together. Little bubbles were showing everywhere, but I could do this. A deep breath. Another one. A third one.

I dabbed at my eyes, making sure nothing leaked up there, and I wiped my hands over my face.

Calm.

Control.

No.

Fake.

Force.

Let's do this.

I stood and came around my desk. "Dean." Damn. My voice was a little wobbly. I swallowed and tried again, hearing it crack before it came out with authority. "I agree that there's no point to our meeting about tomorrow. You've finalized everything already. You just want to cover your ass, tell the board you okayed everything with us if you get called up in front of them."

Reba was still barring me.

My knees were shaky, so thank Reba again.

She was glancing back over her shoulder, and she saw me reach for the desk to steady myself. Yeah. She was staying right where she was.

"What is this, Cheyenne? Why won't Reba let me in?"

"I'm in an indisposed state of undress right now." Totally lying, but I could feel his immediate retreat.

I almost grinned at his, "Oooh! Oh. So sorry. I didn't—I'll knock and wait next time. I promise."

He was skipping over my veiled threat.

"But...uh...Cut Ryder and Hendrix Sanderson are coming in today."

"What?!"

Reba sent me a fierce frown.

"Yeah." Dean was trying to stand on his tiptoes to see me. "It was a last-minute ask. They, themselves, reached out yesterday, and they're set to arrive in an hour. They're coming straight from the airport."

I got that wrong, too. I thought he was already here.

Why won't I ever get my shit together? Be good at this living thing? Not just adulting. I was trying for that, too, but living. Being functional. That was more my goal.

This would be comical to another person, in another setting. I'd laugh at this maybe in a year, but not now. Cut was coming here to work, and I was in this state.

Cue another attack—no.

I had to get on this. Again.

"Okay. I'm guessing that you'll be here to run through every-thing?" Me. I sounded so professional. I also had cold sweat pouring out of me.

"Yes."

Dean sounded like he couldn't wait to gush over both of them.

Reba rolled her eyes at me.

I grinned at that, but asked, still impressing myself with how controlled my tone was, "And you've let Boomer know?"

"I ran it by him yesterday."

Then there was no point in telling me because Dean had no idea about myself and Cut. Only a few did. So that meant since it was a last-minute appearance, he was trying to be extra team-mate-y and not wanting to piss us off even further.

Wanker.

I wasn't English, but that name made me feel better right now.

"That sounds good. I'll be in my office working on a few things."

There was quiet from the door, and Reba still wasn't moving.

A second later, he left and she shut the door before locking it. Then, she harrumphed. "Ridiculous we have to lock it so our coworkers don't barge into our offices. The guys who come and eat here aren't the ones we're concerned about. It's the co-work-ers." And she stopped to eye me up and down. "You okay, honey?"

I closed my eyes, drew in some air, and asked for calmness.

I didn't expect it to happen, but one never knew about mira-cles. I've heard they happened sometimes.

"I'll be fine."

She sat, folding herself into one of my chairs. "I tell you I have a daughter?"

I was taken aback. "No."

She started picking at her nails, running her hand over each end and holding her hands out to inspect them. "No? Well, I do. Had a husband. Got her out of it. Best marriage and divorce present ever. Couldn't care less about him, but her, I'd wrestle a tornado if I needed. You got me?"

"So, it's not all only Netflix and chill?"

She grinned before going back to studying her nails. "She's in college. First year, and she calls me up first weekend she's there. She's having a panic attack. She's been having panic attacks almost weekly. She and I, we're taking the steps we need to, but those things are a bitch."

The anxiety was subsiding, and exhaustion was filling in its place.

But my mind was still spinning. I could tell her how many times she chipped at her nails just sitting there, and I could tell her how many creases she had in her blouse, but she was telling me she understood.

She understood *some* of it.

"You think I'm crazy?"

She gave me a look. "I don't like using that word, but everybody's a little off. If you ain't, then you're part alien. That's my philosophy. Don't sweat it. You do what you have to do to get by, as long as it's legal, you know. Me?" She went to her armrests and pushed up, standing. "I now have to go and rearrange the volunteer schedule because Dean didn't think to tell me he was bringing in two celebrities today. Don't think a bunch of reporters who were coming in on their own would be a good mix since it seems like these two want it on the down-low they're here."

She started for the door but glanced back. "You need anything from me?"

I had to tell her. It wasn't a secret, but I'd just not gone public at work. That was a different thing.

I eyed her back, seeing that she probably knew because she had a whole knowing glint in her gaze. I said it anyway, "I'm in a relationship with Cut Ryder."

Her mouth pressed in before she let out a grin. "Nice. You want me to usher him in here quietly?"

I considered it, but then shook my head. "You know, I think today is a day where it might help to turn my brain off."

"You can do that with those two being there?"

I nodded. "Yeah. Cut's supportive. I'll let him know ahead of time, and he'll understand."

"Gotcha. And already he seems like a good one."

Warmth rushed through me. "He is."

And he was. He also proved it a few minutes later.

ME: Heard you're coming here.

Cut: Yeah. I wanted to surprise you.

Me: I forgot my meds. My mind is spinning more than normal today. I'm going to be out there helping, but I'm going to zone out.

Cut: You're going to do that thing where you work in the back with headphones on?

Me: I wanted to let you know so you don't think I'm ignoring you or anything.

Cut: Are we keeping you and me secret there?

Me: Might help just with my spinning today. Is that okay?

Cut: As long as I get to see you tonight. Hendrix already mentioned having people over to his place to watch the games tonight since we don't play until Saturday. You want to go with me?

Did I? Yes.

That was a normal thing to do, but this was me and I needed to do extra work to try and overcorrect everything.

Still...

Me: I'm in.

I wanted to try to be normal.

48

CUT

I gave Hendrix the 411, but not the why behind it. So when we showed up at Come Our Way, Dean gave us the usual greeting. He was a do-gooder suit. He wears the suit, but he means well bottom line. We've been around enough people to know the difference, and I relaxed a little once I met him. I remembered him from the first night, and a part of me still wanted to rip the guy's head off.

He seemed more placid this time around.

Hendrix thought it was hilarious.

"It's really nice of you to reach out and want to come on your own," Dean was saying, backing up as he was leading us to his office.

Hendrix shared a look with me. Don't know why we needed to go in there, but I had a feeling we needed to give this guy five minutes, or he'd never leave us alone.

He opened his door. We walked in, and neither of us sat.

Shutting the door, he extended his hand. "Take a seat."

We still didn't.

"Oh. Okay." He'd been about to sit at his desk but remained standing. Smoothing a hand down his tie, he leaned forward and typed on his computer. "Mr. Sanderson, you've been here before, so you know the protocol."

"Remind me."

Yep. Hendrix thought this whole thing was hilarious.

"Uh, yeah. Sure." He moved back around, a slight laugh coming from him as we went back into the main area. We were led to a back kitchen section where we were told to wash our hands. Then we were given a hairnet, an apron, gloves. A big black guy came around, wearing a chef's apron, and we were introduced to Boomer. We got the low-down from him, which was basically where to stand and when someone handed you a plate, put a scoop of food on it. That was it. It took me till later to realize Dean was planning on sending Hendrix out ahead of time, keeping me in? Sounded shady, but in our world, worse shit happened.

We met Reba, too, and she stared at me long enough, so I started putting two and two together. When I cut my gaze to Cheyenne once, and back to her, she had a small little smile there. My girl shared. I stifled a grin and focused back on what we were doing.

It was hard not to watch Cheyenne, though.

I could tell she was stressed. There were strain lines around her mouth and under her eyes, but her earbuds were in and she had her phone in her pocket. She'd close her eyes every now and then and she mouthed the words along with some of the songs, but she looked like a regular kitchen worker.

Boomer would watch her progress. When she would be three quarters of the way finished with whatever he had her doing, he'd start setting up her next task. When she'd finish, he'd go over and point her where to go. She'd go over and start up. She always knew what was needed, and he'd start collecting whatever she just chopped, diced, or peeled. Most of the product was put in containers and taken back into their walk-in fridge. He was having her help get ready for a future meal.

Hendrix and I stayed for an hour.

We were both asked if we wanted to stay. Note that it wasn't Dean who asked. He'd been standing around, checking on the beverages, but that lasted twenty minutes. He'd been in his office since, and Reba asked if we wanted to stay. We both did.

I caught Hendrix glancing at Cheyenne a couple times, too, a slight frown. I didn't tell him why she was doing what she was doing, but I could read my right-winger, and he knew something was up with her.

After another hour, some of the stress lines were fading. She was gulping down coffee like it was going out of business, but she kept working. We kept working. And Boomer kept going back and forth between all of us. Reba came and helped out, too.

I could see why Cheyenne loved this place so much, and why Hendrix wanted to come back.

The workers were cool. They were laidback. Funny too. The only guy who had an agenda was Dean, but he came out when we were in our third hour of working, and he seemed to have accepted he wasn't going to get what he wanted, whatever it was. He picked up some of the dessert trays and took 'em around to the people eating. And all the people coming in, they were characters.

Some just wanted the food and wanted out of there.

Some had a story for each person. A few looked ready to collapse, but after being in Come Our Way for a few minutes, they relaxed. A lot of guys stuck around, sharing an extra cup of coffee, and one of the guys went over to the piano. He started playing, and most enjoyed. There were a couple who made cracks about the sound, but those were hushed or told to leave by the other patrons.

Thirty minutes into the piano concert, a guy sat down and started singing.

I glanced back, saw that Cheyenne had taken her earbuds out, and there was a small little grin on her face. Yeah. She seemed a lot better.

"All right, folks." If Boomer wasn't his given name, I heard why it was his nickname. He boomed out on our fourth hour there and held his hand up in the air, "We're good to go. Time to close up shop."

A few guys whined, but most picked up their items and headed for the door.

A couple lingered back, and I saw Reba handing out food in closed containers. When she caught me watching, she winked. Each guy stuffed the container under a coat or shirt before heading out the door. She came over when she was done, putting the empty pan on the counter where I was standing. "That's not legal, but most everyone here's done something not legal."

"Not going to hear a word from me."

She winked again, nodding to where Hendrix was sitting at a table talking to a few of the patrons who were the last to leave. "Enjoyed having you both here. Real nice of you, and even better that no press was called in."

"That happens with some, but a lot of the guys on the team aren't like that."

"That's why you guys will do real good this year. Can already see it." Then, her gaze trailed past me, and I waited, expecting her next comment about Cheyenne. I was surprised when I heard instead, "Don't let him know about you and her. He'll use her, and it'll wear on her after a bit, even if she thinks she can handle him. She can't. None of us can when he's got his mind set on something."

"Noted."

Her eyes moved back to mine. "Watching you watching her today, I can tell you feel a right sort of way with her. Take care of her. She deserves it."

"That was noted a long time ago."

She grinned at me, a slow nod, and moved past me with a pat

on my arm. "You'll do, Mr. Big Celebrity Athlete. You'll do right well, I can tell."

"Thanks."

As soon as she left, Hendrix came over. He nodded in the kitchen's direction. "She's still working. You two coming tonight?"

"Yeah." I glanced back, then to Dean's office.

"He took off."

"He did? When?"

"Five minutes ago, or so. He was rushing out and checking his watch. I was expecting the social media pics at the end, but it seems like he's the only one who would worry about that. He must've been late for something."

"Maybe." That meant I could talk to Cheyenne without leaving and not speaking to her. That felt wrong in a deep-sort of way.

A few of the volunteers came over. They must've got the go-ahead by Boomer, because we were approached for selfies and autographs. Once they left, it was literally the two of us. Cheyenne had gone to her office and Boomer and Reba weren't around.

Boomer then came out, startled at seeing us. "Thought you two would've left long ago."

Hendrix shot him a grin. "I'm on my way out. It was a pleasure, sir. You run a tight ship here."

He held his hand out, and Boomer took it, giving him a slow nod. "You both faired real well. Real well." He said to me, "She's in her office, so you can head on back."

Hendrix and I shared a look.

A low chuckle came from Boomer. "That girl's a looker, and she's got the *it* that guys salivate over. Knew something was up when neither of you asked about her. Knew something was more when I caught you checking on her, and knew something was really up when Reba was giving you a once-over a few times. Deano's gone and I won't say a word. I'm going to head on out myself in a few, but Cheyenne's got keys to lock up. I'm assuming you'll stay to make sure she gets to her car safe?"

That had me frowning. "Does she walk out alone normally?"

"Never. We always have one of the volunteers keep an eye on her, same with Reba. Though, most of the guys who linger around here are scared of Reba. Rightfully so. She can snatch a tongue in three seconds flat." He shuddered, before giving us both another nod and heading into the kitchen.

"Right. There's my cue, and I'm not a third wheel." Hendrix clasped me on the shoulder. "Girl or not, I want to do this again. Okay?"

"Sounds good to me."

"See you at mine later?"

I nodded. "That's the plan."

He was going down the back hallway as I went over to Cheyenne's office and rapped lightly.

There was a second before she answered, "Yeah?"

I bent my head down. "It's me. Only Boomer is here."

"Oh." It was another couple beats before she came over. The door was unlocked, and she opened the door. "Hey."

I felt punched in the gonads.

She looked pale and the strain lines were worse.

I stepped inside, my hand instantly cupping the back of her neck and I shut the door behind me. "You were faking out there."

"I wasn't." But she didn't say anything else, resting her head against my chest, and I worked the muscles in the back of her neck. We stayed like that as I worked around to the pressure points on her face, working over her temples and down the rest of her face. It was a weird sensation your first time, but then it was damned addictive, and relaxing. I kept going when her head grew limp. She was giving herself completely over to me so I bent down, caught her up in my arms, and carried her over to her desk chair.

Sitting down, her on my lap, I positioned so she was sitting sideways, and I kept massaging the rest of her.

We didn't talk.

I massaged her until an hour into it, I realized she'd fallen asleep, and I kept working even after that.

I worked until I just sat there, just holding her, and that's when I knew.

There wouldn't be a day where I wouldn't want to do this.

49

CHEYENNE

I woke to Cut carrying me to his vehicle.

He was putting me inside the front seat when I started to stir.

"Go to sleep. I called and got directions on how to close up, and Reba is keeping your car at her place. I'll give you a ride back in the morning, or whenever you need it."

Oh.

I loved him.

Really, truly.

And I went right back to sleep.

"She's sleeping, so I don't think we'll be coming tonight."

No.

I heard Cut, and I didn't remember what he was talking about or who he was talking about, but I didn't want him to cancel anything on my behalf.

I was also seriously glad we were in my apartment. That meant no Chad, but also, my bed, my sheets, my pillows, mine,

mine, mine. I did like his place, too. He had a bigger bed. More wrestling area.

I wasn't feeling up to wrestling right now, though.

"I'll see you tomorrow. I'm going to watch here." A pause. "No, it's good. She needed the sleep. Truth told, I need it, too."

He hung up after that, and it was starting to come back to me.

I went in reverse.

He locked up for me.

He put me in his vehicle.

He held me, rubbing my face, and I fell asleep.

He and Hendrix had been at Come Our Way.

Me cutting vegetables all day.

Me freaking out.

Me forgetting my meds.

And I remembered that we were supposed to go to Hendrix's tonight.

My limbs felt like cement was in them, but I called on the force of my racing mind and summoned enough energy to sit upright. Then, I rolled.

Then, I staggered to the bathroom.

Then, I used the bathroom.

Then, I brushed my teeth.

Then, I felt a bit more presentable.

Cut was on the couch with a beer in hand when I came out, my blanket was pulled around me because I was that kind of girl tonight.

"Morning."

"Har, har."

He laughed, lifting up a pillow beside him, but nope. I had worked on my insecurity and I went and curled in his lap. I no longer had any shame. I was going to embrace this relationship status we had, whatever it was.

He didn't seem to mind. His arm curled around me, and he lifted me to his other leg so my back was against the couch's armrest. My feet were on the cushions beside him, and as he picked up the remote, turning it to one of the NHL games that was on, I tipped back to watch him.

Seriously. So hot.

Those chiseled cheekbones. Lips that seemed perfect and wanted me to touch them.

He could scowl and my pants would fall off.

I laughed a little at that last one.

"What are you thinking?"

"You're so handsome. You're like the Beauty to my yeast infection."

He'd been about to take a sip of beer, but stopped almost mid-pour. He swung big eyes toward me. "What?"

I laughed. "I'm joking." A pause. "Not really." But I reached up and grabbed his chin and shook it gently. Playfully. "You're so pretty. You're so pretty that if you were a unicorn, you'd shit glitter."

He frowned. "Thank you?"

I was just getting started.

"You're so pretty that if aliens ever invaded, they'd take one look at you and declare you their cult leader."

He groaned. "That's a bad one."

Just getting started.

"You're so pretty that the blind guy at Come Our Way asked for your digits."

"Stop."

"You're so pretty that I look at you and poof, my brain short-circuits." I patted the top of my head. "Do you see the steam?"

He laughed, then shook his head. "You wake up funny like this all the time?"

"Only when I'm around someone as beautiful as you."

He was shaking his head again. "Keep going with the lines and I'll start saying 'em back. You want that?" His arms tightened.

I froze, but my heart started pounding.

Guys hit on me a lot. Looks wise, I knew I was the 'hang ten', but anything past that and fuck no. I was the shark-infested waves. But no. He wasn't going to scare me that way.

I sat up on my knees, staring down at him. "I can quote you line by line from *Night at the Roxbury*."

"Like that scares me."

"That's movie one. *Anchorman* is next."

"Yeah? Well, here's my pickup line." He grabbed me, but I expected him to roll me on my back and him on top. He didn't. Cut was a lot more direct and simpler than me, and I was having flashbacks to the first night I went home with him because he merely anchored me on his lap. One of his hands slipped inside my pants, my underwear, and he had two fingers inside of me in two seconds.

I died.

He started thrusting.

I was gone.

He won.

"How's that?"

I groaned, my eyes rolling backwards as his fingers were already doing magical things. "You're the alien god."

"Damn straight I'm the alien god."

Then, he really got busy, and I ceased being able to think or talk for the next hour.

50

CHEYENNE

I wasn't nervous.

I was nervous.

Not freaking out.

I was freaking out.

Okay...on the outside, I looked calm and chill. I was too-cool Cheyenne again.

My insides: I'm the *Home Alone* dude running around with his arms in the air.

Cut had dropped me off at Come Our Way since he was heading in a little earlier to the rink. Reba lived only a block away, so she said she'd drive my car back for me. And once she came in, we had no time to talk. Dean insisted on a staff meeting. I was guessing my veiled threat filtered through because he made sure we were all okay with what would be happening that day.

Basically, we needed to get everyone cleared out an entire hour earlier, which was going to piss off the regular guys. This was a whole hour argument between Dean and everyone. Everyone included myself, Reba, and Boomer. Gail was rumored to be coming in, too, and when he heard that, Dean backed down.

He was scared of Gail, but it wouldn't push into the time when people would be arriving.

It's clearly on the invite that people can start arriving at six, but no one arrives to an event at six in the evening. Reba promised that she'd have the volunteers start cleaning the room, but no one would be pushed out an hour earlier.

After that, Dean had catering coming in, and they'd start setting up around six thirty. Boomer was asked to have appetizers on hand to cover those thirty minutes, which Boomer said was fine.

The meeting was ended with Dean asking, "Anything else?"

I felt Reba and Boomer's gaze on me, and I felt them because I was firmly looking down at my phone. No. Dean didn't need to know about Cut, about Deek, about Chad (if he showed or not), or— Wait, I had something.

"Yes."

Dean turned to me, his irritation clear. I'd been pushing back on a whole ton more than I usually did. "Yes, Cheyenne?"

"Sasha and Melanie are coming."

"They're not—"

"They're coming." No arguments, dickhead.

He heard the unspoken message from my tone and said, "They're coming, I guess. Anyone else?"

I was back to my own internal monologue. Dean didn't need to know about Natalie, or Hunter, or... I was running out of anyone else I personally knew who could be coming that Dean didn't need to know about.

"We're good to get back to our regular jobs now?"

Reba was the best at sarcasm. She even had a head tilt, and her eyes were bulging out with that comment.

Dean read the room and glowered back at us. "This is for Come Our Way. The funding we can get from tonight could finance us for another five years. I'm not doing this as a personal—"

"Bullshit."

That was Boomer, and Reba and I were suddenly more interested in the conversation.

He added, "You're doing this because you want to rub elbows with the high and mighty from the city. Come Our Way has never done it this way before. We've never needed to do that, and we're your excuse, so don't lie to us. Lie to yourself, fine, but not us." And with that, Boomer stood up and left the building.

He didn't actually leave the building.

I was being dramatic. He only went to the kitchen.

Reba and I shared a look before we both scrambled, not wanting to be around for the aftershocks. We'd gone three steps before Dean's door was slammed shut.

Reba followed me into my office, dropping into one of my chairs as I went to close the door. "How you doing, chickadee?"

Chickadee. I liked that term, and I shrugged, booting up my computer. "I'm good."

"You know what I'm talking about?"

I looked up, locking eyes with her. Yep, she knew.

I sat back with a soft sigh. "He was pretty great yesterday, wasn't he?"

"I'd say so." Her eyebrows were up, and she was giving the look of all looks. "Dean was stumbling over himself trying to impress your guy, but he only had eyes for you. Could tell he cares about you, a whole lot."

"You could?"

Warmth started spreading through me.

"Sure could." Her eyes narrowed and her head moved back a little. "Why am I getting a feeling like you're not believing me?"

I shrugged, reaching forward for some paperwork. I didn't want to have this conversation, and especially not with Reba. She'd be the Boomer to my Dean. "It's just new and..."

"And what?"

"Nothing. It's just new. That's all."

Her mouth pressed together, hard. Disapproving lines curved down around her lips. "My Mama Alert is blaring loud right now. What's going on?"

"Nothing."

"Child."

I laughed. "I'm not far from thirty."

"Come on, tell me what's going on with you."

"It's nothing. I'm just..." My throat swelled. This was an old conversation by now. I was even tired of thinking about it. "It's just insecurities. That's all, and they're dumb."

"Honey." Her tone was soft, but also knowing. She leaned forward. "Insecurities are never dumb. Everyone has insecurities, but not believing something or not letting yourself live your fullest life because of them is what is dumb. That guy I saw here yesterday cares a lot about you. Whatever your insecurities are, you don't need to be listening to them. Got it? He's a big-time athlete, but you'd never know unless you were told. You feel me on that? He's a good guy and he's smart, and he took one look at Dean, and I knew he had him figured out right away. I was impressed with him and the other cutie patootie. I might need to get me some hockey tickets, maybe when my girl comes back for a visit." She sighed, shaking her head. "I don't express it enough, but I look at you like a daughter. If you were my own daughter, I'd do nothing different."

My throat swelled up.

I...never had that before.

"Now." She stood up, coming around to me behind the desk. She took my face in her hands and gave me a big smacking kiss on the top of my head. "I was a bit more distracted by the delicious yumminess that had been here yesterday. You're not the only one who's got work to catch up on. I'll see you later on?" She squeezed my shoulder lightly, giving a soft smile before she headed to the door. Her hand on the knob and she looked back at me. "You going to handle tonight okay?"

No.

I nodded. "I'll be fine. Dean's handling everything, so I'm not even really needed."

"He might ask you to speak."

I shook my head. "He won't. This is his shining moment tonight."

She snorted. "I guess. He might be an annoying, ambitious idiot, but he's our annoying idiot. Right?"

I laughed. "Right."

ME: I need reinforcements tonight.

Melanie: I'm in!

Melanie: What are we doing?

Sasha: Question, should I bring some of the girls with? Juna mentioned wanting to go for a drink.

Me: The charity gala is tonight at Come Our Way. You guys are my dates.

Sasha: Is that a no on Juna and the other girls, or a hell yes?

Melanie: I say hell yes, but I'm not the one calling for reinforcements.

Me: As much I'd love to say yes, I'm thinking no for tonight's event.

Sasha: Cool.

Sasha: In.

Melanie: Ooh! Let's arrive in style, in Matilda.

Me: Doors are opening at six, so come whenever.

Sasha: Time?

Melanie: Are you staying there, or leaving to get dressed?

Me: I hadn't even thought about that.

Melanie: Can you step out for an hour? We can meet at your place and finish getting ready? Go together.

Me: That's a plan. Meet at my place at 5?

Sasha: Cool.
Melanie: Fuck yeah.
I loved my family.

I WAS JUST STARTING to head out, grabbing my purse and shutting my computer down, when there was a knock on my office door.

"Yeah?"

The door opened, and one of the volunteers poked their head inside. "A lady is here asking to see you."

"You know who?"

"She said her name was Natalie? She's rich, that's all I can tell you about her."

Natalie?

But I nodded to the volunteer. "Yeah. Bring her in."

They nodded, starting to leave.

"Hey."

They poked their head back in.

I added, "Don't let Dean see her."

Another nod, and they were gone.

I checked my email quick, looking to see if Hunter had emailed me about anything with Natalie, but no. Our last emails were a running joke about a quokka. We'd moved on from koalas long ago. Now it was pretty much constant smiling quokka memes back and forth. So I had no idea why Natalie would be coming early, and why she'd ask to see me.

The door opened and there she was.

"Hello, Cheyenne."

She looked different. I skimmed over her cardigan sweater, and she was wearing khaki pants, the kind that someone might wear playing golf, but she looked like she was glowing. More natural. Less makeup.

Her brown hair looked lighter, too, but her eyes were Hunter's. Dark almond with specks of hazel and gold in them.

I felt a little kick because this was Hunter's mother, and once upon a time, she hugged me and I felt nice afterwards. That'd been something that I hadn't known I was missing until that hug from her. Donna never hugged me.

"You look younger than you did back then."

"Oh." Her eyes widened and her hand went to her chest. She'd been holding a small clutch in front of her, then she nodded to my office. "May I come in?"

"Yes." I indicated one of the chairs. "Please."

She gave me a small smile, one that seemed genuine, and I was having flashbacks to my mom's funeral. That'd been the last time I saw Natalie, and she'd been so nice to me on that day.

"Thank you, and thank you for the compliment. That's very kind of you." She shut the door behind her, then sat into the chair with grace.

I almost laughed because no one sat down in those chairs with grace.

They plopped. They collapsed. They sank into them, but no one sat down as if they were easing into a tub of boiling or freezing water. And clutching a clutch in their lap as they did so, but this was a reminder of the world that I'd never been a part of, and a world that was coming here tonight.

"You must be wondering why I came to talk to you?"

"Kinda, but to be honest, I've already run through twenty different scenarios, and I'm noticing the different textures of your sweater. I could tell you how many steps you took to sit down, and how many steps it probably took you from the door and through the cafeteria room to here. Not to mention, all the smells and all the different voices I heard when the door opened for you."

"I see." A soft laugh. "So the same Cheyenne?"

"Hardly." Because I was able to mute those thoughts and push them to the back, so they weren't front and center. That's not how I had been back then. "Is Hunter okay?"

She'd been tucking a strand of hair behind her ear at my question and she froze, her eyes latching onto mine. "Of course. Why wouldn't he be?"

"Because he's the only connection between you and me, and I figured I should ask to rule out that he's fine so I'm not worrying about him until you do tell me why you came here early to talk to me."

"Oh." Another soft smile as she stared at her lap where she was resting the clutch. "I wanted to talk to you because my husband and I are coming tonight. I thought I might run into you, and I didn't want any social awkwardness at all."

"Right." The thoughts were pushing at me, pushing to come forward. I knew that was because of Natalie's presence. "Well, it was lovely to see you. I promise not to be awkward tonight at the event."

"I—" Another frown appeared, this one creasing her forehead. "No. That's not— I'm sorry. I'm not explaining myself at all, and I should just say it, right? Yes. I should." Determination fared over her features, smoothing out the frown, making her eyes shine bright. "I came to apologize for how I treated you."

She was struggling, closing her eyes and she let out a breath of air.

"I..." She choked off and had to cough. "Jon's a good guy. He's my new husband. I'm saying this to explain that being with him has made me a good woman, or a better woman. A better person. I—I wasn't when I was with Deek. I'm sorry, but I'm imagining that if something happened to me, and Hunter had to go into someone else's house and if he was treated how you were treated, I'd be heartbroken. Because of how I treated you." She paused, her throat moving to swallow. "The person I am now looks back at the person I was then, at the mom I was then and I'm sorry."

"That would never happen. About Hunter." I didn't want to talk about me, or Jon, or Deek. I didn't care about any of that.

"I know. I'm just saying—"

I waved that off. "No, I mean that would never happen. Hunter's adorable. And he'd be coming from a rich household. He's an athlete. He's good-looking. He has great social skills."

She frowned. "Have you seen Hunter recently?"

"Social media. He hasn't blocked me yet. Please don't block me."

She lowered her head, looking to the side before raising it back up. "You saw him at the hockey game."

My breath hitched. "He told you?"

"He did, and I know that you two email each other. He let me know a long time ago, and that's another thing I am apologizing for. I should've orchestrated more communication between you and your brother, and I didn't. I did nothing. My husband," She had to stop again, looking down at her clutch before sniffing and raising her gaze to mine. She wasn't hiding the regret. It was bright and shining right on the edge. "He was worried for me. He wanted to reassure me, so he did it the way his world does these things. I didn't realize the magnitude of my silence about you until he handed me a file the other day. He knew that Hunter saw you at the hockey game. Hunter talked about it at great lengths with both of us because he was upset with how Chad and Deek both acted toward you. He went so far as to say that if attitudes didn't change, he'd not be seeing his half-brother or his father ever again. It was then that I realized that I was partially responsible for this."

My throat was swelling up again. "He told Chad and Deek this, too?"

She nodded. "Not at the time, but he talked about it more with my husband and me, and he seemed as if he were coming to a decision. I know he has reached out to both and told them this decision, but that's not why I'm here. I had been planning on reaching out before Hunter made that declaration, but also before we got the invitation for the event tonight. I—well, the mother in me is ashamed when I think about it. My husband has a heart condition, and we didn't get good news the other week. I think that, more than anything else, hastened this meeting. Life is short, and we don't know when we may lose people we love."

My damn throat. It was still swelling, and I was someone who mostly lived in my head.

Her words were making me feel things.

"You mentioned a file?"

"Yes." Her cheeks reddened. "That was the moment I realized how my nonaction was coming across. My husband grew alarmed when he noticed that I was never encouraging Hunter to reach out to his sister, so he hired a private investigator."

A P.I.?

I knew these people used to think I was a criminal, but to actually hire an investigator?

Natalie kept on, "I was stunned, not what I read inside, but that he had hired someone to look into you. You have deserved nothing for how you have been treated. Your mother was very sick, and had been for a long time, but I didn't look at you as a child needing love. I was scared. I didn't think I could handle what you might be bringing into my home, and my instincts kicked in to protect Chad and Hunter. In all that time, I never thought that I was hurting a child needing help, that perhaps you had been brought to us for a reason. I turned my back on you, and I'm very sorry for that."

This was a lot.

I was feeling itchy all over, and restless, and my thoughts were almost breaking my barrier. If that happened, I'd be flooded with so much stimulus and information that I'd have to call for a ride home. I wouldn't be able to endure coming back for the evening.

I didn't do my run this morning, or yoga.

I wanted to sleep another hour in Cut's arms and I was kicking myself, but this—who could've been prepared for this to happen?

"It's fine. I went to my uncle's."

"Cheyenne." She scooted to the edge of her seat, leaning forward. She placed her hand on my desk. "You are a very kind and resilient young woman. You are intelligent. You are funny. You are caring. I can always tell when Hunter's read one of your emails. His smile is bigger, and he laughs louder. He's happier. You make him happier." She looked down, closing her eyes for a beat. "And I read that file and I'm amazed at the things you've done, and this place, this place is amazing. You started this place. I'm very proud to say that you're Hunter's sister, and I'd love it if we could form a relationship moving forward? If that is some-thing you'd be interested in?" She paused, sensing my unease, as she then said, "But I will understand if the past is too painful for you. Either way, I want to apologize, and I am hoping that you and Hunter can do more things together. He really adores you."

My forehead was itching.

I kept rubbing at it, over and over again.

This didn't happen to people like me.

People like me, we were messed up and we were scorned, and we were judged. We knew our place. I knew my place. Cut had been chipping at that wall, but her being here, apologizing, saying all these things to me, and I was struggling with my brain getting away from me.

"Cheyenne?"

Panic was rising up in me, taking over, clogging my veins. It was moving into my throat. It was going to close up my throat and I wouldn't be able to breathe.

"You need to go. Now." My ears were starting to pound.

I couldn't distinguish my own voice or the normal volume.

I might've been yelling for all I knew. "Now. You gotta go."

"Cheyenne." She pushed up from her chair and was coming around to my side. "What is it? What did I say—"

The door was pushed open, and Reba was there. "What's going on in here?"

"I—" Natalie's voice broke. I think that was her? I couldn't tell.

My skin was crawling. I felt like there were ticks everywhere and I needed to wash them off of me.

"I was trying to apologize for something."

"Apologize?" Reba pushed her way in my office, shutting the door behind her. "For what? Who are you? How do you know Cheyenne?"

My head was pounding. I reached for my phone, dropping it a few times, and I managed a text to Cut. He'd be done with his practice for the day.

Me: I need you. Come Our Way.

Natalie was speaking over my head, "...Hunter is my son. I only had the best intentions. I swear. I didn't mean to upset her in any way. I'm trying to make up for the past."

"Cheyenne. Honey." Reba was at my side.

Natalie had moved so she was behind the chairs.

When had that happened?

Reba was looking at my phone. "You need me to call someone?"

"Cut—Cut is coming."

I stuttered. I couldn't talk now?

"You're having a panic attack?" Natalie was asking me, sounding panicked herself.

No shit. I hated these things. Another thing wrong with me, Natalie.

Natalie wouldn't want me around Hunter now, now that she was seeing this. She'd take back all the nice and wonderful things she said.

Horror clamped down on me, stifling me.

"Okay." Reba's take-charge voice was coming out. "It was

really nice that you came and apologized to Cheyenne, but as you can see, I think you triggered some old anxiety in her."

"I don't want to leave her like this. I feel awful."

"Ma'am, I think it's best if you go. Cheyenne is kind and forgiving. I feel comfortable enough to speak for her that she's already feeling worse about this than you do. She'll reach out. Give her some time."

My phone buzzed back.

Cut: Outside. I was already close.

Me: Coming out. Stay there.

I showed Reba the phone and she helped me shut everything down. The computer. I needed my keys. My purse.

Natalie watched us, standing back, with her hand to her throat. "I feel so bad. I'm so sorry, Cheyenne. I didn't mean for any of this to happen."

I was fucked in the head. What'd she think would happen?

But I couldn't talk. It was taking so much of my energy to focus and make sure I had everything before I left. Reba went to the door, a hand behind Natalie to urge her out. Their heads were bent together, and I knew Reba was smoothing things over for me.

I grabbed my phone and was locking my office door when I heard Dean's voice.

"Mrs. Carroews! Hello. Are you early for the event tonight?"

I beat a hasty escape, going to the back door and hoping Cut would go back there. It's where he dropped me off, and as soon I was out the door, I was so grateful to see him.

He took one look at me and hit his AC on full blast. Sometimes focusing on that helped settle me.

I shut my door, and he didn't say a word. He was driving down the side alley that led from our back parking lot to the street, and he paused before turning.

I looked up.

Natalie was right there. With Dean. They were coming out from the front door.

They saw me, then Cut turned toward them. He was focused on the street, so he didn't see them.

They saw him.

51

CUT

"I'm okay." Her first words to me after we drove a few minutes. Anxiety wasn't anything new to me. My little brother had anxiety, so I knew she'd tell me what she needed, which she did. She needed me and we were heading out of there, but after that, I wasn't going to bug her for details on what happened.

"You sure?"

She nodded.

I glanced at her, and she was drawing in a deep breath. Her eyes were closed, but she had some color coming back to her face. That was good.

"Stress just kicks things off, and I wasn't expecting that."

"Wanna talk about what happened?"

"Natalie came to see me."

I almost swerved into the oncoming car. "What? Chad's mom Natalie?"

She looked to me, her voice calm. "Hunter's mom Natalie."

"What'd she have to say?"

Her tone got low. "She apologized to me."

My hands tightened over the steering wheel.

That was a good thing. Wasn't it?

"I'm okay. I am. This will pass. I'm just off my cycle because I missed so many days, and I didn't do my cardio this morning."

"You're sounding clearer."

She nodded, but her eyes were still closed. "I'm so sick of this."

I liked that she texted that she needed me. I really liked that I was so close, since I did a late lunch with my agent downtown. And her anxiety, I could handle it. Her other stuff, I could handle that, too. But this, with what I was starting to hear from her, I wasn't getting a good feeling and *that*, I didn't like.

"Sick of what?"

"This." She was pointing to her head. "I have to be fucking perfect to maintain. That's it. I'm just trying to maintain. Then someone walks into my office and says nice things to me and looks at me. I had to text you to come and get me. Fucking pathetic."

"Hey! Don't ever say that. Ever."

She quieted, but her voice came out gravelly. "It's the truth. It's selfish of me to put you through this. You want to team up with me? Having to come and get me at a moment's notice? That's not a relationship. That's a caretaker. I can't fix what's up here, and trust me, I've tried. I have to be perfect just to keep my head quiet at times, and that's not fair to you. You could be with someone normal, someone who can take care of you—"

"Stop talking."

"—and what else? I mean, what if you want to marry me? God forbid. You want this for a whole lifetime? I'll wear you out within the first two years. Children? You want kids? I can't have kids. I can't bring someone into this world and give them what I have. Put someone through the suffering that I endure daily. That would be selfish of me. It's unbelievably selfish of me not to walk away from you—"

"Stop it!"

A fast food parking lot was on our right, and fuck it. I hit the turn signal and made a sharp turn, parking in the first slot I saw.

I cut the engine and turned on her. "I don't want to ever hear you say that shit about yourself. And you don't get to decide for me. I do. I choose. I choose who I want to be with, who I don't, and I choose you. You. Got it?"

A tear fell from her eye, tracking down her cheek to her chin.

Her eyes held mine. I didn't think she knew it was there, and cursing, I reached over to wipe it away.

"I love you." I was holding her face in my hand.

Her eyes kept glued to mine, and she asked, "Why? Again. *Why?*"

I'd never felt this before.

I felt fury. I felt like I wanted to rip an opponent's head off. I felt all those emotions when I hit the rink, but off the ice, I wasn't emotional. Easygoing. Go with the flow. That was me, but not with her. Since that first party, and I just fell harder and harder each time she stripped herself down for me.

"Why?" I repeated her question. Had I heard that right?

A second tear fell and she bit her lip before nodding, her head still in my hand.

"I love you because you have every reason to be angry at the world, and you're not. You wake up smiling, and you stay smiling. You'd choose laughter over anything, all day and every day."

"Except for sex with you. I'd always choose that first."

I grinned, moving closer to her. "Right."

"Six times."

"What?"

"You're an alien sex god."

"We're getting off topic."

"Just saying," she said against my thumb.

I leaned closer and closer. She was almost looking up at me.

"You just proved all three of my reasons."

"Those were good reasons. I'll give that to you."

Jesus. Everything in me was softening for this girl.

I said, my head angling more over hers, "I love you because you're the strongest person I know. All the shit you've had to endure, and you keep going. You will keep going, no matter what happens. Your reasons for not marrying me or having children with me, they're bullshit. Ask me how I know they're bullshit."

I waited.

Pain flared in her gaze, and she tried to look away from me.

"Ask me."

"I can't." Her lip started trembling.

I moved so my forehead was resting against hers. "Because if something happened to Natalie and Deek, you'd be the first in line to take Hunter in. If you got a call that someone's mother died from an overdose and they needed a place to stay, you'd offer yours in a heartbeat."

More tears fell. Her eyes were closed, and her entire body was shaking.

I kept on. "You'd take that child in, and you'd love that child with everything in you. You would deal, because that's what you do. You deal and you keep moving forward, and you try to love everyone on the way. Because that's how you are, and if you really want to know, I'd be fucking lucky to have you as a wife, and I'd be the wealthiest man in the world if you ever decide to give me a child. I'm not talking money. I'm talking *life*. You would be giving me life. So, when I see you and I hear you say that shit about yourself, it kills me inside because it's the opposite of how I see you. The opposite, Cheyenne. I love you because you're you. You open your arms, your heart, and you let people see you. So many people hide, but you don't. You're you, and I respect the fuck out of that."

Now she opened her eyes.

Now she looked up at me.

Now she let me see her.

I smiled down at her, both hands cupping her face, and I ran both my thumbs over her cheeks, wiping away the tears that shouldn't be there in the first place. "There she is. I see you."

Her hands lifted to wrap around my wrists. She whispered, "Cut?"

"Yeah?"

"I love you, too."

I smirked. "I know."

She laughed, but then I was kissing her.

52

CHEYENNE

I was raw when we got to my place, but I was better.

The storm of emotions had passed. Something synced when Cut was telling me all the reasons why he loved me. I would never understand it, but I felt whole. I felt like something fell into place, and instead of feeling disjointed from myself, I could feel myself. I felt my emotions. I understood my emotions.

That had never happened to me before, and drawing in a breath, I actually felt stronger after one of my freak-outs. Like what he said was the truth, that I *would* deal because that's just how I was.

I growled to myself because fuck yeah, he was right.

I wasn't no weak sauce.

My head was swimming with so many different thoughts, but not this time. This time I was going to be driving my own bus, not my freaking brain. I shut it down. One thought after another. I was using all my cognitive coping exercises that I learned in therapy, and by damn, it was going to work. And I would go back to that event tonight. I would see Natalie. I would march up to Natalie, and I'd hug her.

I'd hug the crap out of Hunter's mom, and I'd enjoy it.

Actually, I might not enjoy it, but I'd still do it.

Why was I going to hug her again?

The door buzzed and Cut asked me, heading over to it from the kitchen, "You expecting anyone?"

I was thinking, thinking—my girls!

"Melanie and Sasha were going to come over."

He hit the buzzer and unlocked the door for them. "You want me to get rid of them?"

"No. I'm good." I smiled at him. "They're my homies."

"Yeah, yeah." He was grinning as he came over and brushed me with a kiss right as the door burst open.

"HOLY FUCKING OF ALL FUCKS, Cheyenne!"

Melanie marched inside, holding a carrier of coffee, a humongous bag, and she was brandishing her phone in the air. "You're on the fucking first page of KC's Dirty Rag."

Cut's head went back and a deep groan came from him. "Fuck."

"Hey." Melanie was grinning. "That's my word."

He grunted, grimacing as he pulled out his phone. "Yeah. Well. You're sharing tonight. *Fuck*."

Melanie ignored him, coming to me and she showed me her phone. "Front and center. I don't know where you guys were, but there's a hella lot of pictures on social media. Were you doing soft porn somewhere?"

Another growl from Cut as he put his phone to his ear, his eyes cutting to me. "I'm sorry. That parking lot. I'll get the team's PR to get this all taken down."

I was looking at the phone.

One, I was thinking shocker.

KC's Dirty Rag was the leading gossip blog for Kansas City. It led in everything, be it scandalous, breaking news, or whistleblower stories. People didn't turn on the local news channels if they wanted to know the real story on something. Instead, they logged onto KC's Dirty Rag, and I'd forgotten that it loved spreading the joys of celebrity life, especially the Mustangs' lives. Hendrix was usually featured. Sometimes Crow. A few of the other guys, but not Cut. Never Cut.

I could see Melanie's soft porn comment.

The first picture looked like Cut was giving me breath. His forehead to mine, and we were both panting. The emotion was there. It was pulsating through the screen, and I felt winded just looking at us. Skimming down, there were more pictures.

My head in his hands.

His mouth on mine.

He was bent over me.

They'd been photographing us almost the whole time.

There was even a picture of Cut's face right as he parked. His face was twisted in fury, and I gulped, remembering why he pulled over at that moment. But damn. The angst. The drama. The sexiness.

We were hot as a couple. Fuck yeah.

I wanted to frame this shit, but looking up, I swallowed my words. Cut was furious, and he was heading to the back, his entire body was rigid and tense.

Melanie was frowning at him, too, putting the coffee carrier on the table. "What's his problem? You're not a secret, are you?"

I shook my head. "No, but he's never been on here before. I don't think he likes it for his image."

She shrugged. "Oh well. You're fucking hot in those pictures."

I grinned. I was. I'd take that compliment.

"Look." She took the phone back and scrolled through, hitting another article. It was another website, this one of a more reputable news channel where they were known for only news and nothing too salacious. It was an article on me.

"Whoa. What?"

"Yeah. They wrote up a whole thing about Come Our Way and the grant that you won, how it was a big deal. They put where to donate for the kitchen. That article is getting a lot of buzz, too. People didn't know you're a big deal here."

I frowned. "I'm not."

"You won that grant. Only two other people have won that same grant. That's a big deal, and…" She suddenly got quiet.

I fixed her with a stare. "What?"

Melanie only got quiet for a reason.

She let out a sigh, biting her lip and scrolled to the last part of that article. "They got ahold of the personal essay you sent in for the grant."

My heart stopped.

My body swayed.

My legs almost gave out.

I was reading, and I couldn't be seeing what I was reading.

Grants were tricky. Some were almost scientific and cold. They wanted straight facts, data, and information. They didn't want personal items, but not the one I applied for. They wanted a personal essay for the reason I was pursuing that grant, and what I wanted to do with the money.

I laid it all out.

All. Of. It.

I told them about my mother. My dad. How I was getting my head in order as I went through therapy, but I told them about my past, about what I endured during my time with my mother. It was right there, in print, the essay I wrote, and how I knew what it was like to be desperate for a warm meal when you were locked out of your home.

This was out there.

Anyone could look it up, and they'd know my story.

This news site thought they were doing me a favor. The whole article was about me, but mostly about Come Our Way, but— Oh shit, shit, shit.

Melanie took her phone from me, and my fingers didn't move.

"Babe." She pulled me to her, and I went, laying my head over her shoulder. She hugged me, smoothing a hand down my hair. "I'm going to say something, and I hope you're in the mindspace to hear it. If you aren't, well, I think I'd say it anyway. I know that your past has never been a secret. You've never been ashamed of it, and I know this is a big difference between talking about it with your family and friends, but I've been thinking for a long time that you shouldn't be in the shadows anymore. Then you started seeing Cut and I thought, 'Finally! She's going to get pulled from the background.' And now this is out, and I think, I really think, you need to just own this."

I started to pull away, but she caught my shoulders.

"Your story can save lives. What you went through, it's not normal. I mean, it is, but it's not. From where you were, to where you are now. You're one fucking rad bitch, and you need to tell people about it. About you."

"I'm messed in the head."

"Everyone's messed in the head. Some are just worse than others, and some deny it, some don't even know about it. I'm just saying, you're a fucking beacon of light. You were for me."

"So, you want her to do what? Do a speech at the event in an hour? Capitalize on our private moment?" Cut's voice came from the hallway, and it was low, and I heard the danger there. He was pissed, beyond pissed.

Melanie turned to face him. "No. I'm only saying she shouldn't hide anymore, and she's been hiding. All this time."

He didn't respond, but his gaze went to mine. He had his phone in hand. "The team's PR department is already fielding calls about the articles. They've moved to get what they can pulled down, but they're getting a lot of questions about you. If they're getting calls like that, then I'd assume Come Our Way is getting a ton, too." A pause. The edges around his mouth strained. "A national news channel already picked it up."

Oh, whoa.

I couldn't. I just frowned. "Is this normal?"

"No."

"Cut's never seen with a chick, and now they're finding out about you, I'm not surprised at all. You're made of golden gooey aura and shit. Everyone else will find out now too."

The door opened and Sasha came inside, carrying an outfit, her makeup bag, and she had a bottle of vodka with her. She stopped in her tracks, reading the room. "Apocalypse?"

SASHA WAS FILLED IN, and in typical Sasha fashion, she had a lot of one-word comments.

Finally. Fuck. Fierce. Frenzied.

She didn't elaborate on what the last word meant, no one asked, and we all moved on. It fit in with the theme, but Sasha was behind Melanie's sentiment. She agreed with the 'golden gooey aura' and I needed a moment.

KC's Dirty Rag didn't take down the article, but the other news site did. My very, very personal essay was removed, but I knew it was out there. Fucking Internet.

"I keep my life private, and I keep my image about hockey." Cut came to my bedroom's doorframe.

Sasha and Melanie were using the guest bathroom to get dressed, and both were two drinks in. They had the sounds of Queen filling the apartment, and both were on the operatic part.

I'd retreated to the bedroom thirty minutes after Sasha's arrival because it was a lot. Just...a lot.

Looking up, I said, "I'm sorry."

He shook his head, coming inside and shutting the door behind him. He'd changed, too, so he was wearing an all-black tuxedo. It was that kind of event, and he looked very 007-esque. When I was in a better mood, I'd be teasing about calling him a certain spy's name in bed, but I wasn't there yet. We hadn't moved to the funny part of the day's events.

"But when I first saw that image, I didn't think about me. I thought about you. You were the only thing on my mind, and I was so damned scared that you'd pull away from me because of it." He came forward, standing right in front of me. His eyes were pinning me down, holding me captive by the sheer need in them. He looked almost ravenous. And his voice came out choked, "I cannot lose you. I feel like I just got you. And there's a feeling in me, like I've been searching for you since high school, since maybe that first time I saw you at the locker. I don't know if that's true, but I cannot lose you. You understand me? But having said that, I agree with your friends."

I closed my eyes, my head going down.

But he kept on, his voice so soft and yet, so clear to me. "I'm doubling down on what I said in the parking lot. I'm doubling down on everything. I'm not a person who thinks anyone deserves anything. I've always had the mindset that you earn it, that no one is entitled to anything. Except with you. You're the only one who is entitled to everything good that's coming your way. And now I need to tell you that I got another call. The team's PR would like to officially represent you. They did more digging and informed me how prestigious the grant was that you got."

That damn grant. I was starting to regret being awarded it.

Well, not really.

I thought about the guys who come to Come Our Way, and never. I'd never regret winning that.

"I don't want it. I don't want any of it...except you."

"Your friends are right. People are going to salivate over you. Your entire story is worth telling. You're worth telling. You're worth showing off to the world." He moved closer, bending down so he was kneeling before me.

He put a finger to my chin and tipped my head up gently.

He was right there, staring at me, looking inside of me, knowing me, knowing the struggles, knowing the good, and knowing the love. There was so much love coming from him. I couldn't handle it. I'd never had someone look at me like that, except a dog that followed me around for a time when I was on the streets. He liked the treats I stole for him.

So that dog really just loved the treats I gave him.

He went with Herb, who started feeding him hamburgers.

That dog was kind of a wanker, too.

No, he wasn't. I missed that dog.

I should look up Herb and steal the dog back.

No. I wouldn't do that either—

"Cheyenne."

I'd drifted. "Hmm? Sorry."

"What are you thinking right now?"

"I was thinking about naming a dog Herb."

He frowned. "I'm not asking your train of thought on that one, but can you come back to me? Can you focus on me?"

I nodded. "I will. I'm sorry."

He cupped my face.

I was learning he loved to cup my face, and I was learning that I liked when he did that. No. I adored when he did that. I melted when he did that, and I was melting again. A full pile of goo on the floor, and then he ran his thumbs over my cheeks, and I really, really loved when he did that.

He finished it up with, "I want to show you off tonight. Will you let me?"

I already knew my answer. I think I knew it the first morning I woke up after our night. (Six. Times.) But moving on, I lifted my hands, took his in mine, and I had to tell him everything.

I put our hands in my lap and I looked at them.

"Stuff like this doesn't exist for people like me."

He looked like he was about to interrupt, so I held up a hand.

I kept on, "I don't get the happy ending. I don't get the family. I don't get the mom or the dad. Even my uncle and my cousins, they were okay when I moved here. I think they were relieved. Then you wanting to be with me, or even around me, and that didn't make sense to me. Nothing you did made sense to me, so I ran. I ran twice. But I can't keep running. It's stupid at some point, and now this is happening and I heard Melanie. I want you to know that. I heard her. It's just a lot to take in, but she's right. Sasha's right. You're right. I don't care about the PR stuff. I have no interest in that stuff. I don't even care that KC's Dirty Rag featured us. I kinda think it's cool because I doubt it'll ever happen again. But," this was the hard part, "I need to stop hiding and I need to be okay sharing my story because Melanie's right. It could help someone. It would've helped me back then."

That was the big takeaway from here.

"Yeah?"

I nodded. "Yeah."

"I love you."

He meant it, and I felt it. All over me.

"I love you, too."

The door was pushed open just as Cut's lips lowered to mine, and we heard Sasha's gripe, "You two are so cheesy that I can't even be serious for my girl's revelation right now. I feel like toilet papering this entire apartment right now." She let out an annoyed sigh. "Let's go. I'm drunk and I want to hit the event in my prime buzz time. If Nut-Brother's there, I'm hoping to make a scene."

Cut frowned at her, then me, when she disappeared from the doorway.

Melanie took her place and she was beaming. "I'm so fucking happy. I am also fast going past buzzed to drunk, so I second Sash's vote to get there. I'm so buzzing right now that I'm forgetting why we're all so hap—oh, that's right. KC's Dirty Rag." She turned toward the kitchen. "I think we should stop at Dino's Beans for more coffee. Cassie asked for a latte, too."

Cut was frowning at me as he stood. He reached for my hand, helping me up, too. "I'm getting that the three of you are a package deal, but please tell me you don't have a group name."

My smile was wide and dazzling, because he had no idea.

He saw my smile, and groaned. "God. What is it?"

"We're the Tomcats."

His eyes widened. "Jesus. It's perfect."

Then, Sasha yelled, "Let's fucking go!"

"Can you stop using my word? You know that's my word."

"Fuck."

"Sash."

"Vamonos!"

That was perfect for Sasha.

KOALA BROTHER: You're famous.

Koala Sister: No, you are.

Koala Brother: I'm serious this time. You are. My friends all told me, and Monica wants to get back together.

Koala Sister: Not The Monica

Koala Brother: So The Monica

Koala Sister: Dude

Koala Brother: I can see we're staying in line with our last exchanges.

Koala Sister: Zero seriousness here, except when I tell you that your sister LOVES YOU SO MUCH!

Koala Brother: Right. Dude. No Monica.

Koala Sister: No Monica.

53

CUT

They had valet at the front door to usher people from their cars into the building.

"Hmm. Nope. Nuh-huh." Cheyenne shook her head, pointing to the alley that led to their back parking lot. "No way am I walking in through the front door like this."

I was refraining from grinning because it turns out that Cheyenne wasn't sensitive about being hot. She stood out and she was okay standing out. She was wearing a cream-colored silky sort of dress. It flowed over her body like it was supposed to be taken off.

I groaned the instant I saw it, and both her girls started snickering at me.

I'd be fighting a hard-on the entire fucking night, but it was worth it. Driving all three girls to the event was a show by itself. One, they made no sense. At all. Sasha would say one word, and the other two knew instantly what she meant. Two, they laughed. A lot. And they snorted. And they made dirty jokes more than I heard in any locker room. And three, I now knew I never had to worry about Cheyenne when I was traveling for away games.

These other two took care of her, but it was reciprocated.

They took care of each other. I never knew females could be like that, but they were all a trip when they were working at an energy level of ten.

Cheyenne leaned over, kissed me, and said, "I'm going in with the girls. I need them for the entrance."

The doors were flung open, and each got out as if they were marching toward their own movie premiere, through the back door.

Hendrix was coming out to meet me just as I was opening the back door. His smirk was deep. "Those girls are something else. Holy shit." His shoulders were shaking. "They walked in, and the crowd parted. It was like Dead Sea shit. That Dean guy has no idea what to do."

I grunted. "*You* have no idea. Try being in the same apartment with them when they're all three getting ready together."

He laughed. "I would buy tickets for that."

"Next time, because it's going to happen."

The other guys came over, and we all exchanged greetings.

Going to these events was part of the job, so it wasn't anything special, but I saw that each one went over to greet Cheyenne.

Hendrix noticed me noticing and lifted up his drink. "That article got around already. There's a group chat."

Of course, there was a group chat.

I shared a look with him. "Are they being respectable in there?"

"No one wants to piss you off."

"Good."

The coaches came over.

The team's publicist was next, and she was gushing about Cheyenne. "I have to meet her. Did you ask her about representation? And she's stunning, and she works here and she—" The publicist wanted to meet Cheyenne, so I took her over to introduce her.

Cheyenne wasn't quite ready for the publicist, but Melanie stepped in.

She took her extended hand, shook it, and drew her away from the group.

Then, Margo came over, and it was the same.

Cheyenne seemed surprised that the team's owner had read the article already, but that meant I needed to educate Cheyenne about Margo. Margo knew everything. Then the other people attending the party came over to meet me.

I noticed Cheyenne moving toward Boomer, Reba, and Sasha remained at her side. She was covered.

The next hour blended together. Hendrix took my side, which was normal at these events. We rode them out together. The Dean guy came over.

He was frowning at me. "I had no idea you were dating our Cheyenne."

I really didn't like this guy.

"Our? She's my Cheyenne."

"Yeah." Hendrix interjected, smirking, "She's Cut's Cheyenne. Get it through your head."

He gave me a look the same time the Dean guy decided he was okay with it.

"That's great! Are you serious? How long have you been seeing each other? What are your plans for—"

"If we could interrupt?"

Natalie had made her appearance. An older man was next to her, and first Natalie came to me, holding her hand out. Six months ago, I would've given her a kiss on the cheek, but tonight I gave her a nod and a brief hug. "Natalie."

She stepped back, sending me a small frown before introducing her husband.

He was a fan, and his firm had season tickets, so they'd be attending the games a lot more now. Natalie and her husband introduced themselves to Margo, who came over to join our circle.

Natalie said, "I've known Cut most of his life."

"Really?" Margo cast me a shrewd look.

I knew Natalie had apologized to Cheyenne, extending her an olive branch, but it was too long in waiting. That shit never should've happened, and she could've made Cheyenne's life a lot easier. That was my opinion, and my other opinion was that it didn't matter what I thought.

It all came down to Cheyenne.

If Chad made it right, somehow.

If Cheyenne was cool with it.

If Cheyenne was cool with Natalie.

Once all those pieces fit together, then I'd take up my woman's side. That was all I thought about regarding people I've known since I was a kid, or a teenager in Deek's case.

Speaking of Deek, I saw him now.

I must've made a sound because conversations lulled around me.

Margo's eyes were a whole lot more alert.

Natalie turned, approaching her ex-husband first. The two husbands were gracious toward each other. How fucking fitting.

Hendrix asked under his breath, "Cheyenne's dad?"

"No. It was just his sperm that helped create her. That's all he is to her."

Margo's eyes now had a mean glint to them. She touched my arm. "Go. Do whatever you'd like. I'll run interference."

Hendrix looked in love. "Margo, you are one fierce owner, and if you weren't married, and I wasn't your player, I'd try to get in your pants."

Margo smothered a laugh. "Dear Lord, get lost, Hendrix. I say that with affection." Margo skimmed me over. "But you have a few things to explain, hmm?"

I had lied to her in her office. But I didn't care.

Hendrix motioned for me to walk with him. "I noticed your boy isn't here."

"That's a relief."

"Everything good there?"

I gave him a look. "You know it's not."

Another chuckle from him. "I know, but I'm just double-checking because I'm moving in on the Not-Russian. That okay with you?"

"That's Chad's problem if you make headway, but fair warning, if somehow he pulls his head out of his ass, I will be telling him about you and the Not-Russian."

Hendrix laughed. "I'd expect nothing less. I'm almost looking forward to that."

We headed over to the girls, and I drew Cheyenne to my side.

There was a lot of mingling. The donation buckets were brought around, along with drinks and the food they always had at these places. There was press set up by the corner, and Dean came over at one point to ask Cheyenne if she'd go and talk to them.

"No." Her voice was flat. "Go away, Dean."

He went, and then Melanie leaned over to whisper to Cheyenne, "You can be a beacon whenever you'd like."

Cheyenne started laughing.

The Reba lady made a speech, and a few of the volunteers whom I recognized from my stint here yesterday came in, and each took a turn at the microphone. They all talked about their time helping out, and how they'd been touched or inspired by the individuals who ate there, and also the staff. That seemed to be the general consensus.

Each of the volunteers came over to hug Cheyenne, as well as Boomer and Reba.

I had no clue where the Dean guy went, but I also had ceased giving a shit about anyone except my teammates and Cheyenne and her group. It was at this point that I knew we'd done enough

time at the event. People looked ready to keep drinking and cele-
brating, but I bent to Cheyenne's ear. "Wanna head home?"

Her hand came to my chest and her lips to my ear. "Please."

"I'll bring the vehicle up. Want to ask your girls if they want
a ride?"

"Okay."

I was just leaving through the back door when I heard from
behind me, "Do you know what you're doing?"

I looked back as the door shut.

Deek was standing there, and he looked like he'd been
waiting for me, smoking a cigar. He waved it around, motioning
to me. "You and Chad were friends since you were little, and I
used to think of you as a son. A long time, Cutler. A long time.
Then, you moved on. You joined the NHL and that was around
the time the divorce was happening. I thought to myself, "I gotta
let him go. He's Chad's now." And you were. You had your own
family, good people. Great people. Solid people, but my heart was
being ripped out of my chest."

"Why are you telling me this, Deek?"

"Because of how you're looking at me right now. You look
down on me, and you've got no right. You're a pup still in the
world. You think you know what was happening when I let
Cheyenne go, but you don't. I lost everything. I loved Natalie. I
loved Chad, and I lost both of them. And Hunter. She took him
away from me. I only got to see him every other weekend, but I
love those times with him. I look forward to them, and he's such a
good kid. He'll be a great man someday. He's going to big places.
A big future before him." His voice broke. "I'm proud of him. He's
the best thing I've ever done."

"You're exactly right."

He narrowed his eyes.

"You had nothing to do with Cheyenne and the kind of
person she is today."

He started to sneer, taking a long drag of his cigar. "You're making a mistake with that one. She'll be just like Donna. I already see it, the beginning. Those two friends she's hanging out with. They're into drugs and they're probably hooking on the side. Same as Donna. She ask for money yet?"

I loved hockey.

Deek kept on, "Because she will. Same thing with Donna. Donna waited until Cheyenne was eleven before telling me I even had a kid. After that it was a phone call every now and then, a nice 'do you want to see your daughter?' But then the demands for money came in. She tried blackmailing me, holding Cheyenne over my head."

I loved the competitiveness of the sport. I loved how ruthless you could be on the ice.

"Then she figured out I didn't care." This was the first pause he made, frowning before taking another drag from his cigar. "I should've cared. For that, I feel a sort of way, but then I start thinking that maybe I'm not feeling a sort of way for a reason. Like there's something wrong with the kid, that's why I don't care for her. Donna figured that out, and then it got real. That's when she tried blackmailing me for money. You don't want to know the lengths she went to find out about me to extort. She said nasty things, really nasty things. All untrue too. I'd about had it with her, then we found out that she was arrested and taken to rehab. Social services called me, told me that they found Cheyenne, and she looked like she hadn't eaten in a while. Donna locked her out of the house. You believe that shit? What kind of parent would do that? I'd never. Not with Hunter."

Ruthless. Violent.

It was a controversial part of the game, but I loved the violence.

I wished I were on the rink right *fucking* now.

Deek was almost done with his cigar. "I'm not the best father there is, but I tried. Brought her in. Gave her shelter, food, clothing. I tried. I did, and then I found out what happened with

Chad, and that was it. That was the final straw. Couldn't stomach seeing Cheyenne after."

Violence off the rink was bad.

I needed to keep telling myself that because I was three seconds from snapping. I wanted my stick in hand, skates underneath, and I'd check this guy on the most perfect angle of coming around the goalie's net.

I was envisioning it.

Deek standing there.

Me coming around.

I'd hit him so hard, his head would— "I did what I had to do, and I wouldn't take it back."

I snapped out of my thoughts and I saw Deek was swaying a little.

He wasn't sober, at all. I hadn't noticed.

"What are you talking about?" What did he do?

"Stay away from her, Cut. Love you like a son, like Hunter, like Chad. I never thought I had to look after you, but I do. That's what I'm doing here. I'm looking after you. You stay with her, and your life will be over. She'll ruin you, just like her mother ruined me. It's in the blood. It's between the legs. A cunt. That's what Donna was, what she did with Chad. She didn't think I'd find out, but Chad came home that night and I knew right away what she did. She did the same thing to me. She was going to ruin Chad's life, too."

I started for him, but checked myself.

He reeked of brandy. A mostly empty bottle was on a chair behind him.

He'd been drinking and waiting for me.

He hadn't answered. I lifted my head back up. "What did you do, Deek?"

"She was just there, lying in the bathroom." Deek faltered now, the words starting to slur from him. "I had no clue where Cheyenne was. Donna's pants were still undone, and there was a needle by her. A full needle, but she'd already taken what she needed. She was gone. Off." He whistled, waving his hand in the air. "She wanted to go. I could tell. It was in her eyes, how she was looking at me." Another falter. His gaze grew distant. "I helped her."

"*How* did you help her?" I grated out.

I couldn't believe I was hearing this, but I was.

"I put the other needle in her arm, and I pushed the drugs in...fast."

Another man had never made me physically sick, until now.

"That was the night she overdosed, wasn't it?"

Deek didn't answer. He was gone, off somewhere else in his head.

I had no clue what he was thinking about, but I knew it was the same night.

"Do you know what you just told me, Deek?"

His eyes were glazed over, and the cigar dropped from his hands. He didn't notice.

He whispered, "Yeah."

I looked up, and it was more a sixth sense. I felt her.

She never said a word.

I never heard the door open, or saw it open, but standing in the doorway, just behind her father, was Cheyenne. She'd heard the whole thing.

I reached into my pocket.

I pulled my phone out.

I called the police.

54

CHEYENNE

I thought police stations were supposed to be busy late at night.

Or was it early morning by now?

Either way, the hallway they'd put me in wasn't busy. It was almost abandoned. I was sitting on a lone bench. The lights were flickering and one of the bulbs was out. It must've been a hallway they never used because I'd see people go past the hallway, farther down. Cops. Cops bringing in whoever they were arresting. Other people being led by cops. I didn't know the time so I was only guessing.

I had my purse, but my phone was dead.

They'd taken Cut into a back room for his statement.

Then they asked for my statement, and when I was done, they led me out here.

This was where I still was, waiting. Sitting. Cut was back there.

So that's where I was when I turned and saw Chad walking past the hallway.

He was back.

For sensory-wise, this hallway was nice. A small echo from

the people down there. The low lights were almost soothing. I could've slipped into a trance from the flickering above me. It wasn't hot or cold, but I was also slightly numb. I must've been, which wasn't my usual. I felt all if I went a certain way, but this time, I was numb.

How odd.

Or I must've felt numb because when I saw Chad, I didn't feel a thing.

Those bruises were still on his neck from me. He was here. Someone must've called him or told him to come down here and the police would ask about his bruises.

He'd tell them, because why wouldn't he? He'd gone back on his word to Cut before so I had no reason to believe he wouldn't this time, even though he said he'd 'make it up' to Cut. Pfft. He was a liar.

Like Deek.

Who was a murderer.

They both hurt me. They both hurt my mom.

She was sick. She was a junkie.

She didn't ask for that second needle. Deek decided. He wanted to be rid of her. He didn't do anything for me. That was a sick man's justification, the excuse he was telling himself, but he killed her because he simply didn't want to deal with her anymore. As long as she lived, as long as I lived, he'd have to. And Chad--maybe I wasn't so numb after all? My stomach rolled over thinking about Chad and my mom again.

I'd been blasé before, telling Cut that it hadn't been a 'bad night' in my old world, but it took on a different feel now. Now that I knew what he'd done with her before, and then what Deek did to her later. Everything took on a different feel. A more raw feel. Primitive. I felt scraped open, my insides were on display for everyone to see and judge.

I felt like scum, like the byproduct for what they did to her. They did it to me, too.

I felt like a victim. I hated feeling like a fucking victim.

They took her away and no one questioned it. Not even me.

Someone should've questioned it. Why then? Was it accidental? Had something happened earlier that might've made her do it, if she did it herself? No one asked. It was an overdose and that was it. They were all wrong.

She was a person.

She was my jailer at times.

She neglected me.

She emotionally abused me.

But she was my mom.

She was taken from me.

Yes. The world felt a little different now.

I heard footsteps first, and I looked.

Chad had spotted me. He was coming toward me, and he paused, seeing me look at him. I didn't know what he read on my face, but he faltered mid-step. He stopped. He frowned. He started to turn to leave. He stopped.

He looked at me.

And he looked at me.

And he still looked at me.

The fucker couldn't decide.

Then he must've.

He pushed his hands in his pockets, his shoulders lowered, and he started for me again.

I was glaring the whole time.

This was not Happy Zen-like Cheyenne.

"Hey." He was rigid, waiting.

I bit out, "Hey." *Fuckface.*

He grimaced, then coughed. "I—uh—Sasha called me, told me what happened."

That made me laugh because what *did* happen? A drunk asshole confessed to killing someone. How does that get relayed over the phone?

"Why did she call you? You're not his son."

He flinched, his hand coming out and running through his hair. "I—uh—I don't know." His hand went back in his pocket. "Is that what I should do? I'm not going to call Hunter, but I could call Natalie?"

"No."

That came out as a guttural bark, like it was forcing its way out of me.

Natalie would know—though, maybe she did? Everything went down discreetly, as far as a confession and an arrest. Cut called the police. He waited outside with Deek. He made sure I went back inside, but I didn't leave the door. I stood just inside and Sasha and Melanie stayed with me. I think Hendrix played guard duty, keeping anyone from seeing us after that.

We waited an hour.

It took an hour for a squad car to come over.

The police arrived, no lights were blaring so it looked like a normal car in the dark.

They got out, talked to Cut. Handcuffs were put on Deek, and he was escorted into the car. They talked more with Cut, then one came to find me. It wasn't hard to find me. He opened the door and there I was, and I gave him a brief statement of what I overheard.

That's how Sasha knew. She would've heard me then.

They remained there for twenty minutes, but I didn't know why.

Then they took him and we were asked to come down as well.

That took another hour, longer even.

The drive to the police station.

Going in. Waiting.

Then the statements, and I was back to waiting.

Now Chad was here.

"How did you get back here?"

"What?" He'd been looking the other way, but swung back to me.

He was being nice.

That registered in the back of my mind. Why was he being nice? He was always so mean to me.

"How did you get back here? It's a police station. I doubt they want someone just wandering around."

"Uh..." His mouth was open and he gaped at me a second. "I don't know. I just walked through. No one was out there, and the door coming back here was open. I figured they left it open on purpose."

"I highly doubt that. You should go back out there."

"What?" He laughed.

Why did he laugh? This wasn't a laughing matter.

"Are you serious?"

"Deadly." I chose my words on purpose. I wanted to see his reaction.

He flushed, swallowing, and then he winced once more. "You don't want me around you?"

"When do I ever?"

He frowned, his hand in his hair once more.

Yeah, yeah. I wasn't being normal Cheyenne, well, fuck that Cheyenne. Fuck who that was—"Do people like you think about the people you hurt?"

"What?"

"People like me. People like my mom."

"Huh? I didn't hurt your mom. Your mom, she—"

"She was a goddamn junkie, Chad! You were a teenager, but in that moment, you were the adult--"

"No, I wasn't! I was a teenager—"

"You took advantage of her and you know it. You and your fath—"

He surged toward me, getting in my face. His finger was pointing and he was red. "He's not my father! He's yours!"

"Then why are you here?!" I yelled right back.

The switch was flipped and I didn't give a fuck.

I didn't care about him.

I didn't care about the police.

I didn't care about his neck.

She was taken from me, and that wasn't their decision. Deek wouldn't have come over if Chad hadn't--but he was right, and I stopped because he was right.

"Hey." Cut's voice came down the hallway. He was alone and frowning, his head inclined and moving between the two of us. "What's going on?"

I turned away.

She could've lasted longer.

She might've lasted longer.

She might've—she might've got help, but no. I was lying to myself.

She did get help. A lot of it. And it never stuck.

When would it have stuck?

Or would she have done it herself later on? Would she have pushed the second needle in anyways?

Cut and Chad were talking. I heard their voices murmuring to each other, and then Cut was coming toward me.

I didn't want him near me.

"Hey, hey."

His voice was gentle.

His hands were gentle.

I didn't want gentle.

I whipped around and shoved him back. "Don't!"

"He—what?" From Cut.

Chad had been leaving, but he stopped and turned back.

"This." He had to know. I already told him, but he had to know. "This isn't a one-time shitty thing that happened to me. This is the last in a long list of shitty things that have happened to me, and I thought it was done. I thought when she died, and when I went away, and when I got better, I thought it was all going to get better. I'm still here! I'm still in the police station because my father helped my mother overdose. He killed her, and he had no right! No. Right! NO RIGHT!"

I was remembering those days.

Bits and pieces. They were disjointed.

We ran out of shampoo.

I used soap from a gas station a block away.

I remember my stomach growling, and growling, until it got to a point when it stopped growling. I thought it stopped working at times.

I remember the cold.

I'd forgotten the cold, until now.

I had no blankets.

She took them, but I never knew why. She just did.

And she was cold.

I wasn't talking about temperature.

I just wanted someone to make me warm.

"Let's go home, Shy."

I wasn't numb anymore.

So many thoughts and feelings were blasting me now, but I heard him and I lifted my head.

I was sad. I didn't want to be sad anymore.

"You used my nickname."

He gave me a crooked grin, but to me it was the most beautiful smile ever.

He murmured, reaching for my hand and curling two of his fingers around mine, "I can call you Shine instead? My own nickname for you."

Shine.

I liked that.

Shiny.

A wind funnel formed inside of me. I had my own tornado in me. It was going around and around, and then finally, at the touch of his hand, it started to leave me. I was all empty inside, just the aftermath of that storm.

I curled my hand tight around his two fingers and I held on.

I needed to hold on.

"She was an outcast growing up. She told me that. She stayed an outcast, too, and so was I. She made an outcast, but," a sick little laugh rippled up my throat and left me. I felt like it was pulling the last of that wind with it, leaving me hollow. "I never felt like an outcast back then, but I was." I looked at him, feeling nothing except emptiness inside of me. "I was one back then, but I didn't feel it. I'm not one now, so why do I feel like I am?"

His eyes darkened and he stepped toward me, pulling me to his chest. He curled his arm around me, holding me tight and his head bent down. His lips grazed my forehead. Then my cheeks. Then my lips. Then my throat, and his breath tickled me.

"I can't speak on what it was like for you back then, but I can tell you about now. And now is good. Now is where you have Sasha and Melanie. You have Reba and Boomer at Come Our Way. You have all the guys at Come Our Way. They all care about you, and you have me." He held me even tighter. "You have all of me."

I did.

His breath warmed me.

He warmed me.

IT WAS LATER on the ride home.

We were going to Cut's house.

I don't know what happened to Chad. I didn't care. Cut told me that Chad was going to call Natalie, and he was sure that Natalie's husband would help Deek how he could. It was karma in a way, but Cut also reassured me that I didn't need to worry about Chad saying anything about his neck.

But it hit me around the time Cut was turning onto his road that if my mom hadn't died, what then?

Would I have gone to my uncle's? Got better? Gone to Silvard?

Would I have ended up where I was right now, with Cut?

I'd never know, I guess.

But there were two things I did know.

I fell in love with Cutler when I first saw him, and I still loved him.

I'd love him for the rest of my life.

I lied. I knew three things after all.

KOALA SISTER: I love you
Koala Brother: Same.

55

CUT

Three months later.

"She's adorable."

My mom was whispering/hissing to me, her hand clutching my arm.

"I know, Mom."

She stood on her tiptoes, pulled me down, and yelled-whispered in my ear, "Adorable, Cutler! *Adorable.*"

"I *know.*"

Her hand squeezed harder. "You kept her away from us for too goddamn long."

This was not the response I thought I'd get the day my parents met Cheyenne for the first time.

They flew in for the start of the playoffs. We were going to pick them up at the airport, but they insisted on renting their own vehicle. Dylan and Jamison were with them, and at first they weren't going to stay at the house.

They always stay at the house.

"Oh, no," my mom said to me in our conversation about it. "*You didn't have a lady friend then.*"

"She's not a lady friend. I love Cheyenne. She's going to be my wife one day."

Killer Mama Alice started tearing up, her hands pressed to her mouth. "Cutler!"

"What?"

Her hands fell away and she whispered, "You're going to propose?"

"What?" I rewound our conversation. "No! I mean, not yet. Eventually, yes, but it's too soon."

Her hands lifted back to her mouth and she was holding them in tight, blinking a ton, and then she sniffled. Her hands fell away once again, and she was beaming at me. "She's the one?"

"Yeah." Everything clicked in place then. I hadn't told her we were that serious, but we were. Or I was. I was pretty sure Cheyenne would be, too. "She's the one."

She was crying after that, and we never resolved our conversation, but I called their hotel and canceled their reservation. So I won and they were staying on Chad's side of the house. Chad had moved out, so it didn't matter. Cheyenne moved in a month ago, though she'd basically been living here since that night of Deek's confession. I drove her home, and it'd been our home ever since.

Chad moved out a month ago, and the timing hadn't been a coincidence.

Things had been strained with him. He hadn't been the dick to Cheyenne he had been before, but he'd been quiet. Really quiet. If she was around, he left and he only came around if she wasn't around. The thing was that I didn't think it was because he didn't like her, not like earlier. He'd been different since Deek's confession. Well, he'd actually been different since the night Cheyenne attacked him. He came to me one night.

"Give me a lowball offer."

"What?" I was watching the team we were playing in a few days. I hit pause and leaned forward. "Say again?"

He sat down across from me, dropping into a chair and he scooted forward. Knees to his elbows and a look of determination on his face, mixed with fear.

I narrowed my eyes. Chad had been off, but he'd not been scared. What was going on?

"I want you to buy me out."

I raised an eyebrow. "Of the house?"

A short clipped nod. He seemed even more determined. "You paid for most of it anyways, so give me a lowball offer. I'll take it. Cheyenne is moving in and you'll want some space, and to be honest; I need to get my shit together. I don't like the guy I was when Cheyenne attacked me and I don't like how she was with me at the police station."

I frowned. "You know that her dad had just confessed to killing her mom, right?"

"I know. It's not that. It's not on her. It's who I was for her to have that reaction to. I shouldn't have been that asshole to her, and I was. I kept telling you I would try and I was trying, but old habits die hard. And I've been using your name for my promoting business and it's not right. I gotta do things on my own. I need to be someone that I like and I hate who I am right now."

"You think me buying you out will do that?"

"Yeah. I do. I gotta do things on my own for a while. I need to do some right, too. This is stage one."

"Okay."

So I bought him out, and he moved into a townhome.

He and I got together for a beer every now and then, but it was random. He seemed to have taken his mission to change to heart. Course, he'd been my best friend since we were little and there was a bond there that might've colored my lens, but he seemed like a better guy. Kind. Humble. Time would tell. He was supposed to be coming to the hockey game tonight, so I was hoping no confrontations happened when I was on the ice. Killer Mama Alice had been briefed on the situation and she was ready to activate her kill switch. If Chad came in and started acting a certain way toward Cheyenne, Chad would find himself on the receiving end of Killer Mama Alice and I knew Chad didn't want that. He'd shared with me a few times he never wanted to piss off my mother.

I think the entire hockey nation felt the same.

"I want to hug her. I want to hold her. I want to never let her go." Alice was tearing up, talking about Cheyenne.

They knew about her. There'd been too much news coverage over us, and over her to keep any of it in the dark. News broke about Deek, then he took a plea deal. He was in prison now, and he'd be there for ten years. All those events shone even more of a spotlight on Cheyenne, but she was handling it fine.

In her words, "The masses learned they love a little Cheyenne, so I'm out and about. I might as well be myself. They'll love the wavy train just like you do."

Sometimes Cheyenne said things that didn't make sense to me, but it was her.

I was learning how to translate. I was also loving how much she accepted that I loved her, and if I loved her, then with her way of thinking, everyone else was going to come and love her, too. Which made sense to me because why wouldn't they?

Maybe that's what the 'wavy train' was. I didn't know, but that was Cheyenne.

Sasha and Melanie had been at her side, almost every day. That meant they were over at the house, a lot.

Except today.

Cheyenne told them to hold off to meet 'the fam' until the hockey game. They were watching it in Margo's box, who had fallen in adoration of Cheyenne as well. She was pushing for Cheyenne to do something official for the team, or even to write a book about her life.

The most Cheyenne had agreed to doing was starting a podcast with Sasha and Melanie.

It was called Decking with the Tomcats.

They tried for Dicking with the Tomcats, but there were issues with that name so they changed it. Reluctantly.

It was in the top five most popular podcast in the local area.

The girls were becoming celebrities in their own right.

"You gotta promise me that you won't fuck up this relationship."

We were back to my mom lecturing me about Cheyenne.

"What?"

"You. I know you. I know my son, and I know that you've not had a relationship except for a silly girl in college."

This was uncomfortable.

"I know you kept girls in other cities when you traveled and you'd call to visit them, but there wasn't anything exclusive about it."

"Mom."

She spoke over me, gripping my arm, "I know this because Kathryn Meomeuooux met one of those girls, and do you know who Kathryn Meomeuooux is?"

God, no.

"Do I want to know is the real question you should be asking me."

She ignored me, giving my arm a jerk. "Kathryn Meomeuooux runs a crafting Etsy shop in Pine River. She's across the river. I hold the market in Pine Valley, but not across the river. That's her. She's my competitor, Cutler. And she found out all about your girls and it wasn't a fun scene when she tried to lord that over me at one of our sales events. She had a booth across from me." She let go of my arm, giving it a soft pat and stepped back. Her voice turned cheerful and her whole demeanor brightened. "But, that's all done for now because you met Cheyenne. You realized you'd be absolutely stupid to do anything to lose that girl, because she's one of a kind. I didn't raise you to be stupid. She's nice, and smart, and she doesn't have an ego."

I grinned at her. "Ask Cheyenne about her wavy train."

"That's healthy confidence. You want that in a woman, too. Do. Not. Lose. Her." A pause. A mean glint showed in her eyes. "Ever."

I was a little scared of Killer Mama Alice myself now. "Not planning on it, Mom."

"Good."

Another pat on my arm and she lifted up on her toes. She pressed a kiss to my cheek. "Now go and make your momma proud on the ice. Fucking reap, Cutler. Fucking reap. Named you that for a reason, I did."

Yes. Still scared.

"Got it, Mom."

56

CHEYENNE

The crowd was beyond tonight.

The crowd was always beyond, but it was a playoff game and so the crowd was *beyond* beyond.

You feel me? Good.

I was golden.

I'd embraced my new lease on life, and that was the life of loving and being loved. Not that I hadn't loved before. I had all sorts of golden goodness love for Sasha and Melanie, but being loved by someone like Cut and then his family? That was deep and something I never thought I'd get. But I did. I got it. That was the cherry on top of everything. The goose egg of all eggs, and I was loving life right now.

"Girl."

That was JJ. She, Maisie, and Otis were up in Margo's box with me. Sasha and Melanie were enjoying their seats instead, because they now came to the games a lot with me. In an unofficial way, Margo had taken me under her wing. She wanted all sorts of goodness for me, and she kept wanting me to write a book. I wasn't a writer. I was barely a typist. I could do what I needed for Come Our Way, but that shindig was it for me and writing. Talking. Doing our podcast. Laughing with my girls, that's what was the easiest so I was getting my story out that way.

I turned to JJ. "Girl."

"Gurl." She was beaming at me, and she grabbed my arm. "I am so glad I took that phone call for you."

I laughed, because it was true. I grabbed her arm. "I am, too."

Maisie came on my other side, a beer in hand. She was already flushed, her cheeks all red, and that was just from laughing. They only stepped into the owner's box two minutes ago.

"Otis is tickled pink by this." Maisie's eyes were shining. There might've been some moisture there. "He's been telling his buddies all week he'd be watching the game from the owner's box. They're all green with envy."

Otis came over, a pink drink in hand with a little umbrella sticking out of it.

He was shaking his head, the tops of his cheeks almost matching his drink. "You tell her about my buddies?"

He was asking Maisie, and she nodded. "I sure did. All week."

He focused on me, a somber look coming over him. "We're loving your new friends and all, but in all seriousness, Cheyenne, we're just real happy to see you happy. We're also real glad to have met your friends, the Tits owner and Melody—"

"Melanie." From his wife.

"Melanie, but I swear she told me her name was Melody. I made a joke that it'd be easy to remember, I just needed to sing a tune and she was all for it."

Knowing Melanie, she might've gone with it.

We were all staring at him.

He blinked, and his head popped farther up. "Anyways, moving on to the meat of what I mean to say. We're just happy for you. It's not that you weren't happy before, but you deserve everything good that's coming your way and I've a feeling there's more coming."

And now my cheeks were the pink ones, and I was flushed, and I was a little weepy.

"Thank you, guys. You guys were the best seatmates ever."

"Oooh!" Maisie was gushing and she started to lift her arms to put around JJ and Otis for a hug, but JJ caught Maisie's drink in hand. JJ now had two so as Maisie was throwing her arms up, JJ shuffled in.

Otis threw his free arm around me, and all four of us got close for a group hug/huddle. Hugdle.

"Is this an exclusive thing or can anyone get in on the group hug?"

We stepped back.

Margo was standing there, a wide smile on her face.

"Oh, girl!" Otis pulled her in and we had our second hugdle for the day.

Margo laughed, her head leaning forward. "I'm feeling like we should be devising a plan to take over the world or something."

"We're just gushing to Cheyenne about how she deserves everything that's been happening to her."

Margo's gaze came to mine, our foreheads a few inches from each other. A soft smile came over her face. "I agree, whole-heartedly."

It was after our hugdle that Margo pulled me aside.

She'd been curious when she first met me, then kind and only kind after that. I felt a distinct maternal nurturing from her and there were times I didn't know how to handle it. I loved it, but I also didn't know if I could let myself love it. Cut told me every time I expressed those concerns to open my channels and let people into my river.

That's what I was doing. Who was I to exclude people from the river of love here? It was now a golden river of love.

But I'd never seen her get serious like this. She took my hand, staring at both our hands for a moment before lifting her head. "I need to apologize to you, and it's been a long time coming."

"Apologize? For what?"

"I got a call from a personal friend of mine, who had a conversation with your father. Based on that call, I pulled Cutler into my office and I put him in an awkward position. It wasn't the right thing to do, and even though I didn't know what was going on, there's been a lot of nights that took me longer to fall asleep because I realized later Deek had been pulling strings to try and control you, or try and control Cutler. I don't know the reasons behind why he did what he did, but I do know it was wrong. It was wrong for me to put Cutler in that position, and it was wrong for your father to use personal connections how he did."

I opened my mouth.

She kept going, hurrying, "And I've been waiting to make some calls, but yesterday I got word. I can tell you today that your father no longer has any friends within my social circle. The last one turned his back on him yesterday, so I know that your father took a deal. He'll be getting out in ten years, but you don't have to worry about him. Those doors will remain closed to him when and if he returns here."

He was technically still here. Leavenworth wasn't far.

I squeezed her hand gently. "Thank you for telling me that. It does mean a lot."

A relieved smile came over her, and she blinked quite a few times. "Thank you. Has Cutler ever talked to you about me at all?"

I shook my head. "Just that you're good people."

"I was never able to have children, and there was a time in my youth where I was in a shelter for a bit. It wasn't long, but I was there. That time will always stick with me."

"Oh." Whoa. Super smart big bad boss Margo was in a shelter? "Can I ask what kind of shelter?"

Her smile turned sad, just the slightest bit. "It was one that my mother and I needed to be in, but again; it wasn't for long. I'm sharing that because while I know that Cutler's mother is here and is going to claim you as a daughter to her, if you're with Cutler or not. I'm also hoping that you and I can somewhat have a mentor/mentee sort of relationship." Her hand trembled, a tiny tremble. "It would mean a lot to me. We could do tea, or meet for a walk at Powell's. Or even a weekly luncheon. You could go with me on some of my trips."

I was suddenly dizzy.

Margo was—Margo was amazing.

A lump was forming in my throat. "I'd like that." A lot, a lot, a lot. I refrained from sharing that. I needed to be cool. I didn't want to scare her away.

A gentle chuckle came from her and she squeezed my hand again. "I'm looking forward to it, and also, Decking with the Tomcats is now listened to by everyone on the Mustang staff. I don't know if Cutler's told you, but the three of you are hilarious."

Well, yeah. We were some awesomesauce type of chicks.

"I see that Alice is here. I'll let you have your time with Cutler's mother now." Margo gave me another one of those soft smiles before she went over to greet them. David was coming in right behind Alice, and Dylan and Jamison, too.

It was the head that came in after Jamison that had me gasping.

Hunter.

I had to take a second.

The air suddenly swooshed around me.

I knew Chad was coming to the game. He'd reached out to apologize. He apologized quite a few times, and he promised to steer clear at the game. I was fine with it. He moved out and he'd not been an asshole, trying to give me space ever since the police station.

So that Not-Brother was really a not-issue anymore.

And back to the real-brother. The very true-brother.

He was here. I couldn't believe he was here.

I was definitely weaving on my feet. Swaying.

A feather could've knocked me over, but then Hunter was looking, scanning, and he found me.

A matching smile came over him and he ignored everyone.

He came right for me.

The air was in slow motion, moving around me, and at that movement from him, it all hit me at once and I jerked forward.

I couldn't let my little brother be the one coming to me. I had to meet him halfway. Fuck that. I was rushing to meet him, and we almost collided in the middle of the box.

My arms were around him.

He was trying to hug the life out of me.

He picked me up, and whoa—my brother was strong.

His head was buried in my neck.

I couldn't decide where to hug him best. Around his arms. Under his arms. I wound them around his neck instead and man, oh man, oh man.

This had been too long coming.

Way too long.

Hunter and I had kept in contact, but because of my new media attention and because of Deek's charges, Natalie wanted to wait until things died down a bit before Hunter and I started our visits.

Visits. That's what she said, too.

And she followed through on her dinner invitation from the Come Our Way event. She sent me an invitation two days ago for their Sunday family dinner. I thought the whole thing was ticklish to my insides. I was now the one being invited to Sunday family dinner. So not the outcast anymore.

But Hunter.

I was hugging him, and I pulled back once he set me on my feet. "You've grown two inches since I last saw you."

He blushed.

Blushed!

My little brother was blushing. "Not quite. Just an inch and three quarters."

Right. An inch and three quarters. I needed to get it correct next time, but I was laughing because this was all filling me up with gooey chocolate warmth inside.

Loving life. Yes, I was.

"Can I just say it's about fucking time you and I are hanging out? The emails were fine and all. Texting, too, but enough is enough. I want to see my sister. And you can tell my mom I swore. I don't care. This has been ridiculous." He nodded toward where Jamison and Dylan were standing. Margo was introducing them to Otis, Maisie, and JJ. "But it's been cool seeing Jamison again. I haven't seen him since like middle school. Mom is infatuated with Alice. And a little scared of her, too, but that's between you and me." Then he stopped talking and he stared at me, and he had to blink a couple times, too. It was the theme for the night. "Too long, Sis. Too fucking long."

That lump was back and it just doubled in size.

I was nodding and blinking my own eyes. "I know."

"Not again. You and me, we stick together from now on."

"Got it. You and me." And a memory came back to me, so I held up my pinkie. "We're gonna hang, right?"

He was all serious and he wrapped his pinkie around mine. He nodded. "Hell yeah, we're gonna hang."

We had a little hugdle.

Afterwards, Alice came over and we had our own hugdle, too.

And even more after that, I hung out with my Little Dude for the whole game.

MUSTANGS WON TWO TO ONE.

Cut scored both goals.

EPILOGUE

CHEYENNE

I'd like to say that we had a happily ever after, but that wasn't true.

We were happy. Then things were rough. Then things smoothed out again. Then they were rough, hard. There were struggles. Then smooth again. Happy. Joyous. Back to struggles. This was my life. This was our life, Cut's and mine, because that's how it goes with someone who has what I have.

Every day is a struggle.

But I can say that we laughed. We laughed a lot.

I can say that we loved. We loved so hard.

I can say that we were passionate. Fuck yes. Pun intended.

So all in all, there *were* good times and there were bad, but the good overshadowed the bad. The truth is, it doesn't matter. Whatever struggles a person has, going forward, what is imperative is that they have love and support. Anyone can get through anything, or it can be less frightening, less suffering, if they have a hand in theirs. Somedays that hand will need to be held tight and some days, it'll need to be clung to.

Other days, a light graze was all that was needed.

I found that. So in that way, I got my happily ever after.

It's been ten years. Cut's still playing hockey. My podcast grew until it was so popular that we were having regular celebrities as guests. The highest ratings were always when it was just the three of us: Melanie, Sasha, and myself.

Life was good.

Cut and I married two years after he won the Stanley Cup.

Two more years after and we fostered our first little boy. Next a little girl.

Then siblings.

Teenager siblings.

We fostered a family of five children, ages ranging from seventeen to seven. There was a nineteen-year-old. He wasn't a foster, but he lived with us. He was the sixth in that family.

We adopted four of the children: Rain, Emily, Brian, and Lewis.

We adopted four dogs as well: Cutter, Chadwick, Clitty, and Sucker. Rain named Clitty. (She wants to be a medical doctor.) Emily named Sucker. (She just wants to hit things. She'll probably go into construction.) Cutter and Chadwick came together and got their names because Cutter wouldn't stop humping Cut's leg. Chadwick because he was kind of a douche dog. I never thought dogs could be douches, but he was. That was the phrase around the house, 'Don't be a Chad.' It was the PG version of the other one, '*fucking* Chad.'

Don't get me started on the cats or the birds, or the turtle. There was a pig at one point, too, but when the family of five (really six) was adopted, they took the pig. It'd become a therapy pig by that time.

Come Our Way was going strong.

Reba, Boomer, and Gail doted on all the kids and animals. Dean was still around, but I had no idea how that happened. He did another few events that weren't cleared by everyone, and the board hadn't been happy when I notified them about it. He got reprimanded, was asked to take a leave of absence. He came back three months later with a more 'teamwork' attitude. We never had an issue after that.

He asked to use my season ticket again. I said no.

He's asked a few more times. I always enjoy saying no. My whole 'setting him up' had been a one time feat, and I was glad that I never had to do it again.

Then we met his girlfriend and Dean's new attitude made more sense. She was the sweetest thing. When she walked into Come Our Way, she was a child and animal whisperer. Where she went, they followed in a line. Literally.

Her name was Sunny.

Beep! Beep!

I was in Melanie's favorite place in the world, the bathroom. Since she and Cassie got married, she swears she likes it even more. It's her new Zen place. Though, I wasn't on the toilet. I'd already done that business. Hearing my phone's alarm, I turned it off and looked up at the counter. I was sitting on the floor.

The house was quiet, for once. All the kids were at Mama Alice's house. They bought one three houses down from ours as their second home, which was really their main home since Dylan and Jamison both were living in states close to us. I didn't understand why they kept their first home, but Mama Alice said it had something to do with not giving up any area to a Kathryn Moomoo Lady. The Etsy business was fierce.

I was digressing because I needed to get up. I needed to look at what I didn't want to look at, and I needed to get ready for the wedding.

I couldn't move.

I had a few years until I was forty, and this was the first time I'd ever taken this test.

I shouldn't be nervous. I was.

I shouldn't be excited. I was.

My heart was fluttering everywhere in my chest cavity.

My palms were sweaty.

I had to do some deep breathing exercises before I pushed myself from the floor.

One step.

I smoothed my hands down my pants.

Two steps.

I was there.

The bathroom wasn't that big.

I was standing just over the counter, and—I just had to do it.

I looked.

The pregnancy test was right there, staring up at me. Positive.

Holy shit.

My legs almost gave out, and I grabbed for the counter.

I was pregnant. We were pregnant. I didn't know how it happened. I mean, I knew how, but we'd taken measures so I wouldn't get pregnant. We had many conversations and I'd been torn. Cut hadn't. He wanted a child with me, but me—I didn't want to bring someone into the world that would suffer how I did.

Did.

That was the operative word, because it was better. It had been better since Cut.

But then we got Benji. Then Amelia...and our own pregnancy talk got pushed aside.

But another Cut.

That's where this test came about because the world needed another Cutler.

My throat was tightening up and I was crying. My lips were trembling.

I was full-out sobbing.

I was going to have a baby, one that came from my blood and Cut's.

Fuck.

Wow.

Okay.

Fuck.

Wow.

Okay.

And repeat because... you guessed it. Fuoway. My new word.

Whoa.

A small knock before, "Shine?"

Shine.

If we had a little girl, her middle name was going to be Shine. If we had a boy, Cutler. I was making the decision now.

"Cheyenne? Babe?" He was getting a bit more concerned now. "You've been in there a while, but we gotta go if we're going to make pictures in time."

Right. Because we were going to Hendrix and Sasha's wedding. Finally, their wedding because those two dumbasses took forever to get hitched. They kept getting together, breaking up, getting together, breaking up. I was sensing a pattern with Sasha, but then Hendrix almost died from a car accident and Sasha declared he wasn't allowed to die without her. They got engaged the next day.

Morbid.

"Hey."

The door opened and he stuck his head inside.

I moved, blocking the test, and I smiled.

His eyes narrowed. "You've been crying, but you're smiling at me. You're giving me *that* smile."

I was giving him *that* wide smile, the one I gave him every time I was going to tell him we were about to foster another child or rescue an animal.

His eyebrows pulled in, lowering. "No. We already have a full house."

I was scared. Of course I was scared, but I had faith, and hope, and love, and I really only needed his love to know we'd get through anything.

He was shaking his head now. "Seriously. Come on. Shine. No way. We just found a home for the pet raccoon."

Oh, crap. I forgot about Rocket One.

And about that phone call I got today. He didn't know that we had Rocket Deuce coming.

I'd tell him later.

"Cheyenne. Come on."

He was breaking.

Now.

Now was the time to tell him.

I swallowed my lump that was nerves and happiness and I breathed out. "I didn't get a phone call for this."

He relaxed.

"But..." I reached behind me, grabbing the test. My hand closed around it. "I got a test."

I showed it to him.

He stared at it, his eyes wide and he jerked his head up. "You're—"

I nodded. "I am."

Ten years.

But it's been so much longer than that when I first fell in love with Cutler Ryder.

"Fuck, Shine." He swept me up, his hand grabbing my neck, and his mouth was over mine. "*Fuck.*"

My legs wrapped around his, but then he turned me around, his hands going to my pants.

His eyes were dark, smoldering. Hungry.

His hands were rough. Needing.

Now wasn't the time to talk.

His pants were pulled down. Mine.

He nudged my legs apart, and he lined up.

No one was home.

We needed to leave.

Still.

"Put your hands on the mirror."

A thrill raced through me.

We needed this more.

His voice was low and raw, and as our eyes held in the mirror, he thrust inside of me.

I LIED. We *so* had a happily ever after.

We had a second one before getting to Sasha and Hendrix's wedding.

And we had another one before we both had to give our best man and matron of honor speeches. Though, I shared mine with Melanie.

ALMOST NINE MONTHS later

Hunter Jamison Dylan Ryder was born.

All three uncles were his godfathers.

Alice was now Grandmama Alice.

Melanie was now Auntie Mel.

Sasha was still Sasha.

WE LIVED HAPPILY EVER AFTER.

For realster real.

Go to www.tijansbooks.com for a
Decking with the Tomcats podcast transcript!

ACKNOWLEDGMENTS

I first wrote Cheyenne under a different name for an anthology. It was the prologue, and I never intended to include it with the actual book.

That changed halfway through the book. I felt it was needed, and the name changed for me as well.

The thing with my books and writing, the characters tend to take over and I meant for this book to be more hockey-focused. It is hockey-focused, but Cheyenne's struggles began to grow and grow.

I knew they were always there from the first time I wrote her prologue, and I felt them. But every single time I started to write this book, they became more and more pronounced to the point where I felt like I was Cheyenne. It was a *trip*, but I went with it and I truly tried to put on the keyboard what she wanted me to write.

Initially I did put in the book the actual primary diagnosis that Cheyenne was given, but I decided to take that out later on. I've worked in the psychology field so I understand the struggle between using a diagnosis to help treat someone versus when that diagnosis *becomes* the label for that person.

I didn't want that to happen in this book.

Cheyenne is Cheyenne.

She's a person. She's complicated. She's amazing. She's loved.

I had a blast writing The Tomcats in this book.

I loved writing Cut.

I loved writing Hendrix.

I loved writing Juna.

This book was just so different from my normal, so I really and truly hoped that the reader loved it as well.

Thank you to The Bookworm Box for letting me put The Not-Outcast in this month's box! Thank you to Crystal, Debra, Helena, Kimberly, Amy, Rochelle, Paige, Elaine, and the ladies in Tijan's Crew!

- Tijan

ALSO BY TIJAN

Sports Romance Standalones:

Enemies

Teardrop Shot

Hate To Love You

Rich Prick

Series:

Fallen Crest Series

Crew Series

Broken and Screwed Series (YA/NA)

Jaded Series (YA/NA suspense)

Davy Harwood Series (paranormal)

Carter Reed Series (mafia)

Mafia Standalones:

Cole

Bennett Mafia

Young Adult Standalones:

Ryan's Bed

A Whole New Crowd

Brady Remington Landed Me in Jail

College Standalones:

Antistepbrother

Kian

Contemporary Romances:

The Boy I Grew Up With (standalone)

Bad Boy Brody

Home Tears

Fighter

Rockstar Romance Standalone:

Sustain

Paranormal Standalone:

Evil

More books to come:

Nate

Canary

And more!